THE

"*Myrren's Gift* is a rich, satisfying confection
of vivid detail, engrossing characters,
and their dark doings, all beautifully written."
Lynn Flewelling

"[A] delightful and fast-moving story . . .
Fantasy fans will welcome . . . McIntosh's
gripping first installment in her Quickening trilogy,
a tale of the eternal struggle between good and evil
filled with magic, blood, and jealousy."
Publishers Weekly

"Fiona McIntosh is a seductress. I have not
moved from my sofa for three days,
beguiled by her new fantasy novel, *Myrren's Gift*."
Sydney Morning Herald (Australia)

"[*Myrren's Gift*] establishes McIntosh as a
talented storyteller with the ability to create
strong characters and a compelling plot."
Library Journal

"Fiona McIntosh scores."
The Guardian (London)

"I'm looking forward to reading the next two."
Robin Hobb

Books by
Fiona McIntosh

The Quickening
MYRREN'S GIFT
Book One

BLOOD AND MEMORY
Book Two

BRIDGE OF SOULS
Book Three

MYRREN'S GIFT

THE QUICKENING Book One

FIONA McINTOSH

An Imprint of HarperCollins*Publishers*

EOS
An Imprint of HarperCollins*Publishers*
10 East 53rd Street
New York, New York 10022-5299

This book was originally published in Australia in 2003 by Voyager, an imprint of HarperCollins Australia.

Copyright © 2003 by Fiona McIntosh
Excerpt from *Blood and Memory* copyright © 2003 by Fiona McIntosh
ISBN-13: 978-0-06-074757-2
ISBN-10: 0-06-074757-9
www.eosbooks.com

First Eos paperback printing: February 2006
First Eos trade paperback printing: March 2005

HarperCollins® and Eos® are trademarks of HarperCollins Publishers Inc.

Printed in the U.S.A.

10 9 8 7 6 5 4 3 2 1

For my own special trilogy . . .
Ian, Will, and Jack

ACKNOWLEDGMENTS

One of the most popular questions asked of any fantasy author is "Where did the idea come from?" In this instance I have a friend, Diane Rogers, to thank for sharing her experience of a visit to a "seer." The moment she began to relate her spooky tale, I felt my hair stand on end. I knew I was hearing the seed of a story which would make an exciting adventure and here it is . . . thank you for reading it.

Behind each book is a team of people; some in a supportive role, others who physically contribute to the final product. All deserve my thanks . . . Gary Havelberg and Sonya Caddy, my draft readers, are treasured, as is the wonderful Robin Hobb, who has been such an inspiration for my work. Hooray for the terrific team at HarperCollins Eos for giving me this opportunity for an international audience, especially Jennifer Brehl and my editor, Kate Nintzel, both such a pleasure to work with, and special thanks to my agent, Chris Lotts, for his guidance as well as his expertise in his field. And for any of you who may not believe that such a stature as Fynch's might exist, let me assure you it does by thanking ten-year-old Justin Klimentou for allowing me to borrow his unbelievably slight frame for my gong boy.

Finally to my family and friends, who already know how much their support is appreciated. Heartfelt thanks and love to Ian who keeps the circus of our home and business life rolling forward when I am lost in other worlds and to my sons, Will and Jack, for their boundless understanding and affection.

MYRREN'S GIFT

PROLOGUE

He knew the injury would be fatal. Accepted it at the very moment he caught the sword's menacing glint as it slashed down.

Fergys Thirsk, favorite son of Morgravia, began the last part of his journey toward death as a gray dawn sluggishly stretched itself across the winter sky. He faced his end with the same courage he had called upon for all of his life as General of the Legion.

It had been the King's idea to attack the Briavellians gathered on an opposite hillside under the cloak of night. To Fergys it had seemed somehow ignoble to interrupt the traditional night's peace in which men sat quietly around small fires, some singing, others deep in thought as to whether they might live through another day of battle. But the King had fixed his mind on this bold plan to take his enemy by surprise on a night where dark, brooding clouds eliminated the moonlight. The River Tague, which bisected the realms of Morgravia and Briavel from the mountains in the north to their midlands, had already run red with the blood of both armies earlier that day and Fergys had been reluctant to put the men to the sword again so soon. But his sovereign had persisted and Thirsk had accepted the challenge.

There had been no sense of foreboding as he carried out his monarch's wishes and led the attack. He simply did not like the plan. Fergys was a man of honor and tradition. War had a code that he preferred to observe rather than flout.

Nevertheless he had fought ferociously but had been disturbed when Magnus, his friend and king, going against his wishes, had joined the fray. Without further thought Fergys had planted his feet and grimly dispatched three Briavellians before he was able to make a move toward protecting his sovereign.

"The white cloak's suitably inconspicuous?" he had yelled above the din toward his oldest, dearest friend.

Magnus had ignored the sarcasm and even had the audacity to wink back. "Got to let Valor know I was here when his army was beaten into submission."

It was a reckless act and more dangerous than the King could have suspected. They were fighting on Briavel's side of the river and once the element of surprise had passed, both armies had gotten down to the business of slaughtering one another. Valor's men were no cowards and had worked with a newfound passion to repel Morgravia.

Fergys had noticed Briavel's standard—signaling that Valor too was in the thick of the fighting—and remembered now, as lifegiving blood leaked from him, how he had feared for both Kings.

With Briavel having the advantage of higher ground, Fergys had made the decision to pull back. His army had already inflicted a terrible price on its enemy; no need for either of these sovereigns to die. He knew by daybreak and the inevitable clash that would come later that day Morgravia would overcome its enemy once again. So he had given the order and his men had obeyed immediately.

All except one.

And it was that one man whom Fergys Thirsk had sworn to protect. The one he would give his life for.

As with the Thirsk Generals who had gone before him, Fergys had lived long, so the only regret that surfaced as the killing blow came was his absence from the family he loved. Fergys was not at all used to losing but it seemed Shar had asked more of him on this occasion; his god had asked for his life and he had given what had been requested without hesitation. He had fought so many battles and rarely returned with more than surface wounds.

And this battle had looked to be no exception until he had seen the danger, heard the man's battle cry, and deliberately stepped in front of that slashing sword. Up to that fateful moment only a thin line of dried blood across one cheek marked the closest a blade had come to threatening him. Duty, however, came first.

Fergys had not even paused to consider the implications of pushing aside King Magnus, knowing he would have no time to block the inevitable blow. The only thing standing between the King and certain death was Fergys's own body. The blade struck, fate guiding it ingeniously beneath the breastplate.

He cried out at the pain from the sucking wound in his abdomen but did not falter, too intent was he on dispatching the Briavellian and ensuring the life of his King. Only then did Fergys Thirsk fall, not yet dead but commencing the longest journey of all.

As they had hurried him from the battleground and back over the Tague, he was still calling orders to his captains. Once he had heard the full retreat sounded, he lay back on the canvas that would bear him back to Morgravia's camp. This journey seemed endless and he now used the time to reflect on his life.

There was little to complain about.

He was loved. That in itself should be enough for any man, he reasoned, but then there was so much more. He commanded respect—had earned it too—and he had walked shoulder to shoulder with a King whom he called friend. More than friend . . . blood brother.

That brother now walked in shock by his side, giving orders, fussing for his care, whispering to himself that it was all his fault; his stupidity and recklessness had seen the great General felled. It was all pointless. Fergys tried to tell the man this but there was insufficient strength in his voice to speak above the din of the retreat. If he could have he would have hushed his blood brother and reminded him that Shar's Gatherers had spoken and whether any of them liked it or not he must now answer that call. No regrets. Duty done.

Men were bowing their heads as the stretcher passed by. Fergys wished he could somehow convey his thanks to each. The Legion produced exceptional soldiers, loyal to a man to his command. He spared an anxious thought for how they would accept the new General, yearned for a last opportunity to beg their tolerance. "Give the boy a chance," he would beseech. "He will be all that I am and better still." And he hoped it would be true.

He thought of the youngster. Serious and a firm follower of tradition. Tarred by the same brush, as they say, especially in looks. They were plain, stocky, fearless men, the Thirsks, and this boy was already shaping up as a leader. The Morgravian Legion followed a curious tradition of handing down leadership from father to son. Fergys wondered if it could last. The lad was so young. Would he have time to sire his own heir to continue the Thirsk tradition or would a new family vie for the right to lead the army? Thirsks had led the Legion through two centuries now. It was an extraordinary history for one family that bred sons with warrior capabilities, tempered with intelligence.

The dying man's bearers were nearing the tent that he knew would be his final resting place. Once he was laid down he would have to concentrate on his King for as long as his heart held out. He wanted time to think about his beautiful wife, Helyna, of whom so much lived on in their son. Not her looks, mind. Those exquisite features belonged to their daughter alone. Fergys grimaced, not from pain so much as grief. His daughter was so young . . . too young to lose both parents.

How would his family manage? Money was no problem. They were the wealthiest of all the nobility, perhaps barring the Donals of Felrawthy. He would have to rely on Magnus. Knew he could. What his family needed now was time. Time to grow into their new lives. Peace must be achieved with Briavel until the young Thirsk was ready to lead into battle. That peaceful time would have to be bought and he hoped his life would suffice as raw currency.

They laid him down. The King had insisted he be settled in the royal tent. Physicians hurried to Thirsk's side. He ignored their probing, knowing it would ultimately be followed by a shaking of heads and grave glances. Fergys closed his eyes to the sudden frenetic activity and returned to his ponderings.

The old hate. It all seemed so pointless now. Valor of Briavel was a good King. He had a daughter. Little chance now of a son. Valor had shown no inclination to remarry after the death of his wife; it was rumored that theirs had been a love gifted from Shar. And he was probably too old now, at seventy, to bother himself with trying to sire a male heir. He too needed peace for Briavel's Princess to grow up and grow into her role. The wars had been a tradition in a sense. Their forefathers had fought each other when they were little more than feuding families. Initially it had been a case of maintaining the balance of power between two small factions suspicious of one another. But when the two strongest families established their own realms, and kingdoms were born, the battles were fought to increase power, gain more land, greater authority. Over the centuries, neither managed to claim domination over the region and so their animosity degenerated into squabbles over trading rights or merchant routes—any petty excuse, in fact, until by the time Magnus and Valor had inherited their crowns, neither was sure exactly why the two realms hated one another so intently.

Fergys shook his head. If truth be known, he rather admired Valor, and lamented the fact that the two Kings could not be neighbors in spirit as well as location. United in friendship and mutual respect, the region would be rich beyond dreams and near-invincible to any enemy. Now he would never see that dream come to fruition. He sighed.

"Talk to me," his King beseeched, voice leaden with guilt.

"Send the physics away, Magnus. We all know it's done."

The King bowed his head in sad acceptance and gave the order.

All except his friend had now been banished by Thirsk. No emotional farewells would he tolerate from his captains. He could bear neither their sympathy nor their despair. They had filed out in silence, stunned by the notion that their General might not even see this day's sun fully risen.

Thirsk asked for the tent flap to be left open so he could

see across the moors to the smoke from the distant fires of the Briavellian camp, where soon the sounds of dying men and beasts would be heard again should the battle resume today. In his heart Thirsk knew the two armies were bleeding and wearied; all of the men were now keen to acknowledge the outcome of yet another battle between these ancient enemies and return to their towns and villages. Many would not be going home, of course, and their widows and mothers, sisters and betrothed were mostly from Briavel.

And yet, as Fergys Thirsk slipped further into death's cool embrace, most from his side knew it would be later argued in the taverns that it was the great realm of Morgravia that had suffered the loss on this occasion.

The General looked wearily back at his oldest and closest friend.

"It's over for them," King Magnus of Morgravia finally said.

Thirsk tried to nod, relieved that Magnus had navigated his way out of the shocked stupor; there were things to be said and little time. "But Valor will try to fight on," Fergys cautioned. "He will want Briavel to salvage some face."

The King sighed. "And do we allow him to?"

"You always have in the past, your majesty. Pull back our men completely and let him have the news of my injury and subsequent passing," his dying companion replied, shivering now from pain cutting through the earlier numbness. "It will be a proud moment for them and then we can all go home," he added, knowing full well he would go home shrouded in black linens and tied to his horse.

The battle was won. Morgravia had prevailed as it usually did under General Thirsk. It had not always been so, however. There were centuries previous when Briavel had triumphed. These nations had shared a long and colorful hate.

"I wonder why I give him quarter—a weakness, do you think?" Magnus pondered.

Fergys wanted to tell his King that it was not weakness but compassion that saw today's Morgravia resist the temptation of out-and-out slaughter. That and the fact that Magnus had never had to watch his best friend die before—suddenly the battle had taken second place in the King's priorities. And if compassion was a weakness, then Fergys loved his King for the contradictions in his character that could see him willingly pass sentence of death on a Morgravian criminal while, on the battlefield, sparing the lives of his enemies. It was this enigmatic mix of impulsiveness and honor, stubbornness and flexibility that had drawn Fergys to Magnus from childhood.

Thirsk noticed his own breathing was becoming shallower. He had witnessed this many times previously on the battlefield as he held the hands of the dying and heard their last labored words. Now it was his turn. Death was beckoning but it would have to wait just a little while longer.

There was more to be said even though it hurt deeply to talk. "If there is weakness in this, then it is shared equally among us all," Fergys responded. "Without it, Briavel and Morgravia would not enjoy this regular opportunity to send their young men thundering on fine steeds across the moors to kill each other."

Magnus nodded. Fergys Thirsk never willingly went to battle; he cared too much for the sanctity of peace and the preservation of lives, particularly those of Morgravian men. But history attested to Fergys Thirsk being the most successful of the campaigners to lead Morgravia. He was legend amongst his men.

Through a haze of pain Thirsk scrutinized the grieving man before him, noticing for the first time how gray his King's hair had become. Once lustrous, it framed a strong-looking face, a determined jaw, and eyes that somehow reflected the man's extraordinary intelligence. The King's tall bearing suddenly gave the impression of a vague stoop, as though his big body was getting too heavy for him to carry around. They were getting old.

The General suddenly rasped a laugh. He would grow no older than this day. The King looked up sharply at the unexpected sound and Fergys shrugged, sending a new wave of agony through his ruptured body.

"We've always managed to laugh at most things, Magnus."

"Not at this, Fergys. Not at this." The King sighed again.

Fergys could hear the pain in that deep breath. They had shared their childhood. Their fathers had raised them to be close but the friendship was not forced. Fergys had worshiped the heir and then the King, and for his part, Magnus considered his General a brother in all but birthright. He loved Fergys fiercely and relied on his counsel, had done so throughout his long and flourishing reign. They were as wise together as they were wily.

"What must I do?" the King whispered.

With his last reserves of energy, the soldier squeezed the hand of his King.

"Your majesty, it is my belief that you would no more celebrate the death of King Valor of Briavel than you do mine. Morgravia has nothing to fear from him now for perhaps as much as the next decade—make it so, my King. Call a parley, sire. No more young men need lose their lives today."

"I want to. I have no desire to prolong this battle, as you well know, and if it had not been for my own stupidity, you wouldn't—"

Thirsk interrupted the King's outpouring of guilt with a spasm of coughing, blood spattering his shirt. Death would no longer be patient. The King began to reach for linens but his General pushed the monarch's fussing hands away.

"My death should suffice—it will be seen as a major blow for Morgravia," he said matter-of-factly before adding, "Valor is proud but he is not stupid. He has no male heir, sire. His young Princess will be Queen one day and will need an army of her own, and for Briavel to breed the soldiers of the future, they need peace. But their men, and ours, would do well to dispense with the ancient quarrel altogether. The threat from the north is very real, my King, for both our realms. You may need each other one day."

Thirsk spoke of Cailech, the self-proclaimed King of the Mountain People. In the early days Cailech had merely been the upstart and impossibly young leader of a rabble of hard Mountain Dwellers who rarely left their high ground

among the imposing sprawl of ranges that framed the far
north and northeast. His kind for centuries had kept their
tribal squabbles to themselves, contained within the Razors,
as the range was called. Back then, fifteen or so years ago,
this young warrior, no more than eighteen summers, had
begun to stamp a brutal authority across the tribes, uniting
them. Thirsk had believed for several years now that it was
only a matter of time before Cailech would feel confident
enough to look beyond the mountains and out toward the
fertile lands of Morgravia and Briavel.

"I will continue your strengthening of the Legion to the
north," the King said, reading his thoughts.

"That will help me rest easy."

Both men could hear Thirsk's increasingly rapid breathing.

Magnus had to push back all the emotion welling inside
him. "And so for you, my dearest friend. What can I do for
you before you leave me?" They clasped hands for the last
time in the Legionnaire manner.

"A blood pact, sire."

The King's eyebrow raised. He remembered the first
time they had mixed blood. They had been lads and permitted to witness the ritual being performed between the
former dukes of Felrawthy and Argorn—a special linking
of Morgravia's most powerful duchies in the north and
south of the realm. The two boys had watched the rites
wide-eyed, impressed at the solemnity of the occasion and
the deep commitment between the participants. It had been
Magnus's idea for them to do the same. "We'll commit to
each other," he'd said to Fergys. "You will love me as your
King and I will love you as my General, but we will be
blood brothers above all else."

They had found the courage to cut each other and hold
palms together as the two nobles had done. They had not
been even ten years old.

Thirsk coughed violently again. His passing into the dark
was just moments away. They could sense it.

"Name it, Fergys!" the King growled, his anxiety betraying him. "Whatever you ask is granted. You know it."

Thirsk nodded, exhausted. "The children. My boy, Wyl.

He must return from Argorn immediately. He is already General of the Legion and does not know it. He must finish his training in the palace." A new fit of coughing interrupted him. "Bring Gueryn with him, sire. Keep them close. There is no better teacher for him."

"Except the one who leaves him now," the King replied grimly. "And Ylena?"

"All I ask is that you make a good marriage for her." Thirsk looked toward the table where his dagger lay.

Magnus moved without a word and fetched it. He sat down again beside his friend. The King passed the blade over his palm and did the same to Thirsk. They rejoined hands, mingling their blood.

The King spoke softly as he made his promise. "Ylena will want for nothing. Your son is now my son, Fergys Thirsk."

"A brother for your Celimus," Thirsk rasped as his breathing turned ragged.

"They will be blood brothers, as we are," the King said, fighting back tears. His grip on his friend's hand tightened. "Go now, Fergys. Struggle no more, my friend. May your soul travel safely."

Fergys Thirsk nodded, the light already dying in his eyes. "Brothers in blood," he whispered, breathing his last.

King Magnus of Morgravia felt the clasp of his friend's hand slacken as death claimed Thirsk. "Our sons will become one," he echoed gravely.

1

GUERYN LOOKED TO HIS LEFT AT THE SOLEMN PROFILE OF THE lad who rode quietly next to him and felt another pang of concern for Wyl Thirsk, Morgravia's new General of the Legion. His father's death was as untimely as it was unexpected. Why had they all believed Fergys Thirsk would die of old age? His son was too young to take such a title and responsibility onto his shoulders. And yet he must; custom demanded it. Gueryn thanked the stars for giving the King wisdom enough to appoint a temporary commander until Wyl was of an age where men would respect him. The name of Thirsk carried much weight but no soldier would follow a near-fourteen-year-old into battle.

Hopefully, there would be no war for many years now. According to the news filtering back from the capital, Morgravia had inflicted a terrible price on Briavel's young men this time. No, Gueryn decided, there would be no fighting for a while . . . long enough for Wyl to turn into the fine young man he promised to be.

Gueryn regarded the boy, with his distinctive flame-colored hair and squat frame. He so badly needed his father's guidance, the older man thought regretfully.

Wyl had taken the news of his father's death stoically in front of the household, making Gueryn proud of the boy as he watched him comfort his younger sister. But later, behind closed doors, he had held the trembling shoulders of the lad and offered what comfort he could. The youngster had worshiped his father, and who could blame him—most of Morgravia's men had as well. It was especially sad that the boy had lost his father having not seen him in so many moons.

Ylena, at nine, was still young enough to be distracted by

her loving nursemaid as well as her dolls and the new kitten Gueryn had had the foresight to grab at the local market as soon as he was delivered the news. Wyl would not be so easily diverted and Gueryn could already sense the numbing grief hardening within the boy. Wyl was a serious, complex child, and this would push him further into himself. Gueryn wondered whether being forced to the capital was such a good idea right now.

The Thirsk home in Argorn had been a happy one despite the head of the household having been absent so often. Gueryn had agreed several years back to take on what seemed the ridiculously light task of watching over the raising of the young Thirsk. But he had known from the steely gaze of the old warrior that this was a role the General considered precious and he would entrust this job only to his accomplished captain, whose mind was as sharp as the blade he wielded with such skill. Gueryn understood and with a quiet regret at leaving his beloved Legion, he had moved to live among the rolling hills of Argorn, among the lush southern counties of Morgravia.

He became Wyl's companion, military teacher, academic tutor, and close friend. As much as the boy adored his father, the General spent most of his year in the capital, and it was Gueryn who filled the gap of Fergys Thirsk's absence. It was of little wonder then that student and mentor had become so close.

"Don't watch me like that, Gueryn. I can almost smell your anxiety."

"How are you feeling about this?" the soldier asked, ignoring the boy's rebuke.

Wyl turned in his saddle to look at his friend, regarding the handsome former captain. A flush of color to his pale, freckled face betrayed his next words. "I'm feeling fine."

"Be honest with me of all people, Wyl."

The lad looked away and they continued their steady progress toward the famed city of Pearlis. Gueryn waited, knowing his patience would win out. It had been just days since Wyl's father had died. The wound was still raw and seeping. Wyl could hide nothing from him.

"I wish I didn't have to go," Wyl finally said, and the soldier felt the tension in his body release somewhat. They could talk about it now and he could do what he could to make Wyl feel easier about his arrival in the strange, sprawling, often overwhelming capital. "But I know this was my father's dying wish," Wyl added, trying to cover his sigh.

"The King promised he would bring you to Pearlis. And he had good reason to do so. Magnus accepts that you are not ready for the role in anything but title yet but Pearlis is the only place you can learn your job and make an impression on the men you will one day command." Gueryn's tone was gentle, but the words implacable. Wyl grimaced. "You can't stamp your mark from sleepy Argorn," Gueryn added, wishing they could have had a few months—weeks even— just to get the boy used to the idea of having no parents.

Gueryn thought of the mother. Fragile and pretty, she had loved Fergys Thirsk and his gruff ways with a ferocity that belied her sweet, gentle nature. She had succumbed, seven years previous and after a determined fight, to the virulent coughing disease that had swept through Morgravia's south. If she had not been weakened from Ylena's long and painful birth she might have pulled through. The disease killed many in the household, mercifully sparing the children.

Although he rarely showed it outwardly, Wyl seemed to miss her in his own reserved way. For all his rough-and-tumble boyishness, Gueryn thought, Wyl obviously adored women. The ladies of the household loved him back, spoiling him with their affections but often whispering pitying words about his looks.

There was no escaping the fact that Wyl Thirsk was not a handsome boy. The crown of thick orange hair did nothing to help an otherwise plain, square face, and those who remembered the boy's grandfather said that Wyl resembled the old man in uncanny fashion—his ugliness was almost as legendary as his soldiering ability. The red-headed Fergys Thirsk had been no oil painting either, which is why he had lived with constant surprise that his beautiful wife had chosen to marry him. Many would understand if the betrothal had been arranged but Helyna of Ramon had loved him well and had brooked no argument to her being joined to this high-ranking, plainspoken, even plainer-looking man who walked side by side with a King.

Vicious whispers at the court, of course, accused her of choosing Thirsk for his connections but she had relentlessly proved that the colorful court of Morgravia held little interest for her. Helyna Thirsk had had no desire for political intrigues or social climbing. Her only vanity had been her love of fine clothes, which Fergys had lavished on his young wife, claiming he had nothing else to spend his money on.

Wyl interrupted his thoughts. "Gueryn, what do we know about this Celimus?"

He had been waiting for just this question. "I don't know him at all but he's a year or two older than you, and from what I hear he is fairly impressed with being the heir," he answered tactfully.

"I see," Wyl replied. "What else do you *hear* of him? Tell me honestly."

Gueryn nodded. Wyl should not be thrown into this arena without knowing as much as he could. "The King, I gather, continues to hope Celimus might be molded into the stuff Morgravia can be proud of, although I would add that Magnus has not been an exceptional father. There is little affection between them."

"Why?"

"I can tell you only what your father has shared. King Magnus married Princess Adana. It was an arranged marriage. According to Fergys, they disliked each other within days of the ceremony and it never got any easier between them. I saw her on two occasions and it is no exaggeration that Adana was a woman whose looks could take any man's breath away. But she was cold. Your father said she was not just unhappy but angry at the choice of husband and despairing of the land she had come to. She had never wanted to come to Morgravia, believing it to be filled with peasants."

The boy's eyes widened. "She said that?"

"And plenty more apparently."

"Where was she from?"

"Parrgamyn—I hope you can dredge up its location from all those geography lessons?"

Wyl made a face at Gueryn's disapproving tutorly tone. He knew exactly where Parrgamyn was situated, to the far northwest of Morgravia, in balmy waters about two hundred nautical miles west of the famed Isle of Cipres. "Exotic then?"

"Very. Hence Celimus's dark looks."

"So she would have been of Zerque faith?" he wondered aloud, and Gueryn nodded. "Go on," Wyl encouraged, glad to be thinking about something other than the pain of his father's death.

Gueryn sighed. "A long tale really, but essentially she hated the King, blamed her father for his avarice in marrying her off to what she considered an old man, and poisoned the young Celimus's mind against his father."

"She died quite young, though, didn't she?"

The soldier nodded. "Yes, but it was the how that caused the ultimate rift between father and son. Your father was with the King when the hunting accident happened and could attest to the randomness of the event. Adana lost her life with an arrow through her throat."

"The King's?" Wyl asked, shifting in his saddle. "My father never said anything about this to me."

"The arrow was fletched in the King's very own colors. There was no doubt whose quiver it had come from."

"How could it have happened?"

Gueryn shrugged. "Who knows? Fergys said the Queen was out riding where she should not have been and Magnus shot badly. Others whispered, of course, that his aim was perfect, as always." He arched a single eyebrow. It spoke plenty.

"So Celimus has never forgiven his father?"

"You could say. Celimus worshiped Adana as much as his father despised her. But in losing his mother very early there's something you and Celimus have in common and this might be helpful to you," he offered. "The lad, I'm told, is already highly accomplished in the arts of soldiering too. He has no equal in the fighting ring amongst his peers. Sword or fists, on horseback or foot, he is genuinely talented."

"Better than me?"

Gueryn grinned. "We'll see. I know of no one of your tender years who is as skilled in combat—excluding myself at your age, of course." He won a smile from the boy at this. "But, Wyl, a word of caution. It would not do to whip the backside of the young Prince. You may find it politic to play second fiddle to a king-in-waiting."

Wyl's gaze rested firmly on Gueryn. "I understand."

"Good. Your sensibility in this will protect you."

"Do I need protection?" Wyl asked, surprised.

Gueryn wished he could take back the warning. It was ill-timed but he was always honest with his charge. "I don't know yet. You are being brought to Pearlis to learn your craft and follow in your father's proud footsteps. You must consider the city your home now. You understand this? Argorn must rest in your mind as a country property you may return to from time to time. Home is Stoneheart now." He watched the sorrow as those last words took a firm hold on the boy. It was said now. Had to be aired, best out in the open and accepted. "The other reason the King is keen to have you in the capital is, I suspect, because he is concerned at his son's wayward manner."

"Oh?"

"Celimus needs someone to temper his ways. The King has been told you possess a similar countenance to your father and I gather this pleases him greatly. He has hopes that you and his son will become as close friends as he and Fergys were." Gueryn waited for Wyl to comment but the boy said nothing. "Anyway, friendship can never be forced, so let's just keep an open mind and see how it all pans out. I shall be with you the whole time."

Wyl bit his lip and nodded. "Let's not tarry then, Gueryn."

The soldier nodded in return and dug his heels into the side of his horse as the boy kicked into a gallop.

Wyl remembered that ride into Pearlis as if it were yesterday. It had been three moons now since his father's death and, although he was now used to the routine of the palace and his role, Wyl hated his new life. If not for his overwhelming sense of duty he would have run away.

He scowled as an exasperated Gueryn struck him a blow on his wrist. "You're not concentrating, Wyl. On the battlefield that slip could have cost you a hand."

The soldier deliberately struck again but this time Wyl countered just as ferociously, his wooden sword making a loud clacking sound as he pressed back against his opponent.

"Better!" Gueryn called, relieved. "Again!"

From out of the corner of his eye, Wyl could see that Prince Celimus had sidled up to a few of the flatterers he usually surrounded himself with. Wyl doubled his efforts and Gueryn was prudent enough to not criticize further.

About time, the soldier thought as he increased his speed, stepping up the session to a combat level rather than just a drill. He was pleased to see the boy relax slightly—a good sign that he was no longer concerned with who was watching but fully attendant on defending himself. Gueryn then upped the skills still further, delivering a frighteningly fast series of slashes and thrusts that would have challenged a battle-hardened soldier, let alone a fourteen-year-old boy. Those around them in the practice courtyard had fallen silent and various trainers and other lads wandered over to watch what was clearly a fight to the "death."

Wyl, sweating lightly now in the chill morning, stepped back, feinted, moved to his left, parried, and then dodged back to his original position, feinting once again before he saw the gap and struck hard and fast. He crouched nimbly to avoid the low, normally "fatal" slash he had already anticipated from his wily opponent and then struck upward with force, two-handed. Suddenly Gueryn was on his back panting and Wyl's piece of timber was at his throat.

There was murder in the boy's eyes and if they had been on the field, Gueryn believed he would be drawing his last breath. Gueryn also knew Wyl had genuinely bested him, despite his smaller stature and strength, with a blaze of raw anger. He realized he would have to counsel him on this

and explain that Wyl needed to fight clear-headed. Fighting
decisions were always based on training and intuition rather
than just pure emotion. That approach only worked once;
Gueryn knew that when wave after wave of soldiers were
bearing down, it was the cool, emotionless approach that
won the day.

He stared back at Wyl, forcing him to give way. Onlookers were clapping and whistling their appreciation of the
demonstration. Wyl regained his composure and pulled
Gueryn to his feet. He glanced toward the smirking Prince,
anticipating some snide comment to humiliate him in front
of his peers.

The Prince was predictable in this. "Can you do that with
a real sword, Wyl?" Celimus inquired innocently.

It was Gueryn, smacking the dust from his clothes, who
replied. "Well, I wouldn't want to take him on with a
blade," he said, hoping to deflect attention. He laughed and
clapped Wyl on the back.

"No? But I shall," Celimus interjected, his smile broad
and anything but genuine. The Prince's voice was sly now.
"What do you say, Wyl?"

Gueryn held his breath. This was the most direct provo-
cation that Wyl had encountered from the Prince, who had
spent much of the time since their arrival simply baiting the
youngster.

Wyl regarded the heir to the throne coolly. Gueryn's hand
was on his shoulder, squeezing hard. They did not permit
the lads to drill against each other with anything but
wooden or blunted swords and this rule was especially rigid
where Celimus was concerned.

Wyl looked away, hating to back down from that clear,
defiant gaze. "I'm not allowed to fight you, your highness."

"Oh, that's right," the Prince said, as though suddenly reminded of the palace rules. "You'd better remember it too,
General." Celimus laced the final word with as much sarcasm as he could.

Wyl had never felt such a well of hate rise within himself.
Until recently he had lived life with carefree joy, had hardly
known dislike for anyone. He had been surrounded by peo-

ple who loved him. Now his every waking moment seemed filled with torment. Celimus baited him at every opportunity and if he was not using his cruel mouth against Wyl, then he was laying traps for him with a few of his henchmen. A day hardly passed in which the Prince did not succeed in bringing gloom to settle on Wyl's shoulders. If there were not dead rats in his bed, then there were cockroaches in his drinking water, or mud in his boots. His food was tampered with and his training clothes hidden. Childish and pointless it all was and yet it wore Wyl down, nibbling at his resolve to follow in his father's footsteps.

"Wyl Thirsk?"

A page had arrived.

"Over here," Gueryn replied, nodding toward his despondent charge and grateful for the interruption.

The messenger addressed Wyl. "You're wanted in the King's chambers, General," he said politely. "Immediately, sir."

Wyl looked up at the still-grinning Prince and bowed. "With your permission, your highness, I'll take my leave," he said, carefully observing the correct protocol.

Celimus nodded, his silky lashes blinking once over olive eyes that missed nothing. Everything about Celimus was beautiful. Even at fifteen, when most of the boys were still struggling to fit into their awkward bodies, his looked as though it was sculpted from pure, smooth marble. Muscled and polished, there was not a blemish on it.

In looks, Celimus represented to Wyl everything he personally was not and that realization was painful for a boy born to lead men. Celimus was tall with wide, square shoulders. His hands were large but deft and he carried himself with grace; even his swordplay was elegant and highly skilled. His features were independently arresting but together they formed a face that was destined to turn heads. Manhood was still to settle on him but, looking at the youth, it was obvious an especially striking man was in the making. His voice had already deepened to a timber Wyl could only dream about, while Wyl's own still squeaked and cracked in places—usually at inopportune moments.

He's perfect, Wyl thought glumly to himself, cursing his own shorter stature, red hair, and no doubt blushing face of pale, freckled skin filled with unremarkable features. He tried to mask his despair as the Prince nudged his friends and excused himself, still smirking. The men standing nearby gave polite bows, but exchanged looks of distaste. Celimus may have been a glorious-looking individual whom the young women of the court were already swooning over but he was unpopular among the larger palace community. In this he was his mother all over again. While the King was revered, the heir had no loyalties he might count on from any but the sycophants who hung around him.

"May Shar help us all when that one takes the throne," someone said, and many gave wary nods of agreement.

Wyl strode away, a sense of foreboding now mingling with his hate: King Magnus had summoned him, no doubt to ask questions about his loyalty. It was hardly news that he and Celimus did not get along.

"Come on, Wyl, make haste," Gueryn urged.

They did so, following the page as he weaved a practiced route through the halls of the palace, taking shortcuts via various walled courtyards and sunlit atriums. On the way they stole a chance to wash their faces and rinse their hands in a bucket of water raised from a convenient well while the page hopped from foot to foot in urgent need to deliver his "goods" to the King's secretary.

Wyl had not realized how beautiful the palace of Stoneheart was. Up until now it had been to him an impregnable fortress with solid, gray walls, dusty yards, stables, and a mess hall that was always noisy. A place where dogs, horses, soldiers, and servants scurried about in a small world of their own within the castle walls. This more serene aspect of Stoneheart was as unexpected as it was attractive. He felt like an intruder on a new world.

The dark stone looked suddenly handsome in the many light-filled, elegant spaces especially created within the internal structure of the castle. Wyl began to appreciate that the castle was also a palace in its own right, possessing a distinctive style of which simplicity was the key. Walls were not busily cluttered; instead, one eye-catching tapestry might be the only decoration in a vast chamber. Furniture was practical, always simple, favoring the heavier, dark Lomash wood so abundant in Morgravia. Adana had had no influence here, Wyl mused; there was no hint anywhere that a Queen of such exotic heritage had lived any of her short life in this place. He wondered if Celimus's more extravagant taste would leave its garish mark on Stoneheart when he took the throne.

Hurrying through the corridors and up stairs, trying to keep up with the page, Wyl caught glimpses of carvings of the great beasts. It was believed that every Morgravian was chosen from birth by one of the beasts, and the choice became known when a person made their first pilgrimage to the cathedral at Pearlis. There, the magical creatures were gloriously presented, each holding up one of the pillars of the great nave. Whenever Wyl visited the cathedral, he looked for the famed winged lion—his creature. Now, in the palace, he spotted the taloned bear, the magnificent eagle, the serpent cunningly twisting out of the stone, and the beautiful jeweled peacock. Finally, as they drew nearer to the King's chambers, he saw the mighty warrior dragon, talisman to all the monarchs of Morgravia. Wyl looked at it in wonderment, then thought of his father's creature, the phoenix. There was a symmetry there which pleased him: both Magnus and Fergys were creatures of fire; no wonder they had loved each other so loyally.

"Wait here please," the page said finally, at the top of a second flight of stairs.

"Where are we?" Gueryn wondered aloud.

"Outside the King's private study, sir. Please be seated." The boy gestured toward an open corridor with a stone bench fashioned out of the walls on both sides. The area was flooded with sunlight and by the soft, unmistakable fragrance of winterblossom. It was seductive. They strolled over to the balcony and stared into a small but exquisite orchard. Its beauty and perfume kept them silent in their own thoughts.

Soon enough an older man arrived quietly behind them.

"It's difficult to drag oneself away, isn't it?" the man said, his voice low and friendly. Gueryn assumed he must be the King's secretary. When they turned, he added, "You must be Wyl Thirsk."

Wyl nodded.

"We all loved and greatly respected your fine father, son. He is deeply missed in our community."

"Thank you, sir," Wyl stammered, unsure of what else to say, wishing people would allow him to heal that wound and not keep reminding him months after the hated event. This man meant no harm, though. It was their first meeting and only right that he would make mention of his prestigious lineage.

The soldier beside him cleared his throat. "Er, I am his guardian—"

"Ah, yes, Gueryn le Gant, isn't it?" the man said. His manner was brisk yet kind. "Welcome to you both. Can I offer you something cool to drink? I gather we interrupted your training." The smile was genial.

"Thank you, we'll be fine," Gueryn answered politely.

"I am the King's secretary, Orto," their host said. "The King has requested a private discussion with the young man so I will ask you to remain here, Gueryn. Please sit, we shall call Wyl soon." He smiled again and departed.

Within a few minutes Orto returned. "Wyl, come with me now. You may leave your weapon and belt out here with Gueryn."

Wyl did as he was asked and, with a glance over his shoulder towards his friend, followed the servant.

Massive oaken doors, carved with Morgravia's crest, were opened before them. Wyl looked up at the keystone of the archway they passed through: carved into it was another fire-breathing warrior dragon, signaling that he was entering the private domain of a King . . . his King. The large chamber he entered had windows running the length of it and a stone fireplace at either end, again featuring the royal talisman.

Wyl had lost his bearings in the journey through the palace; he wondered what those windows looked out onto.

But the sound of voices called him back from his distraction and he heard the scratching of a pen on parchment.

"Last one, I hope?" a gruff voice said.

"It is, sire," another man's voice answered, and then the owner of that voice shuffled past them carrying rolls of documents.

"Ah, Orto, you have the boy? Bring him in, bring him in."

Wyl emerged fully into the study and came face to face with the man he had met only briefly once, the man his father had died protecting. Magnus had headed north to Felrawthy almost immediately after Wyl's arrival and this was their first occasion to meet again. He noticed that the King was tall but stooped and he appeared much older, even since their first, very hurried, talk. Magnus, he noticed now, looked very little like Celimus, although the strapping physique was there. A gentle push from Orto, on his way out of the room, reminded Wyl that he was in the presence of his sovereign. He bowed low.

"You look like your father, boy."

It had been meant as a compliment but Wyl's plain looks made him feel that almost any reference to them was a barb.

"He always told me I look more like my grandfather, sire," he replied politely.

Magnus grinned then. "That's probably true, son. But you remind me of how he was when we were both mere scamps together in this same castle."

Wyl could tell the King meant it sincerely. He knew how fond the friends had been of each other and imagined that Magnus losing Fergys Thirsk would be like him losing Gueryn. More than just painful.

"I miss him, sire," he admitted.

The King gazed down at him with soft eyes. "Me too, Wyl. So keenly that I still find myself talking to him now and then."

Wyl regarded the King and saw no guile. He appeared nothing like his son in temperament either, thought Wyl.

"So, Wyl," the King said, sitting down and gesturing for Wyl to be seated too. "Tell me, how are we treating you in

Pearlis? I imagine you must regret not being in that glorious world of Argorn. I know your father constantly did."

"Yes, sire, but . . . I am settling in."

Magnus scrutinized the lad before him, sensing he was cautious like his father—and probably just as unforgiving if he was wronged, judging by that proud jut of his chin.

"I have seen your sister about the place. What a sunny, pretty young thing she is. I trust she is happy?"

Wyl shrugged gently. "I think Ylena would be happy anywhere, your majesty, providing she has her dolls and fine dresses." He smiled. "Thank you for all that you've given her, sire. She is pretty, that's true. She's the lucky one in looks—she took after my mother."

He was startled by the King's sudden laugh. "Don't put yourself down, Wyl."

"No, sire. I'll leave that to others."

"Ah."

Orto reentered the King's study and brought with him a small tray with two cups of blood-red wine.

"Don't tell old Gueryn, eh? He'll think I'm corrupting you." The King winked.

Wyl could not help but like the man who sat before him. He wanted to be wary of him. He was the father of Celimus, after all, but still it was hard not to enjoy his company.

"Now here's to you, young Wyl," the King said, lifting his glass.

"And to your continuing good health, sire." The underlying message was not lost on Magnus.

"Has it been hard settling in?"

"Oh, the usual stuff, sire."

Wyl felt Magnus fix him with his direct gaze. "Tell me about Celimus," the King said.

"What can I tell you, your majesty, that you don't already know?"

The King paused and Wyl thought it was a telling hesitation. "Tell me any good points you've noticed about him."

Now Wyl felt really cornered. "I don't understand."

"Oh, I think you do," Magnus said gently. "I grasp more than people credit me with, Wyl. Celimus has many imperfections. On the outside, however, he is a truly remarkable individual. I freely admit, without any shame, that I think he will turn into one of the finest-looking men Morgravia has ever bred. Shar rest his mother's soul." This last he added perfunctorily. "I don't know whether it's because he lost his mother early, or because he has no siblings . . . or simply because I am a woeful father. Whatever the reasons, Celimus is not so remarkable on the inside. In fact I know him to have a darkness within that troubles me."

Wyl nodded, fearful of what to say to a King making such a frank admission about his own son.

Magnus held him with a light blue gaze. "I've heard the two of you are enemies. Is this true?"

Wyl felt tongue-tied. He had no desire to lie to Magnus who was being so candid with him and he tried to be diplomatic in his response.

"That's a strong word, sire. I am Morgravian. I am prepared to die for my Kingdom and for its ruler. I am no enemy to the King," he assured, horrified to think Magnus might think otherwise.

Instead Magnus grinned. "So like your father. But perhaps you are prepared to die for *this* King, son. How about King Celimus?"

Wyl understood. "You obviously wish me to do something for you, sire."

The King sighed. "Yes, Wyl, I do. And it's not going to be easy. I trusted your father all of my life, and I trust his son now. Moments before your father died we joined our bleeding palms to make an oath. Your father's deathbed wish was that I bring you back to Pearlis and make a General of you. You are a Thirsk and it is your birthright to head the Legion. But part of our oath was that we make our two sons blood brothers."

A blood oath? Wyl felt the slow crawl of a chill through him as Magnus continued.

"I gave my word to your father—my closest friend, my blood brother—that his son would become my son." He paused again. Wyl said nothing, his silent thoughts racing ahead to guess what the King might ask of him. "Do I have your loyalty, my boy?"

Startled, Wyl quickly moved to kneel before the King. He placed his hand on his heart. "Yes, sire. You will never have to question it."

The King nodded. "Good. I am elevating you to your father's revered title of King's Champion. It comes into effect today but I do not grant this position lightly. You despise my son." He held up his hand to hush Wyl's ready objection. "I know this—and he has given you little reason to think highly of him in any way, so I do not hold this against you. However, from now on you will protect the heir of Morgravia with your life, as your father protected me with his.

"As of this moment you will shadow the Prince in all that he does. I don't doubt for a second that any of his activities are distasteful, as I know my son has a penchant for cruel habits. Together we will try to change this. Make a friend of him, Wyl. Influence him. Everything that made your father the fine man he was is embodied in his only son—I know this to be true. Your reputation precedes you, boy. You have the qualities that make a special man, a leader of men, and I want you to do everything you can to imbue Celimus with those qualities."

Wyl tried to object.

Magnus interrupted him. "No buts, Wyl. This is my command. You are already General to the Legion and Champion to the King, and one day you will be called to act for Celimus—at *his* command. In the intervening years, you will befriend the Prince and somehow, child, I pray your humility, your sense of right and wrong, your courage, and your leadership will rub off and help him as he matures. I know I ask a lot of you, Wyl, but this is your duty now—your duty to me."

The King's eyes blazed as he reached forward and grabbed Wyl's wrist. "Swear it to me, Wyl. Make this pact with your sovereign."

Wyl felt his world suddenly spin as he put his other hand over his heart and gave the solemn oath to be "blood" to Celimus.

Magnus suddenly dropped Wyl's wrist and reached for his dagger. Wyl saw the blade glint as Magnus drew the sharp edge across his own palm; bright blood sprang instantly to the surface. Without hesitation, Wyl offered his own hand and the King repeated the process. The knife bit cruelly and swiftly through his young hand until it too yielded up its precious liquid. Wyl did not wince at the pain, but he suspected the King had deliberately cut deep enough to leave a scar—one that would always remind him of this oath.

"You will protect the life of the heir to Morgravia with yours, preferring to die by his hand than save your own life."

They clasped fists, blood to blood.

"I pledge it," Wyl affirmed.

"You and he are to be as one body, one life."

Wyl swallowed silently. "As though my blood runs in his veins. I swear it, sire."

2

IN THE END IT WAS HER EYES THAT GAVE THEM THEIR EXCUSE to hunt down Myrren. Her eyes were bewitching indeed—one a piercing gray, the other an arresting green with flecks of warm brown. Lovely enough in isolation but so ill-matched as a pair that they were alarming to behold. Little wonder then that as soon as those eyes had settled from their newborn blue to their strange final coloring, her parents had fled from the city of Pearlis to the sleepy hamlet of Baelup in the southwest, where they raised their only daughter in relative obscurity.

Both knew this facial oddity would symbolize much to the Stalkers, hungry for prey. Thankfully the family's sudden departure was soon yesterday's gossip and quickly forgotten. Meanwhile, the folk of Baelup were known to be of

liberal mind. The father, a wealthy physic, was a great boon
for a community lacking in any medicinal talent, whilst the
mother, a scholar, was a special boon for the youngsters of
Baelup.

Not prone to the old superstitious fears of their city
cousins, the folk of Baelup welcomed the gentle child,
Myrren, with her strange eyes and shy smile.

So when the Witch Stalkers finally came some nineteen
years later it was such a shock that the physic's weak heart
had given out. He had died at their feet upon answering
their terrifying banging at the door.

The mother was helpless, watching her husband take his
last breath while all she could do was rail at them, cursing
them for having ever been born. She had finally slid to the
floor in despair as she had watched Myrren, now a beautiful young woman, being dragged into the street.

The Stalkers had gone through their usual pointless list
of contrived accusations—everything from disease in the
south to an irritating bunion on the King's foot was now
firmly linked to Myrren's devil craft. No farewells were
permitted as Myrren was taken to the city.

King Magnus heard the first doleful clang of the cathedral bells and his first thought was a sour one. Pearlis
still loved a witch-burning. Nothing could bring the city
folk out faster from their homes than the clamor of the bells
signifying that a witch had been discovered and sentenced
to die for her sins. And it had been more than a decade since
the capital had heard this particular sound; tradition had it
that the brides of the devil could not abide it.

It began with a single bell pealing six times every six
hours for six days to announce the discovery of a witch. Six
was the devil's number. Once the trial began, the rhythm
would change to a single somber peal every six hours for its
duration.

In truth, very few continued to believe in sorcery under
Magnus's rule. However, the older gentry of Morgravia, es-
pecially those whose parents had been seduced by the
Zerques, and who themselves had fallen under Queen

Adana's spell, remained suspicious of any who might show a leaning toward the fey. The now fading tradition of wariness had been grounded in the practice of Morgravian Kings to keep a hag within the castle. An old crone, usually harmless enough, she brewed healing teas for the royals and was called upon at births, marriages, and deaths. She also performed readings and sightings for the King, in order to make prophecies.

The first indication that the influence of hags was waning occurred about one hundred and fifty years before Magnus came to the throne. According to the history books, his forefather, King Bordyn, kept a crone who favored the drawing of blood for her prophecying. After the loss of two heirs and a wife in a series of accidental deaths, Bordyn objected not only to his hag's unsavory practices but to her prophecies of doom and gloom for Morgravia. When tragedy struck again twice in the same year, with first the death of his second wife and her unborn babe after she toppled down the castle stairs, and then the routing of his Legion by the Briavellian Guard, Bordyn declared his hag an instrument of darkness. Branded a witch, she was tortured and burned in order to cleanse Morgravia of her stain. It was the first time in the history of Morgravia that a person had been tried and punished for having magical influence. Uncannily, after the hag's death, life for Bordyn took a turn for the better. The King lived to a ripe age and, taking a third wife, sired a son who outlived him and inherited the throne.

During this period of prosperity, the belief began to grow that hags—or witches, as they were now called—were a blight on society. Many innocent people who had openly practiced the healing arts were hunted down. Around this time, a theologist called Dramdon Zerque emerged, preaching a new Order that claimed Shar himself denounced sorcery because it challenged belief in the god's omnipotent powers. Zerque was a gifted orator with a brilliant mind—skills that worked especially effectively on the gentry, who embraced the radical new religion, along with its message to annihilate all who showed even the slightest talent for those arts considered magical.

It was Zerque who coined the term "witch-smeller," when he proclaimed that anyone who even smelled of magical taint should be brought in and given the opportunity to confess their sins. Using Shar as his battering ram, he challenged Morgravians—and later Briavellians—to take up the fight against witches and warlocks. His influence spread, reaching beyond Morgravia and Briavel across the oceans to as far west as Parrgamyn, where the new Order was embraced with a special vigor. It was this more fervent form of the religion that Queen Adana and her contingent brought back to Morgravia all those years later, turning Pearlis into a Zerque stronghold.

Interestingly, in these more modern times it was the rural areas that dismissed the Zerques as religious zealots, claiming they threatened Shar's gentle teachings far more than any hedgewitch might. Country folk simply ignored the Order's claims and those areas became a tentative sanctuary for those with magical tendencies.

Now, with an enlightened King—who had little tolerance for the gossip that the witch-hunting Zerques might be finding a foothold in the realm again—the opportunities to persecute any so-called practitioners were few and far between. As soon as Queen Adana had died, her death taking with it the last key supporter of the Zerque Order, Magnus had grabbed his chance to stamp out the practice of persecution. It was his cold and cruel wife who had encouraged more of the Zerques into Morgravia; she who had encouraged they make the pilgrimage to this "peasant" realm across the ocean from her own country a long way to the northwest, where life for the lower caste was intolerably cheap. Her father had been determined to do trade with the realms of the eastern peninsula and considered a marriage necessary to build those important bridges where his merchants could move freely among these "barbarian" lands.

Magnus had been seduced by the audacious glamor of the bride on offer. One look at the twenty-one-year-old Adana had seen desire take precedence over prudence and his acceptance was immediate. It was barely a matter of days following the lavish royal wedding that Magnus had first grasped the enormity of his poor decision. His friend and counsel, Fergys Thirsk, had argued passionately against the union in the intervening months. He had suggested that the gap in cultural differences was yawning, not to mention the stunning age difference of almost three decades, and could not envisage how Magnus and Adana would overcome such obstacles.

"I want her!" Magnus had resisted, recalling the dark beauty who had already been offered.

"She is rather young, sire. Your fourth decade is well behind you."

"And you can talk, Thirsk, courting Helyna of Ramon—barely into womanhood," the King had countered, wanting to hurt back, for the truth of his friend's barb had hit home.

He remembered the words of ever-wise Fergys Thirsk as if they had been spoken yesterday. And Magnus had spent the rest of his life wishing that he had listened to his friend's well-intentioned wisdom instead of following what he soon realized was nothing more than lust.

The promised dowry came but Morgravia was already a rich realm. What he had not bargained on were the zealots who followed Adana and, using her influence, weaseled their way into the fabric of Morgravian life, promoting fear and loathing. In truth the Zerques were already well established in Morgravia but Adana's eager priests brought a new verve to their fanaticism.

The royals' dislike for each other extended to the marriage bed. Adana despised Magnus so much as touching her. On their wedding night the King discovered that nothing in his wife burned for him except contempt—and desire for the power he could provide.

He gave her none as a result. She gave him only her derision.

"Your hateful grasping hands and loathsome wrinkled skin could never entice me, old man," she had hurled at him on the very night of her marriage vows.

Twice in their time together he had forced himself upon her and deeply regretted his desperation on both occa-

sions. It remained a wonder that Celimus was ever even
born. His son was conceived in anger and horror when
Magnus impregnated Adana in that second and most brutal of rapes. He never touched his wife sexually again;
hardly touched her at all, save to take her arm as required
on formal occasions.

No one offered more silent thanks to Shar than King
Magnus at the untimely, though suspicious, death of the
Queen. While the rest of Morgravia publicly displayed its
shock, Magnus found himself going through the motions of
grief but inwardly rejoicing. It was a release he shared only
with Fergys Thirsk, and his friend never once reminded the
King of his early advice.

As soon as Adana's body was cold in its tomb, Magnus
had begun systematically breaking down the Zerque structure and in his reign could claim that he had singlehandedly
achieved the destruction of an Order that had been centuries
in the making. But he had made concessions—as one must
during campaigns of change—to give those gentry who
clung to the old ways time to adjust to a new regime.

Magnus had agreed that only in the event that there be
damning evidence brought to bear against a man or woman
would he permit the traditional trial. In the years since
Adana's death only two witches had been brought to trial—
only one of those had burned. He permitted a judge and jury
to be embodied in one man—a fellow called Lymbert—and
gave him the authority to roam the realm with his three
Witch Stalkers, more as an appeasement for the destruction
that the Crown had visited on the entire Zerque Order than
for witch persecution.

"It will keep the traditionalists quiet, Fergys," he had
explained to his friend, who, though proud of the King's
determination to destroy the Zerques, did not approve of
the new twist on the old theme. "We let those who remain
true to the old fanaticism believe we still pursue the
devil's doings. In the meantime we dismantle the structure
that has, for too many decades, brought fear and loathing
into Morgravia."

"And then?" his friend had asked.

"And then we wait for a new generation to finish what we have begun," the King had replied with certainty. "A generation that has not known the terror of the Zerque Witch Stalkers and will therefore hold no faith in them."

Fergys had agreed that a handful of deaths—if any at all—were preferable to the early years of persecution of suspected witches, usually innocents with the unfortunate afflictions of cleft palates or club feet. The introduction of a single Confessor and the binding of the law, which gave the sovereign final say over any cases, was a worthy compromise during the Years of Abolition, as Magnus termed it. Fergys was not fully convinced that granting concessions to those still suspicious of herbwomen or people of irregular features might not encourage the fanatics to take their fervor underground, but he conceded the sense of giving the King ultimate say over who might be brought to trial. He had to trust that Magnus would frustrate the progression of cases to such an extent that the practice of witch-hunting would simply peter out.

Confessor Lymbert, in the meantime, had walked a careful path, never overstepping his authority, and as a result his role quietly continued long after the abolition of the Zerques had been achieved. Magnus regretted this and had made a promise to himself that he would abolish the office of Confessor. The war with Briavel had distracted him, and then his General's untimely death had so profoundly affected the King's health that he had paid little attention to domestic affairs for some time. Lymbert had survived and, sadly, his Witch Stalkers had found Myrren.

King Magnus hated the sound of those bells and he knew as the clangor began that morning that the few remaining Witch Stalkers would be understandably desperate for a trial and a kill. He had hoped the girl Myrren and her family had taken the sensible precaution of fleeing their village but then he knew Lord Rokan to be far too cunning to allow such a thing to happen. Rokan was a senior noble of little consequence, with too many vices for Magnus's tastes, but he was well connected among the nobility. Lord Bench, one of the most influential men in the realm, was distantly related through marriage and Rokan rarely failed to use Bench's status to further his own causes.

Magnus had pieced it together in his mind, even though Rokan had only told half the story. It was obvious to the King that Rokan had made his predictable, albeit unwelcome, advances to this youngster, Myrren, and when spurned had decided to take revenge. He had a long history of indiscretions outside his marriage and this had been just another attempt to get a young woman into his bed. It was a tragedy, Magnus felt, that Rokan had stumbled across this particular girl's village.

The problem for Magnus was that the noble's accusation carried weight in the eyes of the Stalkers and those who still harbored deep-rooted suspicion of any man, woman, or child who might show some physical difference. The Zerques had preached for a century or more that a person born with a caul, more or less than ten fingers or toes, or— Shar forbid—ill-matched eyes must be a member of the devil's clan.

Magnus might have officially dismantled the power of the Zerque Order, but he could not control the minds and hearts of his people. He knew that some in his realm still used the odd warding against sorcery, or wore specific colors on certain days, and whilst these seemed little more than harmless superstitions he also knew how easily they could develop into full-blown fear, a baying for blood. He hoped that any genuine sentient—if there was such a person— would have the wisdom to keep his or her practices secret.

No such chance for young Myrren—witch or not, her case was now very much public. Magnus did not personally believe the girl was guilty of the charges, but only privately scorned those who did. No matter his own opinion, the law—his law—provided for Myrren's trial. And Morgravian justice was not renowned for its mercy where a guilty verdict of devil craft was handed down. Worse, he knew what lewd enjoyment some would derive from seeing her tortured and debased—not least of all Lord Rokan—and there was nothing he could do to stop it now.

Rokan's evidence was persuasive and the law was, sadly,

on his side. When Lord Rokan had called for a private audience with the King and had seemed utterly determined to have this woman brought to trial, Magnus had felt his hands were tied. Odd-colored eyes were the single most damning characteristic a person living in Morgravia could possess. The girl was doomed by the peculiarity of her features. He felt sorry for her, but the time to save her had passed. At the point when Magnus could have intervened, he had instead been distracted by anger toward his son. Celimus's irresponsible behavior was drawing far too much attention and the boy was still only sixteen. Shar help them when he was of an age where his father's height and wrath could no longer cow him. But mostly Magnus had been feeling an uncontrollable rage at the dark news from his physic that his days were numbered. Magnus was fearful it would not be sufficient time to mold Celimus into a responsible heir to the throne, to create a true King from the ruin of his marriage.

His anger was fully stoked by the time Lord Rokan kept his appointment and strode in to formally demand the young woman's death. Celimus had not excused himself either, which would have been the polite choice under the circumstances. Instead he had hung on Rokan's every word, his sly smile creeping wider across his face. He even had the audacity to join the conversation and this was the taper that lit the dry straw on his father's smoldering mood.

"Go ahead, Father," he had jeered. "A witch trial would deflect attention from the Crown's wayward heir and give them something to really talk about." The mocking smile challenged the King.

Magnus knew his son was a young man without love and all his parents had given him, it seemed, was the capacity to be cruel and self-centered. With his impending death, the King of Morgravia realized if he had been a better father, a more affectionate and loving one—even just a father who had been more accessible and keen to exert his influence during the child's early years—it might have made a difference. Instead what stood before him was a clever, avaricious individual who was, to all intents, heartless. A frightening combination for the person who would sit on Morgravia's throne. Today's indiscretion had been the latest in a long line of acts that made his father despair of him, hate him even.

Rokan had continued to bluster through his troubled thoughts and Celimus had egged him on. In a fit of pique, Magnus agreed, if only to get both detestable men out of his chamber. Had he any inkling that he would reign, without succumbing to his illness, for another six years, he might never have let Myrren of Baelup suffer.

ELIMUS WAS FRUSTRATED. HE PACED THE COURTYARD ANgrily awaiting a page he had sent off to find Wyl Thirsk. The Prince enjoyed belittling Wyl but the orange-haired troll was not giving him the sort of smug satisfaction he wanted. He would be King one day and he wanted to see this one in particular cringing early to him. Wyl was Fergys Thirsk's son after all and Celimus had despised Fergys since he was old enough to measure the bond between his father and his General. Perhaps without the famous soldier in the King's life, his father might have paid more attention to his sole heir.

Now all Celimus had to offer his King was contempt.

The major rift had come when his mother died twelve years previous. Whispers around the court had hinted that perhaps her death was not quite the accident it had seemed at first. Try though his caretakers might, they could not protect the sharp, highly intelligent four-year-old from absorbing the enormity of what was being gossiped about. If he valued his father's praise, he worshiped his mother ten times as much. Although he had sensed her cool detachment from Morgravian society and its people—especially his father—Celimus also grasped that this aloofness did not extend to him. Celimus she loved with intensity. He was every bit her child. While his father was golden in looks, the son had her dark, exotic glamor. Olive skin and black lustrous hair meant Celimus was Adana all over again. She granted him his height was no doubt inherited from the King but that was all. Men should be tall, she had argued. For sovereigns she felt it was a prerequisite. She had no doubt that Celimus would be an imposing man in years to come—he was already an arresting child to look at. And with it came a bright and agile mind that she adored. Adana made good use of those early years, manipulating her son's thoughts, trying to poison him against his father—*the peasant,* she called him—but not to much avail. It remained a failure of hers. The infant Celimus craved the attention of Magnus but she was relieved to note the King had neither time nor inclination to level much interest toward the boy. She hated the red-headed General even more and used his presence as a weapon to turn Celimus against the King.

"He loves that Thirsk fellow more than us, child. See how they bend their heads together. Plotting. Always conniving."

Celimus had not understood the grown-up words then but he had grasped her meaning. She accused Thirsk of constantly filling his own coffers at the King's expense; she laughed hard at the shy and reticent creature Thirsk had finally married. "Peasant for peasant!" she had spat at Celimus one day. Although he had thought Helyna Thirsk quite pretty, he was only a few years old, and so believed his mother must surely be right. And when she had finally seen the Thirsks' first child, Adana had attacked the infant's red hair, claiming it was the sign of a warlock. Magnus had overheard her snide comment and his reaction was the closest Celimus believed his father had come to striking his mother. His parents had hardly spoken after that. They had never behaved as a family might—eating together or playing together. Magnus was absent as a father, preferring his war rooms, his soldiers, the hunt, and other manly pursuits.

But despite his caretakers striving to assure the boy that his majesty had little time for anything but running his realm, Celimus knew his father avoided him. He watched other nobles making time for simple pleasures with their families and his mother's words rang true: his own father disliked him, hated them both in fact, and deliberately chose to evade all contact with his wife and his son.

It hurt. And Adana made it her business to prey on her small son's pain and turn it into her own weapon. Her machinations worked. The young Celimus hardened his thoughts; the changes were initially subtle—he no longer asked whether he might see his father before going to bed or whether the King might care to take a ride with him sometime soon. Then they became more apparent. One one occasion, Magnus had sent a message that he would be joining them for supper. Celimus was absent, claiming a stomach upset, but Adana knew better and she rejoiced in his shunning of the King.

It was after the aggressive incident between his parents that Celimus felt compelled—and that he had right on his side—to openly reject his father. Watching the tall man's anger stoke so fast had frightened him. His mother had fallen to the floor as if struck, though he knew his father had pulled the blow just in time. She had shrieked and writhed on the flagstones of that courtyard before rising to cast a final cold slur at the man she despised.

Celimus remembered it well.

"I would rather die than have you touch me again, you pig!"

And the chilling, prophetic reply. "Perhaps that can be arranged," his father had said, just as coldly.

Celimus had not been the only one in earshot of the harsh exchange and so when the hunting accident occurred not long after, it was a small leap for many who had heard the gossip. Anyone who knew Magnus would refute the claim fiercely. Anyone who knew him well enough would know the man was more than capable of such a thing. Whether he had killed his wife or whether it was an accident remained a tantalizing mystery to Celimus. It was a matter never discussed and over the years it had become a buried issue, as cold as the tomb that enclosed its victim.

Celimus never forgot it, however. It festered in his heart to become a dark ball of hate he vowed to one day hurl at the pig who sired him. He had heard his father openly threaten Adana and from the day of her death he had privately sworn to make his father pay. As a child there was little more he could do than remove all contact and pretense at affection, even in public, from the King as best he could. Drawing on memories of his mother, he became utterly cold and detached from Magnus, who, by the same token and at the urgings of Fergys, had begun an all-out effort to bring his son closer. But it was too late.

Too late for the father to give love. Too late for the child to want it, let alone welcome it. In a youngster's warped way Celimus had linked the always present Fergys Thirsk with wanting Adana dead and maturing had not eased the young Prince's attitude toward his father's closest friend. When the news of Thirsk's passing had begun to filter through Stoneheart, Celimus had rejoiced at the old General's death. He had hoped it would drive a stake of pain so hard into his father's heart that he might die of the agony and loneliness. But now he was having to deal with the hated seed of Thirsk's loins. And the son appeared to have the same qualities that the father had showed before him.

Now was a chance to stick another stake into his father's side. Oh, he knew how how his father loved Wyl. Did Magnus think him a fool? Did he not think it was writ all over his peasant face everytime he encountered the flame-haired troll? It mattered not to Celimus that he did not chase his father's affection but he would be damned if he'd allow the old man to love anyone. *You don't deserve it,* he had often raged silently at his father whenever he saw the pair of them together. *I will not permit you that pleasure, that sense of warmth in your last years. You denied it to me and then you destroyed the only person who ever loved me. I shall do the same to you by destroying Wyl Thirsk whom you fawn over,* he promised himself, smiling slyly toward the aging monarch.

Celimus had deliberately never given the Thirsk lad a chance. From the moment of Wyl's arrival at Stoneheart,

Celimus had set about a campaign of destruction, his intention to break Wyl's spirit and send him running home to Argorn. But so far the lad's keen desire to follow in his father's footsteps was giving him sufficient grit to withstand Celimus's cruel schemings. He did not care for the defiance that burned in Wyl's gaze either, that remained even when he was seemingly paying homage.

"I'd like to poke your eyes out, Wyl, and wipe that disloyal gaze from your ugly halfwit's face," he said to himself. "One day I might just do that. Destroy your eyes, destroy you, destroy the pretty, spoiled Ylena . . ." he trailed off as he heard the bells again.

He smiled savagely at what the sound prompted in his mind. The Prince had heard the change in the bells a day or so ago. Discreet inquiries had told him this afternoon was the right time to strike. He had only his mother's reports to go on of how brutal the torture of a witch could be. He reveled in the thought that he would finally witness the brutality she had hinted toward when he was a boy. Persuaded by his bigoted mother, he held the view that those who appeared to wield magic—not that he believed in it—should be hunted down and executed. In truth Celimus cared nothing for witches or warlocks. Their kind had never impacted on his life and his generation had no belief in such folk, yet the idea of wringing confessions using methods of torture from supposedly empowered people did interest him. It interested him in the same way it fascinated him to hear the screams when he bullied and hurt defenseless creatures such as the palace dogs and cats. As a youngster he had enjoyed listening to their pitiful cries for release from his ministrations. He wondered if anyone knew how many corpses he had secretly buried, mostly in the midden heaps around Stoneheart.

He would have to sneak into the dungeon today, of course, but he was counting on no one having the courage to ask a royal Prince to leave—not now that he was a man and tall enough to look down on most. No, he would have a fine afternoon's entertainment, not the least of which was dragging thirteen-year-old Thirsk through what he hoped would be a shattering experience that would show up the General for the cringing child he surely was.

"I'll bring you down, Wyl Thirsk. I shall crush you like overripe fruit and then I will poison your family name. And when I'm King," he muttered to himself, unaware that his words were becoming loud enough for others to hear, "I shall end the reign of the Thirsk ingrates as generals by—"

His rantings were interrupted by the arrival of the breathless page.

"Well?" the Prince demanded.

The boy, sweating from both exertion and his nervousness of having to face the well-known temper of the young heir, stammered that Wyl Thirsk was not to be found in Stoneheart.

Before Celimus could explode the boy tremulously added, "But I have an idea where he might have gone, my lord Prince."

Celimus bent low toward the trembling child. "I don't care where you have to go, you dullard, but you find him and do it quickly!" he bellowed at the youngster. "Don't come back here without Thirsk," he yelled toward the retreating figure. "Or it will be your neck I'll snap!"

The boy fled.

Wyl was not so far away on this particular afternoon but had made himself scarce with Alyd Donal. Fortune had smiled upon him a few months after the meeting with the King. A new boy, the same age as Wyl, had been brought into the group. He too came from a close family and because they were both feeling a similar emotional dislocation the boys became inseparable.

Wyl could tell that Gueryn had done everything within his power to encourage the friendship and had gone so far as to include Alyd in his personal training with Wyl. But Wyl, much to his lament, now spent long periods out of the yards and in tutoring with Celimus.

Wyl had kept his promise to the King and made himself as available as he could to Celimus but nothing had changed in how they felt about each other. But he had forged the ability within himself to simply accept his lot. He would not join in with any of the mischief that the swaggering Celimus promoted and yet, like a shadow, was never very far away. Wyl watched and Wyl protected wherever he could, often warning Celimus of impending discovery of his latest scheme or diverting attention to prevent him from being found out. It was not without its risks and it was obvious to him that Celimus was unaware of the pact Wyl had forged with his father. He never promised he would like the heir, though, or even respect him and Wyl could never fully suppress his smoldering contempt. His friend Alyd warned that it showed.

"Tread carefully, Wyl. He will make you pay somehow."

"I've saved his lot so many times."

"For which he owes you nothing! Don't forget your place or the fact that your pact is with the King alone. One day Celimus will be King . . . what will you do then?"

Wyl could not answer that pointed question. The notion of Celimus ruling Morgravia twisted in his gut all too often. Kneeling to him, swearing loyalty to him—privately he wondered if he could ever do this and mean it.

He knew he was ugly to the heir's beautiful eyes. Celimus took immense pleasure in reminding Wyl of his plainness. Wyl had little choice but to accept the taunts with grace; he knew the Prince was, for once, not lying in this regard. Nevertheless the words stung. It was Alyd who always helped him retrieve his sense of humor and whenever the pair found time alone together explosions of laughter could be heard.

Wyl firmly believed Shar had sent a golden-haired angel to him in the shape of Alyd, for laughter had been rare in his life at Stoneheart before his arrival. Alyd's sharp wit and easy style seemed perfect foils for Wyl's remote, yet very direct manner, and where Wyl was brutally honest, Alyd had the gift of gilding the lily, always prone to exaggeration. Alyd's storytelling powers had become legend, even in his short time at Stoneheart; a minor event, such as Lord Berry's wig slipping when the old fellow napped during a council, took on gigantic, hysterical proportions when retold through the imagination of Alyd Donal.

Wyl loved Alyd for his friendship, his ability to make him laugh out loud, and for his interest in Ylena. It never bothered Alyd on the rare occasions she tagged along with them and he appeared to take as much delight in entertaining her as Ylena did in accompanying them. And while she was blossoming into the same golden beauty her mother had once possessed, the boys had put on some height and bulk. Gueryn had seen to it that if Wyl was not going to be especially tall, then he would have strong physical presence that would impress his men in years to come. He devised for Wyl and Alyd a special training routine that worked on their boyish muscles, and the results were impressive already.

"You'll be my second, I promise," Wyl said solemnly to Alyd as they chewed on apples near the lake that flanked Stoneheart. It was a free afternoon; the day was cold but the sun shone and both boys had nothing better to do than lie on their backs, hidden from the castle's world, and stare up at the sky, making plans as they dreamed of soldiering together in the Legion.

"How do you know they'll allow it?" Alyd replied.

Wyl snorted. "Who is 'they?' I will be 'they,' " he said in a rare show of arrogance. "I am General of the Morgravian Legion."

"Title only," Alyd corrected.

Wyl ignored him. "And in a few years, I will lead our army. My father had total control of the men. And I will have only those I trust as my Captains and Lieutenants."

"But what if—" Alyd broke off as a disheveled and weary-looking page suddenly crested the hillock they lay against.

"Oh, what now?" Wyl muttered. "Ho, Jon!"

The relief was evident on the youngster's face. "You've got to come, Master Thirsk—he commands you."

Wyl grimaced, resigned. He stood. "The Prince?"

Jon nodded, still breathing hard from his exertions. "I've been looking everywhere for you. He's in a hot temper, too."

"Lovely—just how we like him," Alyd said, grinning and standing as well. "How did you find us anyway, young Jon?"

The boy's eyes flicked nervously at Wyl. "Your sister, Master Thirsk. I'm sorry but I had to find you."

"That's all right, think no more on it."

"We'll just run her through with our swords later," Alyd reassured him.

Jon looked aghast.

"He's being witty, Jon. As if he would harm the girl he loves."

It was Alyd's turn to look shocked. He threw his apple core at his friend, then in a blink he knocked Wyl backward and sent them both rolling down the hill with the poor page running after them.

"How dare you!" Alyd accused, not sure whether to laugh or punch his friend.

"It's obvious to a blind man, you fool."

"She's not even eleven, curse you!"

"Yes and when you're twenty, she'll be sixteen summers and equally eligible. Don't deny it, Alyd Donal. You're starry-eyed over my baby sister. But I actually approve—lucky for you."

"I refuse to discuss this," Alyd said but Wyl could see a treacherous red flush at his neck—a sure sign that Alyd's protestations were empty.

He grinned. And then noticed the trembling Jon. "Shar forgive us! Sorry, Jon. I'm coming. Lead the way. See you, Alyd—don't get into any trouble while I'm away."

"Watch your back, Wyl. He's never up to any good."

At sixteen the Prince's stature had undergone a major transformation and it felt to Wyl as though Celimus towered above him, making his own recent spurt of growth irrelevant. The Prince had broadened as well. He was indeed breathtaking in looks, but spoiled by the scowl.

"Don't keep me waiting like that again, Thirsk."

"My apologies, your highness," Wyl said, adopting his usual politeness. "How can I assist?" he added, moving the conversation quickly forward. He knew from experience that if he did not it would follow the traditional path of insult.

"You're well fortunate that I am in a good mood today."

"I am glad of it, highness. How can I make it brighter?" he said, almost smirking at his own sycophantic manner. Alyd had taught him how to say something in a sugary way while meaning something quite different. Wyl had learned that this tactic worked well on Celimus who was too vain and preoccupied to notice. Alyd would be proud of him.

"Back to your duties," Celimus said to the page and Jon trotted off, happy to be away from the growls of the Prince. Celimus returned his olive gaze to the lad his father had implored him to get closer to. He sneered and Wyl wondered what wickedness lay behind it.

"Come along, then," Celimus said chirpily. "I have a special treat for you."

"Where are we going?"

"It's a surprise, Wyl."

Myrren's bruises and cuts had begun healing. She now sat shivering in the dungeons of Stoneheart, where they had brought her days ago. The hunger pangs of near-starvation had recently settled into a numbness. She had refused the deliberately salty food they had thrown into the cell, knowing full well no water would be offered later when her parched throat would scream for it. And after a few days of such treatment the raging thirst would be enough to send one mad, as it had some poor soul a few cells down. She was the only Stalkers' prey in the dungeon and thus inwardly accepted that she would offer the best sport.

They were preparing her for the "trial" that would extract her eventual confession under torture. Myrren could hear the mournful ringing of the bells and was half-tempted to fall to the damp flagstones and writhe about as witches were apparently meant to. That would soon bring them running, excited that she had been found out. It would save a lot of pain, she realized grimly. She could just confess and be done. They would kill her anyway, so why suffer more than was necessary?

A small voice inside begged her to make it easy for herself. Death was coming whichever way she looked at it and it could either be a merciful end by fire after possibly days of agony, or she imagined, it could be swift and relatively painless; a brief confession and a blade into the throat. Myrren thought of the flames. They frightened her more than the notion of torture, which seemed harder to imagine. But she had no trouble picturing herself bound and screaming as the fire melted and consumed her flesh.

The trial—as had been explained to her by a tall, hook-nosed creature who had introduced himself as Confessor Lymbert—had three categories. Lymbert, whose name Myrren had recognized with a sinking heart, preferred to call these categories "degrees." The word made him smile each time he uttered it.

Myrren had already undergone Lymbert's so-called first degree. Apart from the permitted rape by one of his assistants in which her virginity was torn away from her, she had been stripped, bound, and flogged in front of a group of hooded men. They were presumably remnants of Zerques whom, she realized, were far more interested in viewing her naked body in pain than extracting anything more than her helpless shrieks.

Myrren had always believed that King Magnus was not in favor of these fanatics, that he had crushed them and their Order. Her parents had not shared her optimism. They had always warned her to be careful.

"It's your eyes, my love," her father would gently say. "The zealots will not see your beauty or hear the intelligence of your words. They will see only the mismatch of your eyes and all the old superstitions will rise up to frighten them."

She had known since she was old enough to converse with others that she was different and was being protected by her parents. Her mother had once confessed the constant anxiety she and her father held for Myrren. She too had referred to her daughter's eyes and the old fear.

"Poke them out, then!" Myrren had once suggested angrily, much to her parents' dismay. She had not meant to shock them but she was tired of the constant care she took to distract strangers from looking at her full in the face.

Tired of the scarves and shawls her mother insisted she wear when out and about.

It was never going to change. The fear was ancient and, though Morgravians were more enlightened and even openly dismissive of the existence of magic these days, the need to privately ward against sorcery still pervaded. Myrren wished she did possess the power to change the color of her eyes because she had known the Witch Stalkers and their whisperings would hover around her for all of her life. She remembered how she had felt hollow after being so abrupt with the noble, sensing immediately that it could lead to trouble—although she was past caring once his unwelcome hand had slipped beneath her skirts. His drunken breath made her feel ill and his decrepit and desperate desires brought a wave of disgust. Her contempt showed in her rebuke. And now she was paying the price.

Nevertheless, she would give no satisfaction to these men.

And so after the first couple of licks from the whip, which brought her shrill objections, she had clamped her teeth as hard as she could and uttered no further sound. She would give them nothing of herself, not even her groans.

Another woman, far older than her, had received similar treatment simultaneously and she had cried throughout, begging for pity. She was accused of slaying her husband but no one paid any attention to the old burns, the bruises, the limbs that had obviously been broken previously and were now twisted. Here, clearly, was a woman tormented by a brutal husband. It mattered not. In finding the courage to kill him, she would now pay with her own life. The flogging had finally stopped and both women had remained bent over barrels, inhaling whatever air they could drag into their lungs to steady their trembling limbs and shattered nerves. The pain from the bleeding welts on Myrren's back had been so intense and all-consuming it became part of her. She had somehow been able to absorb it and put it aside. Moments later she had been turned and strapped to a post. She recalled ignoring the cloudy messages of pain from her back as it had chafed against the rough timber. The men had then enjoyed watching her body, still naked, from a different angle, but more importantly, she had been able to witness what was happening to her companion.

They had obviously decided, Myrren deduced, that she should be saved for future entertainment—a suspected witch, after such a dearth, was to be savored after all. Myrren had watched mournfully as the other woman had been dragged from her barrel.

"Put her boots on," Lymbert had commanded, bored with this one, and Myrren had closed her eyes. She knew what was coming, for Lymbert had already taken sincere delight in giving her a guided tour of this torture chamber.

The sagging woman had been hauled jabbering toward a bench where she had been pushed into a sitting position.

"Bind her hands," Lymbert had ordered.

"I beg you, sir," the victim had beseeched and Myrren had clenched her eyelids tight and had tried to close off her hearing but could not. She knew there would be no mercy now, not for a killer . . . certainly not for one who would not admit to murdering in cold blood.

Two specially crafted vises had then been clamped around the woman's feet. She had been still too much in a swoon from the pain of her flogging to even realize that more pain was coming. Needless to say it had not taken too many twists of the cruel screws to shatter the shin bone in one of her legs, at which point the victim had screeched a confession, agreeing that she had in fact planned and then murdered her husband without remorse. Myrren could tell that the Confessor had little interest in pursuing the truth, particularly in the cases of common criminals. She understood that Lymbert did not view extracting confessions from thieves, bandits, and murderers as his appointed duty. It seemed he wanted the old woman dealt with as quickly as possible, in order to pursue his real interest—the annihilation of witches and warlocks, what he called the curse of society. Myrren's father had once shared a rumor he had heard that Lymbert's grandparents had been fervent Zerques, whose only daughter had supposedly been killed by a suspected witch four decades previous. As a result, right from childhood Lymbert had harbored a grudge

against anyone who supposedly dealt in matters of magic—
and extended this to herbmen and herbwomen, whom he
believed drew on devil craft for their healings. Fearful for
their daughter, Myrren's parents had gathered as much information as possible about the Confessor. Lymbert was
renowned for being so stringent in his investigations that he
never brought a victim to trial without their conviction
being a certainty—and Myrren knew it would have taken
only one glance at her eyes for him to be sure of winning a
conviction in her case.

Myrren opened those same odd eyes now and fought
back tears at the memory of the older woman's terror. She
remembered how Lymbert had turned and smiled directly at
her as he watched the woman put her mark to the confession and sent her away to die at the end of a rope, no doubt.
The message Myrren received from that cold grin had been
unmistakable. He was reserving her for much harsher treatment. The woman had been carried off and not heard from
again, presumably dispatched that same day.

Lymbert's assistant, the same one who had used her
body, had then untied Myrren, blowing his foul breath into
her face as he had whispered all the other sexual obsceni-
ties he would like to inflict on her. He had deliberately let
her fall when the bindings had come loose and had then
savagely grabbed her by the hair and dragged her back to
her feet but still she had given none of those present the satisfaction they so desperately wanted.

"Back to her cell," Lymbert had commanded, unmoved
by her courage. "The witch, Myrren of Baelup, will un-
dergo second-degree torture in three days," Lymbert had
proclaimed to all present. Then he had looked at her. "That
should give you sufficient time, my dear, to lick your
wounds"—he had chuckled softly at his jest—"and perhaps
loosen your tongue."

So now she sat in the dungeon contemplating the next
stage, when Lymbert and his henchmen would get down to
the real business of torture. Myrren was not sure whether it
was day or night. The cell was small, windowless and airless save whatever fetid air might leak up the corridor and

through her bars. She huddled herself on the ground, naked but for a rough scrap of blanket crawling with biting insects. Nevertheless it was all she had and the young woman wrapped herself as best she could, turning away from the doorway.

She thought of her parents but did not cry this time—it seemed every pointless tear had leaked from her body. But then she thought of the black puppy and tears surged again. He had been a special present and had brought such joy. Myrren had called him Knave. He was abandoned now—she felt sure her mother would not be of a state of mind to care about a dog.

"I wish I could fight back," she whispered. "If I were a witch, I'd seek revenge."

The tears came for Knave and with them a voice in her head.

Fear not, my child. You are no witch but you will have your vengeance.

"Who speaks?" she whispered, terrified, whipping her head around in the darkness.

I am Elysius, the man spoke into her mind.

A few hours later Myrren felt exhausted but at peace. She was amazed that she could think so calmly about the inescapable trauma that lay ahead of her. Elysius had explained much. Now she understood. He had urged her to be brave. She realized she had no choice to be anything but courageous.

Lymbert and his henchmen were preparing to come for her. The Confessor had sent her some items of clothing. Through his aide he insisted she wear them but she soon found out they were nothing more sophisticated than a piece of rough cloth with a hole for her head, and another strip of fabric for a belt. Myrren wondered if Lymbert had suddenly had a change of heart and would allow her a modicum of dignity through her trial. But nothing about Lymbert's conduct so far could convince her that he possessed any empathy for his victims. She dismissed her notion as wishful but gladly donned the garment. In sudden inspiration she used the blunt spoon that sat amongst the congealed mess that passed as food in this place to scratch a message onto one of the stones. It made her feel defiant in these last hours of her life.

Myrren felt grateful that since hearing the voice of Elysius she had felt a strange numbness overtake her body. She recalled his softly spoken words now, repeating them silently to herself.

They will hurt you, my little one. But the pain will be minimized. I cannot save you but I will give you the means to avenge your death. Hear me now, I give you a gift—and he had told her it all.

Why can I not use this gift to save myself? she had asked into this strange void opened in her mind.

Because, child, they will burn you. It will not work. And he had explained why.

She had fought back the initial surge of hope as understanding dawned. He had spoken more but it was of an intimate nature. She had heard his words, his explanation of who she truly was. Despite the shock of it, she had loved him then for sharing the news and she had buried the information within. She would not resurrect that joy and have it tarnished here by these proceedings.

Myrren of Baelup was no witch but she had a gift to give that would unleash a relentless power until it found the true target of her vengeance.

Myrren considered her torture now. Lymbert's choice would most likely be the rack, for his eyes had lit up at its mention during her tour, and probably thumbscrews, which she had seen the Confessor almost lovingly stroke when he had presented them to her.

But Myrren was wrong.

When they led her once again into the main torture chamber it seemed he had reserved something far more special for her. Many more people had gathered, including the smug Lord Rokan, invited no doubt to savor the results of his connivings. In fact the room was crowded with men, none hooded this time, eager to witness her trial and the confession.

Wyl stood rigid next to Celimus in the torture chamber. The men gathered were talking excitedly; some jocular and a few voices raised in obvious anticipation of what was to come. The Prince joined in the animated conversations while Wyl scowled and made a poor attempt to mask his nervousness at being in this place.

Celimus had taken him by surprise with this jaunt. Wyl gathered he was here to witness something unpleasant; he too had heard the bells and Gueryn's solid education told him what they meant. But he had not yet put it together in his mind that he was present to see the torture of a witch. Even now as a hush began to spread around the room, Wyl expected it would be the hasty confession of a criminal that Celimus's warped mind felt he needed to see.

Of course he wondered why so many would be present but his anxiety prevented him from exploring that notion. His question was answered when a man called Lymbert announced himself and the witch Myrren.

Her arrival silenced the chamber and Wyl held his breath when he saw the attractive young woman raise her head and challenge her audience with a compelling gaze that saw most of the men clear their throats and cast their eyes toward their feet. It was a small win, Wyl felt, but he applauded her courage nonetheless and he hoped it fueled her obvious resolve to die bravely.

Rough hands began to tear the flimsy garment from her body and Lymbert's seeming generosity fell into place for the falsity it was: he had insisted on her being robed only in order to make the theater of her torture, beginning with nakedness, that much more dramatic for his audience. Wyl could not know this but he did not need further reason to dislike the man after watching the way he licked his lips at her nakedness and helplessness.

The rents in Myrren's robe revealed her body, just blossomed into womanhood, and the audience's gaze no longer rested in discomfort by its collective feet but was drawn all too hungrily toward her bared skin.

A squealing noise distracted them and Wyl, together with the rest of the onlookers, glanced above where a strange contraption was being lowered from the ceiling. His attention was quickly drawn back to Myrren, whom he also noticed did not give Lymbert the pleasure of her fear. She ignored both her Confessor and the contraption, instead fixing her focus on Wyl.

He could not help but wonder what she thought of him with his crop of bright red hair atop a plain and lightly freckled face, which he knew was heavily written with despair. His own unremarkable eyes were riveted upon her. Not upon her bare flesh but on her own ill-matched eyes. He watched her expression soften as she regarded him and she even dared the barest of smiles. He was so petrified on her behalf he did not have the ability to muster even the hint of a smile in return.

Wyl heard Lymbert making some announcement to those gathered, who nodded and made sounds of approval, led by her accuser, Rokan, but neither he nor Myrren paid attention. Wyl surmised she had lost all notion of embarrassment at her nudity but from her grimace was perhaps more acutely aware of her hands being tied tightly behind her.

A cleric was brought to absolve her of her sins and as she turned her gaze on him, Wyl watched the man recoil at the sight of her eyes. Nevertheless, he prayed to Shar's Gatherers to claim her soul and for that Wyl was grateful.

"Thank you," Wyl heard her utter to the cleric as he began his mournful prayer to guide her soul to Shar.

She looked over the short priest's bowed head, her attention drawn again to Wyl, who watched her gaze shift now towards Celimus and who heard Myrren's sharp intake of breath. Her captors probably thought it was because they had just tested the ropes that bound her hands but Wyl was sure Myrren's sound had escaped at the beauty of his companion and he hated Celimus all the more for having her attention.

That same beautiful man leered at her nakedness and

whispered something lewd to Wyl, who scowled with disgust and blushed furiously. Hitting his mark, Celimus laughed loudly and Rokan nearby joined in.

Celimus muttered, none too softly over the prayer, that the trial had been his idea. People nodded and grinned.

"And it was I who discovered the witch in the first place, my Prince," Lord Rokan added, keen to be included in the praise.

Wyl saw Celimus scowl in Rokan's direction and it seemed the middle-aged noble considered it politic to remain quiet from here on and allow the young royal to have his moment.

"Have you anything to say?" Lymbert's voice suddenly boomed to Myrren above the idle murmurings. Apparently the priest had stopped his praying, not that Wyl had noticed.

He watched Myrren take a deep breath and look around her. "Yes," she replied. "Who is that person?"

Lymbert stepped aside, taken aback by her odd question, and looked at those gathered. "Which one?"

Myrren stared at Celimus. "You."

Wyl did not have to look to know it. He could feel the triumph emanating from Celimus and imagined the smile stretching across his face. Wyl felt disappointment knife through him that she had chosen the Prince for recognition and he looked down while Celimus took a step forward, all easy grace and arrogant swagger.

"My lady," he said, accentuating his words to ensure the insult could not be mistaken for genuine politeness, "I am Prince Celimus."

Wyl glanced toward her. Whether she was surprised to share such lofty company for her forthcoming pain, he could not tell for she managed to keep her expression unmoved, her voice steady. "I understand why the pig-fingered Lord Rokan would bring along his bruised ego and flaccid member for inflation at my expense." There was a series of audible gasps followed by snickers amongst the audience and Wyl reveled in the high color suddenly on the cheeks of the noble who had brought about her ruin. "But why," she continued, "would a Prince of the realm have any interest in this—" she swept her strange eyes around the chamber—"mummery? For that's what this is, sire."

Wyl watched the Prince grin and wondered whether it made Myrren's heart flutter as it did so many of the young noblewomen of Pearlis.

"Lord Rokan's flaccid member aside, madam, I am here in the name of education," Celimus replied and then Wyl felt himself grabbed by the Prince. He struggled but Celimus held him firmly. "This lad here has never watched a witch confess before. As he is soon to lead our great Legion and stand up as my Champion when I am King, I felt it was my duty to expand his knowledge of Stoneheart's ways, which has been sadly lacking in his life. He's a country bumpkin, you see."

This time Wyl twisted away angrily from Celimus's grip and shook his head vehemently so Myrren would know his attendance here was forced. He remained silent, though, imploring the woman before him to understand.

She nodded at Celimus but this time her gaze rested on Wyl. "Thank you," she offered and he knew she understood. "Do what you will, Lymbert. You'll get no confession from me."

"Feisty," Celimus said, running his tongue over his lips. "Pity she had to be broken so. I would have bedded her first and loosened her mouth by a different sort of torture." Everyone around him laughed loudly again, led by Lord Rokan aiming to ingratiate himself to the crowd once more after the young woman's heinous accusation.

Wyl, helpless to stop this terror unfolding, saw the confessor step forward. There was a sparkle in Lymbert's eyes. "Myrren, may I introduce you to the Dark Angel. It's my favorite instrument. I'd like to take a few moments to explain how it works, if you please." He was all graciousness now, enjoying the chance to show off his latest contraption of pain. "Your hands are tied behind you for a reason and now my assistant is attaching the Angel to your bound hands. When I give the word, those three men over there," he said, pointing, but Wyl cheered silently that she refused to look, "will use that pulley to hoist you aloft so you will fly like an angel, your arms outstretched backward like wings," he said, enjoying himself. "Now, Myrren, it's at that point we'll all enjoy hearing your arms dislocating. My favorite sound." He all but shivered with delighted anticipation. "And did you notice the hundred-pound weights, my dear? Well, as you can see—if you would only look—they are attached to your feet now and they, of course, will do their best to fight the Angel to prevent your body leaving the ground, thereby assisting us in dislocating your hip joints. Oh, glorious agony! Incidentally, we have decided to bypass the somewhat tedious second degree and go straight to the third to save time and a great deal of pointless screaming. I hope that's agreeable to you?" He laughed jovially and everyone except Wyl joined him.

Myrren turned her face away.

"Oh, and, Myrren," he added, "I nearly forgot—how careless of me. I thought I'd throw in what I like to call Dark Angel Swoops for good measure. Perhaps you don't know what that is? It's the most exquisite suffering I think I could possibly inflict without actually drawing blood. This is when we will let go of the Angel's ropes—just momentarily—and you, of course, my dear, will fall from the sky. But oh—and this is the good bit—my men will suddenly halt that swoop to the ground by grabbing the rope and you just can't imagine what torment that's going to mean for those suffering sockets and limbs, long past their pain barriers. Now, do be a good girl and confess after the first flight and drop because you should know that by law I have another three times to inflict it. It will hurt a great deal more by the fourth and I do think it's more noble to die by the flames than hanging dead and broken on the ropes, don't you?"

This time Wyl wanted to applaud loudly when she spat at him, but he held his composure watching her turn her back to her tormentor in a last show of defiance. It was but a momentary triumph.

"Hoist the witch—let's watch the Dark Angel fly," he said viciously and his henchmen obeyed, hauling on the rope attached to a pulley.

Wyl felt his stomach contents lurch into his throat as he

heard the inevitable and sickening sound of Myrren's shoulders capitulating almost immediately. As the first of her limb sockets popped, Wyl's midday meal burst onto his boots but few paid him any attention, except Celimus, who pushed him aside to avoid being splattered.

The Prince was laughing, though, and Wyl knew Celimus was revelling in Wyl's obvious squeamishness at watching a woman suffer.

"Trust you're enjoying my surprise, General," he growled for Wyl's hearing only.

This was what he had wanted, Wyl knew, to finally unsettle his Champion-to-be into humiliating himself. It was true that plenty of other watchers looked away or retched at the hideous sound of her shoulders releasing their arms but only Wyl's discomfort counted for Celimus.

No one in that room heard Myrren utter a sound.

They dropped Myrren time and again that afternoon, all the while demanding she confess herself a witch and failing. For several periods she appeared unconscious, presumably from the torturous pain. Wyl could not comprehend how she resisted, for he felt weak from her trauma. He felt sure many were quietly in awe of the courage it took to repel such an assault, for none would be able to imagine the level of punishment her body withstood.

Lymbert, coolly detached, expertly revived Myrren on each occasion with strong smelling salts and a dousing of freezing water. Still her mouth was firmly closed to any sound, although every other opening of her body slackened with the shock of her trauma, and if she were able, Wyl thought she might have even derived some satisfaction from the effect her loosened muscles had. Initially the chamber had smelled of men's sweat and lust. Now it smelled like a cesspit and a few experienced trial attendees held perfumed linens to their noses.

Knowing this was a test of his own nerves but also frozen with fear at what this young woman endured, Wyl remained as still now as one of the statues of Stoneheart. He had conquered the second wave of nausea and panic, fighting back the sour bile. Now he would conquer his fear and be like her; he would not capitulate.

Wyl understood why Celimus had brought him. It was to show him up as a child, a pretender to his father's title. Well, he would not permit Celimus to succeed in this humiliation. Ignoring the stench of his own soiled boots, he lifted his chin and stared at the closed eyes of Myrren, his own new bedrock of determination derived from her refusal to succumb to their demands.

Lymbert had his victim pulled higher so that the weights attached to Myrren's already distended legs and arms could stretch them further. He was satisfied to hear her ankles and elbows give up their resistance. Now every major joint was loosened from its socket and several inches were added to her height, some wit acknowledged.

Naked, broken, and surely dying, she was still true to herself, Wyl realized. He now would prove himself to be just as true to the name of Thirsk. He was no coward and, although this was a shocking, intensely barbaric scene, he would not let himself down again.

As her eyes opened once more at the dousing of chilled water, they seemed to search for his, and in that moment he felt connected to Myrren. Together, united by their personal despair, they would get each other past this torment. It might be a childish view, he thought, but he was somehow convinced she knew he was staying strong for her. Her time was short—that much was obvious—and he promised himself he would see her through to her end without turning his head again.

Look at me only, Myrren, he willed. But she closed her strange and exhausted eyes once again. He wished she was dead but knew otherwise as she retched for the umpteenth time from her agonies, her thin framework of delicate bones in stark relief beneath stretched skin.

She had endured the four mighty drops. Lymbert had begun to scream at her to confess, seemingly demented with his desire to overpower and win this admission from her. Realizing she had somehow, impossibly, won, he looked around wildly and then ran toward one of the braziers, surprising the man tending it. It was obvious that the Confessor could not afford to fail in wringing a confession from the girl, particularly with the Prince in attendance. Wyl could tell that Lymbert had been unprepared for the royal presence; perhaps he had not experienced such an important audience in his work, and having sensed the cruelty smoldering in his regal guest, the Confessor intended to display the full breadth of his skills.

Wyl watched with horror as the man grabbed a nearby glove and picked up a pair of white-hot pincers from the coals. Tearing the flesh from victims' bones was surely not Lymbert's favorite practice but all present could see that there was no other way he might prevail in this battle of wills. Lymbert had already explained that no one resisted the Dark Angel or her swoops yet here was brave Myrren, her fourth drop completed and still adamant.

Wyl's pride surged as did his anger. He had status here, no matter how young he was. *Do something,* he silently screamed at himself.

Reaching for the pale flesh of Myrren, who was hanging unconscious once again, Lymbert was stopped by a loud command into the now brittle atmosphere of the torture chamber. The crazed Confessor turned around, scanning for its owner, his face a mask of fury.

"You will put those down," Wyl repeated. "She has suffered enough punishment by your hand, sir, and she has survived the four legal drops."

"And who in Shar's Name are you to give me orders?" Lymbert sneered, gathering his wits.

Wyl felt his rage focus on this cruel man. And the white flash of anger coursing through him suddenly made him feel stronger, bigger than he knew he was. Even his voice suddenly sounded deeper as he faced down the torturer.

"I am Wyl Thirsk. You'd do well to remember that name, Confessor. It belongs to someone with the ear of our King and I will recount all that I have witnessed here today and the law you are about to break if you do not end this procedure now. Our King would not permit you to step beyond the legal boundaries. The trial is over. Let her die."

Celimus stepped in, the ever-present grin across his

mouth, and was about to take charge of proceedings when something dangerous in Wyl's glare stopped him.

"Your highness," Wyl said. "With respect, I believe it undermines your status to witness these proceedings any further. As your protector I insist we get you away from this place."

Celimus was shocked as Wyl knew he would be. All eyes were on the Prince now. If he remained he would certainly appear the sadistic royal voyeur—as Wyl had cleverly insinuated. He could not risk that.

"Of course, you are right, thank you, Thirsk. I had no idea it would be so ugly," he lied, a murderous look in his eyes. "Lymbert, do as he says: bring her down. Incidentally, let me introduce General Thirsk of Morgravia."

"But . . . but he is a mere lad, sire," Lymbert spat.

"Young, yes," Wyl countered, not allowing Celimus to answer on his behalf. "But my name carries weight where yours never will unless you consider 'traveling butcher' a memorable title. Do as your Prince commands. Lower her!"

It was an audacious order coming from the red-headed youth. Watchers muttered to one another but none challenged him outwardly as it was obvious the lad was with the Prince.

As Myrren was lowered, Celimus shouldered his way through the onlookers but not before whispering to Wyl: "There will be a reckoning for this."

It was as he expected and Wyl sighed, pushing the Prince's threat from his mind, for the woman needed him. Wyl watched the Prince leave and then to Lymbert's disgust he demanded a cup of water be poured from a pitcher. He knelt by Myrren and after gently lifting her head he dribbled a trickle of it into her throat. Her lids fluttered open and somehow she mustered a smile that touched her oddly colored eyes.

"I'm Wyl" was all he could say.

"I know," she croaked through her cracked lips, bleeding from where she had bitten them. "I shall return your kindness with a gift, Wyl. It will avenge me." Her voice was no more than a whisper.

What could you possibly give me? he thought as her eyes closed once again.

"She's for the flames now, Thirsk," one of the dungeoners growled.

He had no choice but to let them drag her limp body away.

"When?" Wyl demanded of Lymbert. He had decided the man deserved no courtesies.

"No time like the present," the Confessor replied and rediscovered his thin smile.

4

HE COLUMN OF PEOPLE SCRAMBLED OUT OF THE CITY TO GET a good view of the Witch Post on the hillock where they held the burnings. Some remembered the last burning, but most of the youngsters had no idea of the horror they would witness. Public executions in Morgravia were usually swift. This was a people forged from a tough, warring background and they had no need for theatrics. Any noble sentenced to death had head and body separated by a quick-falling sword; those of lower caste fell to the axe. Criminals convicted of a crime lesser than murder or treason were hung, and in such cases the King favored the drop method. It was brutal but merciful. He did not believe in death as an entertainment. Unfortunately, the very rarity of a witch-burning turned it into a public spectacle.

Traditionally, the Zerques had promoted a festival atmosphere for a burning and although the open celebration of death had long been wiped out, there remained a strong sense of theater. Lymbert's Witch Stalkers deliberately played off the harmless superstitions of the people, making warding signs as they led the procession up the hill. Many onlookers were bemused to realize that gestures they often performed without thinking—such as crossing their index and third finger should they inadvertently pass someone on a flight of stairs—were rooted in the ancient belief that such a sign in the vicinity of a witch would prevent the devil entering your body.

For the majority of Morgravians, their interest in viewing a proven witch stemmed from plain curiosity, but there were still those in Pearlis—wealthy older folk—whose fear and loathing of magic was very real. Lymbert was counting on this to convince his audience that this woman was a danger. He would fan the flames of those fears and watch them erupt into a desire to see the witch suffer as she burned.

Wyl's mood was as bleak as he could ever remember. With his mother's death and more recently his father's passing, his deep sorrow had been like a darkness over him and he had never felt more alone. But this turn of events involving the young woman called Myrren provoked in him a pure and seething rage . . . an anger he never thought he was capable of. And as always Celimus was at the root of his problems. If not for the Prince, Wyl might be none the wiser about Myrren.

Alyd caught up with him. The news of Wyl's stand-off in the torture chamber had obviously traveled fast.

"Is this wise?" he asked carefully, knowing how determined his friend could be.

Wyl stopped short. "You needed to be there to know why I do this."

Alyd's gaze narrowed. "Do what exactly?"

"You wouldn't understand."

"Why not?"

Wyl shrugged, the rage cooling to a hard determination. Gueryn had always warned him to harness wrath and unleash it only when he had it under control. He felt it was his to use now. His voice was brittle. "It's too hard to explain."

People jostled past them and in the distance Wyl could

see Gueryn striding purposefully toward where they stood. Alyd noticed him too. Time was now very short, for he knew Wyl would say nothing more in front of his mentor.

"Tell me quickly. Let me understand," he urged.

"I need to share it with her," Wyl blurted, rubbing a hand through his flame hair.

"Share what?"

"Her death. I can't describe it any better."

They both glanced toward the grim-faced Gueryn, now only a few strides away.

"Why? You can't do anything for her!"

"She needs me" was all Wyl could say and then the shadow of Gueryn fell over them.

"What happens here, Wyl?" There was no trace of emotion in the man's voice. Not a good sign. It was often easier when Gueryn was stirred to raise his voice.

Wyl told his tale as simply as he could, sticking to the facts in soldier fashion, as he had been trained. "I was forced to accompany Celimus to watch the torture of a woman accused of being a witch."

Gueryn sighed. "I gather."

"She wouldn't confess, didn't even utter a single sound of protest," he continued. "Confessor Lymbert made her go straight to the third stage. They dropped her four times using a contraption called the Dark Angel."

Wyl could see the confusion on Alyd's face and the inevitable question springing to his lips but Gueryn must have seen it too, for he prevented it with his own comment. "I have only witnessed such a thing once in my life. I only wish that I had been around to spare you of such a thing."

Wyl looked down. "I survived. She won't, guilty or otherwise."

"I heard that you assisted her."

"A sip of water." Wyl shrugged.

Gueryn nodded. He had heard all of this from someone who had been present. "That was noble of you, boy. So why are you here now?"

Wyl stayed quiet. It was Alyd who answered. "He says he wants to share her death." He looked back at his friend with an apology in his eyes and could see none was necessary. Wyl would forgive him anything.

Their attention was diverted to the main party bringing the accused.

"Here she comes!" Wyl exclaimed and made a move towards them.

"Leave it alone, lad," Gueryn said, grabbing his arm and spinning him back. "I felt similarly when I had to watch a woman suffer. I felt I should do something to help her but it was useless. They're going to burn her in spite of you."

Wyl's gaze considered Gueryn coolly. "I know."

His expression was now as serious and determined as any his father would strike when he had made a major decision. It was clear he would not be moved. "She needs to know that when she dies here today that her death is witnessed by at least one person who disagrees with it."

It sounded like an accusation. Gueryn let go of his arm. He and Alyd watched Wyl draw up alongside the cart and call to the slumped figure it carried.

"I thought they paraded convicted witches," Alyd queried.

"Normally, yes, but not if they've survived the Dark Angel," Gueryn answered, "and it would be nigh impossible after her swoops."

"Oh . . . is that when they rip all the limbs from their sockets?" Alyd asked, unable to quell his eagerness to learn all the bleak details of torture.

Gueryn answered absentmindedly, more intent on watching Wyl. "After what I've heard they've done to that poor girl, they'll be lucky if she can do any more than lie at the burning pole. Come, lad, if he's determined to see this, we must stay close. I fear it will be his undoing."

Wyl was already a brisk walk away, so his two friends did not hear the exchange between him and the torturer.

"Come to say your farewell?" Lymbert asked Wyl.

"Come to see that you treat this woman with the respect she deserves," he answered.

"Respect! A witch?" The Confessor was amused.

"Not proven, Lymbert. Your vile tortures won nothing from her."

"Watch yourself, boy. I know who you are but your rank counts for naught with me when I am about my business."

"That may be so, Confessor," Wyl replied, scowling at the title, "but officially those are my men behind you escorting this charade and I could disrupt affairs just as easily as let them take their course."

Wyl knew Lymbert regarded him with pure hate, although he was wise enough not to show too much of such an expression on his face.

"Have a care, Confessor," he added. "Do it right. Where is the samarra she is supposed to wear?"

"For someone so squeamish, you appear to know a great deal about the formalities of witch trials."

The barb did not work. Celimus's taunts had ensured Wyl was well used to ignoring insults. Instead he glared. "I am a noble's son, sir. I am well read." Wyl suddenly sounded years older.

Lymbert stepped away to order one of his men to fetch the special cloak. He carried a samarra with him as he travelled the realm but it was rarely seen. Ancient law required that the victim be burned wearing the samarra, which was believed to entrap evil humors emanating from the witch's flesh. The cloak bore a design of flames and dancing devils, with the Zerque sigil of a silver star to denote purity in the face of debauchery and evil. It was crafted by a special tailor, who needed royal assent to produce this garment. In ancient times, the cloak itself was considered enchanted and dangerous, and as such no other tailor could be granted permission to touch it. Lymbert realized this would be the first occasion for its use and grumbled at the price he calculated he would need to replace it. He stalked away from the upstart "General" and awaited his man.

"Myrren," Wyl called gently, trotting now alongside the cart, knowing he had but moments. "Myrren!"

Her eyes opened to slits. He watched her sore lips mouth his name. She tried to say something but he could not hear. He smiled, trying to convey his care, not knowing what to say. There were no words of comfort that could begin to touch what she had endured or would still endure before she met her god.

Wyl reached to her hand and touched it gently, casting a silent prayer to Shar to send his Gatherers for her soul and make her end quick. Then her minders pushed him aside as they arrived on the hillock. A single post had been buried into the ground, rising up to stand taller than the tallest of men. Around it were placed bales of straw. It was a sharply bright afternoon with few clouds. A breeze ruffled everyone's hair and the more wily onlookers took the hint and moved upwind of the promised smoke.

"General, if you please?" Lymbert said with a forced politeness that was all underlying insult. "We have a witch to burn." He hurled the highly decorated samarra at her.

She could not support herself, and so Lymbert's men, with no care for her suffering, pulled the cloak over her naked body before taking her by her stretched and broken limbs and throwing her toward the Witch Post.

"No point in tying her, Confessor, she ain't going anywhere," one commented.

The people near the front of the crowd dared a nervous laugh. Lymbert smiled indulgently and nodded as a priest might to his flock. He stood on a hay bale and began reciting the list of terrible acts Myrren was supposedly responsible for.

Gueryn grunted and muttered. "I see they make it no easier for her."

"What do you mean?" Wyl asked.

"The bushels are damp to ensure a slow burn."

Wyl did not reply but his expression darkened further as he gripped the small sack he carried with him.

The accusations done, Lymbert had nothing further to say other than to acknowledge that the accused woman had not confessed to being a witch.

"However, you can all view her eyes—as ill-matched a pair as you'll ever see." He made a gesture and one of his men pulled up the lids of Myrren's eyes to reveal the disturbing facts. Those closest peered obediently and made warding signs. "Might I add," Lymbert continued, "the mere fact she has survived four flights with the Dark Angel proves conclusively that she wields evil power." The city's bells tolled their dour clangor again—a new series of peals that announced the burning was about to commence.

Myrren had not moved since they threw her among the kindling. This was not what Lymbert wanted for his spectacle. The people had waited a long time for a burning and this wretch was determined to ruin the event. He noticed not a single noble was present, barring the lippy redhead and his hangers-on. Not even Lord Rokan was in attendance. It irritated Lymbert that he was performing for commoners; he ignored the small voice in his head that whispered that it was only they who might take him or the claim seriously enough to be impressed.

He called to his henchmen. "I suspect our fancy cloak need not burn with the witch," he said and chuckled, inviting all the onlookers to join him. Like sheep, they followed, unconcerned that in the absence of the samarra they might be infected by evil humors. Unlike their ancestors, who truly believed in the power of witchcraft, the majority of onlookers viewed the burning with curiosity. A few older members of the crowd made a warding gesture, but their mutterings were ignored.

The samarra, which had covered the girl, was wrenched away, leaving her naked once again.

That should spice things up a little, Lymbert thought to himself, pleased with the effect her broken but still strangely desirable body had on the menfolk. He was especially glad that the red-headed youth had not protested at the cloak being removed, although it surprised him. It seemed the young man's attention was diverted to a sack he was holding. Lymbert cared not. "Burn her!" he commanded.

And then there it was again, that damnable voice.

"Wait!" Wyl yelled, surprising Gueryn and Alyd, who flanked him. He stepped away from them. "Myrren of Baelup has not confessed to being a witch. She remains only accused and convicted. She will die by the flames, yes, but she will die with the dignity she has shown throughout her ordeal."

Wyl lifted out a shirt from the sack he carried.

Lymbert heard a sound and glanced behind him. "As you will, General Thirsk," the Confessor responded through gritted teeth. At least his expensive cloak was spared.

A group of the King's private soldiers moved briskly toward them on horseback. Amongst them he saw the unmistakable figures of Magnus and Celimus. So that was why Lymbert conceded so fast. Men immediately bowed low and the womenfolk curtsied, taken by surprise that their sovereign was present. Magnus said nothing but his face was grim, his jaw clenched.

If you don't like it, stop it, my King! Wyl begged inwardly. But Magnus only nodded once as he and his men continued on, passing by within twenty feet of the crowd. Celimus's expression was dark with his own anger but he managed a smirk at Wyl. It was Wyl's only consolation in this disturbing day that Celimus was clearly not going to be permitted to witness the burning. Perhaps his father had forbidden it. One could only hope. How these people could watch something like this—and cheer over it—eluded him.

It made him think of how, as a realm, they poked fun at the Mountain Dwellers, accusing them of being nothing more than barbarians. His father had cautioned him at leveling that tag so loosely.

We are the barbarians, Wyl thought, *to still be persecuting helpless women in this way. Peasants! Just like Adana claimed.* He looked around at the folk of Pearlis, out for some excitement. There were no nobles present, he was glad to note. Many in the crowd were youngsters, who had never seen a witch-burning before, and so he found it within himself to forgive them their gawking.

The King's arrival had broken the spell. People looked suddenly uncomfortable and Lymbert felt himself lose control of his special event. He grimaced as Wyl, rising from his obeisance to his sovereign, walked over to the girl and placed the damp shirt across her body.

Wyl whispered something again to her and she heard him, raising her face toward the one person who had shown her tenderness.

"My dog, Knave. Promise me you will keep him," she croaked.

"I swear it to you," Wyl said, bewildered at her concern for a beast when her own life was about to be obliterated.

At his response she smiled and her torn, twisted body seemed to relax.

"Farewell, Wyl. Fear not my gift."

Wyl nodded once, wondering why he should be afraid of a dog. He returned to stand alongside his companions, feeling that he had done all that he could for this woman.

Gueryn muttered under his breath, "I see you're well ahead of the Confessor, boy."

"She's suffered enough," Wyl murmured back.

"What are you both talking about?" Alyd whispered, helplessly mesmerized by the torches being lit.

"You'll see," Gueryn replied. "Good work, Wyl."

The torches touched the dry kindling. Immediately the twigs began to burn and Wyl saw Lymbert smile, smug in the knowledge that the straw would be a long time in the burning, his plan being that Myrren's throat would scorch and her insides dry out from inhaling the smoke long before her body would be consumed by the flame.

He watched the confessor take the comforting cup of wine that one of his assistants had poured from a clay flagon and heard the hateful man complain: "Such thirsty work, this burning."

As Lymbert tipped his head to take a gulp of the wine, his attention was grabbed by the sudden whoosh of flames around Myrren.

A spark had landed on the shirt Wyl had placed over her to protect her modesty and the tiny flame had caused the linen to ignite. Myrren, her body aflame now, struggled to sit up. Predictably, she failed. Wyl watched for Lymbert to search him out—the cursed boy—now that he realized that Wyl had doused the shirt with lamp oil. Wyl looked away. His eyes were only for Myrren now. Her lovely hair caught

alight, shriveling about her as flames reached out to lick at
her pretty face and through it all Wyl noticed her eyes . . .
those arresting oddly matched eyes that found his gaze and
locked onto it. She began to tremble as her flesh burned
freely now, the oil clinging to her body and helping the
flames do their work. Her face was charred, her teeth bared
in a grimace of agony but still her eyes held his in a final
embrace of death.

Wyl heard her words again in his mind. *Fear not my gift.*

Now Myrren did finally vent her anger and despair. At
last Lymbert heard her voice and he reveled in her agony.

And at the sound of her final, chilling scream, Wyl
Thirsk, General of the Legion, felt a strange sensation overcome him. It was neither painful nor pleasant but it was
keen and pressing. It devoured him. Then it changed into a
sharp, splintering agony and Wyl felt as though he was losing his breath—his ability to breathe, in fact. He closed his
eyes and bared his teeth against it, unaware of anyone
around him, hearing only the piercing sound of her scream.
When her voice ended abruptly Wyl lost his wits, collaps-
ing into an all-encompassing darkness. A few people
watched him fall to the ground, including Lymbert.

"Some General," he commented, eager to get a final and
powerful thorn driven into Wyl's image. "Imagine him in
battle."

A butcher nearby agreed. "No stomach for death, that
one. He should come and work in the slaughterhouse with
me. We'll toughen him up."

Gueryn and Alyd pulled Wyl's limp body away from the
grim scene and the smoke. A shocked Gueryn ordered Alyd
to find water immediately. His stunned companion wasted
not a second.

"Wyl, my boy. Wyl! Come on now, lad." The older soldier pulled back Wyl's lids and was mortified to see the
pupils dilated so large that there was no color in his eyes
at all.

Gueryn looked up anxiously for Alyd. His glance landed
on a painfully thin boy, scrawny and grubby. The smell
alone emanating from him was powerful enough to make

the hardiest person gasp but in his outstretched hand was a bladder of water.

"It's fresh, sir," the boy said. "And clean. I fetched it just an hour ago from the well."

Gueryn cast aside his doubts and took the water. He threw some of it over Wyl's face and hair before trying to pry open his mouth and get some of it into Wyl's throat.

"He will be all right, won't he, sir?" the boy asked, his face a mask of worry.

The soldier did not answer, his attention distracted by the muffled groan of Wyl coming back to consciousness.

"Ah, lad, you scared me."

Wyl's eyelids fluttered open and Gueryn, horrified by what he saw, sat down hard on the ground in a new wave of shock.

Wyl shook his head to clear the blur. "What?"

"Look at me, boy," Gueryn said, his voice filled with dread.

Alas, the feverish gaze before him was still burning brightly from a pair of eyes that were bewitching indeed—one a penetrating gray, the other an arresting green, with flecks of warm brown.

Wyl closed his ill-matched eyes as Alyd hurried to his side, pushing away the small boy whose water had helped revive his friend.

"Help me get him out of here," Gueryn ordered, too shaken by what he had witnessed to give further explanation.

5

ALYD DONAL COULD NOT KEEP THE SMILE FROM HIS FACE. IT had been his companion since sixteen-year-old Ylena Thirsk had accepted his proposal of marriage. He had been patient; six years of absence from his beloved family in Felrawthy had been made less painful partly because of his fiercely loyal friendship with Wyl Thirsk but mainly because there was Ylena to love. There had never been anyone else for him since the day his red-headed companion had introduced him to his exquisite sister. The strong urge Alyd felt to protect this beautiful creature had surprised him, not that he was such a champion. Ylena had her seemingly fearless brother and the ultimate protection of a powerful King; she had no need of his sword and yet even as a bashful twelve-year-old, confirming the promise of the handsome woman she would become, Ylena had sought out his company. It seemed, even at that age, there was no one else for her either. Still, her shy nod and gentle tears prompted by his proposal had sparked such surprise and intense joy for him that he could not imagine life could ever get any happier than now. Ylena would make the prettiest of all brides. Not wanting to wait a moment longer than they had to, they had set a date that allowed barely enough time to make all the necessary formal announcements, let alone preparations for a nobles' wedding.

General Wyl Thirsk, as head of his family, had not hesitated to give his permission; in truth, he'd wondered why they had taken so long to ask. Out of courtesy Alyd had spoken with Gueryn, who was equally delighted. Finally, Alyd's family messenger from Felrawthy had brought the news granting immediate blessing. The Duke and Duchess were delighted to hear that their youngest son's bride had a strong connection to the royals and came from such loyal Morgravian blood.

Now, with Wyl at his side, Alyd sought an audience with the King. It was fitting that the sovereign give his formal agreement to this marriage, as Ylena's father had entrusted Magnus with the task of making her a good match. The Donals of Felrawthy were an old family with a proud history and loyal to the throne. There would be no question that the King would give his blessing to the union between his closest friend's only daughter and the son of one of his most supportive Dukes.

Magnus, now feeling the weight of his years, welcomed two of his favorites, smiling indulgently at Alyd's excitement as the young man stammered out his request, not as used to meetings with the sovereign as his red-headed friend.

Over wine and wafers the trio chatted in the King's private garden. For an old warrior and a man who in younger years had reveled in hard, outdoor pursuits, Magnus showed a particular tenderness for his prized blooms. In these past years of peace, which allowed for his constant presence in Pearlis, the garden had flourished under his careful touch. It was to be part of his legacy. He left the rest of Stoneheart's formidable grounds to his team of gardeners but this walled square of color was all his and the two young soldiers indulged the old King as he spoke fondly of his latest prize.

"Can you credit it!" he said with amazement. "A blue nifella, normally found only in the northern climes of the realm."

The soldiers grinned. It meant little to them but how the King had encouraged it to grow in the milder climate of Morgravia had everyone with a green thumb baffled.

He smiled over his cup. "You youngsters make me feel envious."

"Sire?" Alyd queried.

"Look at you both. Fine specimens of Morgravians," he said, reserving a special glance for Wyl, knowing how his young General suffered such insecurity over his looks and stature. "I envy you your energy and youth," he added.

Wyl grinned and as he did so Magnus saw that the boy had disappeared. All the round softness had been absorbed and hardened. Before the King sat a man and one who reminded him achingly of his old friend. Muscles fairly bulged on Wyl's stocky frame and the carrot-colored hair was now his signature rather than his curse. His soldiers jested that they would never have need of a standard for their General—they would just scan the battlefield for the head of flame. His freckles had withered beneath the sun's glare, the toughening of the skin and the stubble of manhood. He had not grown especially tall but then neither had Fergys Thirsk, Magnus silently acknowledged, yet both were formidable soldiers and leaders of men. Apart from his own son, he could not imagine a single individual at Stoneheart who could hold a candle to the fighting prowess of Wyl Thirsk.

He had proven himself a doughty soldier and deserving owner of the title of General of the Legion. Honest, forthright, and without question courageous, Wyl Thirsk had over the last few years won his army's respect. He was still painfully young, of course, but then so was most of the army these days. Magnus knew they followed avidly in the steps of the young Thirsk.

It was just such a pity that the acrimony between Thirsk and Celimus still stood. For all Thirsk's polite posturing and his obvious determination to keep his promise to his sovereign, Magnus saw through the veil. There was no love lost between the two. And no one could appreciate such a sentiment more keenly than the King. But, so long as Wyl Thirsk protected the heir faithfully, that would have to be enough. Magnus understood Wyl's feverish loyalty and would not have to question whether the younger man would put his understandable doubts about Celimus before Morgravia.

It would not be long now before they could test this theory. Magnus sensed his own time coming to an end and quietly welcomed it. He was tired. And lonely too. His wife long gone—Shar rot her; his great companion dead and his only son not much more than a stranger. Yes, it was drawing close to the time to hand Morgravia over to the new breed and give Celimus his time. Perhaps it would be the making of him. Who could know? King and General would need to work together, though, as they always had in the past.

Morgravia and Briavel could rarely rest beyond a decade without waging war on each other. Magnus nodded to himself. Old Valor would be feeling creaky on his horse too. Perhaps they should just leave it to their children now, although Briavel had only a queen-in-waiting to govern it and a faint-hearted, fragile one at that. He had seen the Princess only once, at a royal marriage many years ago in faraway Tallinor when King Gyl had wed a civilian of no noble line, the honey-haired beauty Lauryn Gynt. All neighboring realms felt obligated to attend.

Magnus hated traveling out of Morgravia, but Fergys had counseled him gently, reminding him that Gyl's father, old King Lorys, had been an ally to Morgravia many moons ago and a once-powerful sovereign of a vast realm. To snub his line by not attending the royal wedding would be unwise. Magnus had sensibly relented and with Fergys at his side had made the interminably long journey.

He had decided to take Celimus, which came as a surprise to the child's minders. But Magnus, again at the urging of Fergys, wanted to spend time getting to know his son better. Without a mother to love him, the boy needed the strength and affection of his father to reassure and guide him. Fergys argued with Magnus that the visit provided an ideal opportunity to forge closer lines with his son. Embarrassingly, the boy showed an early aggression towards Briavel as Magnus had paid his respects to its monarch. The two Kings had stiffly bowed to each other but their curt salutations had been interrupted as Valor's young daughter had suddenly become near-hysterical.

Granted, Celimus had looked decidedly guilty and the Princess's doll was in several pieces on the flagstones of the reception hall but the racket that had ensued far outweighed the supposed deed. It was only a doll, for Shar's sake, and the child's terrible howling had clearly embarrassed her father. Magnus recalled how the plump, dark-haired girl had been run out of the hall by her maidservant, not to be seen again. He shook his head ruefully. She was no match for Celimus then and he knew she would be no match for the vain, often cruel man he had become. He wondered what would become of Morgravia and Briavel under their respective guidance.

But in truth, what worried him most was the threat from the north. Fergys had begged with dying words for Magnus to pay keen attention to the Mountain King. The Legion knew for a fact—had reported it on countless occasions—that Cailech's people often slipped across the border. They were clever, rarely lingering, doing lightning-fast trips into and out of the realm for trade. He remembered his General's warning: "It might be trade now. One day, Magnus, he'll bring an army. He's testing us. We must never allow him to feel comfortable."

Magnus wondered whether Cailech and his people had made the same sorts of "trips" into Briavel. No doubt. He mused that the best response would be for the two heirs to the southern thrones to marry. Bind the realms, blend the armies. Scare off Cailech.

He laughed to himself at the fanciful thought of Morgravia and Briavel being on friendly terms. It was then the King realized he had been in his thoughts too long and it was only politeness that kept the two young men before him alert.

"My apologies," he said softly.

"No need, sire," Wyl replied, relaxing into the cushions at his back. "Your garden is so tranquil, I too feel myself drifting." He smiled.

Magnus returned it, glad in his heart to see Wyl Thirsk at such ease. There was a time when he had worried for the boy. All that business with the witch several years ago was a distant memory, now, but he still regretted the death of that girl. He had hated witnessing the sight of her battered naked body tied to the witch post. *Bah! Sorcery,* he thought to himself, *a lot of stuff and nonsense.* He was glad he had finally rid Morgravia of the office of Confessor. He had personally dismissed Lymbert the day after Myrren's burning, and with the Confessor's demise the only remaining channel for the Zerques' religious zeal had closed. It had been six years since the last witch-burning and, in another few, most of the older folk—the believers—would be dead and with them their fanatical pursuits. The battle would be fully won and the Zerque Order would no longer hold any influence in Morgravia. The prospect was a relief, for Magnus no longer had the strength to fight that battle in the little time left to him. He was sorry that a young woman had to die to remind him of his promise to rid the realm of the Zerques, and that others—including his General—had also suffered.

Gueryn had still been in shock when he met with Magnus and had described the strangeness that had overcome Wyl during the witch's execution. He had also mentioned the lad's eyes changing color. Magnus stole a glance at them now, relieved to see how ordinary they looked, a murky blue that Fergys had also possessed. The King had not believed Gueryn then and still maintained it was an aberration. When Wyl had regained consciousness properly and with the King's own physics in full attendance, the lad had appeared perfectly normal. Self-conscious but no worse for the curious event.

Those same unremarkable eyes now regarded him with a faint trace of amusement sparkling in them. "A mynk for your thoughts, sire."

The King was pulled from his ponderings, winked at Wyl, and turned his attention to his other guest. "Ah, Alyd. How remiss of me. You see what age does to you, lad? So waste no time, marry this bright young sister of Wyl Thirsk's and my blessing upon you both. May love and laughter follow you in your lives," Magnus said, adding, ". . . and in your bedchamber." Alyd grinned at the King's final comment. "Are we looking forward to seeing the pretty Ylena as a Newleaf bride?"

Alyd cleared his throat and a blush stole across his open,

handsome face, which like Wyl's had taken on a more angular look. His golden bright hair would probably still flop in his face if not for the short manner in which he styled it now. It suited him, together with the short beard and clipped moustache he now favored. Many a lass at Stoneheart would feel her heart break at the marriage announcement, the King realized.

"Your majesty, I can't wait a moment longer. As soon as the royal tournament is done, we wish to make our union formal."

"That soon?" Magnus replied, clearly surprised.

"I've tried, sire, to talk them out of it but there's no stopping this pair, I'm afraid," Wyl admitted. "Ylena's determined to wed Alyd within the month."

"Then so be it. Fare well at the tourney." The King stood, towering over Wyl despite his stoop. He clapped a hand on Alyd's shoulder. "And, Alyd, watch that handsome face of yours if you're to stand in front of an altar a few days later."

"Thank you, your majesty; nothing will happen to me, sire. Ylena and I will grow old and fat together."

Their laughter was disturbed by the arrival of Celimus.

"Ah, father. I was sure I would find you here."

Wyl and Alyd made stiff but courteous bows before the Prince.

"Forgive me, am I interrupting a private gathering?" he asked, the dazzling smile masking his contempt.

"No, son. Alyd here has just won my permission to wed his lovely Ylena. We were discussing the timing of the ceremony."

"Congratulations, Alyd," Celimus said, his smile not faltering. "I had always hoped to taste those rosy lips of Ylena Thirsk myself."

Alyd felt Wyl's stance stiffen yet more beside him. He always grabbed hungrily at the baits thrown him by the Prince. When would he learn to ignore him?

He replied in his usual deprecating manner. "Well, there's such a long list of eligible beauties awaiting your attention, my Prince, I can't imagine crossing Ylena off would matter to you much."

"No. You're right, it's not such a loss really, is it?" the

Prince said, enjoying watching Wyl bristle. "And you, General. What say you to this union? It must make you happy to see your sister off your hands and tumbling into the bed of a very rich Duke's son."

"Indeed, my Prince" was the only thing Wyl could think to say that sounded remotely polite.

"And when does this happy union take place?" Celimus persisted, pouring himself a cup of the wine.

Alyd answered, more than used to the chill that settled around this pair whenever they were near each other. "Soon after the royal tournament. Your father has given his blessing. Your invitation will arrive shortly, my Prince." He gave the heir his very best smile.

Wyl sighed within. Even Alyd's disarming looks were nothing compared to those of Celimus. The Prince of Morgravia had grown into a glorious-looking man, easily overshadowing the handsome youth he had been a few years previous. Taller now than his father, broad and slim-hipped, he could still the tongues of a room full of chatting people simply by his arrival, such was his impact.

"Then I shall have to dream up an appropriate wedding gift for the sister of our esteemed General here," Celimus replied after draining his cup.

Magnus decided to bring the barbed conversation to a close. "Son, you came here to talk with me? Let me just bid farewell to my guests and we can sit together awhile."

"No need, sire," Celimus replied. "It involves these two fine soldiers—in fact their good opinions would be valuable."

"Oh?" said the King, wondering what mischief might be afoot now.

"Yes, it's about the tournament, Father. I wish to make arrangements for us to use real weapons."

The King shook his head and made to move away. "You know my feelings on this, Celimus. I will not risk the heir."

"My lord." For one rare moment, Celimus lost his smirk and the tone which usually accompanied it. There was a plea in his voice now. "It is because I'm to be King of Morgravia one day that I beg this of you. We are not boys prac-

ticing in the bailey any more, father. We are trained soldiers. Thirsk here could cut down any man I know blind-
folded . . . except me, of course." His regular demeanor
made its return. "This is no longer a time for play swords,
father. Let us fight like men because we are men. You may
need us on that battlefield sooner than you think and then
we'll have to die like men at the end of an ugly blade."

Wyl leapt onto the Prince's words. It would be one of the
rare times in his role as General that he would agree with
Celimus. "Your majesty, my Prince is right. This is an exhibition but let's give everyone a genuine insight into hand-
to-hand fighting."

Magnus was cornered. In truth he did not know why he
had fought so hard against the use of real swords; a small
voice told him that it was because he had been afraid that
Celimus and Wyl—even as youths—might have well
fought to an ugly end. But here they stood, strong and bold;
men bristling with barely repressed energy and passion.

He was making a fool of Celimus to make him fight with
wooden weapons.

He nodded, resigned to their plea, and the three in front of
him could hardly contain their pleasure at his concession.

The annual royal tourney was a major festival for Morgravia and the folk traveled from far and wide to partake of the festivities. Around the tournament fields grew a
veritable village of traveling sideshows and marketers of
exotic wares. A seemingly endless queue of gypsy wagons,
tinkers' carts, and country people lined up patiently at the
city gates to gain entrance into Pearlis. Troupes of tumblers,
singers, musicians, and even a small circus formed part of
this line too.

The population on the outskirts of the northern end of the
city where they held the tournament had doubled in two
days, then quadrupled in four. Excitement was building and
the local inns were enjoying their traditional busy season.

Magnus, having learned from past experience, was keen
to ensure the city dwellers did not take advantage of the
poorer visitors enjoying a day's holiday from their back-

breaking toil on the land. He sent out edicts that special fees were to be offered on accommodation, stables, eating houses, and watering holes. Through Wyl he set up a special crew of soldiers to make random checks on the various taverns to see that their ale was not too watered and that their food remained honest. Wyl chose Alyd to supervise this crew, knowing his friendly and open manner would ease the pain for disgruntled tavern proprietors out to double their fees.

Helmets and breastplates, the only armor Morgravian soldiers wore, were polished until they sparkled. Horses were groomed until their coats shone and weapons were oiled and sharpened so that sparks would ignite when they struck each other. The thrill of using real weapons had touched off a fire of excitement. Training in the lead-up to the day had never had a more fierce intensity.

Wyl had to constantly remind his men on the use of these weapons.

"Exhibition only. Don't forget it. There will be ladies of the court present and a wealth of guests from all over the realm. We do not want the women passing out at the sight of flesh being opened by overzealous combatants."

He had more advice on the other skills that would be on display.

"Yes, you heard me right," he said above the indignant mutterings. "Wrestlers, oil up out front this year—I'm assured the women like to watch, and apparently so does Captain Donal," he added, winning a roar of delight from his men, who clapped a furious yet helplessly amused Alyd on the back.

Wyl dismissed the men and caught up with Alyd. "I'd like to take you up on that sparring idea but I'm afraid I'm being reserved for a special piece," he admitted grimly.

"Oh?" Alyd inquired, his mind racing as to what this might be. "Let me guess. The Prince?"

"Correct."

"My guess then is that he plans to hurt you, and what better opportunity than in the name of entertainment at our most public festival?"

"He has to be able to get through my guard first."

"I've watched him too, Wyl. He's good."

Wyl shrugged. "But perhaps not good enough. We'll see in a few days."

Alyd laughed. "And then we'll celebrate at the Alley," he said, a wicked glint in his eye.

But Wyl did not grin. "I need to share something. Celimus is planning more than just a humiliation for me. He aims to hurt me in more ways than physically. He wants to fight for the Virgin Kiss."

"So?" Alyd looked perplexed. "I think I would too."

"Mmm. But which virgin is he most likely to choose, do you think?"

Understanding struck Alyd like lightning. "Ylena," he said flatly and stopped walking.

"Correct again."

"I won't permit it," Alyd said, shaking his head wildly. "I will not allow that man's lips to touch those of my betrothed."

Wyl looked pained. He cast a glance around to see no one could overhear them. "It's worse. He's reintroducing the ancient form of this rite. It's called Virgin Blood. It's far more sinister than the Kiss, Alyd." Wyl had only just been informed about this dark turn of events himself and he was now on his way to the King to seek an audience. "He means to bed Ylena before you."

"Then he'll have to kill me first," Alyd replied, his voice cold and hard.

"No, he'll have to kill me," Wyl answered.

When Wyl arrived to petition the King, Orto informed him that the sovereign was ailing—it seemed Magnus was far more fragile than Wyl had been previously led to understand. He was permitted to see his King, but only briefly, a hollow-eyed physic cautioned before leaving them alone.

"Hello, dear Wyl. I knew I would see you here before long," the old man said.

Wyl was too diverted by the sickly appearance of his sovereign to hear the underlying message in those words.

"Sire, what ails you?" he asked, taken aback.

Magnus was propped up on a mound of cushions and, although his manservant had seen to it that he was perfectly groomed, nothing could disguise his newly sunken, pale visage.

"Can you not guess?"

Wyl was unprepared for this. Suddenly all notion of aggressive petitioning fled. It was clear the old man would not make it to the royal tournament, even less likely to Ylena's wedding.

Magnus allowed his guest's silence for a few difficult moments and then said what needed to be shared. "I am dying, Wyl." The King held his hand up as his young visitor made to protest. "Please . . . sit with me a while. I have some things to say to you." Magnus motioned for Wyl to take the seat next to his bed. Wyl obeyed, his mind running the King's words over in his head. *Dying.*

"Ask me an intelligent question . . . the sort your father would want to know."

Wyl did not feel like playing games but knew he must go along with his King's request. He took a moment to consider before he spoke.

"I believe my father would want to know how long you might reckon we have."

Magnus clapped his hands once. "Good, Wyl. Excellent. That is precisely what Fergys would have asked. No shallow sympathies, no dwelling on what cannot be changed. He would set aside any personal emotion and get on with the business at hand, which is what must be set in place before I depart."

Wyl nodded. "Which in your estimation might be when, sire?"

"Ah well, my physic tells me with luck I may see the next full moon."

Wyl felt as though a knife were turning in his gut, and sensed the person holding that knife was Celimus. It was too soon for the old man to die.

"Does your son know?"

"Another good question. No. I have not seen Celimus

since that time in the garden with you and Alyd—and yet I have seen plenty of you since then. Odd, wouldn't you say?" the old man asked genially. It belied how he truly felt.

Wyl did not know how to respond. He blinked. "I cannot imagine our lives without you ruling, sire."

The King's voice became earnest and his sunken eyes seemed to spark. "You must! You alone must have a vision for the protection of Morgravia because Celimus, though skilled enough in the tools and strategy of war, will not. His mind, sadly, is filled with debauchery just now."

"My King, with deepest respect, I fear you may underestimate the Prince. He is ambitious."

Magnus agreed. "I sense that is not a compliment to him, although you dissemble cleverly, General." Wyl sensibly said nothing. "If he is ambitious, then he hides it well from me. However, I think you are right, Wyl. I too believe Celimus is not as shallow in his thoughts as he would have us all think."

"No, sire. He has a razor-sharp mind, and if I might talk freely?" Magnus nodded. "Then I would foresee that upon your death he will rule with a fierce hand."

"This much is true. He may be subtle but he lacks the finesse and indeed the largesse I hoped he would have acquired by now. He is, however, true to Morgravia, I believe, and in this I commend him. He will not permit it to lag behind its neighbors . . . and neither must you, Wyl Thirsk. Briavel may make a move toward war again in the next few years, when it feels strong again."

"It is the Mountain Dwellers who concern me more, sire."

"Just like your father." The old man sighed.

"He was right, your majesty."

"Yes, he was. You must continue to strengthen our northern forces. Cailech grows more bold."

"The retaliative skirmishes occur more often, sire. In days gone the Mountain Dwellers would flee if they encountered any of our patrols."

Magnus sighed. "And now they stand and fight. Bold indeed. Your father warned as much with his last breath. You must pay attention to the north, son. It may be that Cailech takes on Briavel first, but it's Morgravia that presents the greater challenge. If he can take Morgravia, then Briavel—when Valentyna ascends the throne—will be an easy victory."

Wyl frowned in thought, recalling the most recent reports. "I don't like us taking the Mountain People's lives. It only inflames a potentially lethal situation and I have given an edict that they are to be spared on all counts. Taken prisoner if necessary."

"Thank you, Fergys," the King said, finding an ironic grin. "Oh, but you do remind me so hauntingly of him, Wyl. That's exactly the sort of thing he would say."

Wyl shrugged. "I don't want us at war on two fronts. Cailech right now is controllable if we don't incite problems. Perhaps, if we can calm the escalation, we might even be able to hold talks with him."

Magnus flicked a glance at his General. "A parley with the King of the Mountains. I wish I could be there for that," he mused.

Wyl could hardly believe they were having this conversation. He switched topic. "How do you feel, sire? Is there pain?"

"Of no consequence. It is manageable with the poppy-seed liquor."

Wyl suspected Magnus of withholding the truth but he allowed it to pass. "Your majesty . . . Ylena's wedding. Would you care to hand on the duty of giving her away? Perhaps to your next of kin?"

Magnus's eyes became wide with mirth. "Celimus?"

Wyl swallowed hard. It was pride alone that prevented him from betraying how he really felt about such a situation.

"You are priceless, my boy." The King enjoyed a feeble burst of laughter. Wyl already missed the bellow Magnus was known for. "You would do that . . . allow Celimus, the person I suspect you dislike more than any other, to have that honor?"

Wyl did not hesitate. "I would, sire . . . if it be your wish."

Magnus fixed him with a more somber stare now. All mirth was gone. "Why couldn't you have been my son,

Wyl?" He clasped Wyl's hand. "You are the one who should rule Morgravia." The King's eyes had gone misty.

Wyl cleared his throat. "It cannot be, your majesty," he all but whispered. "You must not speak of this again."

"Yes, but I think it all the time. You are fit to rule. The man who would be King has no compassion. I fear for our people. I fear for you."

"Fret not about me, sire. I have his measure and he has my loyalty."

"Does he, Wyl? Does he have your loyalty?"

Wyl wondered why the King would ask this of him a second time. He paused and searched himself. He came out of his thoughts wanting. "Sire, may I say this? If Celimus rules poorly he cannot expect my respect but I will pledge you this from the bottom of my heart: Morgravia has my loyalty. I will protect her to my dying breath."

The King closed his eyes momentarily. When he opened them he nodded, squeezing Wyl's hand in his own large fist. "It is enough for me, Wyl Thirsk." He smiled. "As for Ylena, I would ask that Gueryn step in for me. He is as good as family to you, and your father would be pleased with such a choice."

Wyl visibly relaxed. "Thank you, sire. I know that Gueryn would consider this an honor."

"Keep him close to you, Wyl. He can watch your back like no other. And now to the real business at hand," Magnus said, looking drained of all energy.

"Sire?"

"Why you came to see me today. I imagine this is to do with the tournament."

"You know then?"

"About Celimus ensuring you and he are the main exhibition piece for swords? Yes. I believe though that you wish to talk to me about the Virgin Kiss and your suspicions that it is Ylena he will choose."

This was a surprise. Wyl had underestimated his King and was reminded once again of what a wily pair Magnus and his father must have made in their prime. "Yes, your majesty. Except it has taken a darker turn. Celimus has announced he is upping the stakes."

"Oh?"

"His plan is to claim Virgin Blood," Wyl said, standing suddenly as his anger surfaced. "It is my suspicion that Celimus wants to bed Ylena before Alyd."

Magnus said nothing, although a deep frown creased his brow. Wyl, unable to be still, paced.

Finally Magnus spoke. "This is very serious."

Wyl spun around. "Can you not overturn it, my King?" he implored.

"You know I cannot. It would gravely undermine Celimus and reinforce his fear that I love and favor you."

"He fears this?" Wyl spluttered.

"How could he not? He and I share nothing but our bloodline," Magnus said firmly.

Wyl could see the King was tiring. He needed an answer and pushed a little harder. "He means to win, sire."

"I realize this. In fact I think you'll find that Celimus will never play his hand unless he is confident of winning."

"So you cannot overturn this decree?"

"And I will not. Celimus is beginning to flex his muscles as the heir. You will have to play to his rules soon enough. This is your first test," Magnus said with regret.

"What can I do? I cannot permit this."

"Then don't play into his hands. Can you best him on the field?"

"Yes," Wyl replied confidently.

"Then you have nothing to worry about."

"And still I do, sire."

"Well, then you have to be even more cunning than he is. Use that wise head on your shoulders. There is a solution to every problem, my boy—those are your father's words, by the way—and by Shar we always found those solutions in the nick of time. How long have you got?"

"Two more days after this, sire."

"One more day than you need, then," the old man said, his eyes glittering now. Wyl could not tell whether it was from the fever or because the King already had the answer. "And when is the wedding again, my boy?" he asked, his voice croaking.

"Month's end, sire."

"Ah, yes, you did say. Perhaps you should go about those arrangements then," he said, again as though passing on some sort of underlying thought. "I am feeling rather fatigued. We shall speak again soon."

And to all intents and purposes it appeared as Magnus closed his eyes that he was already drifting into a drugged slumber.

As if he could see through walls, the physic knocked and made his entrance. "With respect, sir, I would ask that the King be left to sleep now."

"Of course," Wyl said, pondering the cryptic nature of his sovereign's words.

WYL SAT IN A TINY, ELEVATED COURTYARD KNOWN AS THE Orangery, which cunningly trapped the sun, encouraging its fruit trees to grow luxuriantly behind Stoneheart's impenetrable walls. The fragrance of the blossoms was heady and Wyl loved the tranquility of this place, as did Ylena, whose suite of rooms overlooked it. He could never accuse Magnus of not following through on his promise to their father. Ylena lived in quiet splendor with maidservants to tend her needs, among a glorious series of chambers and this courtyard, which Magnus had designed and built for the little girl who came to him all those years ago.

The daughter I never had, he had once whispered to her and she loved him for it. Had loved him ever since. Ylena had never forgotten her father's love but it had been taken from her so early that she had found it relatively simple to transfer it to his highly influential friend, who showered her with gifts and beautiful gowns and just about anything a noble's daughter could wish for.

Wyl awaited his sister, his mind clouded in thought. A black dog sat patiently beside him, his mournful eyes staring up at Wyl, occasionally nudging his hand to remind him of his presence. Wyl stroked the large head absently and Knave complained softly at being so ignored by his master. He dropped his beloved ball, fashioned by Ylena from old linens, stockings, and wool, in the vain hope that Wyl might kick it and begin one of their games.

The dog's ears pricked at the sound of a footfall.

"Looking for a game, Knave?" asked Ylena as she appeared fresh and primped from her rooms, her spicy fragrance mingling with the courtyard's perfume. She duly kicked the ball and sent Knave leaping after it. "Hello, Wyl," she said, tweaking her brother's ear and planting a kiss on his coarse red head.

He pulled her close, loving the joy she found in simple pleasures and hating himself for bringing news to ruin her perfect day.

"You even smell like our mother," he commented, kissing her on the cheek.

Ylena sighed. "I wish I could remember her as you do. I'm wearing her perfume."

"It's lovely."

"Father gave it to me so many moons ago. He said I was to wear it on my wedding night. I've saved it all this time and yet felt reckless today and dabbed a little on. Do you think he'll like it?" she asked shyly.

"Who?"

"Prince Celimus of course!" she said, making an exasperated expression that changed immediately to one of concern at the way Wyl started at that name. "Alyd, you fool—my husband-to-be. Who else could I mean?"

Wyl felt relieved that the subject had been raised inadvertently. He opened his mouth to say what he had rehearsed in his mind but Ylena interrupted him, reaching over to talk to Knave.

"You daft dog, you still have that silly red ball."

"And woe betide anyone who touches it," Wyl said affectionately.

"Other than you, of course," she replied. "What is it between you and this dog, Wyl? He strikes the very fear of the devil into almost everyone at Stoneheart and yet he's like a puppy around you."

"And you."

"Yes, but it's passing strange, isn't it?"

"Not really. He lost Myrren when he was a baby and then I came along out of the blue." Wyl wanted to add that it was probably similar to how Ylena transferred her love from Fergys to Magnus. Instead he shrugged and scratched the dog's ears. "I was the next best thing he had."

"Whatever made you follow her instructions?" Ylena wondered.

"I'm not sure in truth. I felt somehow compelled and perhaps a little obliged after all her suffering. She said he was a gift and I was to use him wisely."

"Do you understand what she meant?"

Wyl shook his head.

"What happened to her family?"

"I heard the father died on the morning the Witch Stalkers came for her. The mother was addled when we met. She listened to my tale and handed me the dog without another word. I don't know what became of her but the house was all packed up when I visited and I presumed her mother was leaving town. She was probably glad to be rid of the burden of the pup."

"Very strange," Ylena admitted. "I'm just glad Knave sees me as friend and not foe." Then she lowered her voice before adding: "He hates Celimus most of all, of course, but then I think he gets that from you."

"Hush," Wyl admonished.

"No one's around."

"Even Stoneheart's thick walls have ears."

"Well, it's true. I think Knave hates anyone you don't like. Think about it, he barely tolerates others who mean little to you but is loyal to those you love. How's that for a fine philosophy?" she said, kicking the red ball, much to the dog's surprised delight.

Their conversation was interrupted by one of Ylena's maids announcing the arrival of Alyd. His expression was bleak as he kissed Ylena's hand.

"Whatever is wrong with you, Alyd Donal? One would think the King had denied permission to our marriage."

"Have you told her?" Alyd asked Wyl, who shook his head.

"Told me what?" Ylena's eyes moved between two grim expressions.

"Ylena . . ." Wyl began.

"Wait!" she said. "This sounds bad." She called to her maid and asked for a spiced cordial to be brought immediately. The maid returned quickly, and Ylena drank her small helping down in one gulp.

"Right. I'm presuming this is connected with our wedding. Tell me," she commanded, her throat burning from the liquor.

Wyl started again. He told her what he knew and of his suspicions. She felt for Alyd's steadying hand as Wyl bowed his head and finished with: "All that's standing between you and the bed of Celimus is my sword."

"But I've never done him a wrong," she said.

"You've never done anyone a wrong, my beloved," Alyd comforted. "This is not about you. This is about hurting Wyl . . . and your family name."

"Are we sure of this?" she asked.

"No," Wyl admitted. "But I know how his mind works. He knows how best to damage me."

Ylena shook her head. "Why does he hate you so much, Wyl?"

"I don't know," he replied, not wanting to repeat what he had learned from the King.

"I do," Alyd admitted. "It's because the King is so fond of you." And when Wyl shook his head in denial, he added: "Everyone's seen it. He had to grow up around the insepa- rable friendship of your father and his. Now you come along and steal the affection that rightly belongs to Celimus."

Wyl shrugged. He did not want to admit that Alyd's argument was, in all probability, very sound. "And so, Ylena, by taking what's so precious from you he humiliates the sister I adore, creating despair for my best friend and a chance to fire my anger sufficiently for an all-out confrontation."

"I see," she said. "Well, I won't cooperate. I'd sooner die."

Alyd nodded. "And although I'm no match for him, I swear I would gladly die trying to stop him laying a finger on you. Wyl, I've been thinking about how we can get Ylena away from here. My intention is to—"

Wyl shook his head. "Alyd, stop! I've told you, there is no escape. Celimus is not one for being thwarted. It would be a cruel blow to his ego not to attain something he has set his heart on—and taking Ylena in the way he imagines is a master stroke guaranteed to hurt both you and me. No, he would hunt you down as easy as blinking. And he is in no hurry. You would be looking over your shoulder for the rest of your lives. The fear of being caught at every turn will destroy any chance of true happiness."

"Then what? What can we do?" Ylena's voice was shaking.

"We have to be smarter than he is, more cunning." Wyl stood and walked to one of the orange trees, inhaling its freshness and stealing a few moments to convince himself his plan could be done.

He turned back to them. "I have a plan. It was a comment from the King which seeded it in my mind, and we have only what's left of today and tomorrow to make it work."

They listened.

7

THE DAY OF THE TOURNAMENT DAWNED SHARP AND BRIGHT over Stoneheart. The rain clouds of the previous day had blown through, leaving clear skies and a cool morning. It had drizzled the evening before so the ground was soft yet not slippery enough underfoot to be troublesome, making it perfect for charging animals and wrestling men. The horses were gleaming and colorful bunting flapped in the light morning breeze around the tournament field.

The carpenters had finished erecting the seating arena and, although damp, the small tents that encircled the field had held firm overnight. Each would become the base for a noble family and it was from here their sons would wage mock war on each other. Another larger and less flamboyant tent would house the jugglers, tumblers, dancers, and other entertainers, including a famous fire-eater and contortionist who was in attendance by express request of his royal highness, Prince Celimus.

The younger ladies of the court would be encouraged to try their hand at archery for the grand prize, from King Magnus, of an exquisite pearl pendant. Ylena, who was no beginner with a bow and arrow thanks to Wyl's training, was looking forward to wearing the pearl that evening. She was sad the King would not be in attendance and, having learned she was not permitted to see him, had sent him a brief note together with a sprig of her orange blossom and some other blooms from her garden. She knew they would convey her love more sincerely to the sick man than the written word.

Despite his sense of caution, Wyl had told Ylena and

Alyd that Magnus was dying. All three could imagine how bleak life would be with Celimus sitting on the throne. But this morning Ylena blocked the thought of the vile Celimus and what he would expect should he win the contest. He made the very blood in her veins chill. Ylena pushed the Prince and his lusty thoughts from her mind. She inhaled the scent from her trees and turned to the man she loved on this her most special of all mornings.

"You look wonderful," she said to Alyd, straightening his shirt front. "Quite the dashing warrior."

He grimaced. "Hardly." Pulling her close, he kissed her passionately. "Let's hope your brother can best him."

"And spare us—"

Alyd hushed her with another kiss. "Say no more. I must away, my lady, or risk the wrath of the famously bad-tempered red-headed General." Ylena laughed but he could see anxiety in her eyes, and knew she was reading the same concern in his. "Come on, where's that famous Thirsk courage?"

"It all lives in Wyl, not me, I'm ashamed to admit," she said, wringing her hands.

"And he has sworn to defend you, as I have, so you need not fear."

"Then why am I starting to tremble, Alyd Donal?"

He tilted her chin up so he could look into her eyes. "I love you. You have to trust that love. And Wyl's plan, of course. We've done everything we can."

She nodded, hoping he would be gone before her inevitable tears betrayed her. After Alyd's departure, Ylena took the final—and, she knew, daring—precaution of sending a page to Orto, the King's secretary, with an urgent request, then sent her maid hunting for her archery gloves.

The morning session of the tournament had proceeded smoothly, with the joust creating much hilarity for the onlookers as various noble sons were toppled. The population of the city had swelled even more dramatically than anticipated. As a special gesture, Magnus—on Orto's wise suggestion—had released several dozen barrels of his ale to be distributed freely at the celebrations together with roasted oxen. All the bakers close to the castle had been harried into action and now the air hung heavily with the tantalizing smell of fresh loaves and meat sizzling on the spits.

The midday feast had begun. Purveyors in the Alley's corridor of tents and awnings were enjoying a brisk trade during this break in the day's events as everyone enjoyed their food and ale. The latter helped them loosen their purse strings.

A mountebank entertained the meandering folk with his colorful patois, hawking a magical salve that promised to ease all aches and pains. To keep their attention and their laughter high, his pet mynah bird hurled insults at its owner, who deliberately ignored it. The contortionist made his audience cringe but despite the squeals they still threw their coppers for more. Children amassed around the confectioner's stall where treats they had only dreamed about were on sale for just two mynks each: fairy floss, toffee apples, caramels, sherbets, and hard shapes of brightly colored sugar that could last a full day if sucked wisely. A group of women had joined forces to sell knitted blankets, woven baskets, even a few rugs weaved by a team of their children. And then, of course, there were the sideshows where, among other frolics, passersby were encouraged to throw wet rags at some poor soul who had agreed to stand in a stock for a share of the earnings. Three direct hits won a flagon of mead. Elsewhere, strong men took their turn at hacking through a log, their times carefully monitored and recorded by a stony-faced man with a piercing stare who chewed constantly on a willow twig, absorbing its painkilling juices for his sore joints.

A small queue formed outside the tent of the mysterious Widow Ilyk, who claimed she could tell people their fortunes simply through touch. Wyl smiled as he strolled by. He liked people who poked fun at Morgravia's old fears. In former years, claiming to have the Sight would would have brought forth a howling troop of Witch Stalkers. He was glad those days were done and ingenious people like this widow could make a living from parlor tricks. If there were any positive outcomes from Myrren's demise, they were that King Magnus had rid Morgravia of Lymbert and his cronies and the Zerque influence had virtually died out. Myrren's death had horrified many younger onlookers, who were more enlightened than their elders and did not fear sentients; in fact, did not really believe such powers existed. But most people were willing to pay a coin to have some-one tell them that their knees would stop aching, or they would indeed marry a wealthy merchant and escape a life chained to a field of barley. Fortune tellers, these days, rarely lacked patrons.

Alyd caught up with him outside the widow's tent. "What are you doing here?"

"Trying to keep my mind occupied."

"Come on. It's time we got you ready."

"Would you pay a bronze regent to learn your fortune?" Wyl mused.

"I'll tell you what, if you pull off the extraordinary today, we'll get drunk and celebrate by coming back here to this very tent—what is it? Ah yes, the Widow Ilyk, and we shall have our fortunes told." He grinned.

"I'm glad you're confident."

"I'm not," Alyd admitted. "The truth is, I'm paralyzed with fear for Ylena."

"How is she?"

"Have you not spoken with her yet?" Alyd looked aghast.

Wyl pushed his hands into his pockets. "I haven't. Is she . . . all right?" he asked sheepishly.

Alyd's expression turned to one of genuine smugness. "Dare I say, since last night she is glowing."

General Thirsk put up his hand in mock defeat to prevent his Captain saying more. "Come, I have a fight to prepare for."

The city bells tolled the commencement of the after-noon's entertainment and, to ensure the throng made its now slightly intoxicated way back to the fields, several pages were sent out with handbells to ring loudly through the Alley.

The court ladies' archery contest was not much of a competition in truth. It was quickly distilled down to Ylena matching her clearly superior skills against Ailen, a ferocious opponent from the House of Coldyn, who not only desired the pearl very badly but had her eyes firmly set on winning the attention of Alyd Donal.

Ailen shot with courage but too much aggression made her aim inaccurate, while Ylena's arrows, gloriously fletched in her family colors, landed true. A clear winner, she did her best to ignore the scowls of the other contestants and to act graciously. Ylena did not need more jewels, but for sentimental reasons she did want the pearl from Magnus. An excited buzz moved through the crowd as King Magnus was unexpectedly helped to the small stage set up for prize-giving. He looked desperately frail and ill, despite his finery. Orto and a surprised Prince Celimus aided him to stand for the presentation, ignoring the murmurings from the folk, who were shocked at the state of their King.

"Father, this is not a good idea."

"Still, it is an idea I like" came the prompt response. "Ah, my lovely," he said, beaming towards his favorite lady. Magnus clasped the pendant around Ylena's neck so the pearl sat at the base of her throat, and kissed her on both cheeks. "This was meant to hang from one beautiful neck only," he said, eyes burning brightly with the fever that would soon claim his life.

Ylena curtsied. "Thank you for coming, my King," she whispered fervently, imagining what it had taken for him to be here.

"How could I resist your request?" he asked, shaking off the arms of Celimus and Orto, forcing them to step back and in so doing winning himself a moment's privacy. "I'm sorry the Felrawthy clan is not in attendance," the King admitted. "They should have seen you shine today."

"I think the Duke is disappointed too, my lord, as is Alyd. His father's clan is too busy in the north."

"Mmm, yes so I gather. By the way, child, don't be frightened," he whispered, knowing she would understand his meaning. "Your brother is more wily than you credit. Now turn so they can all see your pretty prize."

"I shall never take it off, your majesty. It will be treasured and will always keep you close to me."

He smiled as a father to his child, loving her in the same manner. The King straightened to his full height with difficulty. His eyes were damp and he could feel the fever beginning to make his body tremble; knew he must keep it at bay just a while longer.

Ylena stepped away from the podium to rousing cheers and catcalls from the soldiers loyal to her brother, each one of them just a little bit in love with the graceful, golden beauty of the young woman who did not resemble the General in the least.

Meanwhile Celimus moved forward to whisper to the King. His words were cloying and sweet. "Father, it was exceedingly good of you to leave your sickbed for the prize-giving. May I ask Orto to assist you back to your chambers now, sire?"

"Actually, no, Celimus. The fresh air makes me feel brighter just at present," Magnus lied, "and I hear you and Wyl Thirsk are to provide a special exhibition piece. I should like to see this."

Celimus gave a terse yet still elegant bow. "As you wish, Father. I feel privileged that you will witness it."

The old man nodded, despising him. "And I also hear you have a special prize for the victor of this contest. Am I right in understanding that you have invoked the ancient Virgin Blood claim?"

"Yes, sire," Celimus answered brightly, determined not to be intimidated by the sack of bones before him. "I thought it might add some spice to the sometimes dull occasion of two men matching blades."

"It was my belief that the addition of real swords would provide enough excitement."

"In this you are right, my lord. However, I felt inspired to mark this as the most memorable of royal tournaments."

"And why is that?" the King asked, dreading the answer.

Celimus moved closer still. "Because it shall be your last and we need to mark it well, sire. This tourney did, after all, arise out of celebrations of our ancient customs. It is right that we send your ancient body off in ancient style."

Magnus worked hard to keep his voice steady. "Indeed, son. I admire your observation of the old traditions, although I cannot admire the rite you have resurrected, the very one my grandfather worked so hard to abolish. It is, if you will forgive me pointing out at this late hour, barbaric and beneath you to perpetrate such a thing on one of the young maidens here."

"Ah, well, as I so rarely please you, Father, this is but another nail I will gladly hammer into your coffin."

Magnus was shocked at the vehemence in Celimus's words, all muttered only just loud enough for the two of them to share.

"You are clearly in a hurry for me to die, son."

Celimus bent down, his smile to the crowd unfailing but his words chilling as he whispered to Magnus: "I shall give you until Newleaf, Father. If you are not wheezing your last unwelcome breath within that time, I shall personally speed you along to Shar."

Magnus, feeling his strength leave him as he absorbed how strongly Adana's blood ran in Celimus's veins and how he had so completely failed his son, collapsed into a chair that had been conveniently placed behind him by the ever-attentive Orto.

"Your majesty," the servant started softly, his tone reflecting his concern. He had heard none of the conversation between father and son but knew well it would have brought no cheer to the old King.

Magnus did not allow him to finish. "A drink, if you please, Orto. I wish to watch the exhibition."

"Yes, sire," Orto said, a twitch of his fingers sending a page scurrying for a watered ale. "As you command," he added, reaching into his pocket for the small vial of poppy seed liquor.

Gueryn and Alyd had helped Wyl dress in the ceremonial fighting uniform of the House of Thirsk. They stood now admiring him.

"Pity about the red hair," Alyd observed.

"Hush, Alyd," Wyl replied out of habit.

"It clashes so badly with the house colors," Alyd continued, staring at the magenta and deep ultramarine of Wyl's show battledress. He wanted to try once more to convince his friend to wear some armor, but knew it would be in vain. Wyl had already refused on the grounds that the contest was to be purely an exhibition.

"Well, you can blame my ancestors for their blindness to pleasing color combinations. They had red hair too." Wyl scowled at himself in the glass. Gueryn stood beside him.

"Celimus likes to feint to the left," Gueryn cautioned.

Wyl nodded, taking his sword from Alyd and sheathing it.

"And he likes to show you all of his right side—don't fall for the ploy and strike. Swipe hard and low to his left."

"I know this, Gueryn. Be still. There is nothing more I can learn about Celimus's swordplay that I don't know already."

Gueryn knew what was at stake; he knew Wyl must best Celimus to protect his sister, although the consequences for beating the Prince so publicly would be dire.

"When this is over and we've seen Ylena and Alyd married, I suggest you take yourself off to the north. You need to get away from here for a while." He did not notice the glance that passed between the two younger soldiers.

Wyl understood that it made Gueryn feel safer to talk of the future. "Well, only if you agree to accompany me. We can check on the border patrols that so consumed my father."

"That's a promise," Gueryn said gravely. He put his hand over Wyl's heart and spoke the family motto: "As one."

Wyl repeated the gesture, holding his own hand over Gueryn's heart: "As one."

He accepted Alyd's brief hug. "Go, be near her. She will be terrified."

Alyd could only nod. Suddenly he felt his world tipping. He tried to sound confident. "I can already taste our first celebratory ale."

Gueryn and Alyd left the tent and Wyl followed moments

behind, emerging into the glare of the clear, mild afternoon. His friends moved toward where Ylena nervously sat. He walked into the main arena. The master of ceremonies announced the arrival of General Wyl Thirsk and was quickly drowned out by the loud cheer that erupted from the soldiers encircling the area. If the civilians were intrigued by this contest between two such highly ranked combatants, they were fascinated by the promise that the victor would have the right to Virgin Blood.

Many of the shallower, less wealthy nobles had been thrilled at the whispers of this ancient rite being reinstated at the direct behest of Prince Celimus. They felt that if the king-in-waiting chose their unmarried daughter to lie with, it was almost as good as a royal seal of approval on that union. The richer, more cynical families, stung by the cunning of Celimus on previous occasions, wisely kept away from the royal tournament, claiming illness or urgent business in a faraway part of the realm. None of this mattered to Celimus; he wanted to see the blood of only one virgin on his sheets tonight and she was very much present.

He arrived in the arena to wild applause from the commonfolk who knew little of his true character yet. To them he appeared a glorious king-to-be, the dashing Prince of a much-loved sovereign. His fabulously handsome appearance, seemingly humble acceptance of their cheers, and his bright, wide smile did nothing to dissuade them of this fine opinion.

Magnus grimaced and noticed Wyl did the same. The King joined in the charade with a halfhearted clap and benign smile for good measure, but behind it lay his cold fear. His physic had recently reconsidered his estimate on the King's longevity. No longer did he believe Magnus would last until the next full moon—in fact, he had curtailed his prediction so savagely it was now his expert opinion that Magnus would barely survive the next few days. It seemed Celimus would get his wish, Magnus thought grimly. Magnus no longer felt guilty for hoping Wyl might prevail, or that he might have found a resolution. The truth was he needed Wyl to beat Celimus. His son was poised to plunge

Morgravia into its darkest times and he suddenly realized he was powerless to prevent it.

The two men touched the flat of their swords first to their lips and then against each other's blade. The sharp metallic sound sent a shiver of anticipation through all from Stoneheart who knew what a formidable fighting pair they were.

The master of ceremonies had announced that the winner would be decreed by whichever opponent drew first blood. This was sinister news to Wyl. It was his understanding this was nothing more than an exhibition. However, it was too late now to argue the finer points. He looked toward Gueryn and noticed the old soldier's face was a blank contrast to Alyd's open expression of intense anxiety. Wyl had to look away. There was nothing to be done now except to fight with the blade as well as he knew he could.

The King was given the task of dropping the white square of linen. The handkerchief fluttered to the ground and the two opponents immediately drew their blades back and began circling. Wyl knew Celimus would not be long in this foreplay and, rather than waiting, struck hard and fast.

The dance of the swords had begun.

Whatever Wyl gave away in height and strength he made up for with cunning and speed. Celimus was light on his feet and his strokes were so elegant his dance was beautiful to behold. He smiled the whole time he fought. Wyl's face was set as a mask and he stood his ground, patiently parrying, ever watchful for the right opening. Gueryn had always admired the shrewd manner in which Wyl wielded his sword. There was nothing flamboyant in his style, his strokes were neat and economical. Celimus liked to move in a wide arc with large, airy strokes, but this was also part of his skill and Wyl knew it. Wyl appreciated how Celimus was enticing him, daring him to take advantage of the room he provided.

And that would be your undoing. Gueryn's advice rang as loudly in his mind as the sound of the blades rang in his ears. It was all Wyl could hear; the crowd's murmurings had faded away for him. He had become one with the sword, moving with lightning reflexes.

They were well matched and, as the fight began to extend, none of the onlookers could say that either was getting the upper hand. The audience marveled at the grace of this contest. The combatants moved like well-rehearsed dancers who knew every move the other would make. Even Ylena and Alyd, pale with worry, were entranced by the glint of the swords and the speed and beauty of their movement.

Wyl jumped expertly as Celimus struck low, and then, to the surprise of those watching, Wyl spun around one way to stop a harsh blow coming again at his legs and then reverse-spun to parry another. Sparks ignited as the blades crashed together. It was a wonderful spectacle—not that Wyl was in a position to hear the sounds of high appreciation from the crowd. He knew better than anyone that he was in the midst of a death struggle.

The Prince, slightly less focused, did hear the cheers for his opponent and that made him angry. Wyl heard his competitor's subtle change in breathing, provoked by wrath, and felt the first nuances that the balance of the contest had changed. Remembering Gueryn's warning about the dangers of fighting on pure emotion, he pressed harder, feeling his own senses withdraw even further within himself until he could no longer see the Prince but simply the blur of aggressive strokes that he could anticipate and deflect.

The Prince was rapidly becoming prey to his own emotions and his skills suffered.

"Wyl's beating him, isn't he?" Ylena whispered nervously to Gueryn.

"I would agree that Wyl's gaining the ascendancy," the soldier replied dryly, adding, "If he keeps going like this, the Prince will tire quickly, as he is expending far more energy than your brother."

Ylena nodded and squeezed harder on Alyd's reassuring hand.

Wyl leapt forward to thrust, knowing what Celimus would do in reply, and was already feinting left to counter the stroke that inevitably came. He could see the beads of sweat now on the Prince's brow and he too felt his shirt damp against his back. He had no idea of time. As he danced backward the Prince followed, thrusting and slashing. It seemed Celimus had found his balance again and the strokes resumed their whirring grace.

Both now deep in concentration, neither could detect the enthralled silence that had claimed the audience.

The Prince searched constantly for the opening that would allow him to draw first blood and Wyl just as nimbly defended. Celimus suddenly moved wide, deliberately airing his stroke to reveal one side of his torso, which begged to be slashed. Wyl was so tempted—it would be so easy— but he recalled the caution of Gueryn and just as forcefully moved in the same direction as his royal opponent, ignoring the invitation and surprising the Prince with a hard, arm-numbing smash downward.

Infuriated, Celimus began to take short angry jumps forward. Leading with his right leg he hammered at Wyl's blade, reverting to brute strength over his shorter opponent. Did he see a grin on Thirsk's face? Yes, damn him all to hell. Well, he had a few surprises left, and he began a brilliant series of spins and leaps to dazzle the crowd, who yelled their encouragement.

Ylena caught a mutter from Gueryn. He seemed to be repeating something just under his breath. She listened intently and heard it: ". . . the Magician, Wyl, use the Magician . . ."

Celimus was still pushing forward, bearing down hard, beating the General back toward one corner of the arena and apparently winning, when Wyl saw it. Saw the potential as the complex series of strokes of the highly difficult maneuver came to mind. It was possible. Celimus, in his arrogance, his confidence that he was in fact winning, would not be ready to counter, for he could hear applause now, was not concentrating quite as ferociously as a minute or so ago.

Gueryn called it the Magician in honor of Fergys Thirsk, who had designed the maneuver and used it to devastating effect in many battles. The older soldier had counseled Wyl on it, claiming only the very skilled in swordsmanship could make it work in a true battle situation—or would have the courage to use it. It needed constant calculation and readjustment depending on the opponent, and many in the heat of the fight could forget one of the tightly woven moves that made it such a formidable trick.

"Its purpose is to confuse," Gueryn had said during their private practice of this piece of art.

And Wyl would use the Magician to daunting effect now.

He audaciously threw his sword from his right hand to his left. Unbalanced by the curious move, Celimus hesitated. Wyl thrust and the Prince only just blocked in time, but the move pushed him off balance in the other direction. Wyl kept tossing his sword from hand to hand, seizing every opportunity in between to strike. Suddenly it was all Celimus could do to defend and keep stepping away from this blitz of frustrating, seemingly random strokes from both sides.

Wyl could hear the breath coming hard from the Prince now. With one final toss to his left hand he brought his sword from that side, slamming hard from the Prince's right, intending to slash across his fighting arm. Celimus was dazzlingly fast though, and at the last second countered, their swords shuddering to a halt, crossed in front of their grimacing expressions.

It was now simply a test of strength.

Their faces were almost touching as they bent against each other.

"Yield," Celimus whispered hoarsely.

"Go to hell!" Wyl replied.

"Yield to me now or those you love will die. Make it look good, for I shall start with le Gant."

The unexpected threat hit Wyl so harshly that his shocked reaction was immediate. He feigned a trip, stumbling away from the Prince and dropping his sword in the process. The arena was silent. Everyone held their breath, wondering how the General, after such a brilliant display, could be so suddenly clumsy.

"Good decision, Thirsk," the Prince uttered just loud enough for his opponent to hear. He smiled broadly before whipping his sword expertly from the top of Wyl's shoulder in a diagonal stroke across his body.

Through the rent in Wyl's shirt bright red bloomed.

"First blood!" Celimus called proudly and encouraged the crowd to honor his achievement.

In their bewilderment, they did, throwing their caps into the air and cheering wildly, although not one soldier present joined the celebration. Their eyes instead lingered on the anguished figure of their General. Gueryn was first at Wyl's side. He knew the cut was a surface one, exquisitely laid for maximum visual impact. Wyl would wear the scar forever but the stinging cut would no more threaten his life than would the prick of a rose thorn.

"Do what you must," he urged Wyl.

Wyl gathered his fractured thoughts and found the wherewithal to bow to his opponent, pick up his weapon, and then touch swords once again to lips and blades. It signaled the end of the contest.

Celimus began to strut around accepting the accolades.

"He said he'd kill you if I didn't yield." Wyl groaned, shaking his head with despair.

"I expected something like this," Gueryn admitted as the master of ceremonies began speaking. "Come on."

"Your majesty," the announcer said, bowing to Magnus, who barely acknowledged it. "My Prince"—he turned, bowing now to Celimus. "My lords, ladies, and all gathered here for this festive occasion. I ask you once again to show your appreciation for the most impressive display of swordsmanship I think any of us will ever witness. I'm sure you'll agree that if this is the standard of our young Morgravian warriors, then Briavel and all who challenge us had better think twice!"

The crowd erupted at the deliberately provocative words. When the noise had died down a little, the man continued. "As you know, there is a special reward for the winner of this particular contest." A murmuring broke out among the crowd. "Prince Celimus, with the permission of his majesty King Magnus, has reinstated the ancient rite of the claim to Virgin Blood."

The murmurs turned into discussion. Ylena felt her knees tremble as Celimus slyly glanced in her direction. The cool air surrounding his hot body had caused a gentle drift of steam to lift from him and he stood, proud and regal, his shirt opened to reveal his broad, hairless chest. Ylena was not the only one to notice his disheveled and yet still sensuous appearance. She was, however, one of very few—perhaps the only one, in fact—among the ladies of the court that day who did not feel her blood stir at the sight of this beautiful man.

The master of ceremonies had finished his explanation of the rite: ". . . which now leaves me with nothing more to say than to invite our esteemed Prince Celimus to make his choice," he concluded.

Wyl, hardly noticing the burning sensation from the slash on his body, glanced cautiously towards Alyd.

Celimus quietened the excited crowd. "This is a difficult choice for me. Cast your eyes among the beautiful young women of the court and you will see that every one of them defies being ignored," he said grandly.

Magnus, exhausted and sorrowful at how things had turned out, looked at the square of linen on the grass. He could put a stop to this incident by simply raising a hand, but after his death there would be no one to stop his son and he must consider the repercussions of humiliating Celimus. Magnus knew he would most likely be dead within days, perhaps this very night. He needed to pass on Morgravia in a strong state. If he overruled Celimus now, who knew what might occur and who else—including Valor of Briavel—might consider it plausible to attack when the boy was still vulnerable. No, he needed to hold his tongue and allow this terrible event to take its course. Celimus must ascend to the throne feeling invincible. He was popular with the people after this most public victory; it would be prudent, for the time being, to let sleeping dogs lie. Despite Magnus's own misgivings about the outcome of this contest, if Wyl was going to stage a coup then it must be his own decision and happen in his own time frame. Only Morgravia mattered now, and this would be the old King's final sacrifice for his realm. He prayed it would be the only time Celimus would employ the old rite. Yet, as powerless as he felt, Magnus reached toward a way he might ease the balance of power between new King and General in the light of this contest. Wyl would not be easily consoled should Celimus unwisely select Ylena as his prize. Magnus left his ruminations and returned his attention to Celimus's gallant speech.

". . . and so may I ask for the indulgence and indeed forgiveness of all of these adorable young ladies today that I can't choose each and every one of them." The Prince grinned, his arms sweeping across the platform where the nobility sat and enjoyed the titter of amusement from the girls who had clearly gone to some pains—or at least their social-climbing mothers had—to make themselves as alluring as possible.

"I choose the Lady Ylena Thirsk of Argorn," he said, his dark eyes finally coming to rest upon the one woman who would sooner die than give up something so precious to this fiendish man.

Ignoring her slump-shouldered, bleeding brother and the outraged Alyd Donal, the Prince walked to where she stood not far from King Magnus, who had closed his tired eyes at the mention of his ward's name. Celimus ensured his own hand was outstretched graciously toward her in what, to the audience, looked like a charmingly beseeching manner and yet to Alyd appeared purely predatory.

The Prince had no intention of wasting any time. He would take her to his bed this moment and relish the opportunity not only to loose his passion on someone so comely but to drive a blade into the heart of the two men he knew hated him more than any. Those who might defy him would learn a hard lesson today and it would serve them well for when shortly he took the throne.

Celimus bowed formally. "My lady," he said, unable to contain the delight at his conniving brilliance.

"Prince Celimus," Wyl said, stepping up and bending low before the royal. He turned toward Magnus. "Your majesty, if you'll forgive my intrusion?"

Magnus opened his eyes and nodded, hardly daring to

believe that Wyl might have taken his hint as to how to foil Celimus's plan.

Wyl straightened. "Sire, apologies, I do believe there has been a misunderstanding here."

"Oh?" Magnus replied, hope suddenly flaring in his heart.

Wyl nodded gravely. He looked at Celimus. "My Prince, as her only living relative, I cannot permit you to choose Ylena."

Celimus's smile faltered, turning into a sneer. "I'm not sure your familial ties override the royal claim, Thirsk. Step aside."

Gueryn's eyes narrowed. He had no idea what was going on here and he could only pray that Wyl knew what he was doing.

"No, my Prince, I'm afraid I cannot do that. You are not grasping the full import of what I say. It is not I who forbids you to lie with my sister. It is the law of our land."

Celimus could no longer brook this delaying tactic. He was tired and sweaty; lust was already coursing through his veins for revenge on the Thirsk family, as well as the sweet release that lying with the young woman who stood before him could achieve. "Law! Which law would that be, Thirsk?"

"The sanctified law of marriage, my Prince," Wyl said, his face deliberately portraying one of troubled confusion. "I'm sorry, sire, did no one here know?"

"Know what?" spluttered Celimus, looking between his father and the increasingly smug expressions of the Thirsks.

Alyd stepped in. "Perhaps I can explain, my Prince. You see, it is I who forbids you to lie with my wife."

"Your wife!" Celimus roared, his body shaking with the rage he now felt.

Gueryn, behind him, began to smirk as he pieced together what must have occurred.

Alyd nodded. "Yes. Ylena and I are married. Apologies to all—we thought the loose-tongued priest would have let the whole of Stoneheart know by now," he said, grinning and taking Ylena's hand. "We were too engaged in marital pursuits to broadcast our happy news, although we did intend to make formal announcements later today."

Wyl thought he might laugh at Alyd's sugary manner.

"Fetch the priest," Celimus demanded and a page was sent hurrying to find the man. "In the meantime, Ylena, please tell me when this marriage occurred."

Ylena curtsied to Celimus. "Our wedding took place yesterday, my lord Prince, a little earlier than planned." She looked toward the King as she spoke, rather than Celimus.

"And I can certainly vouch that my wife is no longer a virgin, probably already with child," Alyd said, standing a bit taller.

"You knew of this?" Celimus said flatly to Wyl. His voice was harsh and low.

"My Prince, you must forgive me. I gladly gave my sister away to her betrothed, an honor that was also sanctioned by the Crown. I had no inkling that she would be your first choice. But then, as you yourself have mentioned, every young maiden here is delectable in her own right. I know you will have no trouble choosing another."

The priest arrived, pale and shaking. His pudgy hands kept moving across his mouth nervously.

"Answer me in a word, priest. Did you marry Ylena Thirsk of Argorn to Alyd Donal of Felrawthy?" Celimus demanded.

"Yes," the priest answered, trembling, then added for good measure, "In Stoneheart's chapel."

Celimus closed his eyes briefly in what looked like pain. "When?" His tone was acid.

"Yesterday morning, your highness. It was a private ceremony, attended only by the bride, her brother the General, and Captain Donal. This was done in accordance with General Thirsk's wishes," he said, turning to look at the King beseechingly.

"You may depart," Celimus responded, barely able to contain his rage. "Father, you are legal guardian to Ylena. I presume you have given your signed permission to this union?"

Magnus considered how best to answer his son without betraying the Thirsk family. He looked toward Orto and it was his calm and collected secretary who came to the rescue.

"Sire," Orto said gently, "I recall the papers being signed two nights ago. It was a brief session, for you were very unwell. If my memory serves me right, you put your signature to only two parchments. This sanction was one of them."

"Ah, there you have it, son," Magnus said, but Celimus had already turned on his heel and pointed to one young woman from the nobility, much to the delight of the crowd. He strode away from the Thirsk party.

Wyl glanced toward Magnus, who nodded almost imperceptibly, a wry smile of relief barely touching his mouth. *Cunning indeed, young Wyl,* he thought. He turned to his manservant. "Come, Orto. I believe we have some pressing paperwork."

"Yes, sire," the man said, his solicitous expression unchanged. "Allow me to assist you."

8

RECKLESS MOOD HAD HIT ALYD AND WYL THAT EVENING. With a number of soldiers, they broke the Legion's drinking record, leaving an increasing number of the men retching in the street and doomed to sleep where they had fallen, too intoxicated to help themselves. Tournament night alone was the only occasion on which this sort of indiscretion by the Legionnaires would be tolerated.

"Leave them," Alyd called over his shoulder, swerving into Wyl. "Weak sods that they are. Now, hear me, men still standing," he bellowed, "I gave my word to General Thirsk that I would take him into the Alley and have his fortune told."

Sounds of hearty agreement ensued and Wyl, his spirits still soaring from Ylena's close escape, made no protest at being swept along on the merry, drunken tide of happy soldiers prolonging their tournament revelries. He had managed to put behind him Celimus's diabolical threat to hurt those he loved, and was even feeling slightly foolish at falling for it. The group wended its way into the Alley, which was itself still a lively hive of activity.

"Right, lads. We need to find the Widow something or other," Alyd said, grinning crookedly, eyes vague and red.

"Widow Ilyk," Wyl corrected, far less in his cups than his friend.

"First one to find her gets a silver duke for his trouble," Alyd yelled, brandishing the coin.

Soldiers departed in various directions, more out of fun than a need to earn more coin to drink with.

A small boy with a curious smell about him emerged from the crowd and grabbed at Wyl's shirt. "General, sir, I know where the widow's tent is."

"Then you can earn the duke," Alyd said, unsteady on his feet. "Could you take us to it?"

"Follow me," the boy said brightly.

"How old are you?" Wyl asked, suddenly noticing that Knave had appeared with the lad.

"Ten summers, General, sir."

"Call me Wyl."

"I couldn't, sir."

"Then what do I call you, young guide?" Wyl said, ignoring the odd aroma and taking his small hand.

The youngster eyed him. "My name is Fynch, General."

They walked on, Alyd calling to some of the men to stop their search and to follow.

Wyl looked at the lean child, who had large, seemingly all-knowing eyes. "Do you live in Pearlis, Fynch?"

"Yes, sir. And I work at Stoneheart," he said proudly.

"I see. And what is your duty?"

"I'm a gong boy, sir," he said proudly. "I've been cleaning the sewer tunnels at the palace since I was four, but I've recently been promoted to take care of the royal apartments' dropholes, so I can assure you I am earnest in my work."

"Well now, that would explain the rather individual smell you carry around with you, Fynch," Alyd said, not unkindly. "And you will no doubt be very busy tomorrow, as Prince Celimus's privy will be getting a right royal workout tonight, I'll wager."

Fynch did not understand the jest but he joined in the men's laughter, thrilled to be in the company of the General he had admired for several years, and pleased that this was the first person ever who had not made a comment on how tiny he seemed for his age.

"Here we are, sir," he said presently as they came to the tent, which now looked even more mysterious with its candle lanterns of many-colored glass strung along the awning, sending flickers of red, blue, and green into the darkness of the Alley.

"Do you believe in this fortune-telling stuff?" Wyl asked him.

"I think the widow does this purely for fun," Fynch admitted. Then he fixed Wyl with a direct gaze. "But if you ask me whether I believe in some people being able to see things . . . whether some people have the Sight, then yes I do."

"Blasphemous child!" Alyd said theatrically. "Look out for Stalkers," he added but stopped that line of jest at Wyl's pained expression. "All right, who's first?" Alyd called. The men all raised their hands at once and drunkenly pushed into the tent. Alyd flipped the boy the coin. "Thanks, Fynch."

"Thank you, Captain," he answered. "Can I assist with anything else, General?"

"No. You've been most helpful. I'm sure we'll see you around the castle."

"That you will. Would you mind if I waited for you?"

Wyl smiled. He suspected that the boy had no home to go to. And he was intrigued at how Knave stayed close to the boy. "I don't mind at all. You can walk back with us later. I might need help with my friend." He glanced towards where Alyd swayed at the entrance.

"I'll wait out here then, sir," Fynch said, seating himself crosslegged on the grass next to the General's large black dog.

Wyl and Alyd were the last to be seen by the fortune teller, by which time the rest of the soldiers had staggered out, still drunk and seemingly none the wiser for the counsel. It did not surprise their Captain. No one took a fortune teller seriously.

"Fairground tricks, General," he said, a dazed grin on his face. "All a bit of fun for the lads."

"Come in" they heard the woman call.

Wyl threw a resigned expression toward Fynch before he and Alyd pushed open the drapes and entered the dimmed space within.

"Welcome," she said.

Wyl stared at the old woman standing before them who called herself the Widow Ilyk. It came as a shock to him that she appeared to be blind, her eyes almost white from whatever afflicted her. The rest of her face was forgettable. A collection of ordinary features that had seen much weathering by sun and wind on her travels. As a result she was tanned and her skin looked like well-worn leather. She wore no adornments and her clothes were simple, well-patched garments of dun brown. For some reason he had expected her to be gaudy of dress and dripping with charms and bracelets.

It appeared that the same thought had struck the Captain through his liquor haze. "What, no fancy costume for us, Widow?" Alyd feigned disappointment.

"I'm tired of it," she replied, her milky gaze never leaving Wyl. "I wore it all day. Those clothes are hot and heavy." She grinned, revealing gaps in her stained teeth. "Ah, but the people do enjoy the theatrics. I like to please. Would you prefer that I climbed back into them?"

"No," Alyd answered, holding up his hands. He looked very unsteady. "No bother. I've brought my friend here—just for a laugh." Alyd belched, rocking on his heels.

Wyl decided it was time to get him home. He looked back at the fortune teller, a little embarrassed. "Do you travel alone?" he asked, for want of anything better to say.

She hobbled toward a chair, feeling for it. "My niece helps me. She is not here this evening," she replied, seeming to stare at nothing now. "You two men were here earlier today, weren't you?"

"How can you know this?" Alyd slurred, teetering dangerously.

"I'm guessing." She chuckled to herself and changed the subject. "Young man, would you be kind enough to hang the sign you see beneath this table outside my tent? I think I am done for the night."

Wyl obliged. When he returned to the dimly lit area where the widow sat, Alyd had placed himself opposite her and she was holding both of his hands in her large, wrinkled pair. Blue veins traversed their old journeys across the backs of her hands and her oversized knuckles suggested she suffered the disease of the joints.

As if reading his thoughts, she spoke. "Ah, but the pain in my fingers is bad today."

Alyd winked crookedly at Wyl. "What can you tell me, old woman?" he mumbled.

"What would you like to know?"

"Tell me about Captain Alyd Donal, the luckiest husband in all of Morgravia," he said expansively, all but falling off his chair.

"Well, I can see that you have consumed too much of the King's fine ale today. And in the future I envisage a mighty headache and fragile humor," she said, a smile at the edges of her mouth.

Alyd tried to focus on her, his expression confused. "Do you know, I think you're right, Widow." He hiccuped, a sign of impending doom. "You are indeed a woman of insight," he said, suddenly overcome by nausea. "Would you excuse me, I think the ale wants to be returned." And he ran from the tent.

Wyl spun around in surprise to watch him stumble out and then awkwardly turned back to the woman. He wished he could leave as well.

She chuckled again. "And so to the quiet friend," she said, the white eyes resting somewhere over his shoulder.

Wyl shrugged. What harm could it do? He sat and offered his hands but she did not take them.

He risked a personal question. "Are you blind?"

"Almost. I see everything as a blur. Still, I have never

needed the sight of eyes." The tent felt suddenly still and tense as Wyl absorbed her meaning. He felt a disquiet take hold. Talk of magic made him uneasy.

She seemed in no hurry. "Where do you come from?"

"Argorn," he replied. "And you?"

"Not these parts. My home is in the far north—a little-known town called Yentro. Now, what would you like to know?"

Wyl shrugged at her question. He was here now and suspected she would not permit him to leave without some sort of reading. He wanted to say he knew this was just for fun but her intent, serious expression compelled him to play along. "Why not tell me my fortune?"

"Pah! I'm no sideshow fortune teller. I put on that act for the revelers."

He took his chance. "Perhaps I should leave, then?"

"Stay. You intrigue me. There is an aura about you."

Now Wyl laughed. He could hear loud, sickly groans coming from Alyd outside and thought it best to make his departure.

"I promise you, Widow, no one has ever found anything intriguing about me."

She did return his smile this time. "Tell me, do you believe in otherworldly things?"

"Such as?"

"Having the Sight," she said, carefully this time.

"No. But here is the regal I owe you for permitting us to visit your tent. I think I must go see to my sickening friend."

Wyl pressed the coin into her hands and was taken aback at the alarmed manner in which she shrank from his touch.

"What's wrong?" he said, indignant.

She did not reply. Instead a low moan issued from her throat.

"Widow!" he called. "What ails you?"

The old woman began to sway and then she spoke a soft, mysterious chant in a language Wyl had never heard.

He recoiled from her. "I will leave now."

She seemed to come out of her strange reverie. "Wait!" she hissed. "You must be told."

"Told what?"

"Let me hold your hands."

"No! I want no part of this. I don't know why I let myself come here tonight."

"Because you were relieved."

"What are you talking about?"

"That you foiled him," she answered, her milky gaze locked on his astonished face now.

Wyl sat. "Tell me," he commanded.

She shook her head, her blank stare moving to look past him. "None of that is important. Neither is the fact that I know. Only one thing matters."

Wyl was confused now. "You're not making sense to me."

"Listen to me carefully, Wyl Thirsk," she said, her voice low and grave.

"I didn't give you my na—"

"Hush! I am in much pain and have the strength only to say this once. Pay attention to me. I am a seer and I speak only the truth to you. Keep your money—I give my advice freely to a man touched by magic."

Wyl balked but she grabbed his hand this time. Her grip was harsh. "You walk a perilous journey, son, and on it you are accompanied by something dark and friendless."

Wyl's eyes narrowed. He felt a hollow open in the pit of his stomach.

"Heed me well," she continued. "It may destroy you or you may use it wisely to your own ends. It has no loyalties no rhythm of its own. No care for anything but itself."

"Woman . . . what are you talking of?"

"I talk of the Quickening," she snapped. "It is Myrren's gift, which she bestowed on you as she died. You must take great care, Wyl Thirsk."

Quickening? Wyl repeated in his mind. "What is it?"

"Some might consider it a curse but Myrren made it her gift."

Until that moment Wyl had never considered that Myrren was anything more than a beautiful and tragic young woman. To hear this stranger infer that she was empowered was unnerving.

"Her gift to me was a dog," he said flatly.

She nodded now. "He is part of it. Knave will protect you and the true gift she gave."

Wyl pressed her. "How can you know all of this?" He shook his head, bewildered; how she could know his name, his dog's name, even Myrren's name? He took a steadying breath. "How must I use it?"

"That I cannot advise. It is your gift to wield as you see fit."

"When will I know of its existence?"

"It is already within you. It exists now." She coughed raggedly.

"What do I do with it, woman? Tell me!" he begged, frightened now by her words.

"You will know when the time comes, although I see swirling about you a woman of note. She needs your protection."

Wyl was baffled. "You have to tell me all that you see."

The widow coughed again and dropped his hands. When she had recovered, she said breathlessly, "I see only this. Those you love will suffer. Keep the dog and its friend close."

The world was spinning for Wyl. He could not tell whether it was the effect of the ale making him dizzy—although he felt suddenly sober—or the strange sticks that burned their spicy fragrance in her tent.

"You lie, old woman."

Her voice was hard now when she spoke. "I never lie in what I see. Your friends are vulnerable. There is a woman—she's important—who needs your help."

He wanted to ignore her, wanted to run. Instead he grabbed her arm, caring not for the way she flinched again from his touch or perhaps from the pain he might be inflicting.

"Get gone, woman. We have no need of you here."

"Take care, Wyl Thirsk. Beware the Mountains. The other friend I spoke of is already known to you. Keep him close."

Wyl shoved her arm aside and strode from the tent.

9

FYNCH WAS FOUR WHEN HIS FATHER FIRST PRESSED HIM INTO service as one of Stoneheart's gong boys. His wages, a pittance though they were, had helped to keep the family from starvation and, although his daily grind was about as unsavory a task as any could imagine, the young Fynch had quickly taken pride in his work. So much so that his diligence and commitment to his lowly task over the past six years had come to the attention of the King.

Before his illness forced him to his bed, Magnus had enjoyed morning walks around the palace, during which he had come across the hardworking lad. Both were creatures of habit. Fynch found himself toiling in the same place at the same time most days, and likewise the King followed a preferred route through the grounds. The regularity of their encounters meant that a nod of greeting eventually ensued, which turned into a few polite words and then into a daily discourse, brief but engaging. Magnus, in his later years, had become interested in the young. It was his eternal regret that he had not played a greater role in shaping Celimus and that he had, in effect, lost his own child. He had found Fynch, despite his low status and serious nature, to be intelligent beyond his years.

One summer morning when the uncleared refuse from the royal lavatories had become particularly ripe in the heat, the King had complained to the seneschal about the unreliable nature of the youngster in question and suggested that young Fynch was the lad for the task. Fynch was promptly moved from one of the lowlier tunnels to the main royal apartments. It was a meteoric rise in status for one so young. From then on his wages had quadrupled, for the gong boy to the royals was expected to be discreet.

Fynch had taken his promotion very seriously—as was his way—and there had never since been cause for complaint with regard to the keeper of the royal dropholes, for either his tongue or his toil. But now that the King had taken so ill, Fynch missed their fleeting chats; Magnus did too.

Since his new appointment both of Fynch's parents had died in a cart accident, leaving the family of four children with its eldest barely thirteen years old. Like Fynch she was a serious child and took to the task of caring for her brood with vigor. Fynch's wages were now of infinite importance to ensure the younger ones could count on at least one daily meal and he considered himself the man of the family.

Even at ten Fynch remained a painfully slight child. He ate as little as the bird that inspired his name. His sister, who loved him well, had given up on scolding her brother with regard to his poor eating habits. Even though she still fretted that if he fell ill the family would perish, she had the sensibility to realize that Fynch was not driven by his belly as were so many lads working around the castle. Yet, in spite of his woeful leanness and stunted growth, he continued to thrive. His size also meant he could continue in this line of work for many years yet, which further secured the family's well-being.

At the time of his promotion to the royal dropholes, Fynch struck up another curious relationship—this time with a big black dog. It was an unremarkable autumn dawn, misty and chill. But the gong boy was about his work early to ensure the King's and the Prince's individual dropholes were cleared and freshened before they had risen for the day. While shoveling he had noticed an immense black dog emerge from around one of the castle walls. The dog had stared at him for a long while. He had whistled to him, knowing this beast looked too well fed and shiny to be a wild dog and glad of the small distraction from his filthy work, but the dog had remained motionless, watching him carefully through dark, intelligent eyes.

When he did finally approach, he was swift and without warning. The boy had stood his ground but felt nonetheless terrified.

This was an enormous dog and when he had arrived to stand boldly in front of Fynch, he was only just able to look down upon him. The dog had neither blinked nor flinched when he had tentatively reached out to touch him. But as he did so he had felt as though he were being blinded as a torrent of information had flooded into him. It took his breath away and suddenly he had a vision of Wyl Thirsk. The vision had dissolved as quickly as it had come and he had found himself staring into the liquid eyes of the dog.

Taking a deep, steadying breath, Fynch had sat down to regain his wits. The dog then settled by him and allowed him to absently scratch his ears and stroke his huge head while he thought about what he had experienced. When the dog suddenly barked, the huge sound frightened Fynch so much he fell backward. As if to reassure him, the dog had licked his face before bounding away. The next day he had returned for more of the same. Just as Fynch had struck up an unlikely relationship with King Magnus, he had now become friend to this dog.

Fynch often felt, in fact, that the beast could sense his thoughts, although he would never admit to such a thing. He was privately convinced that he and the dog did communicate on a deeper level than the ordinary man-to-beast relationship. It became important to him to learn its name and who owned this fine canine and so he followed it back one afternoon and found the dog playing and gamboling around the red-headed General, of all people. More than just coincidence, then, that he had experienced that strange vision. He knew very little of Wyl Thirsk but since that alarming vision and through his interest in the man's dog— whom he noticed paid scant attention to anyone in the soldiers' yards except the General—he began to learn more about him.

He quickly discovered the dog's name was Knave and realized that he did attend a few other people, including the older soldier Gueryn, the General's sister, and the always smiling, friendly Captain Alyd Donal. For almost every other individual, barring himself, the dog reserved a menacing stare or low growl.

Fynch was a born observer, unconsciously absorbing vast amounts of visual and spoken information each day. Then, without even realizing he was doing it, he would sift through it all of an evening, taking from it what he wished. Although he never used this talent beyond his own interest, the lad had gathered an enviable wealth of information on just about anyone who wandered Stoneheart. He knew their habits, their friends, their lovers. He shared his information with no one, but his memory for detail only grew more intense as he matured. Fynch realized he could extract items from years gone by, bringing them into instantly sharp focus.

Over the months since he had befriended Knave—their familiarity now stretching to sharing his midday meal with the dog—he had begun to loosen from his memories various whispered conversations and scenes involving Wyl Thirsk and had soon produced a comprehensive picture of a man he now liked immensely. Finally he had plucked up the courage to speak with him last night, on the evening of the tourney, but that was not the first time he had been that close. No, the first time he had seen Wyl, he was new to his trade as gong boy. The General had collapsed at the witch-burning. Fynch had gone to the scene out of a childish curiosity. It was his first witch-burning and, appalled by the horror and the excitement of the adults around him, he had quickly decided it was to be his last. He was just four summers when he witnessed the terrible sight but what he saw afterward would make an even deeper impression on his mind.

Although the soldier, Gueryn, thought no one else had witnessed the phenomenon, Fynch, who happened to be carrying his tiny water bag and offered it to help the young man, noticed that when Wyl Thirsk regained consciousness his eyes were of a chilling and strange hue.

It had frightened him. But the General's eyes had reverted to their normal color, blue and unremarkable. He did not know what to make of all that.

Now, at dawn, as he made his way through the grounds towards the royal dropholes, he mulled over the previous evening's events. He had been surprised when General

Thirsk had burst from the tent of the Widow Ilyk and ordered them back to Stoneheart. The General had been distracted and solemn as he grabbed his sore-headed friend and with Fynch's assistance had helped the semiconscious Captain back to the castle, Knave trotting happily ahead.

The General had tossed him some coin and thanked him for his help that evening.

"Are you all right, sir?" Fynch recalled asking, a reflex to the man's suddenly vacant stare.

He remembered how the General, only an hour earlier so jovial, had finally focused upon him. "I am well. A little startled from what I learned," he had admitted and then fallen abruptly silent as though regretting he had said as much as he had.

Fynch had instinctively understood not to press further. "I am but a lowly gong boy, sir, but I am at your service at any time of the day or night should you need."

"Gallantly said, thank you" he recalled the General saying and had flushed with pride at the remark. Then the soldier had added curiously, "I see, Fynch, that my hound has taken to you."

"Yes, sir. We play together each day."

"Is that right?" the General had commented, clearly surprised, adjusting his snoring friend into a prone position on the grass. "This is passing strange."

"How so, sir?"

"Because Knave is deliberately contrary to all but a few. I can't explain it better than saying he is just short of vicious to almost everyone."

Fynch had nodded then. "That's true, sir—to all but the people you love." At this he recalled that Wyl Thirsk had stared at him, obviously taken aback and so he had quickly added, "I think he likes to protect you, sir."

"Yes," the General had admitted, "he is an odd animal but he likes you well enough, which pleases me, for you are a good lad."

"He hates the Prince, sir," Fynch had suddenly blurted out. "I sometimes know when the Prince is near simply by the way Knave behaves."

The General's eyes had narrowed. "You notice much for a gong boy."

"Perhaps I should not have said so much. Forgive me."

He pondered now, as he came to the royal drophole and immediately set to shoveling, how Wyl Thirsk had smiled at this and then nodded. "Good night, Fynch. I'm sure our paths will cross again."

"Sleep well, sir," Fynch had said and then watched Wyl hoist a complaining Captain Donal and throw him over his shoulder.

He had continued watching until the General had disappeared after a few quiet words with the gatekeeper and had not been surprised to see a familiar shape reemerge from the darkness. Fynch had stepped back into the shadows as much out of sight of the guards doing their rounds as he could.

"Hello, Knave," he had said quietly. "Come to say good night?" The dog had nudged his hand and Fynch had knelt then to hug his friend. A soft sound had issued from the dog's throat. "I know. You want me to look out for him, don't you, boy," Fynch had said gravely, stroking the dog's ears. "Though I don't know how."

The dog had nuzzled closer to the small boy and they had remained entwined for a few silent moments.

"You'd better go now, big fellow. I need some sleep too. I'm working on the Prince's drophole tomorrow. He hates it if it goes beyond a day or two and I promised myself I'd clean further up the channel. Not very nice but it will be fresher for my efforts," he had mentioned brightly to the dog.

Knave had then growled. Even the mention of Celimus made the dog's hair bristle.

Fynch came out of his thoughts and sighed to himself. He had made the pact with himself that today he would get on with the muckiest of tasks. Ignoring the eye-watering smell he bent to look up the drophole that led to the privy attached to the Prince's apartments. It was filthy and desperately in need of a good brushing out.

He put down his shovel and after casting a quick glance around he took off his shirt and trews to reveal his pale, painfully thin body. No point in getting his clothes all putrid; his sister would scold him harshly and at least he could wash the muck off his body in the nearby lake before he went home. He carefully folded his clothes and tucked them away in a small bundle.

At that moment, Knave padded up softly and Fynch brightened.

"Guard my clothes, boy," he said seriously and was bemused to see the dog settle itself by his garments. "I'm going up there, Knave," he explained, pointing up the drophole. "Nasty work, so don't distract me, all right? I need to get it done quickly and my body washed because the stuff up there stings my skin. But I'm very glad you're here—it will help."

Knave barked playfully once. Fynch was quite sure the dog understood.

"I'll see you in a while," he said, just stopping himself from waving at his friend.

He picked up his sturdiest brush and, naked, ducked into the opening. Indentations in the vertical tunnel had been cleverly hacked out by the stonemasons of ages gone for this very purpose of climbing to clean. Fynch flinched as he felt the first cold touch of the slime covering the walls of the drophole. He smiled grimly in spite of it, taking a fierce pleasure that most gong boys only had a short lifespan at this job because they grew too big for it within a year or so. Not him, though. His all but skeletal frame still fitted Stoneheart's dropholes with room to spare.

Fynch had long ago learned to distract himself from the nauseating odor of his work. He had taught himself how to breathe through his mouth but nothing was more effective than his unique ability to lose himself in his thoughts. He glanced down and saw the outline of Knave's dark head staring back at him and that made him think of the General again.

Climbing instinctively now with slow care he gave himself over to his "information," as he liked to call it, and delved into where he kept his details on the General. There was no way that General Thirsk should have lost that contest to the Prince. Even a dolt could see that Thirsk had the heir well and truly beaten and still he had yielded. And then that business with the fortune teller later in the evening. That was most odd. Fynch was sure she was only a fairground fake and yet something had happened in that tent to rattle the General.

He was not that far from the top now and he slowed down to consider the connection he had suddenly made between the General's strange behavior last night and that equally odd moment when Wyl Thirsk had collapsed at the witchburning and how his eyes had changed color. Fynch had to admit it. Curiosities definitely surrounded Wyl Thirsk, not the least of which was his mysterious dog. He had gleaned from overhearing some of the soldiers talking that Knave was a special gift from the woman who had died at the stake, in exchange for his small kindness to her. As Fynch brushed away the slime he laid out tidily in his mind all of the information he had gleaned, including his disturbing experience when he first touched Knave.

His agile mind picked its way across all that he knew and finally, disturbingly, it crossed Fynch's consciousness that perhaps the General was somehow touched by an enchantment. The woman who burned was called a witch, after all. Fynch did believe in sorcery, though he could never admit to such a thing to others. The idea of enchantment was whimsical, he granted, but it nagged. He continued his slow climb upward and as he toiled he came to the conclusion that Knave was somehow part of it. When all was said, Knave was the witch's dog.

An enchanted General. A fanciful notion, he chided himself, but one he could not let go of as he looked up to see dim light coming from the small windows hewn out of the stone walls of the privy above. Soon he would be able to slip his fingers over the lip of the drophole and start his more vigorous cleaning, steadily moving downward and back to Knave, whom he could sense was still watching him. Just as Fynch was about to heave himself to the opening, he heard an unmistakable low rumble coming from below. It was the dog. Knave made many sounds and, as strange as it seemed even to him, Fynch believed he could understand many of them. It was as though the dog were speaking to him. And this sound was unmistakably the growl that Knave reserved for Prince Celimus.

He was warning Fynch that the heir was near.

Fynch ducked to cower in the darkness. Surely the Prince did not need to use the privy now! Worse, he was afraid of Celimus and wholeheartedly shared Knave's feelings toward the man. Carefully, Fynch began lowering himself as he too could now hear footsteps. His first thought was to let go and jump. Whatever breaks or bruises occurred, so be it. He could not bear the thought of being caught like a peeping tom by the Prince—Shar alone knew what the man might do to him.

The growl intensified and then Knave fell silent and in that moment Fynch froze. He heard it too. Speech as well as footsteps—and it was not just one voice. Fynch recognized Celimus but he was talking to another man and they were in the privy. *Why?*

He carefully and silently lowered himself to where he thought he was in sufficient shadow to be hidden and then he listened intently. It was uncanny how clearly he could hear them.

It was the other man who was speaking. "—Yes, but why here?"

"Because it is the only place where I feel we can speak plainly without risk of being overheard," Celimus warned. "The walls are made of thick stone, my friend, but most of them have ears."

"All right," said the other. "Your privy it is then. Why am I summoned, my lord?"

"Because my sources tell me you are the best."

"I am competent in many things, your highness. I wonder to what you are referring?"

"Don't be glib with me, Koreldy. You are a mercenary, am I correct?"

"Yes."

"And an assassin for the right price?"

There was a pause and Fynch felt himself holding his breath for fear of them hearing even his heartbeat.

Finally the other man replied. "It depends on who and how much."

"Several hundred crowns," said the Prince without hesitation.

Fynch's eyes widened in surprise. Even to the wealthiest noble, this was a fortune.

"You must want this person dead very badly, your highness," said the assassin, politeness in his words although it was clear he was not daunted by the Prince.

"I make no jest. Will you do it?" Celimus sounded impatient and seemed not to have noticed the man's direct manner.

"When?"

"Soon. I must arrange a few things to ensure your job is easier—see what a considerate employer I am?" said Celimus.

"And payment?"

"Half this very minute, if you agree. The gold is in my chamber."

Fynch heard the other man whistle low and softly.

"Who?" he finally asked.

"General Wyl Thirsk."

Fynch felt the shock shudder through his tiny frame. He almost lost his grip on the slimy wall.

"Ah, I knew it could not be that easy to earn so much," the man said, resignation settling into his voice.

Fynch could hear Celimus move around the confined space. He was agitated. "He is but one man and unsuspecting. Surely you can handle it?"

"Yes, of course I can handle it, your highness," the assassin replied smoothly. "The trick is in feeling comfortable about doing it to a man I respect."

"How about five hundred crowns—will that help ease your guilt?" asked the Prince, just a hint of sarcasm edged in his voice.

Again there was silence as the man considered.

Celimus filled the quiet. "You are falling for history, my

friend. Wyl Thirsk is no more of a hero than you. You're from Grenadyn," he pressed, "how can you care?"

The man replied so softly that Fynch's excellent hearing had to strain to catch it. "My family is originally from Morgravia, sire. Before our families moved away from these parts, my grandfather fought with his. I hear old Henk Thirsk was a fearsome warrior and a fine commander—apparently this one takes after him."

"You seem to take a strong interest in history," Celimus said.

"I remain Morgravian at heart even though I was born across the oceans," the man said coolly.

"Well, you hear tales, I'm afraid. This one is a coward who throws up his dinner at the sound of a bone breaking," Celimus said.

"Is that so?"

"Yes. Which is why I want him dead. He is useless to me and threatens the safety and security of Morgravia. As a mercenary I assume you have no allegiances?"

Fynch presumed the man must have shaken his head because Celimus continued.

"Good, then you should feel nothing at his death and I am paying you a vast sum of money to suffer no regret. We follow a rather quaint and, if I might add, senseless tradition of promoting the Thirsk males to Generals without so much as a thought to whether they are any good at it. This one, it appears, does not bear comparison to his predecessor you speak of."

"Can you not demote him, your highness?"

"Only when I am King."

"I gather that may occur soon, my lord."

"Not soon enough," Celimus spat.

"I see," the man replied, and again Fynch was amazed at how direct he was with the Prince. "Why not have him killed by one of your own, then? It seems extravagant to spend so much on a foreign assassin if the man is so incompetent. Surely one of your own soldiers would do your bidding for one tenth of what you would pay me?"

Fynch waited, willing his numb fingers to hang on. The

mercenary was no idiot and the boy marveled at the man's composure in front of the Prince, who intimidated most.

"It would not look good. I'm sure you understand," Celimus answered, disguising his discomfort with a harsh chuckle. "I do not want Wyl Thirsk's blood on any Morgravian's hand. The Thirsk family is revered and closely connected with my own."

Fynch imagined the canny mercenary's eyes narrowing at this. The Prince's reasoning sounded thin.

"What is your plan?"

"I will brief you shortly. In the meantime I have hired some foreign soldiers to accompany you."

"Can they be trusted?"

"No. But they will do my bidding or they will not get paid. And they will be paid handsomely for following my direction. Greed alone binds them to us. They will have their own orders that do not involve you. Your task is simple: dispatch Thirsk."

"Where must it happen?"

"Not on Morgravian soil."

"Half now?" the man finally said.

"And the other half when I have proof that he is a corpse," the Prince replied, the familiar slyness back in his voice.

"Agreed."

"Good. Come, now, let us drink to our pact."

Their voices began to recede and Fynch felt relief flood as he risked moving his body and flexing one of his hands. He heard the soft growl again and froze: the Prince had returned.

"Pour me one," Celimus called. "I'll be right out," he added and proceeded to rid his bladder of its contents.

Fynch closed his eyes and quickly looked down just before the hot liquid hit his bent head, stinging his face. In his humiliation mixed with despair at this newly learned information, he barely heard the soulful ringing of the cathedral bells, the particular rhythm of which signified the death of a sovereign.

10

MAGNUS DIED IN AN OPIUM-INDUCED STUPOR AS HE GAZED absently through his beloved arched windows into the cold, bright autumn morning.

The night previous, sensing death was standing at his bedside, he had met with as many of his counselors as Orto considered important. He had also met briefly with his son; they had little to say to each other, although Magnus had certainly tried to speak about his vision for Morgravia, hoping against hope to reach his son on some level where the two might find common understanding.

His painful effort was in vain.

A wintry smile had passed across the Prince's face, as cold as the heart that beat inside him, as he once again wished his father a speedy death. Then he leaned toward Magnus and for one blinding moment of hope the dying man thought his only son might be offering a hug of farewell. It would be enough, Magnus had thought in that shining second of anticipation. And then he had grimaced wryly as he realized how wrong he was—indeed how desperate he was for his son's love. The King's was a dark smile of sudden and complete acceptance. It was his final surrender to the sickening notion that he truly hated Celimus as much in return.

The young man had bent only to tug on his father's hand, pulling viciously at the large ring that bore the seal of Morgravia. The sovereign felt the bile rise to his throat.

"You have no further need for this, Father."

Magnus had then summoned such a withering look it had made Celimus step back. His son's reaction had given the King a final sense of power. "And your reign will be cursed.

You will die hated as I make my final prayer to Shar that your crown is somehow wrested from you. Get away from me! Let me walk toward Shar looking at the palace dogs rather than you. Leave!"

"I'm gone, you useless old fool. By nightfall the kingdom will be mine to do with as I please and I swear to you, Father, it will bear no resemblance to your weak reign. My mother was right. You are a peasant. Good riddance to you and all who swore fealty to you."

Celimus had departed then but not before he deliberately paused to spit at his father. "That's all you've ever meant to me. Die lonely and with the thought that Wyl Thirsk will fast follow."

And Magnus, too helpless now to even call loud enough for a runner to Wyl, had watched in horror as the Prince strode gracefully from his chamber, leaving behind his saliva, which slid down his father's face and mingled with the tears that freely came.

When Orto had arrived a short while later he found the King slipping away. His servant knew it would be only minutes now. With his knack for making intuitive decisions, Orto had sent his speediest page to fetch Wyl Thirsk and a second runner for the physic, who arrived first.

"I can give him a draught that will send him peacefully on his way," the man had offered.

"Do it after Thirsk arrives," Orto suggested.

The physic nodded and silently went about his business of preparing the lethal concoction.

Wyl arrived breathlessly and Orto welcomed him softly. "I think I'm right in suggesting, General, that yours might be the last face our dear King Magnus might wish to look upon before he leaves us."

"Celimus?" Wyl asked, knowing it was an empty question.

Orto shook his head. "They have spoken. It left him disturbed. Please, General, the physic would like to give him a draught to soothe the pain and make his journey end."

Wyl nodded, his chest tightening with sadness. He knelt by the large canopied bed and took his sovereign's hand. He kissed it reverently.

"Sire, it is Wyl."

Magnus struggled through his rapidly vanishing wits to reach the brightness where daylight shone and beloved Wyl Thirsk's face smiled crookedly at him through damp eyes.

"My boy, my son," he whispered, trying to squeeze Wyl's hand in return but knowing he failed.

The physic handed Wyl the cup and nodded. Inside was a shallow amount of a dark, strong-smelling liquid.

Wyl held the cup to the King's mouth. "Drink, sire."

Magnus knew what it was. "Yes, time for me to cross over, Wyl," he mumbled.

"Now you and my father can be together again," Wyl whispered, holding back his tears.

The King swallowed the contents of the cup and his head fell limply back against the cushions. The physic was dismissed by Orto. The King turned, eyes suddenly blazing with clarity.

He spoke haltingly as if each word pained him but he was clear from the slur that plagued only moments earlier. "Wyl, the blood promise I made you give years ago, I take it back, all of it. You know what I speak of. You alone have the power to take Morgravia. The Legion is loyal to you."

Wyl looked toward Orto, shocked by what the King said. Orto's expression glimmered with triumph. Wyl hoped his loyalty was true.

"Sire, you must not speak of such treachery. Please—I—"

"No time! Get Ylena away. He means to kill you. Leave now—"

The King's voice trailed to murmurings and then nothing. His eyes stared blankly over Wyl's shoulder as he took one last look at the bright sun shining on Morgravia. A final shuddering breath issued from his sunken chest and then he was gone.

"I must fetch the priest," Orto said quietly.

"Orto—"

The man turned back. "I am loyal to Magnus, not to Celimus, sir. I heard nothing but the shallow breathing of a man drifting in the poppy seed liquor to his death."

"I am in your debt."

"I will be leaving the palace, sir. Soon it will not be a safe place for me to be. You may care to take similar precaution. I shall find a way to send word of my whereabouts, should you ever have need of contacting me."

A look passed between them over the corpse of Magnus. Wyl stood and shook Orto's hand. "I'll send word for the cathedral bells to be rung."

Orto nodded. "Good luck, sir—until we meet again."

Fynch shivered, his teeth chattering against the biting chill of the lake. He had scrubbed his body raw of Celimus and still he kept ducking his head underneath the surface until it ached so much he felt his eyes might pop. And all the time Knave paced at the water's edge, agitated and barking over the sound of the bleak drone of bells.

"I'm coming," Fynch called through numb lips, his mind like stew after the shocking revelation he had overheard.

Would Thirsk believe him? Likely not. His story would sound too farfetched. And him just a gong boy—who would listen to him? Knave barked again, louder this time, and Fynch swam his weary way to the bank, using the dog's strong tail to heave himself out of the water. As he did so the vision blazed in his mind again: it was General Thirsk, a sword being pulled from him, the light dying in his eyes. It vanished and his head hurt once more. A fresh wave of nausea shuddered through his tiny frame and the boy retched. Earlier panic had made it hard for his normally agile mind to think coherently. He knew to wait until the dizziness dissipated.

Knave's rough tongue licked the droplets of water from him repeatedly. The dog's breath was warm and gradually Fynch found his wits again, coming out of the frightening vision. His head pained him but he ignored it, rubbing himself vigorously with his shirt before he pulled on damp clothes. There was no time to lose. Convinced now that his vision was a warning, a premonition, Fynch knew he had to find Wyl Thirsk, tell him what he had overheard, and somehow make the General believe him.

"Come, Knave. Let's find him," he said, knowing he

would be risking his job by entering the main palace grounds. It mattered not. The life of a man he was mysteriously connected to was at stake and he alone knew.

The dog bounded off and Fynch ran behind, not knowing he was already too late.

Wyl paused outside the new King's chamber. Celimus had not even had the courtesy to wait for his father's body to cool. Tradition required him to hold off claiming kingship quite as blatantly until the old King had been laid out in the cathedral. He should wait until the stone had been laid on the tomb to be actually crowned but Celimus stood on no ceremony. He wanted the crown so badly, Wyl imagined, it was probably already glinting on his head.

It had been only an hour since he had kissed the dead face of Magnus. In that short time, the body had been washed, presumably would now be moved to the chapel, and Celimus had apparently swept into power and his father's chambers. It was sickening.

Wyl took a deep breath and wondered what Celimus was up to by summoning him so soon. He wished Alyd was there to accompany him, but he had not been able to find his friend, not even in his chambers—which was odd considering Alyd's state the previous eve. Ylena too was elusive; perhaps she had been cross at her husband's drunkenness and taken herself off on a shopping expedition in the city. More worrying was the news that Gueryn had been posted north during the night. Wyl was extremely unhappy about this and felt guilty that he had been reveling with his soldiers and therefore unable to prevent the sudden departure of his mentor. The posting had the King's signature on it, but it smelled wrong to Wyl. Magnus would have been in no fit state to be signing off on dispatch orders. That piece of maneuvering had Celimus stamped all over it and Wyl meant to get to the bottom of it. Celimus's threat to him at the tournament began to niggle anew at his mind.

The soft fragrance of winterblossom wafted in through an open window and reminded Wyl of former days—happier times—when he had stood at these massive oak doors awaiting entry to see King Magnus. Now the King was dead, taken by Shar's Gatherers to be with Fergys, he hoped. Wyl felt alone indeed as one of the doors opened and a man he recognized as one of Celimus's most loyal servants stepped out.

"At last," the man said. "The King does not like to be kept waiting."

Any number of retorts sprang to Wyl's lips but he bit them back. This one did not warrant his attention and so he gave the fellow a look of disdain.

"Hurry up, then. Announce me."

The doors were opened fully and Wyl stepped inside to wait. His gaze was drawn to the carved keystone he had marveled at as a child. Once again he was reminded that the fire-breathing warrior dragon signified he had entered the private domain of a King—but this time, one he detested. The man returned soon enough, a scowl settled on his face.

"King Celimus will see you now."

Wyl ignored him and strode past to where another servant led him into the study.

Wyl knelt, his whole being privately protesting at having to pay homage to Celimus.

"My King," he said, not looking up but glad his voice was firm.

"Ah, Thirsk." Celimus did not invite him to stand. Wyl could just see the feet of an aide step up to the King, who had obviously motioned for him. Celimus whispered something and then the feet disappeared. Wyl remained kneeling, saying nothing although he heard other people had, as quietly as possible, arrived behind him. Out of respect, soldiers were required to remove all weapons when in the private chambers of the royals. He wished now he had not observed the protocol so honestly. Gueryn had oft warned him to conceal a small dagger.

As Celimus finally stood and walked around him, Wyl was grabbed. He struggled valiantly, crushing a nose with the back of his hand. That assailant staggered backward, and Wyl then bent low enough to fling another over his own back. He swung around ready to face the enemy only to feel the razor-sharp tip of a sword at his throat. He felt it break his skin.

"I wouldn't," its owner said smoothly and Wyl, perceptive to such things, picked up a Grenadyne accent.

While men Wyl did not recognize chained his wrists and ankles, the stranger's smile never left his face nor did he remove his blade until the General was twisted around to face the King. Wyl now looked more closely at his burly attackers; their beards and the way they wore their hair marked them as foreigners. He dragged his gaze away from them as the King spoke.

"I'm wondering, Wyl, how loyal you are," Celimus commented from the large picture windows at which he stood.

"I am sworn to give my life for Morgravia and her citizens, sire," Wyl answered, breathing hard with fury at this treatment.

"That's all well and good. But a new King must surround himself with people true to him first and foremost. I cannot have my own General plotting against me."

Wyl was silent.

"Speak freely," Celimus encouraged. "They don't care," he said, shrugging and gesturing towards the foreigners. "They are loyal to money only."

"I am your servant, sire. I am your General and yours to command."

Celimus smiled now and Wyl hated him for that sudden easy way he could become so casual and friendly.

"That's good, Wyl. It seems both our fathers had high hopes that we might run the realm as they did. Do you think it might work as they dreamed?"

"I see no reason why not, your majesty," Wyl said, glancing around again, wondering at his options for escape. His mind was already racing to how he could get word to Ylena. Old Magnus had been right to warn him. Celimus knew Wyl was dangerous simply by the power he held over the soldiers of the Legion. Wyl had been the one too slow to recognize it. And now here he was, helpless and captive.

"Well, I'm impressed by your optimism, General. But I

need something more than words. Words sound hollow when there is no action as tangible proof of sincerity."

"How may I prove it, sire?"

"Simple. I have a mission for you, Wyl. And if you can carry it off successfully for me, then I think you will have gone a long way toward proving your words are not empty. I realize we can never be friends but I would value your loyal service."

Wyl nodded. "Tell me what you wish me to do."

"Please, sit," Celimus said, waving his beefy henchmen back.

Wyl preferred to stand but felt it was best to do as he was told. He noted Celimus remained standing by the window, looking out into one of the small courtyards. He also did not give any order for Wyl's hands to be released.

"It's a delicate mission that requires your touch—or at least your family name," Celimus said, not turning. "I want you to lead a small company of men into Briavel and win an audience with King Valor."

Although he tried not to, Wyl knew he showed his surprise at the audacity of what Celimus suggested.

The King continued. "You will make him an offer."

Now Wyl was intrigued. "What is my offer, sire?"

"An offer of marriage between myself and Valor's daughter, Valentyna. He is an old man now and would see the sense of joining our two realms, for no young royal—especially one as flighty as I gather she is—would choose war over peace and prosperity. I alone can give her that security. Or I can bring her interminable grief as I will systematically wage war on her realm until it falls."

Celimus stopped talking and turned around, his dark gaze resting languidly on the General. Wyl felt strangely heartened. Was he really hearing right? He saw the King was patiently waiting for his response.

"Your majesty, your idea is inspired," he admitted. "It would bring peace after centuries of war," he added, hating that he was stating the obvious and yet still unable to contain his pleasure. "I will gladly take this mission and I will not fail you, sire." Wyl stopped, realizing he was gabbling.

"I'm glad you like my plan," Celimus replied, looking at one finely manicured hand.

Wyl's brow creased again. "But why did you think you'd need to bind and subdue me to hear such a promise?"

Celimus glanced up. "Because I don't trust you, Thirsk, that's why."

"And do you now?"

"Perhaps. I have assembled the company you will take with you." He looked past Wyl's shoulder and nodded. "You've already met Romen Koreldy. I have appointed him your second."

Wyl's gaze fell again upon the tall stranger. The man had dark features although his eyes were of a particular silvery gray. They had a laughing quality to them. Hair dropped thickly to his shoulders and a closely trimmed moustache followed the line of his neat, wide mouth. When he spoke his salutation it had the same amused quality in its timber that his eyes held. This was a man who was clearly comfortable in his own skin; confidence and surety seemed to ooze from him.

Wyl stood. "Alyd Donal is my Captain, your majesty," he said quietly, firmly, swinging back toward Celimus.

"Not on this sensitive mission, Wyl. In fact you'll be taking none of the Legion with you."

"You would send me into an enemy kingdom without my own men, sire?"

Celimus opened the window. "Entering our enemy's kingdom so boldly is precisely why we will not send Morgravians other than yourself. The mere presence of the Legion would be like a spark to kindling. I cannot risk it."

"And you trust foreigners to the task?" Wyl said, looking again toward Romen Koreldy, who smiled back, his manner infuriatingly relaxed.

"You are no foreigner, Wyl—you are a proud son of Morgravia. The foreigners will be briefed and fat purses await each on their return from a successful mission."

Wyl wondered if it was his imagination that Celimus's grin had a new wolfish quality to it. *Mercenaries,* Wyl thought, grimly. *Both our fathers will turn in their graves.*

He set his expression gravely, bracing himself for the repercussion of what he was about to say. "No, sire," he said, "I regret but I cannot do this without the men I trust around me and I must recommend that you reconsider this plan."

Celimus's voice was now laced with a sharpness. "This is not about you or what you want," he snapped. "This is about achieving peace between two realms through a strategic marriage. You are its negotiator."

Wyl bristled. "I am a soldier, sire, not a politician. Perhaps I am the wrong man after all."

Celimus shook his head as though in the presence of a stubborn child. "Valor will trust no other name. He may be our enemy but his respect for your father is well known."

"And yours too, sire," Wyl countered. "It might be more appropriate for you to go in person and ask her hand."

Celimus swung around from the window now. He could no longer disguise his anger. "Are you afraid, Wyl?"

"No, sire. I'm just not stupid," Wyl said, instantly regretting his choice of words and what they intimated. He pressed on. "These men are strangers and I do not trust them with my life or anyone else's."

"And if I guaranteed your safety?" Celimus asked. Wyl opened his mouth to speak and then shut it again. He knew now this was a trap. "I have, of course, sent a diplomatic messenger ahead to request Valor's cooperation in entering into peaceful talks with my envoy," the King added.

Wyl shook his head, determined not to show the shock he felt that Celimus had obviously begun orchestrating this plan when King Magnus was still alive. Trusting Celimus was laughable. He was as cold and as unpredictable as a snake. "I regret it, but no, your majesty. I will not head this mission for you under these circumstances and I would respectfully warn—"

"And this is your final answer?" Celimus interjected.

Wyl nodded, fearful now of what his decision might promote, but he remained resolute. He would risk neither his office nor his family name conspiring with mercenaries.

Celimus sighed dramatically. "As I thought. So now we

must find new ways to encourage your loyalty." Throwing open the other window, he turned to the burly men standing near. "Bring him," the new sovereign commanded.

Wyl was dragged to the window, his eyes helplessly drawn to what had previously held the rapt attention of Celimus. Kneeling at a block was a man. Above him stood an executioner, his hands on a large axe, the blade resting menacingly between his feet.

The prisoner's hair was grabbed, his head pulled back. Wyl felt his knees buckle. It was Alyd staring back at him pitifully from a shockingly swollen and bruised face. He recognized Wyl and through puffy, smashed-up lips he managed to scream Ylena's name before one of his keepers cuffed him hard. The fight went out of the prisoner and he was dragged back from his prone position in the dust where he coughed out more teeth and blood. Once again Alyd's head was forced to the block.

Not even the memory of Myrren, which came sharply back into his mind, could frighten Wyl as much as he felt at this moment.

"My King, please, I beg you—" Wyl cried.

"Too late, General Thirsk. I am not someone to be trifled with."

Celimus raised his hand.

"Celimus!" Wyl beseeched, forgetting protocol. "For the love of Shar, man! That's the captain of the Legion out there. He is loyal to Morgravia. His father—think of his family, my King, I beg of you. Felrawthy would give his life for you. Alyd must be spared." He knew he was blathering.

A choked cry from Alyd calling Wyl's name urged him on, his heart beating hard with panic.

"I gave you a task, you denied me your service," Celimus explained, almost gently as one would to a child.

"My lord King, if you would allow me to take my own good men, then I—"

"I don't make bargains with my General, Wyl. You forget that you serve me."

Wyl opened his mouth to say something. His mind was

spinning with what he could possibly negotiate but it was already too late. Celimus had no intention of sparing Alyd's life. This was all a ruse. He had meant to have him killed from as early as the moment he found out his intention to bed Ylena had been thwarted.

Wyl watched with horror as the King's hand dropped, giving the signal. His eyes switched with terror toward the courtyard, where an axe rose and then fell. Wyl watched, mute and devastated as his friend's life was cut tragically short. Even the use of the axe was an insult to his friend's noble status.

A choked sob escaped him. "You evil bastard!" His voice broke as he shouted at Celimus, struggling against the men who held him and the chains that prevented him from striking out.

Celimus had barely batted an eyelid at what he had witnessed. "It's your fault that he had to die, Wyl. If only you had followed your King's instructions without question—isn't that what you're supposed to do? Isn't that what your father did for mine?"

"My father did not follow the orders of a lunatic," Wyl spat, realizing too late how calamitous his words were as his mind raced toward how to keep his sister safe, how he might negotiate with this cruel, bloodthirsty man.

At Wyl's insult, Celimus turned back to the window and gave another signal.

Only then did it occur to Wyl that his sister was no longer safe. "Where is Ylena, Celimus?" Wyl whispered, petrified.

"Right here," the King replied, menace in his voice.

Wyl dared to look out again and despair wracked his body for the second time as he saw his distraught sister being pushed into the courtyard. She saw her husband's headless body slumped against the block and she began to scream.

Fynch stopped running abruptly as his mind swam with a vision of blood. *We're too late, Knave, too late!* he screamed inwardly and slumped against Stoneheart's cold walls, his distress too much for him to bear as he succumbed to a small boy's tears. His four-legged companion seemed to understand and allowed Fynch to bury his head against him.

Don't do this, Celimus." Wyl was begging now as he watched Ylena slipping in Alyd's blood as they carelessly booted her husband's body aside. Alyd's corpse toppled to the dust and Ylena had to step around his legs before they pushed her face toward the wet block. He could see her body shaking as she stopped her screaming and began to wail.

"I've had her dressed in virginal white. An ironic touch, don't you agree?" Celimus asked.

The King raised his hand to give the signal and Wyl begged harder, straining against the hands that restrained him. At a look from the King the men holding him loosened their grip to allow him to fall to his knees. He did not even notice the pain as he fell.

"Celimus, I beseech you. Spare her. I will do whatever you ask."

"Whatever I ask, eh?"

Wyl nodded mutely, blood from where he had bitten his own lips mingling with the helpless tears streaming down his face.

"Dear me, look at the state of you, General. One item of sorrow in your life and you fall apart. I wonder what your father would think of you?" Celimus said, deliberately rubbing salt into the wound. "How can I possibly believe you are the man to watch out for the security of Morgravia?"

Wyl could not focus on anything but winning a reprieve for his beloved Ylena. If Celimus asked him to chew off his own hand, he would try—anything but bear witness to her being hurt again.

"I am, sire," he beseeched. "I am the right man. I will do this job. I accept your mission." He broke down again as he spoke the words.

"On your sister's life, yes, you will!" Celimus said viciously. He turned back to the executioner. "Take her back!"

Ylena was roughly pulled back to her feet, her face and

gown soaked with Alyd's blood. She was alternating between shrieks and whimpers now. Celimus laughed.

Wyl gathered himself and took a risk by calling out to her. "Remember who you are, Ylena. As one!"

She did not even look up at the family motto being called.

Celimus was highly amused by her state. "Wait! Make her carry her husband's head back to the dungeons. He can keep her company, and tell her if she drops it, she'll be flogged." He turned back to Wyl. "I'm glad you saw reason. Ylena will remain in the special accommodation I have chosen for her until you complete the mission we have discussed. Is this clear?"

"Yes" was all Wyl could trust himself to say as tears began to dry on his cheeks. He made himself remember the sensation of the salty rivulets hardening on his face. It would remind him of Alyd. One day Wyl would avenge his death by killing Celimus.

Magnus had alarmed him just hours ago by echoing his own conviction that Celimus must die if Morgravia was to be saved. Wyl looked at the new King now with renewed hate and knew he alone would be the one who must do it.

"Excellent," Celimus replied. "I have already taken the liberty of briefing the men, and have sent a messenger to Briavel to advise of your impending arrival. You leave immediately. Romen will accompany you to the stables. Don't worry about packing, it has already been arranged."

"May I see Ylena?"

"No. You will see her when you return. Until then, she remains a guest of Stoneheart's dungeons. Questions?"

"What if Briavel is not disposed to your proposal, sire?"

"Then you will have failed me, General, and not only yours but Ylena's life will be forfeit, as will your wealth and landownings."

All that mattered was saving Ylena.

"Anything else?" Celimus asked politely.

"Yes," Wyl said, trying to think straight. He gritted his teeth before he spoke. "Gueryn. I will need to get word—"

"Ah," Celimus said with a hint of regret. "I should have

mentioned this before, Thirsk. My father asked your friend, le Gant, to go on a special mission deep into the Razors. A task requiring experience but also, I suspect, involving certain death. Le Gant, to his credit, accepted the mission without hesitation—a brave man indeed."

It was the final crushing blow and Wyl could not hold in his gasp. "This is surely a jest," he said, eyes wide with disbelief. "What special mission? Why was I not told about it?" he demanded.

"A secret mission," Celimus repeated. "Not *everything*, General, is cleared through your office." His voice was filled with sarcasm.

"Gueryn is *not* dead," Wyl affirmed.

"Not yet," the new King said, and Wyl knew now that Celimus had him completely. Once more he recalled Celimus's threat at the tourney and realized now that it had been a true warning.

Magnus was dead. Alyd was dead. His sister had been imprisoned and, Shar forbid, his beloved Gueryn had been sent on a death mission.

Wyl's world fell apart. He nodded and bowed his head, refusing to bear witness to the King's glee.

11

HE COMPANY MOVED OUT OF STONEHEART'S EASTERN GATE in a frigid silence. Celimus had masterminded his plan with brilliance and all news of Alyd Donal's death, Ylena's imprisonment, and the coercing of General Wyl Thirsk was contained. Meanwhile, the city bells continued to mourn the death of a monarch and Morgravia's proud flag was being lowered in respect for the passing of a great man. Five official days of mourning prior to the King's full ceremonial burial would now take place. This would include the closure of all drinking houses, eateries, brothels, and indeed any establishments of entertainment.

Any nonessential workplaces would close. Throughout the Kingdom no animals would be slaughtered during the coming five days and Morgravia would live on vegetables and pulses in a further sign of respect. People would not be about the city. The dwellers of Pearlis would be encouraged to remain at home or attend chapel to pray for the soul of Magnus to speed it to Shar.

They should be rushing to church to pray for deliverance from Celimus, Wyl thought bitterly as he steered his horse through the great stone tunnel and beneath the gate. Celimus's timing was perfect. The fact that Morgravians would be off the streets and Stoneheart had effectively become a ghostly place meant no one of any note knew this party had left.

That is, all except a small boy and a large dog who followed at a safe distance. Fynch had cautioned Knave to stay quiet when he noticed the dog's tail wagging as Wyl passed by. As usual Knave appeared to understand the warning and now they moved at their own pace, keeping the last rider's dust in sight. Fynch's plan was to catch up to them by nightfall and he also hoped by then he would have found a way to convince Wyl of the truth of the plot he had overheard.

Fynch had gotten word to his sister not to worry about him. He had recently been paid so he knew the family would be fine for a while. He had run all the way home to fetch the family mule, their only asset, and pack a stock of dried food, oats, and water. Fynch had no idea how long he might be gone or what indeed he might be able to do. All he could think about right now as he followed discreetly was reaching Wyl and warning him of the trap Celimus had laid.

Stoneheart was behind them now and the signal was given to increase the pace. Fynch noted that the horses quickly put more distance between them.

"Come on then, Knave, we must stay with them, boy." He moved his heels against the mule and the sweet-natured beast obeyed his wishes and broke into a canter, Knave bounding easily alongside.

At the head of the column, Wyl rode in stony silence next to Romen Koreldy. Everyone except Wyl was armed, although there was no further need to hobble him. Celimus knew Wyl would give full cooperation with his beloved sister as security.

"Thirsk, this is not personal," Romen finally said when they were resting the horses with a trot.

"It is for me," Wyl snapped.

"I understand. I'm sorry about your friend."

"Why would you care?"

"Because it was unnecessary, frivolous even. No man should lose his life for a whim. It was obvious that you would have agreed to almost anything if Celimus had simply threatened your sister. If it means anything to you, it sickened me."

"You don't know the new King as I do, stranger. He has no scruples. If there's an ugly way to do something, that's the way he prefers. Killing Alyd was settling an old score—it was convenient that it looked to be serving the purpose of coercing me." Wyl looked away, disgusted.

Romen nodded. "I see. We have a code, us mercenaries. We kill only if it pays."

"I am the General of the Legion of Morgravia, stranger. Mercenaries are the dung that clings to the bottom of our boots."

The man sighed. "Yes, it would seem that way, although it also seems that we have our place in the world, doing the unsavory tasks that you more superior soldiers prefer not to take on."

Wyl's head snapped back to look upon the handsome foreigner with the easy manner. "I do not kill for money," he spat.

Romen smiled sadly. "Oh, we all ultimately kill for riches of some sort. It's just a matter of perspective, Thirsk."

"Who are you, Koreldy?"

"Just someone who fell by the way. Let's just say I

wasn't cut out for traditional soldiering. Our two grandfathers fought together, by the way—my background is Morgravian."

Wyl was surprised. "All the more reason for you to find this task despicable."

It annoyed Wyl to see the man grin. There was no unkindness in it. Just a wryness he could not interpret.

"You need me, Wyl Thirsk, because I'm the only one who can control this lot following us. Don't look upon me with such disdain—we are not so different, you know. I don't care for Celimus's tactics much but I agree with what he's trying to do. Morgravia and Briavel will end up destroying each other without this marriage, leaving themselves open to genuine threat from the north. His rationale is sound but I admit the way your new King goes about his business is certainly brutal."

Wyl grimaced. "He's a lunatic." Anger boiling again, he changed the subject. "What do you know about the threat from the north?" He hoped Koreldy might throw some light on Gueryn's chances of surviving this death mission.

"I know Cailech grows strong and more confident by the day. He will test his army. The raids will become more bold, more frequent. Mark my words."

"A barbarian will not take Morgravia," Wyl countered. "Even someone as deranged as Celimus will not permit it. He has an intense dislike for Cailech anyway. I'm not sure how it has grown to such a festering sore but he hates the barbarian—been telling us all for years how he'll rid us of him once he became King."

"Don't be too sure about what the Mountain King is capable of. He is far more sophisticated than you give him credit for," Romen warned.

Wyl's voice sounded condescending. "You know this firsthand, of course."

"As a matter of fact, I do," Romen replied, not at all offended at his companion's tone.

"You've met him?"

The mercenary smiled again in his disarming way. "I fought alongside him for a while." Before a surprised Wyl could pursue the conversation, Romen had called the men to pick up the pace again.

And so it went. For a few hours Wyl was able to let go of the powerful grief that he felt so assaulted by, allowing Romen to talk in his carefree style about life amongst the Mountain Dwellers. He was impressed with the man's knowledge and the sheer audacity of how he had navigated his way into Cailech's stronghold.

"So where is the famous rock fortress—does it even exist?" Wyl wondered aloud.

"Oh, yes, it exists, and impressive it is too. If you could ever see it, you'd be surprised by its sophistication." Wyl looked at him, was tempted to smirk but could see Romen meant what he said. "I hope you do see it, just so that you know I'm not a liar."

"But why were you there? I thought it was forbidden for any stranger to even get within leagues of the fortress."

Romen hesitated and his expression darkened momentarily. "Oh, family business," he replied, not convincingly, Wyl noted, and stored it away. "I'm from Grenadyn, as you know. We traded with the Mountain Dwellers. Let's just say I managed to find myself on reasonable speaking terms with Cailech."

"Will you tell me about him?" Wyl was intrigued.

"He's an enigma." Romen grinned. "I think I recognize some of my own traits in Cailech but he is certainly someone you wouldn't want to make a hasty judgement on."

"What do you mean by that?"

"That he's unpredictable." He shrugged. "Cailech is larger than life. He's heroic and devoted to his people. That makes him dangerous if he's crossed or senses any form of betrayal. He rewards loyalty and wins it easily from his warriors. He is at once easygoing and relaxed but in the next breath will trap you with cunning."

"Go on," Wyl urged.

"What else can I tell you? He thinks deeply on most subjects. His decisions might appear impetuous but they are often far from it, yet his personality is spontaneous. He lives by instinct."

Wyl blew his cheeks out. "You sound impressed with him."

"I am. Believe me. I don't know another who can be as ruthless to his enemies as he is generous to his own. I fear for his temper, though. He can be more cruel than you can imagine if someone has crossed him or he feels threatened. But his creed is really quite simple and I admire that. Mostly I admire his subtle mind. He is intelligent enough for ten men."

"A Mountain Dweller," Wyl mocked gently.

"Don't be fooled, Wyl. This is no ignorant, ale-swilling barbarian. This is a man born to be King."

Wyl pondered the advice. "What can you tell me about the fortress itself?"

Romen laughed. "Plenty, but it would be a betrayal for me to tell Cailech's enemies his secrets. He paid me well for my service. In return he enjoys my discretion."

"A mercenary with morals," Wyl jeered.

"You'll be surprised," the man replied softly. "Stop here, we make camp."

Fynch and Knave caught up with the group long after the campfires had burned down to embers. The horses whinnied nervously as the huge black dog melted silently out of the darkness. Fynch had had the presence of mind to unsaddle and tether his mule some way back. She was munching happily on her oats and seemed disinterested in the dog that frightened most other animals of her ilk. The boy waited in the darkness and watched as Knave padded up to Wyl and licked his master's face. Then the dog disappeared as silently as he had arrived, back into the shadows where Fynch crouched, and they both waited.

Wyl sat up and looked about him, shocked at the arrival of his dog. Most of the mercenaries in the camp were snoring; there was no need to post lookout guards in this part of the realm.

"What is it?" Romen asked quietly, his eyes still closed. He was clearly a light sleeper.

"Um—I have to go to the, er—"

The man sighed. "I'll come, wait a moment."

"No! That is, I have to empty my bowels."

Romen yawned. "All right. You know I'll have to leave one of your hands tied behind your back—can you manage to—"

"Yes, I'll be fine."

"And I'll have to tie this other length to your ankle—I'll keep a hold on this end here so you don't go wandering off into the night."

"I'm not going anywhere, Koreldy. My sister's life depends on me staying right here with you."

"Off you go then."

"I may be a while—I've got cramps."

"Take your time," the man replied, yawning again.

Wyl left the fireside, one leg trailing the long rope, the other end of which was tied to Romen's wrist. Just over the hillock he was overjoyed to be greeted by Knave but even more surprised to see the wide-eyed gong boy waiting for him too.

Fynch put his finger to his lips before whispering: "Just listen."

He told him everything he had overheard while hanging in the drophole and then all that had happened since, leaving out only his unsettling visions. He was brief and precise. Wyl listened grimly, his rage and bitterness settling into something cold and intractable within. Celimus would pay. *Somehow, Shar help me*, he thought, *I will survive this and he will suffer*. He surfaced from his angry thoughts and heard Fynch still whispering intensely.

"—we can follow you and perhaps plan an escape."

Wyl shook his head violently. "Your turn to listen," he whispered back and proceeded to tell Fynch all that had occurred this past day. He quickly realized that the little boy had not known of King Magnus's death, being too young to understand the significance of the particular mourning bells. The lad looked distraught hearing of Alyd's death and then Ylena's plight, but Fynch was a plucky boy and pulled himself together quickly for Wyl's sake.

"Hurry up, Thirsk," Romen suddenly called from behind them.

"Coming," Wyl replied. "You must go now," he whispered to Fynch. "Keep Knave close—and go home, back to Stoneheart. Forget about me."

The boy bit his lip. "I won't. We've come this far to help you."

"Go back, Fynch! I don't want you near me!" Wyl said deliberately viciously. He did not want the blood of this courageous boy on his hands, and blood, he believed, would flow soon enough. "You cannot help me. You are— a—a nuisance," he spat under his breath, hoping now to hurt Fynch, force him to leave.

Wyl watched the child's eyes narrow in pain as he patted Knave farewell. He turned and did not look back.

"Feel better?" Romen asked sleepily.

"Remind me not to eat squirrel again," he replied, laying his head down and recalling the strange Widow Ilyk and her caution to him about keeping Knave and his friend close.

Had she meant Fynch? How could she have known?

He pondered this as he drifted into an unsettled sleep in which he dreamed of himself being killed and yet somehow remaining alive.

There was no sign of Fynch or Knave as they entered Briavel's western border the following midday and by late afternoon they had been met by a contingent of its soldiers, who were clearly expecting them. Wyl suspected their party had been trailed anyway since the moment the first horse's hoof set foot on Briavel's soil. There was no possibility that a party from Morgravia could enter this realm—and vice versa—without its guard being put on alert. The mercenaries agreed with the Briavellians' edict, without a murmur, to make camp a few miles from the beautiful walled capital city, Werryl. There they would remain under a thin supervision of the Briavellian Guard. Romen had already briefed Wyl on their plan. He had foreseen them being met and taken under escort to King Valor. And Wyl knew he was trapped. So long as he was seen to be cooperating, then Ylena was safe. He realized he too would remain safe until he met with Valor. He hoped Shar would smile on him and grant him a private meeting.

Werryl's palace was indeed as breathtaking as fabled stories had it. Very few Morgravians had seen it with their own eyes but the palace lived up to the famous tales of its beauty. In stark contrast to the somberness of Stoneheart, it was built from the palest of sandstones, so light in color to be almost white; it sparkled on a hill.

The city of Werryl stretched out among the safety of the palace's walls. Smaller than Pearlis, it was no less sophisticated and its architects clearly had a keener eye for vanity. Even the bridge leading to the portcullis was superbly constructed, with statues of former Kings and Queens carved in marble and holding torches that lit the way at night.

Daylight was fading by the time Wyl and Romen arrived at the bridge and the keepers were just touching flames to those torches. Their escort led the way into the crowded city and through its pretty cobbled streets to the palace entrance on a rise. A messenger had gone ahead and various dignitaries were awaiting them.

After introductions they were politely shown to a private bathhouse where they might tidy themselves after their two-day ride. It was a courteous touch.

Soaking in a tub of hot water, Wyl began to relax for the first time. After hearing Fynch's tale, he now accepted that he would probably die on this journey but he had no intention of losing his life without saving Ylena's. Celimus would kill her anyway, whether Wyl succeeded in his mission or not—of this Wyl was now sure. He looked at Romen, who soaked in the scented waters of another tub, as still as a statue; eyes closed, long lashes touching his tanned cheeks. His long, freshly washed hair was slicked back and Wyl admired the chiseled profile.

"Why do you watch me?" Romen asked softly.

Wyl, in spite of his gloom, smiled. Romen was every bit the soldier he pretended not to be. Even soaking in the bath the man was alert to every movement, every nuance around him. He was impressive.

"I was just wondering how adept you might be with the sword."

"My favorite weapon—although I am devastatingly good at throwing knives," Romen replied, still not moving.

"Where did you learn that?"

"Oh, far away from these parts."

"You're well-traveled then?"

"And bone-weary from it."

"Why do you do it, Romen? Why sell yourself like you do?" Wyl asked, genuinely searching for an answer.

"Why not?"

Wyl could tell his companion preferred to remain a mystery. "How did Celimus find you?"

Now the man did open one one eye. "Do you know, I don't know the answer to that. How very annoying," he said. "It was via a mutual acquaintance, apparently."

"How much is he paying you to kill me?"

At this Romen did stir; opening both eyes, he looked at Wyl, the silvery gaze suddenly penetrating. "Not enough."

"Is there anything I can—"

"No," Romen interrupted. "I never go back on my word. But I'll do this for you, Wyl Thirsk. I will save your sister."

It was Wyl's turn to stare. The sickening pit in his stomach lurched. What could he mean? "Go on," he said.

"The King of Morgravia kills for pleasure. I don't like that. Whatever it is between you two, I sense you have the same hate for him as he does for you. I will not take sides. However, what he did to that young woman, clearly an innocent, was unforgivable."

"He's going to kill her no matter what the outcome here," Wyl said.

"That's obvious. But you can go to your death knowing I will not permit it."

"You'll forgive me if I don't find your words as reassuring as they sound," Wyl admitted, pouring a cup of water over his short red hair.

"You should be reassured. I am guaranteeing your sister's life. Meanwhile, you are a soldier and death eventually comes to all who carry the blade, including myself. There isn't a more noble death for a soldier than to die fighting."

"Except I won't be fighting, will I?"

"Yes, you will. When you have done what we set out to do, I will hand you a sword, Wyl Thirsk, and we will duel. If you kill me, you are free. If I kill you, I collect my extravagant reward."

Wyl thought about this. "But if I kill you, then my sister is not saved."

"Ah, well, that is a hole in the plan, but you too can save her. You have the Legion on your side. Collect your men and overturn the King. He will ruin Morgravia if you don't."

Why do I like this man! "It's a pity we meet under these circumstances, Romen. I would love to have you on my side."

The man smiled and sank deeper into his tub.

12

LATER, WHEN VALOR'S CHANCELLOR MET WITH WYL AND Romen he explained that the King wished to meet with General Thirsk privately. Romen said nothing initially, although his eyebrow lifted in its perpetually cynical manner.

"I shall wait outside," he finally said to the man. "I am the General's personal bodyguard on Briavellian soil. It is not worth my life to leave him—unsupervised," he added, choosing his words with care.

Wyl grinned, once again wishing he and Romen might have met in a different time, a different place.

The Chancellor, Krell, pursed his lips as though gravely affronted. "General Thirsk is under no threat in Briavel while here as a diplomatic envoy, sir. We have laid out a supper for you—"

"No need, my friend," Romen said, casually resting his hand on the man's arm. "I mean no offense but I have my orders, isn't that right, General?"

Wyl adopted a contrite expression, secretly delighted he would have time alone with the King. "Perhaps Romen could take his supper outside, Chancellor Krell?" He looked hopefully at the man.

"You mean outside the chamber where you are meeting the King," Krell replied dryly. It was not a question.

"Well done, you have it right," Romen said, now clapping the man on the back. "Thank you. A meal would be most welcome," he said and dismissed Krell by turning to Wyl. "I shall be right outside, *sir*—if you need me."

"Thank you," Wyl answered and made to follow Krell, who had already shown Romen his back.

Romen caught Wyl's arm and muttered under his breath, "No tricks, eh, Thirsk? Or the deal's off."

Wyl nodded.

Wyl was shown into a large, splendid chamber where a table had been set with a sumptuous cold supper. Awaiting him was a tall, and seemingly as wide, man. Wyl was announced and the two of them were left alone.

"Shar's Balls, you look like your father, boy."

Wyl bowed deeply. "I shall take that as a compliment, sire."

"And my spies tell me you're maturing into every bit the good man he was too." King Valor took Wyl warmly by the shoulders and looked at him. "Welcome to Briavel, son."

It was confusing. He liked this portly sovereign immediately. This was the enemy his father and Magnus had plotted against for most of their lives and yet he felt they should have all been the greatest of friends.

"I feel privileged, sire."

"So what news from Morgravia that doesn't break any secrets in the sharing?" Valor asked genially, pouring two cups of wine from an exquisite decanter. He held one out to Wyl. "Your health," he added, raising his glass.

Wyl followed and they both took a mouthful. It was excellent wine and, looking at the spread before him, Wyl could see no expense was being spared for the Morgravian envoy.

"Some grave news, sire," Wyl said and when the King raised an inquiring eyebrow he told him of Magnus's passing.

Valor stopped drinking, putting his cup down. This had clearly come as a shock. "That is a sorrow. Was Magnus not in good health?"

"No, sire. He had been ailing for a few moons beforehand. I think it was the wasting fever."

"Ah, a vicious thing it is too. I am deeply sorry to hear of this, Wyl. We were enemies but I respected him enormously—as I did your father. They were very good men, despite being Morgravian." A small smile curled at the edges of his mouth. "I understand now, why news of your arrival came from Celimus. I thought it was the Prince getting more involved in royal duties. Shar strike me! I can't imagine the old rogue's body is even cool yet—the son wasted no time grabbing his new status?"

Wyl said nothing but his silence spoke volumes.

"I see. Let me drink to Magnus, then," Valor said, raising his glass high. "May his soul speed to Shar's Light." They both drank. "Now sit, Wyl Thirsk. We have business to discuss and then supper to enjoy. My daughter, I hope, will join us shortly."

Wyl's expression must have been one of query because the King added that his daughter had been asked to attend but no one—just at this moment—could find her. Wyl decided not to pursue it. Valentyna, in truth, was all but irrelevant to an arranged marriage.

"Sire," Wyl said, steeling himself, "did Celimus give you any indication of why I am here?"

"The messenger merely advised me to expect a delegation from Celimus. I have to tell you, Thirsk, I am not in the habit of being told to expect anyone in my own realm, least of all a Morgravian." He noted Wyl nod and continued. "Your new King's choice of words were a trifle condescending, to say the least, which is why I have insisted on seeing you alone. I trust it gave some offense?"

"It did, thank you, sire," Wyl said, daring a grin.

Valor joined him. "Good. And I'll tell you this: it's purely on the strength of who your father is that I have even permitted entry for you and your companion."

Wyl nodded again. "I think my King counted on this occurring, sire."

"And what else did he count on?"

"Your Majesty?"

Valor leaned forward, his silver hair a halo about him. "Why are you here, Wyl? What is it your King wants of Briavel, son?"

Wyl felt annoyed for giving such a dim impression of himself. He decided to be direct—the soldier's way. "Your daughter, sire. He wants Valentyna."

The King started, first at the shock of his words and then at the woman's voice that came suddenly from a secret door behind them.

"Who wants me?" she said.

Wyl jumped up from his seat, also startled by the arrival of the striking woman, covered in dust and dressed in riding clothes—men's riding clothes.

Valor sighed. "My dear, why do you continue to use that secret entrance into my chambers? You know it annoys me."

"Because it is secret, darling father, and because it annoys you and has since I was a little girl" came the amused voice. She walked across the chamber on long, lean legs and planted a dusty kiss on the old man's cheek. "You must be the envoy," she said, turning to Wyl and eyeing him from her considerable height. "A bit short for a politician, aren't you?" she said, deliberately facetiously. "Aren't they normally bred to be tall and imposing in order to intimidate?"

"Valentyna, hush! This is Wyl Thirsk. He is no less than General of the Morgravian Legion. Do him honor please," the King admonished but not without some private amusement between the two of them.

Wyl felt himself blush. She appraised him again and after a simple bow, finally held out her hand for him to kiss. It smelled of leather and horse.

He bowed and as neither of the familiar scents offended him, he gladly kissed her hand. "Your highness," he said, feeling unbalanced by the dark blue gaze that impaled him from high.

"Apologies, General Thirsk, Princesses will have their jests," she said, leaving her hand in his. "Forgive me. I shall clean up and then I shall remind you of the conversation you were having before I arrived." She grinned at Wyl from a generous mouth. "By the way, Father, dear old Norma birthed the most beautiful black colt this morning. I'm still delirious with happiness he is alive and suckling. He almost didn't make it, you recall?"

Her father nodded. "Yes, my dear, and I suppose you were there among all the drama?"

She hugged him. "I delivered him in the early hours. I want him too—I've already named him because I was first to touch him. He's called Adamant. Thank you, Father." She said all of this in a contrived rush to befuddle.

"Valentyna, he is a prize stallion, you can't—"

His daughter had strode away and closed the secret door, leaving him mid-sentence.

"I think she can, sire," Wyl said, gulping.

"That girl will be the death of me," Valor admitted, shaking his head ruefully. "But she's irresistible. Come, Wyl. She'll be back quicker than you can imagine. Not one for taking long over her toilet or the usual primping of other women, you understand."

Wyl nodded, not understanding at all, considering his sister took several hours to prepare even for a day without visitors. He still felt as though he needed to catch his breath from the whirl that was Valentyna but he forced himself to find his previous train of thought.

"Celimus wishes your daughter's hand in marriage, sire."

"I gather," Valor said, appreciating his guest's brevity. He refreshed their glasses. "I imagined it was something like that. Let us not speak of this yet, then. Valentyna must hear it too."

Wyl was surprised but was happy to relax by the fire and let the delicious wine work its own particular magic while they waited.

"Tell me, Wyl, why Celimus sends you with mercenaries as escort and, more importantly, why you accept that."

He had been ready for this. "Ah. Well, he believed it would be inflammatory to send any soldiers from the Legion."

"And you are comfortable with this?"

"No, sire," he admitted. "I am not comfortable with it."

"So you are here against your will?"

"Some might think that."

Valor's eyes narrowed as he considered the young General's obviously careful choice of words. "Would it be truthful to say that Celimus on the throne does not please you?" he asked, making it easy for Wyl to simply nod if need be.

"Yes."

"And so you are here on a political mission under guard and you are being used because your name would open doors?"

Wyl nodded and put his finger to his lips.

"This room has walls twice as thick as our heads, son. They may hear voices but nothing we speak of in here can be eavesdropped with any clarity."

"Sire. In spite of how I personally feel about Celimus, I am as loyal to Morgravia as my father was. I consider this offer to be a stroke of genius. It is how those of us who crave peace can win it bloodlessly for the two realms. More importantly, your majesty, is the threat of Cailech from the north. A marriage between our realms would stop our senseless warring between east and west, allowing both southern kingdoms to focus a joint effort on quelling the Mountain King's potential to raid either of our lands. I think you'd agree, sire, that we'd all prefer the enforced company of each other to the barbarians."

The old King smiled at the gentle jest but sighed. "In this you are correct. There are skirmishes on our northern border that, each year, seem to intensify. I've strengthened our forces up there but I worry for Valentyna when she reigns. I too wish peace for our nations—perhaps we can work together against the Mountain King. I'm not sure why we need to despise each other so much. The reasons go back centuries and Magnus and myself simply perpetuated the old hate. Young bloods do that, I suppose. We should have stopped it years ago and bound our two heirs to each other by plighting their troth. I'm sure neither of us wishes our youngsters to continue this senseless cycle of battle."

"So, am I to take away from this meeting your agreement to the marriage, your majesty?"

"Yes, of course. However, that is not worth even a pinch of salt until Valentyna agrees to it." The King smiled when he saw the surprise and confusion register on Wyl's face. "Valentyna is my heart's joy, Wyl. She pleases me immensely, not just because she's my daughter but because she has turned into the person who is everything and more I could have ever hoped she would be. She sensed from a very young age that I might have somehow failed Briavel by giving them a female heir. She deliberately set her sights on becoming every bit as good as the son I didn't give Briavel. She rides better than most men I know; she can shoot a deer cleanly with a single arrow and then skin that same beast faster and more adeptly than I could at twice her age. She has learned sword skills and battle strategy—neither of which I hope she ever needs to use.

"There is nothing soft or sappy about this woman, Wyl, and yet she is the most beautiful person with a gentle heart and a desire to rule Briavel firmly yet with a largesse only a woman can possess. She has genuine empathy for her people's needs. She will make a fine ruler if she's permitted to sit on the throne. Which is why I will encourage her to make this marriage and bring peace to Briavel at last. I fear without our agreement, Celimus will choose war again."

Wyl nodded. "That's my understanding too, sire."

He felt relief flooding his body. As the King spoke, his mind returned to Ylena in the Morgravian dungeon, knowing she was now safe. He had no doubt that Romen would keep his word and rescue her from Celimus. It was Valentyna's arrival once again that dragged him from his thoughts.

Both men stood and turned. Wyl's breath caught in his throat. Gone were the men's clothes, the dusty hands, and the mud-smeared face. Tangled hair that had been carelessly caught under a man's hat had been smoothed and now gleamed dark and shiny past her bare shoulders. She had attired herself in a simple gown with no adornments, but its ruby color showed off her creamy skin and raven hair to their best advantage. She wore no coloring about her face, which was polished to a healthy glow from nothing more complicated than a vigorous scrubbing.

Valentyna was tall and willowy—too slim perhaps, Wyl thought, recalling the almost boyish physique in breeches. And yet she carried herself with supreme grace as she glided across the room to kiss her father once again.

"Ah, that's better, now you look like a Princess, my love," he said, smiling indulgently.

"But I prefer how I was before," she said. She turned to Wyl. "This more glamorous attire is for your benefit alone, sir."

Wyl, finding it hard to speak, mumbled something about how glad of it he was and then cringed at how awkward he felt and sounded.

"Shall we eat?" she offered brightly and the men joined her at the table.

Wyl spent the next couple of hours in a swirl of confusion. Beneath the table his body betrayed him frequently as Valentyna's sharply swooped neckline showed off the alluring swell of her breasts every time she reached across to help herself to food. And when she turned her blue gaze upon him, Wyl's breath caught in his throat. He realized he could feel his own heartbeat and the drum of blood through his ears. All of it creating a dizzying and yet a pleasurable sensation as Valentyna, always animated, talked about everything from her new stallion to her plans to check the fences on the northern end of some vineyards.

"Goats, sheep, wild horses, you name it. They just wander in and eat our fine grapes," she complained. "I'll be gone most of the day, Father," she added.

He looked at Wyl with a pretend despair. "You see I have no control over her," he admitted.

"You have come the closest, sire," she answered affectionately, "but I have to tell you that no man ever will."

And it was at those words that Wyl knew in his heart that he must prevent the marriage of Valentyna to Celimus at all costs. She was too bright, too beautiful, too headstrong, too talented, and far too much her own person to be wasted on the arrogant, cruel Celimus. They would hate one another and a new type of war would break out between the realms.

It would be as it was between Adana and Magnus, history repeating itself. Except Valentyna was neither cruel nor calculating. She would instead be smothered. He looked at the soft pulse he could see at Valentyna's throat and he thought about Celimus touching that pale skin. It made him feel sick.

Wyl interrupted the conversation to ask whether there was a privy he could use. Valor, wondering at the General's sudden paleness, pointed him to a small door cunningly concealed behind a tapestry. He gathered his wits in the privacy of the privy, dabbing his face with cool water from a pitcher and shaking his head ruefully at the position he found himself in. He was having to make a choice between Ylena and Valentyna. It occurred to him to bargain with Romen; perhaps he could still save Ylena?

"Are you well, Wyl?" Valentyna inquired, touching his hand as he returned to the table. Her warm touch sent a shocking thrill of pleasure through him.

"Pardon my mentioning it, but that is the widest drophole I've ever seen," he said, trying to make light of his sudden departure from the table and overcome his desire to take her hand and kiss it. The King and Valentyna laughed, surprised by his turn of topic. "Well, the dropholes in Morgravia are far narrower." He shrugged, embarrassed.

"Very savory chatter at supper, I must say," Valentyna quipped, her bright eyes sparkling with amusement.

"Forgive me," he said, and meant it but she waved his apology away.

"No, don't. I much prefer that to the usual stuffy conversations I have to suffer through with Father's friends. I like you, Wyl. I like your discomfort at being here," she said and he felt her smile drift over and through him like sunlight.

"I am but a soldier, highness," he said truthfully. "I shouldn't be here."

Valor cleared his throat. "Which brings us to why you are here, Wyl. Valentyna, my dear, the General has brought an offer of marriage to you from the new King of Morgravia. That's what we were discussing earlier."

Wyl noticed she stopped chewing but that was the only sign that gave away her startlement.

"And what did you both decide about this?" she asked levelly, again disguising any personal feeling.

"Only what you'd expect us to—that such a union would bring peace to two long-warring realms, both in need of a release from the cycle of battle and death."

Valentyna put down her fork and eyed the King. "I have not met him, Father—unless you count that one occasion all those years ago."

"Oh, come now, child. You were just an infant and—"

"Very fat, yes, I know," she interrupted. "But—"

"I was going to say . . . and easy to tease. You've come a long way since then, child. You are a most remarkable young woman and highly accomplished in ways I would never have dreamed. You make me proud and you will make a dazzling Queen for any King."

"Thank you." Her eyes softened. "But we don't know him, Father."

"Well, here we have the perfect person at our table to tell us more. Come on, Wyl, explain to my precious girl why Celimus might make her happy."

Wyl reached for his goblet and took a long draught. In that brief moment he asked Ylena to forgive him what he did. "I cannot, sire," he said, putting the goblet carefully back in its place.

"I beg your pardon?" It was the King's turn to be startled.

Valentyna's gaze landed with weight on Wyl's profile. He felt the side of his face burn with its intensity and he felt his heart hammering with desire. It made his breath shorten and he felt suddenly lightheaded. Was it possible to fall in love with someone so instantaneously? His mother had believed so. She had told him as much, smiling every time she recounted to Wyl of her first meeting with Fergys Thirsk.

"I was so young, Wyl. Not quite sixteen—" she would begin.

"My three sisters and I had heard such tales of King Magnus—we knew he was tall and dashing with golden locks. We could hardly contain our agitation for the two days leading up to his visit. And the food! We roasted an ox in his honor but there were also delicate fish dishes and meats, pigeon and duck. On and on the list went, Wyl. I thought the kitchen would explode from all the hysterical activity."

And then she would sigh. "All of us girls wanted to attend the King, but Mother said it was appropriate that I do so, as youngest. We didn't know, of course, that he was courting Adana by then. I think we all had starry-eyed hopes of Magnus taking one look at any one of us, falling hopelessly in love, and making her his Queen." She would say this dramatically and Wyl would always laugh.

"And now to Father," he would say, eyes shining, knowing what was coming.

"Yes, to Fergys," she would reply. "When the royal party arrived on that bright afternoon in summer we were only permitted to watch from a distance. We could see the stories were true, though: Magnus was every bit the handsome King. That evening we dressed in all our finery and we were presented to the royal party. When my name was announced, I was so nervous that I caught my foot in the lining of my gown and stumbled."

"It wasn't the King who caught you, though!" Wyl would chime in.

Helyna would smile indulgently. "No. When I gathered my wits sufficiently to look up and thank him, it was not the King I saw but his stocky, red-headed General, a man with genial eyes and a smile that lit my world."

"And you knew, didn't you, Mother?" Wyl would say at the end of the story.

"Yes, son, I knew. This was the man I would marry. My heart was already his at the first gentle sound of his lovely voice and his shy smile."

Wyl came out of his thoughts and realized there had been an awkward silence while King Valor and Princess Valentyna awaited his response. If his mother could fall instantly and helplessly in love with his father, then why could not he with Valentyna? She was an impossible dream but one he would permit himself.

Wyl took a steadying breath, looked first toward Valor and then at his daughter, both waiting expectantly. And he found the courage.

"He is no match for you, Valentyna." He turned to the King with an expression of deep regret. "I'm so sorry, sire, I came here today to win your daughter's hand in marriage for King Celimus but, having met her, I realize such a union would be a grave mistake."

Wyl blinked into the initial shocked silence before being brave enough to return Valentyna's grateful and just a little bemused gaze. Valor began to splutter his surprise.

13

THE BRIAVELLIAN GUARDS DIED SWIFTLY. THE ATTACK, AS VIOlent as it was unexpected, was over as quickly as it was begun and the mercenaries were adept at killing silently. Celimus was playing a slippery game. While Romen thought he was spearheading this band of soldiers, another of them—a man called Arkol—with a ransom on his head and little else to lose from murdering more people had agreed to run a killing raid.

Promised immunity from those who hunted him, as well as an irresistible sum of money, this killer had bigger prey on his mind than General Wyl Thirsk. His orders were to murder the King of Briavel. Celimus's evil mind had concocted a plan to leap all the obstacles in the way of his getting precisely what he wanted. Having met the man, he judged that Koreldy would not agree to assassinate a King for little other reason than he might not agree to marrying off his daughter. Arkol lacked even fundamental scruples, it seemed, and Celimus noted this immediately, deciding he was definitely the person for his third tier of the mission.

His threefold aim was this. First he would use Thirsk to open doors in Briavel. Celimus felt convinced that Wyl's name would win the audience, and get his men into Briavel without suspicion. He also rather hoped Wyl might win Valentyna's hand for him—not that he cared either way. Marriage was not to his liking but it was necessary—and it was essential with this supposedly plump and fragile Princess of Briavel.

With or without Wyl Thirsk, he would get his way with marriage—of this Celimus was sure. But the second aim of the mission was to ensure Thirsk was off Morgravian soil when he was killed. It was just such a neat plot to use Romen Koreldy to rid Celimus of the annoying presence of Wyl Thirsk—once his task was done in winning Valor's trust, that is.

And finally, his favorite of all the intertwined plots was the slaying of his neighboring King. If he could he would lay that peacetime atrocity at Thirsk's feet, further damaging the family name. However, his main achievement would be to dispense with any necessity to deal with Valor. If the Princess did not submit immediately to his demands to marry and thus join the two realms once and for all, then he would bring the full might of Morgravia crashing down upon her inexperienced and no doubt hysterical shoulders. He would take Briavel by force and he would see to it that she died in the process.

In killing Thirsk and Valor he believed he could lay open a path of hopelessness and indeed helplessness for the young Princess of Briavel. Without her father she would be nothing but a whimpering, spoiled Princess. And staying married to her—even if she did agree—was only ever a temporary situation; an immediate way to satisfy his burning desire to straddle the two realms. Celimus had full intention to rid himself of the cumbersome wife after a couple of years, perhaps by which time he might have sired an heir to genuinely sit upon a single throne ruling both Morgravia and Briavel. The irony of its comparison to his own parents' marriage and siring of an heir was not lost on him.

He loved the way his own mind worked. Killing Thirsk among it all was his master stroke. Being able to bring the Legion entirely under his own command was his dream. And then why stop at Briavel? With both realms under his rule, he could look to other, weaker kingdoms. Celimus already saw himself—in his daydreams—as some sort of Emperor in the making. It would mean disposing of the self-proclaimed King of the Mountains, of course, but for some reason this did not impact Celimus as being particularly troublesome. Oh, he had listened to his father flap his gums about the threat from the north but the barbarian's capacity was unknown in truth. How could he possibly put together a raggle-taggle fighting unit that could even begin to match the well-drilled prowess of the Morgravian Legion? Celimus had from early adolescence entertained himself with notions of empire that had eluded his father—the seeds of which had been planted by Adana in the bright youngster's mind. Magnus, he thought, sneering in a way his mother would be proud of, had only ever wanted to keep Morgravia safe. It had never occurred to the old fool to look beyond her borders. Why not take Briavel? Take the north?

So while the King of Morgravia lost himself in pleasant thoughts of killing Cailech, King of the Mountain Dwellers, Arkol in Briavel smiled as he surveyed the mercenaries' handiwork.

"Good work, men. Now muffle your horses' hooves and any weapons. Get rid of anything that makes noise—we move silently toward the palace."

"How do we get in?" someone asked.

"The messenger who arrived ahead of us is one of ours. He will kill the guards on duty at the gate and open the portcullis."

"That easy, eh?"

"It's better than easy. King Celimus has planned for another company to raid into Briavel and create a disturbance on the northwestern fringe of Werryl. Those men will draw away most of the Briavellian Guard while we storm the palace."

"And the others left behind?"

"Will be drugged, if our man can pull it off. Either way, they will not be expecting a direct strike and we will only move when the night is late. We'll catch them in their cups."

The soldiers laughed.

"And Koreldy?"

"Will die by my sword," Arkol cautioned. "No one else is to take that arrogant, ever-smiling bastard. Understood?"

They nodded and got busy with their horses.

Deep in the shadows of a small, nearby copse, Fynch shuddered. Despite Wyl's cruel words of the previous evening, he had doggedly followed and watched with horror as the recent events unfolded. Having heard the mercenaries' plan he knew it was up to him alone to save more lives tonight.

"We have to get to Wyl," he whispered to Knave.

They set off ahead of the soldiers, using the trees and undergrowth for cover and cutting across the fields so they could get to the palace before the killing spree began.

Wyl gambled everything. Appetites lost but glasses refreshed, he began to tell Valor and Valentyna of how he came to find himself here at their table. A shocked stillness had descended about the room as they absorbed the enormity of the General's sickening tale of Celimus's brutality and betrayal. When he haltingly described how his sister had been paraded among her new husband's blood, Valentyna took Wyl's hands in her own and when his voice broke, telling them of how Ylena was forced to carry Alyd's blood-soaked head back to the dungeon, she moved to hold him close and even held him to her as she wept for people she did not know.

When Wyl had finished speaking, Valor stood and paced. "And that man you came with, who is he to you?"

Wyl desperately wished he didn't have to move away

from Valentyna's sweet embrace. As he pulled his emotions together, he noticed with gratitude that she did not let go of his hands.

"My murderer," he said flatly.

"What!" she exclaimed. "This is preposterous!"

He explained everything he knew about Romen and the deal they had struck regarding Ylena's safety.

It was Valentyna's turn to stride distractedly around the room. "No! There has to be another way. You will not bargain with your life."

"My life is all I have to give," Wyl admitted.

"Father!" she begged. "What do we do?"

"Celimus is obviously certain he will win our permission for the marriage," Valor replied, looking to Wyl for confirmation.

Wyl nodded. "One way or another," he said, ruefully. "As I think about it now I realize he will win it either way—with your consent or by force."

"So it's Briavel he wants, rather than my daughter?"

Before Wyl could respond they heard a commotion coming from behind the tapestry.

"What in Shar's Name—" was all Valor could get out before the privvy door burst open and a small boy covered in something unspeakable and smelling just as unpleasant toppled in breathlessly through the opening.

Wyl regained his wits first. "Fynch!"

The youngster had run so hard he could hardly speak. "It's a trap, Wyl. They're coming to kill you. Koreldy and the King also. A man called Arkol leads them!"

"Who is this?" Valor demanded.

Wyl swung around to Valor. "Someone to trust. Where is the Briavellian Guard, sire?"

"On hand, I'll rouse them."

"Too late!" Fynch said. "Those who were supervising the mercenaries are all dead. And the bulk of the palace guard has already been lured away. Look out your window if you don't believe me."

Valor and Wyl did just that, while Valentyna had the presence of mind to slide the two huge bolts into place over the main door before running out of the secret door, returning moments later with her men's garb. She threw the bolts on that door as well, for a few in the palace knew of it and might be persuaded by pain to reveal it. She could hear the two men making noises of despair at the window.

The boy was telling the truth then, whoever he was.

Putting her finger to her mouth, she unbuttoned the gown, ripping it in her impatience and to Fynch's wide-eyed surprise, stepped out of it and proceeded to pull herself into her preferred working clothes. By the time her father and the General turned back from the window, she was just fastening the buttons on her shirt.

"Right, that gets rid of the Princess," she said grimly and turned toward a cupboard. Opening it with a key from a nearby drawer she took out three swords. "I hope you keep these blades keen, Father." She locked the cupboard from habit as she spoke.

"Sharpened each moon, child."

"Good," she said, turning toward the two men. "We're going to need them."

Wyl began shaking his head. "Not you, highness," he said to her, moving quickly across the room.

"Don't you dare, General Thirsk," she cautioned, her eyes glittering with anger. "This is Briavel, not Morgravia. The women here do not shirk from duty. I may be a Princess but I am my father's daughter. I fight alongside him."

She's magnificent, Wyl thought. He wanted to kiss her then and there and almost laughed at the realization that he would probably have to stand on tiptoe to do it. "I meant," he said gently, "that we have to get you away from here, Valentyna. You are too precious to risk."

"He's right," her father commanded. "My death is coming soon anyway, child. We have already discussed this."

Telltale tears began to leak from her eyes at her father's words but she fought them down. "No! We both flee if we must. I am not leaving without you, Father," she said.

Valor shook his head and smiled. Then his face became gravely serious. His voice cold. "You will do exactly as I

command, Valentyna. I am your King first. Don't forget
what I have always taught: you embody all of Briavel's
hopes for its future."

Valentyna bit back the words she was about to hurl at her father. There was no mistaking his tone. This was no longer her
indulgent father talking to her. A sovereign was speaking now.

She folded her arms defensively. "There is no escape,
anyway. Not from this chamber. If they have the front
gate—" her words trailed off.

Fynch looked around at their beaten, resigned expressions. "There is a way out," he blurted. The trio turned back
toward the small boy. "The same way I got in," he added,
shrugging.

"Of course!" Wyl said. "Fynch, you are an inspiration.
Quick, your highness, follow the boy. Is Knave down there?"
Fynch nodded. "Good, tell him to protect her with his life."

Valentyna was still contemplating the ugly passage out
when she asked, "Who's Knave?"

"My dog. Believe it or not, he will understand the message. Hurry, Valentyna, this is our only chance."

They could now hear the fighting raging beneath them. It
would not be long before the mercenaries reached this
chamber. Banging had started on the door. The King looked
at Wyl, wondering if it was already too late.

"It's Romen, ignore him," Wyl said grimly. "We'll deal
with him later."

They stepped inside the privy.

"I'm not sure I can," Valentyna admitted, looking down and
feeling disgusted by the thought of what encrusted the walls.

Wyl had no time for this. "He did it to save your life.
Now you'll do it, your highness, or I'll throw you down
there myself. Don't be misled by my height—I am far
stronger than you credit."

She could tell he meant it, and she appreciated his force-
ful directness—in fact, she admired this Morgravian General for everything he had said and done here this night. But
still she hesitated.

"Don't make me pick you up, Princess," Wyl threatened,
urging her down the drophole.

"He is damnably strong, your highness," Fynch echoed. "Please, I'll go first and you can follow. Breathe through your mouth—it will help."

Valentyna nodded, fighting the urge to scream. She glanced toward her father with a pained expression as Wyl helped her to clamber into the drophole. It was more than wide enough for the Princess's slim frame.

"You're next Father," she warned, her eyes peeping over the edge as she gulped air, not daring to breathe through her nose.

The King nodded his encouragement at her, knowing full well his bulky body would not be able to fit the width of the opening. Wyl knew it too and diverted her attention by telling her to concentrate on the small footholds in the stone. She called down to Fynch in the shadows and he whispered his reply as she began her descent.

The banging on the door increased and now Romen was bellowing at Wyl. They ignored it still, focused only on Valentyna's safe journey down. They could not see her once she was consumed by the darkness but they heard Fynch call up the all-clear.

"I have her. She's safe, sire."

"Father, be careful, it's slippery."

There was a pause.

"Father?" Her voice traveled eerily from the dark beneath them.

"No, my darling. I cannot."

Before she could raise a noise, Wyl interrupted and his tone was firm. "Valentyna, listen to me, now. The opening is too small for the King. But I will remain with him and I swear I'll die trying to fight him safely to freedom. You must, however, for all our sakes, follow our plan and flee. Listen to Fynch. He will guide and protect you. I am dropping a purse, Fynch—use it to hide yourself." The King disappeared and reappeared with a larger pouch, which he warned he was dropping.

Wyl continued: "Princess, you must hide your hair, disguise all features that might give away who you are."

"How will you find us?" her voice called harshly up from the depths.

"Somehow, I will. Knave will find us—be assured. The mercenaries won't remain here long. They are a raiding party—whether they succeed or not, they will not tarry. Now run!"

"Father—"

"Go, child. Remember who you are and that I couldn't love you any more than I do."

"General," she said, her voice trembling, "thank you for being honest and a friend to Briavel, despite your loyalties. Keep your promise and save him or die trying!"

Valor and Wyl thought they heard a stifled sob but it was Fynch's voice that whispered up now. "Good luck, Wyl."

"You're a brave lad, Fynch. I thank you—and I'm sorry about last night. I didn't mean a word of it. I just wanted you to be safe."

Fynch's spirits lifted as he heard the words. Then he turned and took Valentyna by the hand, looking for Knave, who suddenly emerged from the shadows, startling his companion.

"Don't be afraid of him," Fynch whispered. Then he spoke to Knave softly, telling the dog what had happened and explaining that their task now was to protect this woman.

The three of them began to run, heading through the orchards and on toward Crowyll, north of Werryl. Valentyna was glad of the dark so none would see her tears.

The King looked at Wyl. "Save yourself, boy. You can. It's your chance."

"Perhaps. But there is unfinished business here, sire. And I will not leave you here alone."

Valor felt the swell of admiration for the young General. "Whoever thought a Thirsk would fight on the side of Briavel, eh?"

Wyl had to smile at the irony of it but there was no way he would let this good man perish, knowing what he did about his own faithless and conniving King. He would not be able to hold his head high if he did nothing to help. Anyway, how would he ever face Valentyna?

He walked to the door. "Romen!"

"It's a trap" came the resigned reply.

"How many?"

"All ten, I think."

"They're under orders to kill you. Arkol apparently," Wyl warned.

"Hmm—I suspected Celimus might do something like this."

"And still you came?"

"A seer once told me I would lead a dangerous life," Romen replied and then barked a laugh. "I guess this is its end, then."

Wyl unbolted the door and dragged a surprised Romen in. "No. If we die, then we die honorably, fighting the enemy."

Romen was taken off guard. He had not expected the General to permit him entry. He had already accepted his own death. He bowed to Valor. "Your majesty, I would not have been a part of this had I known who the real target was."

"But you would accept payment to murder a man just as good, just as valuable to his kingdom," Valor snarled.

"Well, right now it looks as though we'll all die fighting for different reasons, sire. Forgive me if I don't enter a philosophical debate with you just now."

"When this is over, mercenary, if I still breathe, I'll kill you myself."

Romen let it be. He looked to Wyl. "How did you find out?"

Wyl shrugged. There was no way he would reveal Fynch.

His companion grinned his acceptance of Wyl's reticence. "All right. Our deal sticks. Just so long as you understand I never go back on my word," he said, taking the offered sword.

"So you keep reminding me. Now hush!" Wyl cautioned. "Here they come."

Clutching their weapons, they faced the door. It was only a matter of time before several axes and some beefy shoulders would smash through it.

Valentyna had run until the breath burned in her lungs. She stopped, sitting down heavily against a boulder, hardly noticing her clothes' ripe smell. Knave trotted back and licked her face. It was that tiny show of affection that broke her heart. The Princess buried her head in her own lap. Fynch, breathless too, tiptoed back and sat alongside her. They were both filthy but she no longer seemed to care, he noticed, about what clung to their clothes and boots.

"Why, Fynch? Why? They're going to die. I know it." She banged her fist against the ground in anger.

"We're safe here for a while, your highness. You can rest." He did not know what else to say, had no words of comfort, for he too believed Wyl and Valor would perish.

"Who are you?" she asked.

"A gong boy. I work the royal apartments at Stoneheart."

She gave a bitter laugh. "I'll bet you've never made Celimus climb down his drophole."

"No, but then I wouldn't offer to save his life, highness," the boy replied gravely.

Valentyna considered him more intently now. "Wyl was just as surprised to see you as we were," she said and let it hang.

Fynch nodded. "I'd overheard the conversation between the Prince and Koreldy, who accompanied Wyl. The plan had been to use Wyl's name to win the audience with your father."

"And then kill both of them," she finished, angrily.

"No, highness. I knew only of one planned assassination—of Wyl. I followed with Knave and managed to get word to him of the plot."

"And still he came here," she said, slightly in awe of Wyl now.

Fynch shrugged. "Not sure he had much choice, your highness. He was trapped, really. He had to win the audience to save his sister."

"Yes, but what you don't know, Fynch, is that he told us the truth. And in so doing doomed his sister."

"Oh," he replied. "That would have been a horrible decision to make. Wyl worships Ylena."

"She's lucky to have him," Valentyna said softly. "I think I am too."

"Yes, you are, highness," he answered, confused as to

Wyl's intentions but unable to be anything but direct and honest.

"There's a stream nearby here. It will be freezing but I'll chance it if you will," she offered.

"I'm so used to the smell, highness, but yes, let's clean ourselves. We'll have to rely on Knave to keep us warm."

The three lonely figures headed toward the stream Valentyna spoke of and in the cover of darkness, stripped their clothes and washed them and their bodies. Later, shivering, damp, and naked, Valentyna—who knew these lands better than any—guided them toward a tiny copse.

"It might still be standing," she said.

"What might be?" Fynch queried.

"One of my camps. I built it years ago. Come."

It was still there and she breathed a sigh of relief.

"It's stood the test of time, highness," Fynch said, his approval obvious.

"I was taught how to build it by a master," she said, finding a smile for her private thoughts.

"Who was that, highness?"

"My father," she replied sadly. "Follow me. It's cramped but it's dry and sheltered. We can rest safely here for a while."

Fynch felt numb from the cold and allowed Knave to push himself in between them. His large body gave comfort as much as warmth. Even Valentyna finally laid her aching head against the dog.

"He's enormous, isn't he?" Valentyna said.

Fynch smiled, enjoying the earthy smell of the hide. "He terrifies everyone at Stoneheart except a few who are true to Wyl."

"Tell me about Wyl," she said, unable to think of what else the two of them had in common. She needed idle chatter to stop her from feeling as if she might just fall apart.

Fynch shrugged and, bringing together the items from his vast storage of information, he began to impart some of that knowledge on General Wyl Thirsk from his earliest days to the present. In spite of her gloom Valentyna found herself fascinated by the story of Wyl and amazed by

Fynch's recollection of the General's life. She was especially interested to hear that Wyl's dislike for Celimus went
so far back.

"So he's never liked the new King?"

"No, Princess. He has always despised him."

"How can he serve a man like this?"

"He has not had a chance, to tell the truth. King Magnus
died the same day Wyl was dispatched on this mission."

"Well, that means Celimus has been plotting it for a
while; his intention always to rid Morgravia of its influential General. You say Wyl controls the Legion?"

"Completely. If he chose, he could overthrow Celimus in
a blink."

"And this business with the witch. You actually saw his
eyes change color?"

"One gray, one greenish. It was very alarming but it disappeared so quickly, I hardly dared believe what I saw."

"And Knave belonged to her?" Valentyna asked, deliberately double-checking the more curious facts of Fynch's tale.

"He was a pup apparently. She gave him to Wyl just moments before her death. I hope you won't consider me
loose-headed, your highness, but it is my belief that Knave
is somehow enchanted."

"How so?" she asked, her interest irresistibly piqued now
as she stroked the big dog's head, though completely disbelieving of Fynch's claim.

Fynch told her everything he could about the curiosities
of Knave.

"Well, well, you certainly have my attention now," she
said, nodding while Knave groaned with pleasure as she
scratched his ears. "How strange it all is," she admitted.

"Do you believe in magic, your highness?"

"I don't. I've never been exposed to anything magical,"
she admitted. "I believe only what I see."

"I'm the opposite, your highness. I do believe." The boy
shrugged. "I'm used to his oddities now. Knave really hates
other people unless they are somehow linked favorably to
Wyl. That's why he likes you."

She smiled at the serious little boy. "You are very loyal to him, Fynch. He's fortunate to have you in his life."

"I am compelled, your highness. Knave chose me."

She frowned in some bemusement at this, then grinned sadly. "Fynch, I've been thinking—I must return to the palace. I can't believe I ran away in the first place. I have to go back and see my father."

"No, your highness! I promised to take you away, to keep you safe," her small friend implored.

"I can't stay in hiding. It's cowardly, Fynch, surely you appreciate this?" Her voice had a pleading tone as she beseeched the grave-faced child to understand.

"I don't, your highness. It is *not* cowardly to protect yourself—the heir to the throne—against killers."

"Then I shall fight them—alongside my father!"

"And you'll die," he said quietly. "You'll be useless to Briavel."

"How dare you!" she raged, jumping to her feet. "Who are you to order me about?"

Fynch shook his head and she saw his despair. "Forgive me, your highness. I am a nobody. A gong boy who clears the sewers and not fit to so much as be in your presence. But I am charged to protect you and I would sooner die than let anyone harm you."

It was his sincerity that broke her anger and she was on her knees in a moment, hugging him and apologizing for her haughty behavior. "Fynch, I didn't mean it. You and Wyl have been true. Say you've forgiven me, I beg it."

She was so distraught that Fynch could tell she was drowning in a sea of emotions, from grief to guilt. Perhaps there was a way he could alleviate her despair. "Your highness, what would you say if I asked you to remain here a little longer? Knave will stay with you."

"And where will you go?" she asked.

"I'll go back to the palace and see what I can find out. It is not dangerous for me."

"I would thank you, Fynch, and ask you to leave immediately."

"You must give me your word, your highness, that you will not leave this place," he cautioned.

"Not until I hear back from you."

Fynch looked at Knave and realized the dog already understood what was required of him. He bowed to the Princess. "Knave will keep you safe, your highness."

Valentyna had no doubt of it as she watched the little boy run off into the night.

The fighting was ferocious in the confined space of the chamber. Man after man had burst through the door only to be slain by the superbly balanced and supremely skilled pair of Wyl and Romen, fighting back-to-back. Valor could only watch for the time being, for Wyl had cleverly blocked the entrance with his attacker so that the men coming from behind would have to wait for the outcome. So far he counted four corpses.

Romen called over his shoulder: "Six more." Then he grunted as he leapt over a fallen chair and spun on his heel to strike low and viciously with a two-handed slash. The fifth fell, one leg almost chopped through at the thigh. Romen kicked his sword away, knowing a major artery was severed. The fellow would be dead within a minute or so.

The King could not help but marvel at these two beautiful fighters. Both had contrasting styles. Wyl was dogged, a real thinker. To Valor it seemed that Wyl had interminable patience; he was content to parry and block, feint and twist. But now two of his opponents were dead, testimony to his skill.

Romen was far more flamboyant, preferring to be the aggressor and taking the fight to his enemy. Romen would never give ground, Valor observed. He continued to push his opponent with a barrage of scintillating cuts and thrusts where the man found himself with no option but to defend constantly. And Romen was fast: lightning speed in his strokes, which was probably the reason why his third attacker had just taken a mortal wound. Valor watched Romen kick the dying man's sword away. The groaning man already forgotten, Romen stepped over him to engage his next opponent, leaping through the door.

Except this time two came through. Valor knew his time had come. It had been too many years since he had lifted a sword in battle but he did not hesitate. With a roar he lifted his trademark sword with its intricate and beautiful carvings on its hilt. He raised it over his head and brought it down with a second roar, a battle cry this time. Sparks flew off the two swords as they met and Valor once again fought for his life. He was a match for his opponent—where the mercenary had brute strength, Valor had height—but the man who grimaced back at him was far younger.

Valor knew immediately he would have to dispatch him fast if he was to survive or, more likely if the fight continued, he reasoned as he went through a series of hard blocks and parries, that he would need one of his younger companions to finish it for him.

He did not mean to lose concentration but his thoughts helplessly fled to Valentyna. She was still so young and yet with the right people around her there would be no better sovereign for Briavel. She possessed his courage and genuinely loved her people and this land of theirs with a fierce passion. But she was headstrong, like her mother. That would need to be controlled or at least channeled in the right way. He felt sure Valentyna would be willing to lead the charge onto a battlefield if she could—if it meant one more Briavellian might be protected. But war must be avoided. He wished now—as he recalled her look of despair as she climbed into that drophole earlier—that he had counseled her about Celimus. He should have said that no matter what, the marriage should still be considered if peace was to be achieved. And yet Wyl's advice was so alarming. He hoped he had gathered the right people around him these past few years who would advise her well, should he fail today. She would need strong counsel—shrewd counsel in the decisions ahead.

Valor felt a dazzling blaze of pain at the top of his sword arm. He yelled and winced but did not have time to look at the damage. He knew that cut would not have made it through his defense had he not lost concentration. Angry with himself and spurred on by the throbbing pain, he now used his height to beat the man back. Already, though, he knew he was in real danger. Apart from fatigue, so shockingly swift in its claim over his body, his muscles in that all-important arm felt weak and a numbing tingle was edging its way toward the fingers that gripped that famous hilt. He intensified his effort. He would not be able to fight for much longer; the man must fall soon.

Wyl realized as he killed another mercenary that the more cunning amongst them had held back. With each new opponent greater skills seemed to present themselves and this had been a clever ploy. Using the less skilled "hackers," they had worn himself and Romen down, making them perhaps easier prey for the more talented fighters coming through. He hated that one had managed to engage the King and as he grimaced at this thought, it seemed Romen read his mind.

"Valor has taken a serious cut. He'll tire quickly" was all he had time to say.

"Two left," Wyl said in reply, chancing a look towards the King.

There was no doubt the King was exhausting his last reserves of stamina. Blood flowed freely and fast from a particularly nasty slash at the top of his arm. Wyl understood immediately that muscle had been severed, which would mean Valor would be rapidly losing all strength in that fighting arm. He wondered if the old campaigner had trained himself to use either arm. He thought not. Many had scoffed at the suggestion but the new breed of Morgravian soldiers—such as Gueryn—had insisted upon the level of skill being upped in the non-natural hand. Wyl knew no different. Although his right arm was strongest, he was certainly adept with his left.

He glanced toward Romen. "Can you hold them off?"

Romen grunted his reply and slashed his man across the throat. "Help Valor!" he roared, kicking his opponent over and out of the way so he could see what was rushing toward them.

Just as Wyl turned to deal with the man intent on killing a King he heard the monarch cry out.

Valor staggered backward, another, deeper sword wound

evident at the top of his shoulder, slicing diagonally through major vessels, blood flowing in a torrent from it.

"Protect our Queen, Wyl," was all he had time to say before he hit the floor.

Arkol, who had struck the blow, laughed and spat at the prone body of the King of Briavel. Romen had dispatched his own opponent with a high slash that nearly decapitated the man. He turned around to see the wrath on Wyl's face and the familiar figure bleeding on the fine carpet.

"Wait, Wyl! He's mine," he said. "There's one more outside, probably hiding."

As Wyl dropped back, Romen even found time to thank him and with a grim smile on his face went about pitting his skills against his would-be killer. Wyl had already been amazed at Romen's swordplay. His own abilities aside, if he thought he had seen the best fighter in Celimus then he was wrong. Romen was indeed superior and he felt sure it would not be long before Arkol's smile was wiped once and for all from his ugly mouth.

Wyl and his final opponent ended up fighting in the hall. The man soon discovered that despite his own high skills he was no match for the General, but he knew how to defend and so it was simply a case of wearing his man down. Wyl cleared his anger as he had been taught. He found his focus, withdrew into himself, and began a flurry of attacking strikes, one finally finding its mark to sever an artery. He left the man bleeding to a swift death and returned to the King's chamber to see Romen all but toying with a savagely wounded Arkol, struck in many damaging places, but none fatal yet.

Wyl dropped on one knee by the King and felt for a pulse, knowing it was useless. It was a momentary joy to find a faint heartbeat but good sense told him it would disappear within moments. Valentyna was about to become Queen of Briavel. He cast a silent prayer for her safety as he heard Arkol gurgle to his death, Romen's sword thrust through his throat.

"Help me get Valor on the settle," Wyl said. "No King should be left like this."

Romen grinned without his usual humor. He was not even out of breath, although his face and clothes were spattered with other men's blood. "Do you always do the right thing, Thirsk?"

"I try," Wyl said, heaving at the old man's body.

They carried the dying man and laid him on a couch. Wyl took his hand. "Sire?"

Valor opened his eyes, their sight already blurring as more of his life force leaked out onto the couch. His breath rattled through his throat as he struggled to speak. It was little more than a mumble. "You must protect her, son, despite your loyalties."

Wyl nodded. "I will give my life for her, sire. I promise."

"Even better than your father," the King slurred and then in one last rally of strength he whispered, "Overthrow Celimus. Take the crown!"

Valor, King of Briavel, died holding the hand of the General of Morgravia, leaving between them a thought of such treachery that Wyl caught his breath. Valor was the second King now to urge Wyl to commit a traitorous act. But Wyl could not bring himself to think on that now. He rubbed away the dampness that blurred his vision, deeply upset that he had failed to save this man's life, and his thoughts rushed toward Valentyna. Once again, as if reading his mind, Romen echoed his thoughts.

"Where's the daughter, by the way?"

Wyl realized Romen had not seen Valentyna enter her father's chamber, having used the concealed internal entrance. Romen was perhaps not even aware that she had been in their company.

He told the truth. "I have no idea."

"And what did Valor say to your suggestion?" Romen asked as he settled one of the old man's legs that had slipped from the couch.

Wyl folded the King's arms across his chest and then leaned down to kiss the man on both cheeks. Romen held his tongue. He watched Wyl stand up and waited for an answer to his question.

"He agreed with my reasoning that such a union would bring peace to both realms." He did not lie.

"Congratulations. Your part of the bargain is kept, then," Romen said, reaching for his sword. "Now I must keep my side of it." He flicked Wyl's sword from the floor into the air and Wyl deftly caught it. "Unfinished business, my friend."

"We don't have to do this, Romen," Wyl said, desperately hoping he could persuade the man not to duel.

"We do, Thirsk. We have a deal. I have a purse to collect— and a score to settle."

"And if I best you?"

"Then you must settle it for me. You hate him enough to do it."

"I promise," Wyl said, realizing his hopes of them both surviving were very much in vain. One of them would die in this room.

"And so what can I promise in return?" Romen asked, tapping his sword against Wyl's.

"Aside from your original promise to take care of Ylena?"

Romen nodded. "I will marry her, if I must, to give her security. It would hardly be a chore. She is very lovely."

Wyl considered and then dropped his sword to speak solemnly. "I want your word that you will offer your services—your life—to Valentyna."

Romen was amused at this. "To the new Queen? Why? You kiss your enemy King while you hate your own. Passing strange, Wyl, for someone who claims to be a loyal Morgravian."

"Swear it, Koreldy!"

"Or else?" he said, the smile back.

"I won't fight you. You'll have to just run me through in cold blood and I know you are too honorable. Nobility runs in your veins, Romen. It is obvious."

"You would change your loyalties? A Thirsk wanting to protect the Briavellian monarch? Oh, this is rich."

"Swear it, Romen."

"Yes, yes, I swear," he agreed as if weary of a pointless conversation.

In a flash, Romen found a sword leveled at his throat, reminding him not to underestimate the prowess of the short but powerful man who stood before him. "Mean it!" Wyl yelled.

Romen's silver-gray eyes darkened. He slashed his blade across his palm and, relieved, Wyl immediately followed suit.

"I swear it, Wyl Thirsk. I will protect the Queen of Briavel with my life," the mercenary said, joining his bloodied palm with Wyl's. "Now fight for your life."

Wyl kissed his blade. And Romen smiled. A new dance had begun.

14

WYL AND ROMEN FOUGHT IN FRIGID SILENCE. Silence as the castle at Werryl grasped the shock of attack—fifteen of the palace staff were dead, another dozen were injured and the rest lay in their beds, drugged. Silence as the Briavellian Guard raced back to their King upon realizing that the threat that most of them had been dispatched to deal with was a hoax. Briavel was not under attack and their clash with a strange company of mercenaries was little more than a skirmish, the foreigners fleeing having barely crossed swords or lost a single man.

And silence as both men, professional fighters, lost themselves in a battle for their lives. The only sound, in fact, was the harsh ring of their blades. Faces set with grim determination, they dueled in synchrony. Romen, Wyl realized, was indeed a superior swordsman to Celimus. He did not let his emotions get in his way and, like Wyl, he fought with cunning, although with little patience. Lots of bravado and flamboyance, yet each move was lightning-fast and deadly.

Everything Wyl threw at him, every trick he had learned from Gueryn, every stroke he had taught himself, Romen countered. He was fast, agile, strong, but most of all, Romen was a strategist. He could think several strokes ahead, was planning moves in advance of where he was fighting now. If Wyl could have stopped their duel, he would like to tell his opponent how much he admired his skill, but there would be no halting now, no more sardonic banter, no more quarter given.

Romen clearly intended to kill, Wyl knew, unless he could strike the death blow first.

They fought on, both their minds blanked of thought other than the focus on their opponent's weapon and movement. The moon had risen high and the Briavellian Guard had almost returned to the city gates. Aides would have come looking for their King if any were alive or well enough to do so. The pair of swordsmen had no witnesses to their life-and-death struggle.

Both were showing their fatigue; hair damp with their efforts and faces shining with sweat, they knew it would be only moments now before one made the fatal error. Tiredness prompted mistakes and, although they redoubled their concentration, their bodies were beaten and could not respond as well as they hoped. Evenly matched, neither was getting ahead. Each recognized the signs in themselves of slowing down and knowing this alone would probably cost them their lives. It was the first time in their lives either of these men had felt true fear that the other man might prevail. It showed on their grim expressions. Gone was the almost permanent amusement Romen Koreldy carried on his face and Wyl had long ago withdrawn completely into himself.

It was Wyl who ultimately made the bad decision. He knew it the second he lunged hard after feinting twice. He saw the slight opening and decided if he was fast enough, he would have Romen impaled on his blade. He made his attempt but although his mind still worked at a high speed, his body was no longer working in tandem.

Romen anticipated what was happening. It was as though he were watching Wyl come at him at a speed ten times slower than normal. His mind was playing tricks but he had heard men say that when the death blow comes, the world around you slows down. It was happening to him now. This was the stab that would kill him. Somehow—Shar alone knew how—he managed to drag himself just enough off balance to dodge the blade so that it only skimmed his side, ripping through surface flesh. And then, as Wyl followed through, Romen struck.

Romen's blade ran General Wyl Thirsk of the Morgravian Legion through, its fierce tip emerging on the other side of its victim's body. Wyl's eyes widened in shock and pain but mostly from the realization that he had lost his fight.

It was up to Romen now to save the two women Wyl loved. "Keep your promise," he gurgled as he dropped his sword and Romen pulled his own back and out of the dying man.

Wyl slid to the floor, closed his eyes and waited for his heart to stop beating and the pain in his belly to leave him. Death felt welcome.

But a new sensation suddenly gripped his body, and without knowing it he arched his back high from the floor in a spasm of that acute pain. At first he thought this was how death must feel as it gathered him into itself but the intensity of the surge forced him to open his eyes—his two ill-matched and alarmingly different eyes.

Romen too was staring at him in shock, but bent double in his own agony. It was as if they were sharing the same convulsive pain. Wyl felt himself lifting now; all that was him was being pulled, dragged from his shell in a tearing, ripping sense of departure. If this was death, why was Romen wearing a mask of such terror and agony?

The suffering mounted toward a crescendo and just as Wyl knew his life was about to pass over to Shar's keeping, he glimpsed what he grasped was the soul of Romen Koreldy as it too crossed over in terror and disbelief.

But Wyl was not passing to Shar. Only Romen's soul was being given up. And Wyl himself—all that made him in mind and spirit—was actually crossing into the body of Romen Koreldy. He thought he mouthed something. Could not be sure if he had, yet he wanted to say something to Romen.

Was this death or life?

The sensation of pain and confusion continued for what felt like an eternity until Wyl suddenly became aware that he was still standing, arms forward with a white-knuckled-grip around the sword hilt. He was the one who staggered backward to clutch at the table, letting go of the weapon, dragging in his breath. No longer drowning in pain, he looked down upon the body on the floor.

He was unaware that he stared through ill-matched eyes but he did know that he looked down upon the corpse of Wyl Thirsk.

Wyl held out his shaking hands. They were the long, neat fingers of Romen, not his own short fingers with the soft ginger hair just below the knuckles. And then he looked at his side where he bled. This was the near miss and testimony to how close Wyl's blade had come.

No! *His* blade had come, damn it!

It was true, then. Beneath him, his own body was already cooling and with it, he believed, it had taken the soul of Romen.

Dumbfounded and disoriented, he stumbled around the room taking in the scene of death. He heard voices, men's voices; guards were running through the corridors. In the bedlam that was his mind he realized they would hit the stairs in moments and he would be trapped. Forcing himself out of the chaos of his thoughts and not daring to think anything through further, Wyl grabbed the arms of his previous body and dragged it toward the privy. It was his only chance.

He threw his sword down the hole and then heaved the corpse over the lip. He heard it land at the bottom with a sickening crunch. The voices were at the top of the stairs now—he was just moments from discovery. No time to climb down with care. Wyl clambered into the drophole and, holding his breath instinctively against the assault of its smell, he let go. He too hit the bottom of the drophole hard, having jumped from such a height. But his landing was softened by the body. His true body.

With no thought beyond the moment and working purely on instinct, he settled Wyl Thirsk's corpse on his shoulder and set off at a labored trot. Moving awkwardly in Romen's body, he wondered what in Shar's Name had happened to him.

15

WYL TOOK COVER IN A SMALL GROVE OF TREES HE REMEMbered passing on the journey into Briavel. It was the first time in hours he had taken a rest.

One stroke of luck a little earlier was coming across the mercenaries' horses and a mule that had seemingly meandered over to join them. It occurred to Wyl that this had to be Fynch's animal. He had untethered two of the horses and slung his corpse over the back of one. He would take the other horse for himself and not wishing to abandon the animal that had effectively saved his life, he attached the mule to the horse carrying the body and the small party set off. Food was in the saddlebags and life-giving water too. It was urgent that he get the body to Pearlis. If he could just cross onto Morgravian soil, he would feel safer. When he had spotted the grove, he had cried out with relief. His nerves were in shreds, his mind felt stewed from the shock of what had occurred, and during the journey thus far he had spent the hours keeping up a string of nonsense-talk to the animals to deliberately stop himself from thinking on the shocking events. He had resisted glancing toward the body. His body.

Wyl slid the corpse off the horse and unsaddled the animals. Exhausted but still not prepared to think on his troubles, he spent time rubbing the beasts down. He finally hobbled his companions with a generous length of rope and lay down, hoping to drift off before he was forced to face the bleak truth. The moon was fat and high in a cloudless sky, denying him the total dark he craved, and despite his exhaustion sleep refused to rescue him. And so he finally confronted his fear—the terror that was surely Myrren's gift. Her true gift, he now realized with a deep sob.

He stared at his hands, eerie in the moonlight, and accepted that these were indeed the large, well-kept hands of Romen Koreldy, still wearing the small, elegant signet ring. Wyl tentatively reached those long fingers to the face he now wore. His touch told him the once-familiar roundish features were now angular. He possessed a neat, clipped beard and moustache.

He could not help but enjoy the lustrous feel of his hair when he loosened the thong that bound it and it fell to his shoulders. He recalled admiring it when he was an orange-haired General with his own, coarse thatch. Wyl knew his eyes were now a clear silver-gray. He even allowed himself the rueful grimace that his features were no longer ordinary and forgettable but were now remarkably striking. A face to turn heads.

Romen's smile had been bright and quick. He tested it now, daring to touch the smooth, even teeth he recalled grinning back at him from the mercenary's generous mouth. And his legs! Now Wyl did make a sound. It was a nervous laugh but nonetheless genuine as he stared at the new length of his legs, which now surely stood him as tall as Valentyna—taller than Alyd—perhaps even taller than Gueryn.

He thought of these people now and the wave of grief he had kept at bay crashed against his mind. Both the men he loved were dead, or as good as, while both the women he loved were living through enormous fear and loss. Ylena, he imagined, was probably still unable to come to terms with what she had witnessed in the courtyard—perhaps she never would. Valentyna, his love, was no doubt wondering whether her father still lived as life's strange turns threw her onto an unknown path. Loving her so immediately and with such intensity frightened Wyl but he knew his heart belonged only to her now.

He remembered how he had made Romen promise to protect her, swear that he would lay down his life for her. Romen had given that oath with blood. It would now be up to Wyl to keep it.

He considered the man he had known so briefly and wondered if there was anything left of him inside. He probed gingerly and was rewarded with a vague touch on memories and ideas, thoughts and inclinations. It was not easy to reach and his instincts were to pull away and yet he glimpsed that the private nuances which made the man were still there, albeit dimly. It was similar to how a woman, walking past, leaves that faint, tantalizing waft of her scent after she has gone.

And yet the very essence of Romen was long gone. His soul had passed to Shar. Wyl remembered it crossing to die in his shell as his own life force entered Romen's body. Wyl decided to seal away what was Romen for now. He was not ready to delve into his life. In this shocking time of confusion he needed to sort out his own life first. He felt the first feathery touch of sleep and yawned, welcoming its escape.

It was a cold, hard bed tonight but he was alive. And he was angry. Angry and confused. He recalled the dream he'd had about dying, and yet not being dead—it seemed now to be a premonition rather than a nightmare.

Wyl pushed his confused thoughts aside. He had plenty to do in this new body, not the least of which was finding Valentyna and Fynch, but first there was unfinished business back in Morgravia. As his eyes closed he whispered a final farewell to Romen, an assassin Wyl could not help but like—and the man he had now become.

As he gave in to sleep, it was suddenly as clear to him as

the sharpness of the moonlight that there was only one course of action he could pursue. He would take his own body back and present it triumphantly to Celimus, going through all the motions required of him. He would trick the King into believing the Crown was rid of Wyl Thirsk. And then as Romen he would collect his purse, make provision for Ylena—*please, Shar, let her live this long*—and then depart Morgravia to formulate a plan to make Celimus pay for his sins.

Its King slain. Its heir missing. Werryl was silent and stilled with shock.

Commander Liryk sat with Krell, the dead King's Chancellor. Krell was a man of few words but when he spoke he made sense and people paid attention. He had been in Valor's service for more than two decades and was the former sovereign's most trusted counsel and confidant. He tried to comfort the old soldier, who sat now in his study with his head in his hands.

"I've lost her," Liryk whispered repeatedly.

Krell had allowed the man his sorrow. They were all grieving, all shocked at the previous night's events. It was Krell who had had the presence of mind to contain the damage within the palace walls as best he could. As soon as Liryk and the main Briavellian Guard had returned from the hoax, Krell had insisted Liryk dismiss all but his most trusted men.

"I would appreciate your thoughts," Krell said evenly into the silence.

The soldier looked up from his hands, face puffy from helpless tears shed intermittently these past hours. Dawn was threatening and decisions needed to be made.

"What do we have thus far?" he replied.

"The diversion of the Guard was deliberate, we know that now. That and the drugging of the palace staff suggests this was a well-planned raid."

"Which succeeded," the old soldier said bitterly.

Krell nodded. "Or did it?"

"What do you mean?"

"Others know the truth, I suspect. There were two other men here this night past, the most important of our visitors, and their bodies are not among those dead."

"So?"

"Who do you think killed all the mercenaries? Hardly our King, I'd suggest."

Liryk nodded. "Valor was a fine warrior in his time, but no, he could not have taken on ten men singlehandedly."

"Valor, aided by Thirsk and possibly Koreldy, despatched the foreigners."

"Why would Thirsk travel with a mercenary?"

"That is a mystery. I can't imagine that he would agree to come onto Briavellian soil with anyone but his own men."

"A trap by the Morgravian King?"

"Possibly. I'm thinking that if Thirsk was forced to travel with mercenaries on his mission, it would account for the thanks I read in his eyes when I separated him from what to all intents and purposes looked like his captor."

"But you think they fought alongside Valor."

The Chancellor nodded. "I do. And I suspect they may well have helped Valentyna escape."

This shocked Liryk. "Was she inside with Thirsk and the King?"

Krell smiled. It was the first reason to do so in many hours. "That headstrong young woman comes and goes as she pleases. She knows the secret passageways better than any. I know her father expected her to attend the supper so I suspect it's highly likely she was present."

"But surely Koreldy could have smashed through the door with the other mercenaries?"

"Yes, he could have. But there are three swords missing from the case." Krell tapped his lip. "No, I'm guessing the King or Valentyna furnished the men with swords—Thirsk worked with Koreldy and they both fought with the King's agreement."

"Set aside their differences, you mean?"

The Chancellor shrugged again. "I'm guessing. Perhaps the new Morgravian King is more cunning than we give credit."

"A double cross?"

"On Thirsk, for sure. I don't think for a minute that Thirsk came here to take the life of Valor."

"What was he here for then?"

The old man gave a slight shrug. "Perhaps he came for Valentyna," he suggested carefully.

Liryk was startled. "Valentyna?"

"Rumor has it the new young monarch is ambitious. Perhaps he sent Thirsk here with a proposal." He sat back, satisfied he had released the thought that had been gathering momentum in his mind for a few hours now.

Liryk looked stunned. "How can you be certain of all this?" he asked, impressed by the Chancellor's confidence. And watched that confidence evaporate as his companion gave a wry smile.

"I can't. It's possible is all I'm saying."

Liryk dismissed Krell's uncertainty and stood. "Plausible. And so?"

Krell shook his head. "Not much else. Thirsk and Koreldy kill the mercenaries, but let's say the King is too injured, or perhaps he died before they could save him. The pair have no choice but to escape with Valentyna."

Liryk rubbed his face distractedly as he paced the room. "But how . . . where?"

"A good question among too many that we still have to answer." Krell sighed. "There is only one certainty here: Valentyna must be found—that is our priority. And when we find her we will convince her of the sense of a union with King Celimus."

"What?!" Liryk swung around on Krell. They were of an age and had both served Valor faithfully over many years. Neither felt the other had rank. "Allow Celimus to get away with this?" The soldier's voice was hard, barely more than a whisper.

"There is more to this than we know," Krell appealed. "What we can safely assume, however, is that should Briavel start a war with Morgravia right now we are lost. Our Queen is young and incapable of waging a long conflict with our neighbor. She is in no position to withstand Celimus and, frankly, neither is Briavel. The marriage will save our people. We walk a tightrope of diplomacy now."

The old soldier nodded thoughtfully as the implication of Krell's words sank in. "You play a frightening game, Chancellor."

Krell held the old soldier's gaze steadily. "We must find Valentyna before he does."

They did not have long to wait, for at that moment a small boy was escorted through the study doors.

With the corpse slung again over the second horse and a quick glance toward the sweet-natured mule, Wyl ignored his hunger and set off towards Pearlis. They had met several curious onlookers along the way over the past two days and now as they drew into its outlying villages he gave none sufficient eye contact to invite questions about the shrouded body. It was nearing evening when he finally drew near to the magnificent stone arch that welcomed visitors to Stoneheart.

The guards eyed him suspiciously and he could hardly blame them, considering his odd company: a mule and what was obviously a corpse. Wyl felt a pang of sorrow upon recognizing a couple of his own men as they held up their hands to stop his progress.

"Ho, there. You, man, what is this?"

Wyl had to remind himself of who he was. "A dead body. I think you'll recognize him if you take a look." He pulled back some of the shroud from the head.

The men stepped closer and Wyl read the dismay on their faces as they noted the flame-colored hair first.

"It can't be," one spluttered. "No!"

"I'm afraid so," Wyl said in Romen's wry manner. But he was glad of their pain. It reassured him that his men knew nothing and were not in on Celimus's elaborate intrigue.

Suddenly their swords were drawn and pointed at this throat.

"Who are you?" one of the guards demanded. Wyl saw dampness in the man's eyes.

This is it, he told himself. *Remember who you are.* In that

moment of hesitation, he realized he had held himself too
tightly within this stranger's body. He knew he must loosen
himself and embrace it; must own it if he was ever going to
avenge his own murder. Wyl opened himself up to what was
left of Romen and felt all that was Wyl Thirsk flow into the
lithe and graceful stature that Romen had once possessed.
Now the voice, the easy style, and even his mannerisms
came effortlessly to Wyl.

"I am Romen Koreldy of Grenadyn. You can see which
son of Morgravia I am returning home. I think you'll find
King Celimus is expecting me," he said confidently.

An urgent runner was sent with a message. More soldiers
had gathered, most in silent shock, just to lay their hands on
the beloved General. Wyl was touched by their grief.

"What happened?" one asked, not at all shamed by his
wet cheeks.

Wyl was ready for this question and intended to make it
difficult for Celimus to squirm out of endorsing the explanation. "The palace at Briavel was attacked by mercenaries
posing as soldiers from the Morgravian Legion."

New shock claimed each face around him.

"But what was he doing in Briavel?" more than one cried.

Wyl shrugged. "I gather he was on business there for your
King and became helplessly embroiled in the problem."

The soldiers muttered among themselves.

"He gave no word—he just left. It's had the whole company baffled," someone said.

Wyl nodded. "Probably on a secret mission then, for
Morgravia."

"How do you know they were mercenaries?" one wily
campaigner asked him.

"There was no mistaking them," he said and then embel-
lished with: "I was there on private business myself but
when the attack occurred I found myself fighting on this
man's side. What is his name again?"

They answered as one grief-stricken chorus.

And then for good measure and a chance to escape further scrutiny he grimaced, adding, "I was wounded and am
in need of some aid."

Hands rushed to help.

"My mule—well, she is not truly mine—is exhausted. The beast has run all day to keep up with the horses."

"We'll take care of her, sir, don't you worry now," a kindly voice offered.

A messenger appeared. "Sir, the King will see you immediately."

"Could someone put his body on my shoulder, please?" Wyl asked. He had, in truth, not realized his own wound had re-opened until he had drawn attention to it.

"We'll bring him," a guard said, a tremor in his voice.

"No. I've carried him since Briavel. I'll deliver him to his King as I promised him just before he died," Wyl lied, hating himself for it.

A look of reverence crossed their faces now. The man who seemed most senior nodded. "Do it," he said and once again hands clamored to assist.

Wyl settled the body and followed the messenger, as did several of the guards.

"Was Captain Donal with him, may I ask, sir?" one said. "A fair-haired fellow, always smiling?"

"That's him," the man said eagerly.

"Dead," Wyl replied. "I'm sorry, I just could not bring the both of them back," he added, truly despising himself.

More pain and sorrow, but he needed to craft this tale perfectly. He must trap Celimus into supporting the story and he also did not want the Legion rising up yet or doing anything rash.

Wyl could not speak any further as he labored up the narrow stone staircase that led him to that favorite open walkway where the familiar scent of winterblossom drifted up from the garden below. It reminded him once again of his first meeting with King Magnus. He fought the memory away and waited while the same courtier who had sneered at him not so long ago did the same again, this time eyeing his load with disgust.

"Follow me," the man said coolly.

And Wyl did, taking a deep breath and bracing himself for Celimus. He wondered in one isolated moment of fear whether the King would see through his facade, see that this was not the hired killer but his hated enemy in a clever glamor. The notion passed as quickly as it arrived. He was Romen Koreldy and he would wield his disguise to brilliant effect. The nonchalant style of Romen was part of him now as he entered the chamber. Passing through the heavy-curtained arch he emerged fully into the familiar room and his silvery gray eyes met the hard, disbelieving stare of King Celimus.

"Leave us," the King ordered his aide. "I could not believe the messenger when he told me you were here," he said to Wyl.

No, I bet you couldn't, Wyl thought, watching the aide bow and leave, his face pinched at being dismissed so plainly. Wyl could not enjoy it, returning his gaze to Celimus almost immediately. When he heard the door shut behind him he eased the corpse from his shoulders and dropped it to the floor.

"I bring you the body of Wyl Thirsk, sire, as ordered."

He waited.

Celimus did not flinch, did not look down but held the stare. Wyl imagined a dozen or so scenarios were flashing through the King's mind now as he tried to work out how his carefully laid plan had gone so terribly wrong, how it came to be that Romen stood before him and not Arkol.

"The other men you took." It was a statement but the question was clearly there.

"Dead, sire, all of them," Wyl reported.

At this the King's eyebrow raised slightly. He had not expected such news.

"Including their treacherous leader, Arkol," Wyl reinforced, hoping the King would bite.

He did. "Ah, yes, what of him?" Celimus inquired innocently but still the penetrating gaze held Wyl firmly.

"Died screaming, your majesty, as I ran him through. It was either that or be killed myself. It was their plan, you see—or so I think I've worked out—that they would deliver Thirsk's body and share the purse themselves. I cannot think of any other reason for their betrayal."

He could see the King relax just slightly after Wyl had

deliberately given Celimus the room he needed to maneuver himself away from all links to Arkol's band.

"Really?" Celimus said. "Treacherous indeed, Romen. I'm glad you were able to save yourself."

"But not the King of Briavel, sire. Arkol murdered him."

There was only a moment's hesitation. "I had hoped as much." Celimus could not keep the excitement from his voice.

Wyl ignored the admission, responding flatly. "I saw him die."

Celimus became suddenly conciliatory and Wyl could sense the way the King's agile mind moved around his problem. In the end Celimus decided to use a half truth. "I mean it sincerely, Romen, when I admit my discomfort at not sharing that intention with you. I sensed you would not be a party to it if I did."

"And you would be right, your majesty. I do not kill sovereigns for any amount of money. Will you be attending the state funeral?"

"I doubt they'll hold a public ceremony, thank Shar! The Briavellian commander, if he is wise, will not want to see the people excited to war just now, would he?" Celimus said, clearly delighted. "After all, the rabble would immediately point the finger at Morgravia and start baying for blood. But the Guard is in no position to fight. Not with the Queen so young, so vulnerable. Poor child. How lonely she must be. Ripe for the plucking."

Wyl hated his King with such fury, it took all of his control, every ounce of determination he could muster, not to strike the man standing before him—kill him barehanded, in fact, despite the guards who could be summoned with a single call.

"But you do not hold it against me, surely?" Celimus queried, sensing the sudden tension.

It was an odd question. Wyl narrowed Romen's eyes and forced the body he inhabited to relax. "It is your decision, sire. I do not interfere in politics or affairs of state. Arkol succeeded with your task and I'm presuming you had good reason for giving the instruction. I did not kill Arkol for that action," Wyl lied. "I dispatched him for turning on me. I imagine he may have even killed more of his own men to keep a bigger share of your money."

"But I was paying them gold to do our bidding," Celimus said, all innocence and offended pride. "They have betrayed us both."

Wyl appreciated how cleverly Celimus used the word "us," artfully depicting them as partners.

"Yes, sire, but men like these can rarely be trusted. I told you that when you hired them," Wyl said, amazed at where that piece of information had bubbled up from.

"That you did. Hopefully I can trust you."

"I am a man of my word. I promised you the corpse of Wyl Thirsk."

"And you have delivered!" Celimus said magnanimously, his pleasure barely concealed. "I am indebted to you, Romen Koreldy," he added, bending down now to roll over Wyl's body and reassure himself how very dead it was. He lifted the head by its orange hair and then banged it down carelessly.

Wyl blinked back the fury. "What now, sire?"

"For him? A state funeral, I suppose. Morgravia will honor her proud General and its Legion will grieve deeply. I will declare a day of public mourning in his honor. We will exalt one of our favorite sons and bury him with pride and pomp alongside his father. The people will weep and their King will shed his own special tears," Celimus said before sneering, "of joy."

Wyl could only nod.

"Come, Romen, sit and join me in a cup and help me celebrate what is surely one of the happiest days of my life."

Wyl had no choice but to accept the goblet of sweet wine that the King deigned to pour from a chalice with his own hand.

"Tell me everything," Celimus said, his dark eyes gleaming with anticipation.

And Wyl did, carefully reconstructing the story and sticking as much to the truth as he could, leaving out Fynch's involvement.

"So Thirsk was supping alone with Valor?"

"No. I learned afterward that the daughter joined them—arrived through some sort of concealed entrance or other."

"Ah, I assume, though, you discovered the outcome of Thirsk's conversation with the King?"

Wyl smiled inwardly. Celimus presumed Valentyna was a simpering Princess without a notion or opinion of her own. If only he knew.

"I did, sire," he admitted, leaning back in his chair as Romen would. "He assured me he had won the King's agreement. Then he tried to bargain with me for his life."

Celimus threw back his head and showed his perfect teeth in a full-throated laugh. "But you killed him all the same. I like you, Koreldy. You are my man."

"Didn't think twice about it," Wyl answered, and joined the King in his mirth, wondering what it would feel like to slash the betrayer's throat.

"Tell me how I can repay you for this stupendously good deed."

Wyl's expression turned into one of Romen's favorites, a cynical raising of an eyebrow. "Apart from the promised purse, you mean, sire?" he asked dryly.

"Of course. I am feeling generous and you are responsible for this lighthearted mood. On top of the gold, ask a boon of me and let me grant it," Celimus offered, sweeping his hand expansively as though nothing could be too large a favor.

"There is something, majesty," Wyl said.

"Name it!" the King said, walking around his desk to retrieve two leather sacks, one larger than the other. He returned and banged them down on the table. They had the unmistakably heavy sound of gold. "They're both for you. I am giving you all the money, including what was intended for Arkol and his men."

"That wasn't the boon, sire," Wyl said carefully.

"I realize. Tell me," Celimus commanded.

"The sister," he replied.

The King looked momentarily confused and then understanding dawned. "Of Thirsk!"

Wyl nodded. "I want her."

"Shar's Balls. What will you do with her, man?"

He said nothing but allowed one of Romen's sardonic smiles to drift across his face.

Celimus began to laugh and then to clap slowly, his delight evident. "This is priceless. Oh, it is too much fun to know Thirsk's executioner will now bed his much-beloved sister. It's an even more perfect sentence than I could have imposed myself," the King admitted. "Take her, Romen, with my blessings. And when you've finished with her, you're welcome to kill her. You'll rid me of a problem—I'll inform the dungeoner immediately."

"Good," Wyl said, only barely holding on to his emotions now. He gripped the goblet and deliberately forced himself to raise it. "To secrets, sire."

"I'll drink to that. You'll be my best-kept one." And he swallowed the contents of his own goblet in one draught. "I see you are hurt," he said.

Wyl shook his head to show it was nothing serious but took his chance to escape. "A legacy from Thirsk, sire, but I will take my leave if you'll grant it and have it seen to."

"Of course. But tell me before you go of the Princess."

This was a critical part of his plan now. In order to protect Valentyna, Wyl knew he must make her irresistible to Celimus. Much as it galled him, he must encourage the King's amorous attentions and thus keep him from waging any strikes on Briavel.

He deliberately rearranged Romen's permanently amused expression into one of seriousness. "She is breathtakingly beautiful, your majesty. A more exquisite woman I have never laid eyes upon nor will I." It was all truth.

Celimus's attention was riveted on him now. "You mean this?"

"I do, sire."

"Describe her for me," the King commanded, perplexed, as he remembered only the hysterical, plump child.

Wyl brought Valentyna fully into his mind and felt the thrill once again of looking upon her.

"She is tall, sire, like yourself. Her raven hair is glossy and falls long and wavy. She has intelligent eyes—blue as a summer sky—and her wit is bright and quick."

Celimus was shaking his head with disbelief.

Wyl continued. "She is lean, your majesty, but shapely," he lied, remembering her almost boyishly narrow hips, "Her breasts are high. Her skin flawless, creamy in complexion."

"Stop!" Celimus said. "This is surely not the same person?"

"Sire?"

"Oh, never mind," he said impatiently. Celimus's brow creased in thought.

Wyl decided to press his case.

"Sire, far be it from me to presume anything even resembling a political stance but, if uniting these realms is your intention, not only is marriage to this woman a most feasible option but she could not fail to please your eye, your majesty. More than your eye, in fact," Wyl added conspiratorially.

Celimus caught the dry comment and exploded into laughter. "My bed would be ever warm, you mean?" he encouraged.

Wyl shrugged slightly; it was a nonchalant gesture yet clearly one of agreement.

The King banged his hand on the table. "Damn you, Romen, I'd enjoy having your company around me. Can I persuade you to stay?"

"No, sire—though it is a generous offer. I have business elsewhere to attend to."

"More assassinations?" the King suggested.

Wyl shook his head. "Your purse is substantial enough, sire, that I will not need to pursue such employment for a long time. No, majesty, the good life beckons. I should return home and inquire after my family. It has been too long since I have enjoyed the rich meadows and lush wines of Grenadyn."

He hoped the King would not ask him his intentions for Ylena.

Celimus had already forgotten her. "But you will stay for the funeral? In fact, I demand you do. It will look right that the man who brought General Thirsk back to his King sees him buried."

Wyl did not want to but he could see the set of Celimus's jaw. It was obvious the King wished to enjoy his company just a little longer. He could also see the sense of it and it might help impress upon the men of the Legion that he was to be trusted. It could come in handy later.

"Of course, sire. It will be my pleasure to remain until the business of Thirsk is fully behind you."

The King nodded. "I will send for my physic to see to your injury." Celimus pulled on a cord, which brought back the courtier. "Koreldy is to have the full generosity of Stoneheart available to him. See to whatever he needs. And call Physic Gerd to his chambers." The man bowed as Celimus turned back to Wyl. "Until later, then."

Wyl, putting the two sacks under one arm, took the King's elegant hand in his. Although he hated to touch his enemy, he liked it that he was finally tall enough to look Celimus directly in the eye. He bowed but the King did not see the smile of satisfaction on Romen's handsome face.

16

WYL ALLOWED THE KING'S PHYSIC TO SEE TO HIS WOUND. HE was impatient, twisting under the doctor's ministrations. The injury was uncomfortable but the slash was clean and a few sutures closed it with ease. Whatever that fellow gave him to drink to deaden the pain of his needlework was making Wyl feel like he was drifting but there was still something important he had to do. He splashed his face with water and was pleased he had been provided with a valet—albeit one still in training—to see to his needs. The youngster had carefully laid out fresh clothes. Wyl told him he would only be needing the shirt for now and that he would require a bath later. Keen to please, the valet said he would arrange for a tub to be brought up.

Feeling only vaguely refreshed, Wyl made off for Stoneheart's dungeons; he needed no help in finding his way down there but asked the guards for directions all the same, just in case he was being watched. As he arrived he was reminded of that day years ago when as a boy he had been tricked into coming to this place of despair. It was as though that terrible scene of torture had occurred only yesterday, so vivid was his memory of Myrren's suffering.

They had expected his arrival but not so soon. The man on duty asked him to wait. Wyl's thoughts sped once more back to Myrren, marveling at her resolve not to capitulate under the most enormous pain and torment. She knew she would die, would not escape their ultimate punishment, and he wondered why she had not just admitted the sin regardless of the truth. *Why suffer such immense anguish?* Why indeed, if she was empowered, did she not save herself? He could not answer his own questions.

His thoughts wandered further to Knave. Myrren was determined—persistent even—to win Wyl's assurance that he would take the pup and make him his own. *Is Knave connected with the enchantment?* Certainly the dog had mysterious ways. *And Fynch,* he thought. *Where does he fit in all of this?*

Wyl recalled the Widow Ilyk's strange words of caution. Keep the dog and his companion close, she had warned, adding that he had already met the companion she spoke of. *It has to be Fynch.* The lad had showed immense courage and tenacity. It would have been so easy for Fynch to return to Stoneheart and forget everything he had seen or heard. But he had not. Instead he had saved Valentyna's life and, to some extent, Wyl. Wyl was just beginning to wonder how he would ever convince the boy of the truth of whom Romen Koreldy now was when the guard returned with the man in charge of the dungeons.

He was a good man, Wyl recalled, who took no part or pleasure in the torture of the inmates on the rare occasion it occurred. In fact he was known for showing leniency to all of his "guests," as he liked to call them.

"Sir," he said, nodding a brisk bow towards Wyl. "I'm sorry for the delay, we were not expecting you so soon."

He dismissed his guard, leaving them alone.

"That's quite all right," Wyl said. "You know I am here to take Ylena Thirsk from your—" he searched for the word, "care."

The man smiled. "Yes, sir. And I'm glad of it. That fine young lady does not deserve this treatment. Er—do you mind if I ask what your interest in this woman is, sir—you being a stranger and all?"

It was an impertinent question and one Wyl knew he could have the man flogged for. Instead he made a promise to one day seek this man out and thank him for protecting his sister's interests.

Right now, he returned the smile to show no offense had been taken but it died as soon as he spoke. "I had the misfortune to witness what they did to Lady Donal—and to her husband." He was glad his voice didn't choke on the last. "I have offered help and been given permission to extend it."

"I am grateful to you, sir. If I might speak freely, it was a wretched thing they did to those two young people," he confided. "Follow me." As they walked, the dungeon's keeper cautioned him. "She is not in a very good—um—state, I should warn, sir. This is no place for young ladies."

He said no more but turned a large key in the cell door. It was the only prison cell with a full, thick timber door rather than bars. This prisoner was clearly not on show.

Stepping inside, Wyl was immediately assaulted by the smell. He saw her and anger warred with pity. Still wearing the same bloodied clothes, Ylena was crouched in one corner. She had soiled herself and her hair was filthy and lank; it fell across her face and she ignored it. Ylena's once-soft lips were chapped and her eyes, formerly so full of amusement and the joy of life, were hollow shadows of their former sparkling glory. She was expressionless and rocked to and fro on the balls of her feet, softly voicing a tuneless hum.

"Ylena?" he whispered, knowing she would not recognize the voice of Romen.

She did not even stir. Instead she seemed to be gazing

past him. He followed her stare and stumbled against the dungeoner, horrified to see the remains of Alyd Donal's head mounted high on a spike. The lids were half-closed, his expression still seemingly reflecting the horror of his last moments. Wyl held back the cry of anger that rushed towards release.

The dungeoner shrugged. "King's orders, sir. I'm sorry, did you know him?"

Wyl ignored the question. "What did they do with the rest of him?" he barked.

"Burned, I think. We are under strict orders down here. Not a single man of the Legion is to hear of her situation or even that Captain Donal was executed, I was told under penalty of death. It is only myself that knows who has been incarcerated and in fact, sir, it is my orders that I must shroud the lady when she leaves."

Again all Wyl could do was nod. "Do it," he said. "Can she walk?"

"Best I carry her, sir."

"Right. Follow me and bring that as well," he said, indicating Alyd's head. "I will see it gets a proper burial."

Wyl seethed all the way back to his chambers at the state in which he had found Ylena. His only consolation was that she lived. He said farewell to the dungeoner outside the door, taking Ylena from him and pressing a gold coin into his hand.

"No need, sir," the man said. "I'm just happy she's back where she belongs."

"Let me assure you it's not here," Wyl replied and the man nodded at this before leaving him.

The young valet's eyes matched the size of his open mouth when Wyl staggered in carrying a woman.

"Lord Koreldy, sir!" was all the boy managed to get out.

Wyl laid the catatonic Ylena on his bed and the sack containing his friend's stinking remains in the corner.

"Jorn, fetch hot water. Do we have bath oils?"

The lad nodded.

"Good. Hurry now."

Jorn was at the door when Wyl called him back. He flipped him a gold coin, knowing the youngster would not have held such a fortune before.

"There is nothing illegal about what we do but please don't go wagging your tongue outside of this room. I have the King's permission to care for this person, who is the sister of the dead man I brought back to Morgravia with me this morning."

Jorn nodded. Word of Wyl Thirsk's death had ripped around Stoneheart like wildfire. "Yes, sir. You wish me to say nothing of the lady's presence," the boy replied seriously.

"Good boy. Discretion is the highest-valued ability of a valet and I will mention that special quality of yours to the King."

Now Jorn's eyes were sparkling with pride. "Thank you, sir," he gushed and tumbled through the door in his rush to fetch the hot water.

He was surprisingly fast. Wyl had only just drawn the curtains around the bed in time to hide Ylena before two servants arrived with Jorn, dragging buckets of water. Satisfied that they were too busy with their chores to wonder what might be behind those drapes, he dismissed them with brief thanks, then suggested Jorn go in search of some suitable clothes. He directed the lad to Ylena's former chambers and then he set about the task of cleaning up his sister.

She seemed so entirely lost to him. Wyl wondered if he could find her again, whether he would ever see her smile again. Softly singing an old lullaby she loved as a child, he began to wash her. Very gradually the familiar features began to emerge from beneath the filth and he saw her thin shoulders begin to relax as the warmth of the water worked its own magic. Orange and violet oil in the water smoothed her skin under the sponge he moved gently about her, and then he soaped her hair, slowly removing its tangles and dirt.

By the time Jorn returned with some garments, Ylena, now wrapped in Wyl's huge shirt, looked like a new person. Wyl had just finished combing her still-damp hair and the young lad offered him a ribbon with which to tie it back. Then he gently laid her again in his bed and covered her.

"Thank you, Jorn," he said with genuine feeling. The boy had been a great help. As well as clothes and footwear, Jorn had brought toiletries and grooming implements from her rooms.

"I also found this, sir," he said, handing over a box.

Wyl smiled. Jorn had brought Ylena's jewels. They were mostly their mother's but he was pleased to see a brooch he had given her and the pearl from the King. She had been allowed to wear her wedding ring, he noticed.

"Argorn jewels," he whispered. "You've done her proud, Jorn. I think what she needs now is sleep."

"What happened, sir?"

Truth was best. "She was a guest in his majesty's dungeon while he suspected Wyl Thirsk of treachery."

"And is it true that Thirsk was treacherous?"

"No. As it turned out his loyalties never wavered for Morgravia—the King knows that now," he lied. "Which is why Wyl Thirsk is to be honored with a full state funeral and his sister has been released into my care."

"And you, sir? You too look badly in need of rest. How about your bath?"

Wyl yawned. "I think what I need most is some food," he said, realizing he had not eaten for two days. "And then I shall sleep. Forget the bath. Wake me early and we'll see to it then."

Jorn once again hurried off, this time to the kitchens, where he refused to be drawn out on the subject of the dashing stranger who had brought home a favorite son.

Wyl woke early from his hard bed on the floor but Jorn was ready for him with the promised bath and a very hearty breakfast. Ylena had seemingly moved only once through the night, turning to face the window from which she could see the sky, a sight lacking from the dungeon. She remained listless and silent, although Wyl sensed her eyes followed him.

He went about his ablutions and then ate hungrily in silence. When finished, he stretched and looked over at her. She was watching him, as he suspected she might have been.

"Good morning," he said in Romen's bright way.

The answer came so softly that he had to lean closer. "Who are you?" she repeated.

He would have to spin his best tale yet now. "I am Romen Koreldy, a noble and a long way from my home in Grenadyn." He made his voice especially soft, so as not to disturb her. "I accompanied your brother on a special secret mission into Briavel." Wyl would have liked to have taken her hand or held her close for the next part of his tale but she had shrunk beneath her covers, only her face above the blankets. He sighed. "Lady Donal, it is with a heavy heart that I must tell you we were attacked and although he fought bravely he was cut down. Wyl died of his injuries but I've brought him back onto Morgravian soil—back to Stoneheart."

Her even expression did not betray her true thoughts. "Wyl was the most superior swordsman of the Morgravian Legion. No man could cut him down."

Wyl nodded, loving her deeply for her loyalty. "This is true, my lady. We were set upon by many and he made sure he took the last one with him to death."

He saw her clamp her jaw hard. She was working hard at remaining calm. "Wyl is dead." Ylena fixed him with a heartbreaking gaze. "So what makes a complete stranger do this kind deed, sir—of bringing him back, I mean?"

She watched Romen Koreldy shrug.

"I too would be dead if not for him. He gave me life. I owed him this much."

Ylena nodded. "And me? What is your interest?"

"A promise," Wyl said, sitting forward and now chancing to take her slender hand from beneath the covers. "I promised your brother as he died that I would rescue you from the dungeon." He steeled himself against the tears and pressed doggedly on. This needed to be said. He needed Ylena's trust and the only way was to use her memory of Wyl. "He told me what happened in the courtyard," Wyl said, carefully avoiding mentioning that Romen had been present during Alyd's execution. "He made me swear I would win your release."

She wept quietly as the frozen memory of Alyd's last day began to thaw. As her body began to tremble, Wyl put Romen's arms around her and drew her close, hugging his sister.

"Did he tell you everything?" she mumbled against his broad chest.

"Yes. I know about Celimus's betrayal but I find myself in a very dangerous position, my lady. I have but one aim and that is to get you away from here and fulfill my promise to your brother. We will get you to a safe place but I am under supervision, you could say, until your brother is buried. The King promises a theatrical funeral."

"Wyl would hate it knowing Celimus was smiling at his tomb."

"I understand. May I call you Ylena?" She nodded. "Well, Ylena, we must get through the funeral and then we leave. That is the only way I can guarantee our safety."

"I am not going. I will not watch Wyl be buried. I have suffered enough death."

Wyl was relieved to hear it and sat her back down. "Right now I want you to eat and get some strength back."

She touched his arm. "Romen, did you by any chance see—in my dungeon—"

"Yes, Ylena. I have brought him." Now she cried again. "We will bury him properly."

There was a knock at the door.

"Who is it?" Wyl called.

"Jorn, sir. You have a visitor."

Wyl grimaced. He went to the door and opened it a crack to get rid of whomever it was but the door burst open and the body of Romen Koreldy was knocked to the floor and straddled by a huge, very excited black dog.

"Knave!" he and Ylena both shouted as he hugged the dog.

Jorn had pulled in the dog's companion; and now Fynch, wearing brand new clothes and a terrified expression, began to wail.

"Murderer! Assassin!"

Wyl was on his feet in a second and clamped his hand across Fynch's mouth. The little boy began to kick and struggle, desperately trying to scream beneath the pressure of Romen's large palm. Chaos broke out in the room. Ylena, terrified, managed to sit up, Knave was still growling with pleasure and leaping to put his paws against Koreldy in welcome while Jorn was so startled he flattened himself against the wall.

"Everyone, quiet!" Wyl roared. "Do you want the whole castle in uproar?" He glared at each. "Down, Knave! Now you, Fynch, silence! I will not hurt you if you stop struggling—stop!" The boy went limp. Wyl breathed out with relief. "Jorn, be at ease. This can all be easily explained," he said, unconvinced he could explain anything. "Ylena, please—eat and rest. You are familiar with this beast?" he asked, looking with bemusement at the dog, whose tail was wagging furiously, his front paws leaning on Romen's shoulders.

"Yes, he is my brother's dog. I . . . I don't understand."

Wyl nodded to cut her short. "I will leave the dog here with you. Fynch and I have things to discuss."

"What did this boy mean by calling you an assassin?" she asked.

"A mistake. I will explain later but let me talk to him first. He has been through much, my lady."

Ylena shook her head, not understanding any of it. "Knave seems attached to you," she said with equal confusion. "And yet he hates everyone."

"I have a way with animals," Wyl said, hoping that would suffice for now. "Excuse me," he added and dragged Fynch from the room, his hand still over the lad's mouth.

A chamber at the end of the hall was mercifully empty. Wyl took Fynch inside.

"I want you to promise me you will not scream but listen. I have news you must know. I understand you were a good friend to Wyl Thirsk. Please, I know about Valentyna and your escape. Just promise you will listen."

Fynch nodded wide-eyed from behind Romen's hand. When Wyl released him, Fynch scuttled away, breathing hard with fright.

"I know about you," he accused. "I know you were hired to kill General Thirsk."

Wyl sighed. He felt it was suddenly useless to try to convince Fynch he was anyone but Romen Koreldy—for now anyway. No one, not even someone who allowed for magic, would believe him. His mind raced; he must persuade the lad to trust him.

"Fynch."

"How do you know my name?"

"Wyl told me."

"Is it true—is he dead?"

Wyl nodded, hating to lie to the courageous lad. He watched Fynch fight back his inclination to weep.

"They say you brought him back," he said, contempt glittering in his damp eyes.

"I did."

"But you killed him."

"No," Wyl lied, knowing it was Romen's skilled arm that had killed his body. He decided he would never be able to explain and pressed on with crafting a new lie.

"Wyl told me what you'd overheard. It is true and he and I spoke about it. After you and the Princess had escaped, he warned me not to trust Celimus. He told me everything and then when the attack came, I realized my life was dispensable too—that Celimus had almost certainly ordered my death together with Wyl's. In the end we fought on the same side, Fynch. We both protected King Valor—"

"Valor's dead!" Fynch hurled back.

"I know. I watched him fall to the blade of a man called Arkol, who then turned on me. Wyl and I had already dispatched most of the mercenaries to their gods but Wyl was cut down by two men. He took one with him at the same time as I killed Arkol. I was wounded and if not for Wyl's courageous slash from the ground where he was bleeding to death, my life would be gone too. He distracted the last man long enough for me to gather my wits and finish him off." Fynch was crying now and Wyl hated himself deeply for the lies.

"Wyl died in my arms but not before making me promise that I would get his sister to safety. I had already given my oath that I would protect Princess Valentyna."

Fynch looked up, disbelief crossing his face. "Did you?"

Wyl nodded. "I gave my promise with blood." He showed him the wound on his palm. "So you see, Fynch, I am on your side. I came back for Ylena and to see that Wyl Thirsk gets the burial he deserves. I made sure the Legionnaires saw his body and knew that he had been sent on a special mission to Briavel by the King. Celimus cannot squirm out of that now. He must hail Wyl as the hero he was for Morgravia. I have deliberately seen to it that the Thirsk name is not sullied. Do you believe me?" He just stopped short of begging.

The small lad sniffed. He considered for a long time, long enough for Wyl to feel uncomfortable in the silence. Finally Fynch spoke. "I will trust you for one reason only."

"And that is?" Wyl asked, Romen's eyebrow lifting in its habitual manner.

"Because Knave does. Knave knows things that I don't understand. He knew we had to come home. I followed him even though I would have preferred to stay in Briavel. Knave made me come back."

"Do you talk to him, then?" Wyl asked, a chill crawling up his spine as Myrren's gift returned to his conscious.

"Not exactly, but he does communicate things I don't fully grasp. And when we got to Stoneheart, he knew where to come. I find it passing strange that he didn't go in search of General Thirsk's body but deliberately slipped into corridors and tiny entrances until he found these stairs. He came straight to your chamber. And I don't understand why he was friendly toward you when three days ago he would have gladly ripped your throat out."

Can Knave really have done this? Wyl wondered. "What are you saying?"

"I don't know, sir. Except that I will trust his instincts over mine, which are to run from you."

"You saw Ylena. She is yet to recover from what she has been through, but she trusts me."

"I trust only Knave and Valentyna now," the boy admitted.

"Fynch, where is the Princess?"

"Where she belongs, sir. She is no longer Princess but

Queen of Briavel. She is returned to Werryl to bury her father and—"

"How is she?"

"Physically fine, sir. Broken over her father's death. She is even contemplating war against Morgravia."

"No!" Wyl shouted, startling Fynch. "She must not, at all costs, do this."

Fynch shrugged. "I am only a gong boy, sir."

"Much more, I fear," Wyl said, shaking his head. "Fynch, you have to go back. You must slip away from Stoneheart and return to Briavel. Give her a message from me. You and I must prevent war—there is a way."

"Where are you going?"

"First, I must get Ylena to safety and away from the King's line of vision or even thoughts. He is fickle and will forget her easily but not if she is anywhere near. I will return to Briavel, I promise. You know I have given my word to Wyl Thirsk to protect Valentyna," he reassured, holding up his palm so Fynch could see the blood oath scar again.

Fynch nodded. "I shall leave immediately."

"Have you a horse?"

"Yes, Valentyna gave me one. I lost my mule in the troubles back there."

For the first time in what felt like ages, Wyl smiled for the pure pleasure of being able to say something positive.

"Oh, I think I found her. A gentle beast who accompanied us back to Morgravia."

"That's probably her!" Fynch said, clearly pleased. "I must return her to my family."

"Come," Wyl said. "I'll give you money for the care of your family while you are gone. Then you must leave with haste. Get away from Morgravia and remain in Briavel until you hear from me."

"And the message for Valentyna?"

"I will write her a letter."

"And Knave?"

"You two must stick together. He will keep you safe, Fynch."

17

WYL EXPECTED TO BE FINE AT HIS OWN FUNERAL BUT HE WAS far from it. He had seen Fynch off in the early hours. The mule had been retrieved and Fynch was on his way back to his family's cottage four miles from Stoneheart, his pockets bulging with coin that Wyl had insisted he take to his sister. He also carried with him a handwritten letter from Romen Koreldy to Queen Valentyna.

Wyl had explained the gist of it to him and Fynch had approved. "She'll like that. But she is scared and untrusting— you'd better not leave it too long to present yourself," he had cautioned.

Wyl had decided in the end that by the time Fynch had met with his family and finally got on the road to Briavel, the formal part of the funeral might well be over. With this in mind, he opted to keep Knave by Ylena as protection; he had no desire for anyone to come snooping around his chambers and discover Ylena. No one would dare trespass with the black dog to negotiate with. He could then send Knave on to catch up with Fynch, who, Wyl was surprised to note, seemed confident that the dog would understand all instructions.

Jorn had been a godsend, quietly going about his business of caring for Romen and Ylena, so Wyl felt confident when he left Knave outside his chambers, guarding his sister, that he would get through the funeral formalities without a problem.

It was easier said than achieved.

A large crowd had already swelled, lining up quietly, and Wyl found it easier to join them rather than enter the cathedral via the "noble doors."

"Why not take the faster route?" a woman said, nodding toward the magnificently carved entrance.

"Thirsk claimed he was a soldier before he was a noble. I pay him respect by using the common entrance," Wyl replied.

She smiled back, obviously pleased. "He was a good man. Always good to my girls he was. Such a shame."

Wyl suddenly recognized her for one of the city's brothel owners. She looked different without her fancy gowns and face colorings. He recalled how she had once asked for protection for the women working in the brothel and how grateful she had been when he provided the girls with a permanent guard who would escort them home when needed.

"Did you know him?" a much older man directly ahead of him asked.

The question made Wyl feel suddenly vulnerable. "I did."

"I knew his father. I was the great man's runner for many years."

"Oh?" Wyl said, taken aback.

"Yes. And they say the youngster was shaping up to be every bit as good as Fergys Thirsk."

"I believe it would have pleased Wyl to know people thought this of him."

"Sticks in my craw, that whole Briavel thing. What was he doing there anyway?"

"A mission for the sovereign, I gather."

"Then it was a dirty mission, I presume," the man whispered and was hushed by someone nearby.

"You'll get your tongue cut out for less," his friend warned. "There are rumors about our new King."

"What is being said?" Wyl asked keenly.

The man grimaced. "I'm not saying this is truth, mind, only what I've heard. There's talk of killings in the castle—secret killings and torture. Let's not forget who his mother was," he added and fell silent.

Wyl knew he would get no more from the folk around him, but he was pleased to hear they were getting an inkling that beneath Celimus's handsome exterior lived a cruel and heartless soul.

As the group stepped across the threshold of the cathedral doors, the anticipated silence hushed all whispering.

Built by the stonemasons and craftsmen of centuries previous, the cathedral inspired awe in all who entered it. Wyl, who had stood beneath its soaring ceiling on many occasions, never failed to marvel at the beautiful carvings and exquisite stonework. Each of the thirty or so internal pillars was supported on a plinth carved out of the famous gray stone of Morgravia to depict one of the famed mythical beasts that were believed to choose an individual at the time of birth. It was said that the spirit within the birth-beast would protect its own, which was why Morgravians made their first pilgrimage to the cathedral at the youngest possible age.

As worshipers entered the cathedral now, the procession split into smaller groups as people moved toward their particular stone beast to touch its head or limbs in quiet reverence for a few moments.

Wyl's chosen creature was the winged lion. Fearsome, snarling, majestic. It had captivated his imagination at thirteen when he had first set foot in the cathedral and now he paid it just homage, waiting his turn to lay his hand on its cool, magisterial mane. He loved to touch its wings too. He did so now feeling not just overawed, as he did each time he was close to this beast, but absorbing the deep sorrow of the occasion that seemed to be reflected in the lion's expressive eyes.

"I wonder which creature General Thirsk chose," a lad whispered nearby. His mother hushed him.

Wyl could not help himself. He grinned at the youngster. "It was this one," he said softly.

The boy's eyes widened in pleasure. "Truly?"

Wyl nodded, glancing towards the lad's mother to reassure her that it was all right to whisper. He crouched to be at eye level with her son. "I knew General Thirsk, and you, him, and myself all share the same mythical beast."

"That makes us brothers, then," the youngster said proudly.

"It does." He touched fists with the boy in the Legionnaire manner.

The woman smiled back and nodded her thanks. Wyl knew he was lingering now to avoid what he suddenly felt he did not want to confront. He had no choice, though. The flow of people was pressing forward and he could not resist that swell for much longer.

He turned and stared toward the front where a bier stood in a cleared space. Atop the bier was Wyl Thirsk's corpse.

Wyl felt undone when he laid eyes on his own cooled and pale body. It was naked save for a binding of muslin about the groin and a wreath of the national flower about the head. Celimus had ordered that the General's corpse be presented in this fashion—an honor reserved for nobility held in the highest esteem by the Crown. He looked at the crimson imolda—the prettiest of all wildflowers—wryly noticing how it clashed with his hair color.

Wyl had deliberately arrived early yet there were already many dozens of people shuffling past the corpse, paying their final respects to a young man cut down in his prime. He overheard someone mutter their observation that the last of the Thirsk men had perished. A lump formed in his throat as a blitz of sorrowful thoughts crashed into his mind and he began to feel the depth of sadness around him.

He stumbled slightly when he drew close to the body, which he saw was covered lightly with gingery hair. *Passing strange I never noticed that when I owned that body,* he wondered. He noted all manner of tiny details that had not occurred to him previously. Now that it was slackened in death's peaceful repose, he saw that his face was not as ugly as he had always presumed. Plain, yes, but not ugly. He noticed that his despised freckles had all but disappeared, that his face, though pale with death, was tanned like the sunburned arms, once thick and strong. For some reason he held a vision of himself possessing a boyish face and yet now that he looked at it he could see that in the years since his arrival at Stoneheart, he had undergone a transformation.

That face was much squarer now, the jaw and brow more pronounced. He had possessed workmanlike hands, something he had never taken account of, and these were now crossed over at the chest, but even so they did not hide the livid wound where Romen's sword had penetrated. It was a warrior's wound, one to be proud of, and some people touched it in veneration. A collective sorrow had gathered itself about the line of mourners who made a slow but steady revolution of the body. He stepped into the line finally and followed suit, resting Romen's large, elegant hand ever so briefly on Wyl Thirsk's wound, remembering that exquisite agony and sense of disbelief as the sword had run him through.

Upon touching his own corpse Wyl experienced a breathlessness as he felt his own emotions rising up. His body looked small and helpless lying there; it made him think of his father's and then Magnus's death. It reminded him that Alyd and possibly Gueryn were dead. All he had left was Ylena to love and Valentyna to protect.

A loud fanfare of trumpets sounded, signaling the monarch's entry into the cathedral. Celimus was earlier than expected. Wyl grimaced with Romen's mouth. He had hoped to be in and out before the King arrived. People about him were dropping their heads and bowing low—as Celimus demanded apparently—yet Wyl could not do the same. Something hard and unforgiving prevented him from paying this treacherous bastard any homage. He could see Celimus striding down the main aisle of the cathedral, his heels clicking loudly and arrogantly on the flagstones, resounding all the way up to the magnificent arched ceiling.

The King made his way to the opposite side of the nave from where the winged lion resided. Celimus stood before the stone dragon, his alone until he died and a new King inherited the throne. Here he paused in quiet reflection, not caring that all were required to remain bowed until he had seated himself. He finally extended an arm to touch the dragon's clawed foot, its rearing head—as befitted the King of all beasts—being too high even for one of his height to reach.

Then he turned and clicked his swaggering way back toward the stone throne at the front of the cathedral. No one was yet permitted to straighten. It was ludicrous, Wyl protested inwardly. Magnus had never asked for such a lengthy and theatrical obeisance. *What is happening to the Morgra-*

vians? And how much worse will it get, for these are such early days in the reign of Celimus?

He realized the traitor had spied and was now watching him; the King had reached his chair but was not seated yet. The olive gaze stared hard, demanding that Romen Koreldy of Grenadyn bow to the King of Morgravia.

Bow! Wyl urged himself but Romen's body would not obey. He knew this was not Romen at work. Romen was gone. This was his own spirit rising up against the evil that looked back at him now from that devilishly beautiful face. Celimus cocked his head slightly to one side. He was asking a question of Romen now. Wyl understood he was pitting his wits against the most dangerous of opponents. All that he had planned would come undone if he threw away his one chance to escape after the funeral.

Obey him, bow to him!

It was his neighbor who broke the spell, the old soldier who had been standing in front of him in the line outside the cathedral.

"Bow, damn you," he growled beneath his breath and mercifully grabbed Romen's arm to pull him not only downward but to his senses as well.

Wyl dropped to Romen's knee and bowed fully to the King.

"Thank you," he whispered to the soldier.

Seemingly satisfied but wearing an unreadable expression, Celimus at last sat. Soft music immediately erupted from a choir on the gallery level above. Their voices soared in the cathedral as though angels were singing. People stood straight and the line resumed its shuffle around the body, the music provoking tears.

At the head of the corpse Wyl looked down upon the closed eyes, the ones that hid the mystery of Myrren's gift. Ginger lashes lay like soft down against the tops of the dead man's cheeks—his cheeks. How deeply sad he suddenly felt for himself.

Dead but not dead. Trapped as Wyl and yet free to be Romen.

Grief betrayed him now and Wyl had to recover quickly

lest King Celimus notice genuine sorrow in Wyl Thirsk's assassin. He strode away from the body, pleased to escape, throwing a glance toward the King, who chose not to look his way.

Many nobles had gathered. He noticed the Duke of Felrawthy was not present, probably still shoring up defenses in the north, as was his duty to the Crown. The Duke's absence was probably a blessing in the circumstances, considering his son's fate, although the King still desperately needed the support of the influence Jeryb Donal wielded in the north. He wondered what lies Celimus had contrived to send to the Duke regarding Alyd's death to avoid jeopardizing that relationship. Perhaps the King was beginning to regret his vengeful decision to end the young man's life?

The service began and pulled Wyl from his musings. The holy men said all the usual things and then the King made a flowery speech lauding the virtues of Morgravia's favorite man of the military. Music, pomp, ceremony—just as Celimus had promised. Once the body was finally shrouded, later to be laid in the family vault at Stoneheart with all the other Thirsks who had served Morgravia, the service concluded, and was followed by a funeral feast that stretched long into the afternoon.

"Sit next to me, Romen," Celimus offered as a rare generosity, obviously excited by the closing of a chapter. He was free now to dominate the Legion.

Wyl reluctantly joined him, wondering how quickly he might make his escape. He pretended to eat the food and sipped frequently from his cup yet hardly took any of the wine into his mouth. He would need a clear head later.

Celimus leaned toward him and whispered, "I've a good mind to burn the body."

Wyl pushed away his startled expression. "Oh? Why?" he asked in Romen's casual way.

"I hate them all grieving like that over him. I wish to rid Morgravia of his memory."

Wyl felt ill. *Would Celimus really open the tomb later and burn my body?* Burning was considered unsavory by all

Morgravians. It was reserved for witches and traitors. The irony was not lost on him.

He slung his arm over his chair, a typically uninhibited pose of Romen's. "I wouldn't, sire. You may just incite trouble. Why not simply send the corpse to the family home? Where does he hail from anyway?"

"Argorn," Celimus said, curling his lip. "A sleepy, hideously backward region of the realm, which yields halfwits and ugly, red-headed ingrates like those of the Thirsk line."

How Wyl held his temper he would never know. Bile rose in his throat and his fingers twitched near a fork that he would have gladly stabbed into the King's throat.

He managed a derisory response, however, that even Romen would have been proud of. "All the more reason to send the little troll back to where he belongs. Let him lie in exile," he offered, twirling his cup of wine instead of his fork.

And now Celimus looked fully at him, just a tinge of gratitude in his expression. "Again you surprise me, Koreldy—this time with your insight."

"Oh, and when was the previous occasion I surprised you, sire?" Wyl asked, knowing almost immediately it was a trap.

"This morning, in the cathedral, when you took a sincerely long time to pay me due respect. Should I be worried about your loyalty?"

Wyl took a silent steadying breath and then grinned expansively again. "I have none, sire . . . except to gold," he said. Celimus did not smile back. "To tell the truth, your majesty, I thought I was going to faint in the cathedral," Wyl said, his mind moving fast now.

"Why is that?"

"I'm not sure, sire. I made little of my wound yesterday but the physic said it was deeper than I thought and he sutured it. He gave me two draughts of some potion. One to take during his ministrations and another to take this morning. I fear this morning's concoction was a little too strong, and my apologies, majesty, but it took all of my wits to stop myself from falling cold to the ground."

"I see. Perhaps falling to the ground would have pleased me more than what appeared to be deliberate flouting of Stoneheart's protocol."

Wyl shook his head vehemently. "No, sire, never. I am in your debt. And also to my neighbor, who helped me when I asked for it. He assisted me to my knee."

And as fast as Celimus's anger stoked, it passed, much to Wyl's relief. Already the incident seemed forgotten. The King waved away the apology and asked for a refill of their cups.

"So tell me, Romen. Have you ravished the Lady Ylena?"

Wyl coughed but masked it well. "Not yet, sire. She is still in some shock and behaving as much a corpse as her husband. She also smells as ripe as he."

Celimus did laugh at this. "So you are showing great patience, my friend. Is that right?"

"I've given her until tonight, sire. Then I shall take her from behind if necessary so I don't have to look upon that terrified, filthy face." He had never hated Celimus as much as he did at this moment.

The King laughed again. "And when do you leave us?"

"With your permission, your majesty, I thought I would enjoy your hospitality for another day," Wyl lied. "Tomorrow eve perhaps?"

Celimus nodded. "Good. Let's take a ride together tomorrow at dawn. You can see my falcons at work."

"Excellent, sire, now you must forgive me," Wyl said with absolutely no intention of remaining more than another hour at Stoneheart.

"Oh, leaving our table early, Romen?"

"Yes, majesty. I beg your indulgence. I am still feeling a little weak. I would rest and get ready to ride with you."

Celimus raised his cup to Romen and sipped. "Until tomorrow."

"I shall see you at dawn, sire," Wyl said, Romen's disarming smile winning hearts around the table but not where it counted.

As he strode from the hall, Celimus beckoned to one of his men. He had already formed an inner circle of sorts who clustered about him as private guards. None were from the Legion.

"Your majesty?"

"Jerico, do you see that man leaving the hall?"

"Yes, sire."

"He is preparing to depart Pearlis tomorrow eve—perhaps with a woman in tow. Once he leaves the city gates, I want you to follow him with several of our own and kill him. Kill them both if she's with him. Do you understand?"

The man nodded.

"No trace is to be found of either, except his finger wearing the signet ring. That you will return as proof of your successful deed. He will have much gold about his person. Whatever you find, you may keep and split as you see fit."

The man called Jerico grinned. "Thank you, sire."

18

YL AND KNAVE NAVIGATED THEIR WAY TO A LITTLE-USED courtyard with a tiny arched entrance and a direct exit beyond Stoneheart's walls. From past experience Wyl knew it would be patrolled only minimally. It was getting on to dusk, so light was rapidly failing, and he was able to distract the single guard in conversation long enough for Knave to trot through the opening. The guard spotted the movement, however, and reacted predictably but Wyl just raised his eyebrows and said something derogatory about Stoneheart having too many dogs.

The man looked worried and then explained that he recognized the dog as General Thirsk's beast and perhaps he should have stopped him.

"Well, don't blame yourself, lad," Wyl said, reassuringly. "He's making his bid for freedom. He no longer belongs here, what with his master dead." He shrugged.

"You're probably right, sir. He was a fearsome mongrel anyway. So are those directions helpful, sir? Can you find your way back to your chambers now?"

"Definitely. My thanks for your help."

"Don't mention it, sir," the guard said and returned to his post.

Wyl had decided he would use the exit through this court-yard to get out of Stoneheart later, when night would give him the shadows he needed. Another shadow, one that could move and melt easily into the darkness, was waiting outside. Knave had his instructions. He would be ready for them.

Jorn had packed their few belongings into a cloth bag. He had also tossed in some fruit, cheeses, nuts, and a couple of loaves.

"Just to tide you through, sir," he said and Wyl realized the lad looked sad.

"Jorn . . . look."

Wyl's tone gave the youngster the courage he wanted. "Take me with you, Lord Koreldy, sir. I'll be no problem, I promise. I can care for the Lady Ylena so you are free to do your business, sir."

The boy looked so desperate Wyl almost relented and then he remembered all that lay ahead.

"Jorn, you're a good lad and you're needed at Stoneheart. Here," he said, handing him a parchment. "I've written a high recommendation to the seneschal—make sure he gets it soon," Wyl warned, knowing the name Koreldy would be blackened shortly but hoping the lad would be forgotten in the scheme of things. "I can't take you with me. Where I'm headed I need no companion, son. I hope you understand."

The youngster nodded but the disappointment was evident. It was Ylena who rescued Wyl. "When I get back to my family home, Jorn, I shall send for you. You will continue your training with us at Argorn."

The lad brightened immediately. "That would be grand, my lady, thank you. Where are you headed?"

Wyl shook his head. "Not sure yet, Jorn. Probably north-west, somewhere very quiet. Rittylworth perhaps." He knew it was a mistake to have said that much. It put the lad in danger and compromised their security too.

Jorn nodded. "I shall wait to hear, sir." He bowed to Ylena. "My lady."

She glanced at Romen and smiled sadly. Wyl wished he could ease her pain, just a little, by telling her that it was him, her brother, smiling back.

Once Knave heard the low command whistle from his master he put on a big show for the terrified guard, growling and barking, running toward him at an insane speed and then swerving away. The man finally mustered enough courage to pick up rocks and hurl them into the darkness to where he thought the beast might be; then, rattled, he went to get help.

In those few moments Wyl and Ylena slipped through the gate toward freedom. They were well-clothed for travel on foot and their soft boots made no sound. Wyl knew Ylena would not be able to travel very far before needing rest. She was undernourished and still weak but he hoped she might at least make it to the next town, where he could buy suitable horses. His aim was to walk as far as they could under cover of darkness and they did so in silence for a mile or more until Wyl felt himself relaxing as Stoneheart was put behind them.

Knave emerged from the shadows of a hedgerow, a huge dark figure. "Good boy," Wyl said, patting his head.

"I have no idea why that dog likes you. He hates just about everyone," Ylena commented absently, her voice still an otherworldly monotone.

"So I hear. I guess I have the touch."

She remained silent.

"Knave, now you go and find Fynch. Take him to Bri-avel. Keep him safe." He knelt down now and looked up into the large dog's eyes. "Watch over her for me, boy." Wyl felt odd talking to the beast with such confidence, yet he felt strangely certain that the dog understood. The animal seemed to be as touched by enchantment as he was himself.

The animal lingered just long enough for Ylena to touch his great head affectionately and then he loped off into the dark, presumably to catch up with Fynch.

"Do you think he misses Wyl?" she asked in her faraway voice.

No point in answering. "Ylena, about your husband," Wyl said gently. "Where would you like us to lay him to rest?"

She did not hesitate in her reply. "He must go home, Romen, to Felrawthy in the north. His family must know of this outrage. The Duke will respond as he sees fit."

Unlike his sister, Wyl did hesitate. He knew it would be unwise to incite an uprising of the nobility right now. There were too many unknowns. Who would replace Celimus? Would the nobles support such treachery—and why should they trust Romen Koreldy? And he had still to convince himself that, when it came to it, he could betray the Crown to which he had sworn unswerving allegiance. He returned his thoughts to Ylena. "Will you allow me to take him to his home?"

"You would do this for me?"

"Surely. You have suffered enough."

She considered his offer. "I would appreciate it but I will need you to tell the Duke and his family that I will travel to Felrawthy as soon as I can." Her voice turned hard. "We will mourn together and then we will make plans to make Celimus pay."

Wyl left it alone, as much as he wanted to caution her. "Good. Now, about Argorn."

"Yes?"

"I would prefer if you don't return immediately," Wyl counseled, expecting a harsh reaction.

It was not forthcoming. She spoke calmly. "Celimus will follow . . . is that your suspicion?"

He nodded, impressed that she was, in spite of her weak and still addled state, able to follow the train of his thought. "Once we're discovered gone I cannot imagine he will just shrug his shoulders. Our sneaking out of Stoneheart will confirm that Romen Koreldy is a traitor to him. We can easily argue that you were forced to come with me but your life means nothing to him. Yes, I think he might follow the obvious trail to Argorn but it's my intention that it will be a cold one."

"Where then do you suggest?"

Once again Wyl was grateful for the glimpses of Romen's memory that remained. "There's a little-known monastery at Rittylworth."

"Ah, yes, I recall you mentioned it to Jorn."

"Hmm, I wish I hadn't, to tell the truth. The fewer people who know the better."

"For how long would I remain there?" Ylena asked evenly. Wyl was proud of her composure.

"Long enough for your recall of recent events to dim, little one," he said.

She looked up at him strangely.

"Is something wrong?" he asked.

Ylena shook her head as though clearing it of a bad thought. "Yes . . . well, no. That was Wyl's pet name for me. He always called me 'little one.' " She smiled sadly. "After our father died I used to climb into Wyl's bed and he'd hug me tight and tell me not to cry. And then he'd spin me great tales of how I would be the most beautiful maiden in all of Stoneheart, with one of its towers all to myself." Ylena choked back a quiet sob.

Wyl wanted to bite his own tongue out. "The monks will be ever kind to you at Rittylworth, I promise," he said, not that he could know this for sure. All he could pull from Romen's mind was the name of the monastery—none of its inhabitants, though—so it was surprising this was where he felt inclined to flee. Fortunately he knew how to find Rittylworth itself. "Four to five moons perhaps and then we can bring you to Argorn. By then I will have organized proper protection for you as well," he added.

"Your plan is wise, Romen. I will do as you suggest, thank you."

He breathed out with relief.

"And you?" she said, unexpectedly. "Where will you go?"

"Back to Briavel. There is unfinished business there but first I must find a seer."

Ylena actually laughed. "Why?"

"Oh, just call me superstitious. We all are in my family," he lied.

Ylena managed to make such good distance through the night that they reached Farnswyth in the early hours of the next day. They took a room at its least expensive inn in order to remain as anonymous as possible in the relatively small village. Wyl realized that Romen had been a man who could fit into most situations—as comfortable around royalty as he was simple folk—when he took so easily to swapping ribald jests with a pedlar who was treating himself to a night in a bed at the Ship Inn. It was not an especially clean establishment but Ylena did not make comment. She moved swiftly up to their airless room and threw open the small window; her only request was for fresh water in the jug.

They slept for several hours and, after eating heartily of a surprisingly delicious lamb and potato stew, Ylena returned upstairs to rest again while Wyl headed out to buy horses. His choice was limited but he was not looking for quality animals. Right now he needed two serviceable nags who would get them to Rittylworth. He stocked up on food and water too, explaining to Ylena when he returned to the inn that he had no intention of risking being seen between this village and Rittylworth. This was usually a three-day ride but probably twice that if they did indeed go across country.

"This is where I intend that our trail will go cold," he told Ylena. "I can't be sure that tongues will not wag in this place if they are threatened with a pair of pincers," he added grimly. "We are not so forgettable, I'm afraid."

Ylena made no protest and Wyl felt once again proud of his sister as she resolutely climbed upon her dun-colored horse and followed his lead.

Wyl knew he was looking for something, a landmark of

some kind, and hoped his sense of Romen was leading him correctly. Several hours' brisk trotting from Farnswyth he found a well-concealed path. It was little more than a deer track but he instinctively knew this was what he had been searching for. Once they were shielded by the undergrowth, he stopped the horses and returned to the main road. Using a thin branch of leaves, he deliberately moved back a hundred paces or so, sweeping away their prints. Whatever new hoofprints came down that road would now predictably continue on to the next major town of Renkyn and lead any followers astray, while they would now swing northwest. He even took the precaution of bending a pair of saplings in front of the tiny pathway. It would not fool an experienced tracker but in poor light it was a reasonably effective concealment.

As it turned out, they spent six uneventful and tranquil days traveling mostly across country, avoiding humanity as much as possible. It was a blessing for Ylena, who was not easily reemerging from the darkness of her mind into the sunlight of Morgravia's spring. She certainly smiled more often and conversations lengthened but then Wyl knew how much she used to smile and talk. The old Ylena had been lost on that terrible day of blood and death. They ate sparingly but well, supplementing their supplies with whatever nuts and wild fruits they could gather.

Wyl realized one late afternoon that Romen was in fact as deadly with a knife as he had been warned when the mercenary was alive. He found the knife in the bottom of their sack and once again thanked the lucky stars that had guided Jorn to them. A rabbit was soon roasting over their campfire after a swift and accurate flick of the blade.

On the seventh afternoon Wyl trusted what was left to him of Romen and reemerged onto a road. This was not so frequently used as the road to Renkyn but he felt instantly familiar with it. They followed it for another four miles or so and as they crested a small hill they looked down into a picturesque valley in which nestled a series of squat stone buildings set some distance apart from what appeared to be a village. Ylena squinted to get a better look at the small houses dotted here and there.

"That's Rittylworth," he said, relieved.

"It is a serene place," Ylena admitted.

"Somewhere for you to enjoy some peace, my lady."

She nodded and they moved on. Monks busy tending the gardens around the monastery straightened their backs from their toil. Someone waved and one, they noticed, yelled something and then disappeared into the building. He returned dragging an older man, and a broad smile stretched across Romen's face.

"Someone you know?" Ylena asked.

"Er . . . yes," Wyl replied, confused. Romen obviously knew and liked this man but he could not dig the old monk's name from his host's memory.

The monk grinned back, clearly pleased when they walked their horses into the compound. "I knew you would return one day, Romen Koreldy."

Romen jumped down and the men embraced. "It's good to be back," he said carefully.

"Brother Jakub promised we'd not seen the last of you, Romen," a breathless young man said.

Jakub! Wyl thought, silently thanking the enthusiastic young monk for giving him the name he sought. "Jakub, I want you to meet someone very precious to me." He helped Ylena down from her horse. "This is the Lady Ylena Thirsk of Argorn." Wyl deliberately said nothing of her being Lady Donal just yet. Ylena either did not notice or she trusted him to make whatever decisions were required.

"Welcome, my lady," Brother Jakub said, bowing along with all the other monks.

Ylena curtsied. "Thank you, brothers."

The young monk who had first spotted them offered to take their horses. "I see they haven't shaved your pate yet then," Wyl said, desperately trying to uncover names and why these people were special to Romen. It was of no use. Romen's memory was too clouded now.

"Not long now," the young man grinned. "I'm counting the days."

"Pil will be ordained in four months. He deserves it," Jakub said gently with an indulgent smile that Wyl seemed to recognize.

"Come, let us offer you some refreshment," Jakub said, taking Ylena's arm.

"I think what my lady would appreciate most of all is a bath," Romen suggested.

"Of course!" Jakub looked chastened that he hadn't thought of that when they clearly had dust on their faces from days on the road. He introduced Ylena to a young lad, asking that she follow him and assuring her of privacy. "We will freshen your traveling clothes, my lady, and then perhaps later you may care to join us for a hearty meal."

Ylena could not help herself. She kissed the older man's cheek and her thanks were sincere.

Wyl grinned at her. "Enjoy. See you very soon, little one."

"Thank you for this, Romen . . . for all that you've done." She kissed him too and Wyl had to stop himself from hugging her back.

Ylena left with the eager Pil trailing her and the youngster, and Wyl turned to Jakub. "I need your help," was all he said. Directness was best here, he figured.

"I suspected as much. Come, let's walk."

Wyl found himself guided to a beautiful herb garden arranged in concentric circles with a sundial at its heart. As he and Jakub settled themselves on a bench beneath a huge old lemon tree, a tray with a jug and mugs was delivered. Its bearer left without a word.

"Our latest vintage is superb, Romen. See for yourself," Jakub said, handing Wyl a cup.

They drank in companionable silence for a few moments and Wyl appreciated not only the delicious wine but the chance to gather his thoughts, although his nerves were on edge. He prayed to Shar to guide him now. What was left of Romen's recall was yielding little to him of this place, except its intense familiarity.

"She has the look of one who has suffered terribly," Jakub finally said.

He heard Romen sigh. "Too much and too recently," Wyl admitted.

"At whose hands?"

"At his majesty's pleasure. The new King."

"I see. And how are you involved with him?"

"A long story, Jakub. Suffice to say if we meet again, we'll be holding blades at each other's throats."

"Ah. And how is the Lady Ylena involved in this intrigue?"

"She is the sister of someone who begged me to help her as he died. He is a man I respected."

The family name of Ylena suddenly fell into place in Jakub's mind.

"This is the sister of Wyl Thirsk?" He spoke with some awe.

Wyl nodded sadly. "Fergys Thirsk would turn in his grave if he knew of what she has suffered at the hands of the Morgravian Crown."

"And you can't tell me more?"

Wyl decided to trust the old monk. "Only that we carry a sack and in it is the head of Ylena's recent husband, Captain Alyd Donal."

"Of Felrawthy?" he said, eyes wide.

Again Wyl nodded. "I need you to keep it for me. Have it preserved. One day I'll come back and claim it . . . do the right thing. You must never reveal to Ylena that the head is still here. She believes I'm taking it directly to his ancestral home. I can't, of course—the Duke would immediately rise up. I cannot risk that . . . not yet."

"Romen, what has occurred?" Jakub whispered.

Wyl felt suddenly guilty for bringing his troubles to this peaceful place. Already he had told Jakub enough to incriminate him should Celimus trace them to Rittylworth. He hoped he had covered their tracks well enough. "Murder, deceit, betrayal. Celimus will throw Morgravia into perilous times. He chases the crown of Briavel, and pays lip service to marriage with Queen Valentyna, but a toad has more sincerity than this newly crowned King." Wyl stopped for fear of saying too much.

"And you and Ylena?"

Wyl looked at Jakub, surprised, and then he understood. "Friends only. My bond is with the brother."

"A brother and sister. Are you seeking redemption, Romen?"

"No!" Wyl said, far too abruptly, wondering at his own vehemence and what was couched in Jakub's words.

"You protest too strongly. There is no shame in it, my son. Shar will bless you for it."

Wyl was too confused to pursue this conversation that suggested secrets from Romen's past. He should find out but in trying he might also reveal himself to be an impostor. It was too dangerous. "I gave a blood promise, Jakub. She is in mortal danger."

"What is it you wish of us?" the older man asked, sensibly leaving alone whatever topic underpinned his previous comments.

"Your protection. No one knows we are here—well, only one but he is a mere valet. I have covered our tracks well. Our trail goes cold at Farnswyth and none of the villagers of Rittylworth have seen us."

"We offer it gladly to the Lady Ylena. Does she know?"

"That she will remain here for a while? Yes. I know she will be happy and she does understand the danger of returning to Argorn. I have already counseled her on this. She needs time to recover from the atrocities she has experienced. Beware, Jakub, there are moments when she strikes me as unstable. Traveling with her, I saw flashes of more than just anger at what she has been through." He could hardly say he was so familiar with Ylena that he could tell something had changed deep at her core. Instead he had to rely on Jakub accepting his friend's sensitive intuition. "I sense she could unravel entirely if she suffers further shock. She needs to be protected—from all stresses, not just the King."

The old man nodded as if to say it would be done. "And you, Romen. Where now for you?"

"I am chasing down an old woman I met recently at Pearlis, a fairground fortune teller. I have a message for her from her family," Wyl lied. He did not want to share his plan to travel to Briavel; the old monk would not approve. He moved on hurriedly, hating himself for being so unfaithful to this good man. "Then Felrawthy to return Captain Donal to his family—although I cannot predict when that will be."

Jakub's rheumy eyes studied Romen's and Wyl squirmed under the scrutiny. If only he knew more of Romen's background. Instead Wyl just nodded. "I will send word."

"As you wish," Jakub said. "Just remember, my boy, you cannot outrun your demons. They will catch you. Best face them."

Wyl was astounded by this comment and could do little more than reach for his cup and swallow a deep draught.

"What's different about you?" Jakub wondered aloud.

"More gray hairs?" Wyl offered, just a little too quickly.

The old man sensibly held his tongue, though his eyes, expressive as always, said plenty. "We will preserve and keep the head in the secret grotto beneath the monastery, which I'm sure you remember," he said and winked. Wyl had no idea what the innuendo meant. "It will be safe."

19

FYNCH AND KNAVE MADE IT BACK TO BRIAVEL ON FOOT, AFTER several days of traveling. The horse had gone lame not far from Sharptyn across the border. Fynch had left the majority of the money Romen had given him with his sister, but the small portion he carried with him allowed him to pay the stableman at the village to take care of the horse until he could return for it. Fynch had no idea when that might be but he was not prepared to sell the beast, for it had been a gift from Valentyna. To avoid any questions about why a commonfolk child should be riding a horse and carrying a purse, Fynch told the stableman that he was taking the beast back to Briavel for a merchant and the coin had been provided for the horse's care. The man had shrugged, uninterested, merely handing over the bronze disk he would need to reclaim the horse.

A family of tinkers gave the boy and his dog a ride out of Sharptyn, but Fynch could tell that Knave made his hosts nervous and after half a day's ride he had thanked them and struck out on foot into open country.

The morning they arrived, Valentyna was on the battlements and speaking with Liryk, head of the Briavellian Guard—a good man, loyal to her father. The soldier inwardly marveled at the Queen's composure and once again considered how unlike most women she was. It did not seem to matter to her that at this moment her hair was being torn from whatever clasp was supposed to hold it back and was now whipping about her face. He recalled his fears for her, which he now realized were unfounded. Valentyna was self-assured and comfortable in her role. He had to remind himself that she had been roaming around the palace battlements since she was old enough to talk and, since the incident in Tallinor when Magnus's son had broken her doll, had preferred the games of men rather than the more genteel pursuits expected of women.

He was not alone in his admiration. All of the Guard were in awe of how well she masked her grief. Everyone, not just in the castle, but in Briavel itself, knew how Valor had doted on his daughter . . . and likewise how she had revered her father. She was every bit a worthy successor despite not being a son. In fact most people forgot she was a woman until she attended formal events where she was forced to take on a more gracious appearance. Then she became breathtaking—a far cry from the tomboy they were used to. And now she was their Queen and Liryk wondered whose duty it might be to remind her that the sovereign was to be protected at all costs. She would no longer enjoy the freedom of riding the moors, disappearing on hunting trips, spending nights in the woods.

He heard the cry go up from the watchtower and waited for news. The runner came soon enough. Liryk excused himself from the Queen.

Returning, he smiled. "The boy and his dog are back, your majesty."

"Fynch!" she exclaimed and turned to leave. "Excuse me, Liryk. Perhaps we could finish our discussion later?"

He bowed his agreement and Valentyna departed, issuing orders that the visitors were to be brought to her immediately at the Bridge—a small walkway between two of Werryl's shorter towers. It had been one of Valentyna's favorite haunts as a child because there she could hide from her nursemaids and later her tutors, as well as anyone else who attempted to force womanly pastimes upon her. It was still a special place for her now. A haven where she could cast her thoughts aloud to the wind.

"Your majesty!" said a familiar voice and she saw Fynch coming toward her, although Knave was faster and at her heels within a bound or two, stretching up to lick her gleefully.

"You wretch, Knave," she said, laughing and wiping away his salutation.

Fynch was more reserved in his greeting but Valentyna was having none of it—they had been through much together. As soon as he was done bowing, she scooped the little boy into her arms and hugged him fiercely.

"I didn't know if you'd return to me. I've been so worried for you."

"No need. Not with Knave close by, your majesty. Did it all go all right?" he ventured awkwardly.

Valentyna knew he referred to her father's burial. "I got through it. It was very private for good reason, which helped." She took his hand. "Sit with me at this bench and tell me everything."

His face became serious. "No good news, majesty."

"Nevertheless, I must know all that you do."

He told her everything, watching her become crestfallen and then anxious as his story drew to a close.

"So you were right; he did not betray us and now he's dead," she said, looking out across the moors.

Fynch shook his head. "I never doubted it, majesty. Wyl Thirsk stayed true to the end. He and the mercenary, Romen Koreldy, fought side by side to protect your father."

Her eyes watered at the mention but she refused to cry any more over her situation. The King was dead. No tears would bring him back. She was now the Queen and she would not let Briavel down. Crying had no place in her life.

"And you trust this Koreldy?"

Fynch shrugged. "I . . . I don't know what to think, your majesty. I am trying to work only with the facts. He carried Wyl's body back to Morgravia in what was clearly open defiance of Celimus. I have no doubt he walked back into direct danger by returning to Morgravia and I can only wonder at how he survived. He assured me he told enough of the Legion his story so that Thirsk's name could not be darkened by any of Celimus's lies. I saw Wyl's sister with my own eyes. She was willingly in the care of Romen." He paused and then added carefully, "But more than anything, your majesty, I trust Knave."

She turned from looking out toward the moors to stare at the boy beside her. Her brow creased in query.

Fynch continued. "You know how I've told you about Knave's strange behavior towards others."

She nodded.

He took a deep breath. "Well, I now truly believe that this dog only trusts those who were true to Wyl."

Valentyna wanted to smile; she felt the urge to ruffle the lad's hair and tell him it was all in his imagination. But something stopped her. Something about Fynch forced her to pay attention and treat him as one should an adult. His ability to gather and interpret information had astounded her in their brief time together. And it was Fynch who had kept her from falling apart in those early hours. He had acted with a maturity beyond his years, standing up to her to make her realize the danger should she rush back to the palace before her safety could be assured. This little boy, a Morgravian no less, had gone to the palace alone to discover whether it was safe for her to return, and had found the courage to face her men—who, no doubt, had been disbelieving and perhaps even derisive of his claim that he had Valentyna in a secure place. She recalled now how he had found her again, this time with her guards in tow, and urged her to come out of hiding. He had held her hand as she—Queen now—emerged to face her Commander, Liryk, and counseled her to remain strong despite her grief. "Briavel needs to see its Queen as a tower, even though she might feel like crumbling," he had whispered. She had not forgotten those brief yet inspirational words of encouragement.

Everything about him was brave and, yes, serious. One could hardly treat him as the child he surely was when faced with the knowledge of all that he had personally done to help Wyl and then herself. No, she would not ruffle his hair or speak down to him.

She noticed he was watching her reaction. "Go on, Fynch."

He shrugged again. "It's hard to explain, your majesty."

"Try," she encouraged.

"Knave is possessed of magic—I no longer suspect it, I know it!" he blurted out. "That's my way of explaining it." She had not expected this and fought to hide the look of surprise on her face. He continued. "I told you once how Wyl's eyes changed color at the witch-burning."

She nodded. Valentyna could still hardly imagine it, for Briavel had outlawed witch-burnings so long ago.

"I saw it occur," he said gravely. "And so did one other person but he is now dead, according to Romen. I am the only living witness."

"So what are you telling me?" Valentyna felt frustrated by the mystery.

"From the moment of Myrren's death when she closed her ill-matched eyes and Wyl opened his to reveal the same, I believe Knave became connected to Wyl and those he loved in a way that is powerful . . . far more than friendship."

She did not even want to think beyond hearing the word "magic" spoken. It just sounded too far-fetched. "And how do you relate this to Koreldy?"

"I don't. I'm baffled by it because Knave treated Romen

in the same way he would Wyl. In fact—and I know you'll think I am imagining this—but Romen greeted Knave using the same mannerisms that Wyl used to."

She made a deprecating sound. "I think you may be stretching now, Fynch." Valentyna could not help her skepticism, but when she glanced toward Knave, the dog gazed back with such unnerving intensity it made her look away.

"Possibly," Fynch said a little sadly. "But I can't explain why or how Romen Koreldy—a stranger, a mercenary, a man hired to murder the General—would know Wyl's dog." Fynch began to tick things off aloud now as his mind began to organize the facts. "When we entered the room, he yelled out the dog's name. How would he know it? He had never seen Knave before. And, more to the point, if Knave is hostile to anyone who Wyl did not care about, then why would Knave even tolerate someone who might threaten Wyl's life, let alone lick him and roll over for him? The truth is, your majesty, I have witnessed Knave growl at people who are known and not necessarily disliked by Wyl."

He looked up, questions written on his serious little face, but Valentyna had no answers for him. In fact, she felt disturbed that he was asking her to base all trust, from here on, on the notions of a dog.

"Fynch . . ."

"No, listen to me, your majesty," he said, not intending to be rude. She let it pass, caught up in what he might say next. "There is something strange going on here. I can't put my finger on it but every bit of me senses that a curiosity has occurred—something that defies logic and all that we know. I can't give you a proper reason but I sincerely believe we must trust Romen Koreldy and I know that he will not do you harm. He made a blood promise to Wyl Thirsk to protect you. I feel Romen has somehow"—Fynch rubbed his hands through his hair distractedly as he tried to search for the right words—"that he has somehow taken on Wyl's duties . . . desires . . . I don't know, your majesty. It's as though Wyl Thirsk is still with us."

There, it was said.

Valentyna was lost for words. She looked back at Knave and once again it was as though the dog was seeing through her, into her, touching her thoughts. She felt riveted by his intense gaze and somehow knew it would not release her until she agreed.

Finally she nodded. "All right, Fynch. I know *you* mean me no harm—so I trust you. I trusted Wyl and I know Knave somehow protects us both. I can't explain it either. Shar help us, but we will put our trust in Romen Koreldy."

Valentyna saw the brave little boy's body relax and at that moment Knave suddenly stepped up, placed his paws on her shoulders, and looked into her eyes. Then he was down on all fours and sniffing around like any other dog, as though nothing had passed between them.

"That dog *is* very strange."

"He knows more than we do, majesty. Trust him."

"Anything else you need to tell me?" she said, wanting to move on from this disturbing conversation.

"Yes," he said, delving into a small bag. "Romen sent you this letter. He said it would help explain a few things."

She took it, happy to have something tangible from the mysterious Koreldy. She would read it later in private. "And what will you do now?" she asked, hoping to hear that he would stay.

"I am not going back to Morgravia, your majesty, unless duty to you calls for it. If you will accept me, I will serve you in any way you see fit."

She hugged him. "Fynch, I wouldn't part with you for anything. You are an honorary Briavellian from today."

He beamed, a rare grin on his face.

"In fact I must grant a special role to you. I shall make you the Queen's spy," she said, arching her eyebrows, hoping to hang on to that so infrequent smile of his.

Fynch liked the sound of this. "No more dropholes then, majesty."

"No more cleaning them, anyway," she replied conspiratorially. "Now, whenever my heart feels this glad I like to feast. Come, let's get you refreshed and then we shall share a meal together and I can tell you all that has been happening since you left. If you are to be the Queen's spy, you must have all the facts."

It was several hours later that the two of them, followed by Knave, stretched their legs by going out to visit another of Valentyna's newborn foals. Over some of the best food he had ever been presented with, Fynch had learned the true depth of his Queen's grief at her father being murdered and how after a hasty and private coronation ceremony she had ridden alone through the streets of Werryl so her people could share her sorrow and understand that she was so very alone now and needed their support.

It was an inspired decision by Valentyna to do this against her advisors' wishes. And as a result, a new sense of patriotism was burning fiercely in Briavel. The people would stand behind their Queen and seek revenge for the outrage of their King's death.

Valentyna had also deliberately fired and then fanned the rumor that the killers were mercenaries only posing as Morgravian. She had decided to play Celimus at his own game. Although going to war had been her initial reaction, she had changed her mind when her blood rage at her father's death had calmed and she had begun to think clearly. The blame for Valor's death had been deflected from Morgravia, so her own people would not expect her to seek vengeance on the neighboring realm. She had encouraged her people's sense of patriotism and now she hoped to direct it toward supporting her. A Queen had never ruled in Briavel. She needed them to trust her, to support her claim to the throne and her right to rule. All of this aside, her army was not yet strong enough to fight, and she herself not experienced enough . . . but that time would come. No, war would *not* be her first choice—but cunning was.

Much later that night she remembered the letter from Romen Koreldy. Sitting by a small fire in her chambers, she broke the seal. Valentyna permitted herself some tears as Romen Koreldy spoke of the final minutes of her father's life and how he and Wyl Thirsk had fended off the attackers to protect Valor.

He told her how bravely her father had died, his last words for her, and that just before Wyl had succumbed to his wounds, he had wrung a blood oath from Romen to swear fealty to Briavel and protect its Queen against Celimus. Romen assured Valentyna that he would come but that she was to burn this missive in the meantime. He promised his help . . . and his blade. And in the firmest of language he implored her to keep Fynch and Knave by her side.

There it was again. This curiosity about the black dog. Well, Knave was nothing if not protective of her, she thought, looking down by her feet where he now lay. He opened an eye to look at her as though sensing her scrutiny. She would do as Romen asked and she would also wait for him. He asked her to make no direct moves and show no aggression. She was pleased to note they were of the same mind.

. . . Don't play into the hands of Celimus by responding— fend off any attempts at contact with the message that you are grieving. Let your father's body cool in peace and his memory fade slightly while you build your loyalties about you. I will come soon—I am yours to command, my Queen. My loyalty to you will never waver. In the meantime I give you a special gift. I give you the dog Knave, who will be true to you. Trust him alone and his faithful companion, Fynch. They will protect you.

Be brave, beautiful Valentyna. Yours, Romen Koreldy.

She was shocked at his final words. How could he know what she looked like? They had not met. She dismissed her query as pure vanity on her part—no doubt Fynch had been overly descriptive of her to this Koreldy fellow. Well, she could do the same. She would rely on Fynch's brilliant skills of observation to describe him to her tomorrow.

That aside, she felt comforted by his letter—the tone was courteous but there was strength in it. This was surely a leader of men conspiring with her. Valentyna threw the letter into the fire as instructed, then drifted into a doze as she watching the parchment burn, her hopes surging in tandem with the bright glow of the flames.

By the time she woke, Knave had disappeared.

20

FOR THE FIRST TIME IN MANY DAYS WYL FELT HIS SPIRITS LIFT. Saying farewell to Ylena had not been as difficult as he had imagined. She seemed peaceful at the monastery and Brother Jakub had seen to it that her accommodation was cozy if not elegant and in an especially quiet wing. Her rooms, although small, were airy and Jakub had deliberately chosen those that overlooked the orchard and the hills in the distance. She had not cried when Wyl said goodbye but she had hugged Romen hard and told him to hurry back. Ylena had pressed her brooch, the one Wyl had given her as a present, into his hand.

"It will bring you luck," she had said.

As he rode away he tried to put aside the nagging thought that the youngster, Jorn, might yet undo his plans by revealing Ylena's whereabouts. He worried at the possible repercussions, not only for his sister but for these good men who cared for her. And still he knew he had made a sound decision in bringing her here first where she might recover among kind strangers who understood to keep a distance. Too much familiarity, Jakub had agreed, could bring her back to herself too quickly and the memory of her suffering might be too vivid.

"Burying the reality is her way of defending herself against the pain. We can't all be heroic like you and ride off into more danger after such adversity," Jakub had said carefully.

Wyl did not understand what was couched in that final statement but he was determined to get to the bottom of whatever it was that sat between him and Jakub. He suspected it had something to do with the reason Romen Koreldy had left Grenadyn and turned to the dangerous life of a mercenary but there were no clues left for him within Romen.

Jakub had insisted on swapping the nag for a decent horse—a lovely roan—and, despite his hot protestations, the old man had finally agreed to accept some money from his friend, which he insisted could only be taken as a donation. Wyl had readily agreed and loved the feel of the horse beneath him. It seemed an age since he had ridden an animal of such quality and yet he realized that it had only really been a matter of days. How quickly one's life can change, he thought, and how strange his had become in that short time.

He had searched his mind long and hard for any clues to the old woman's whereabouts and it had only come to him very recently that she had mentioned hailing from the north. Even if it turned out that she had not returned home, it was worth trying; he could comb the towns and villages of the region, for they were few and far between that close to the Razor Mountains.

He urged the horse into a steady canter and once again headed across country to avoid being sighted. Wyl was well stocked and his intention was to travel for several days keeping the woods to his left and then come out into a town called Orkyld, known for its specific talent for crafting swords and knives. Master craftsmen from around the realm considered it the high altar of their trade and only the very best were picked to do their apprenticeships at Orkyld itself. It took him almost four days and in the end he had to carefully walk the horse into Orkyld as it had taken a stone into its shoe two miles back.

He paid for a room at the Old Yew Inn and was grateful that this part of the realm was used to strangers. No one paid him a second glance and the roan was cared for immediately. He treated himself to a jug of ale and several roasted pigeons before finding the local baths, where he gave himself a second treat of a leisurely dip. For those who could afford such luxury, a "smoothing" could be enjoyed for just a few more royals. He was sorely tempted because his muscles protested from being in the saddle so much. Wyl promised Romen's body that luxury soon enough.

Right now he needed weaponry and a new pair of stout boots. The boots came first and as an afterthought he added a warm shirt and cloak to his list. The north could be very cold even at this time of the year.

Wyl's inquiries led him to a master craftsman called Wevyr, who was supposedly one of the three most talented artisans in Orkyld. He recalled his father mentioning this man's name but had never met him. At Wevyr's workrooms twenty or so young men were diligently applying their skills to blades of all shapes and sizes. One stopped his work and moved to the counter.

"Yes, sir?"

"I'd like to buy a sword," Wyl replied.

"I shall fetch Master Lerd for you, sir. May I give him your name please?"

"It's Koreldy," Wyl replied.

He waited while the youngster disappeared into a set of rooms beyond the main workroom. Another man reappeared as the first fellow returned to his seat.

"Are you Romen Koreldy, sir?" this one asked.

"I am."

"In that case, follow me, please," he said, turning.

"Why?" Wyl asked in Romen's casual way. It amazed him how Koreldy could do this without giving offense.

"It's Master Wevyr, sir, he prefers to take care of his clients in his private room."

"Thank you," he said, impressed, and followed.

The man took him into a small yet light-filled room where a very old man was inspecting various weapons.

"Hello, Romen," he greeted him, not looking up from his work.

Wyl nodded even though it wouldn't be noticed. "Wevyr."

"Don't tell me you've lost them?"

"Er . . . no," Wyl said, carefully. He presumed they were talking about weapons. He took the risk. "I had to give them up at a round of cards."

"Shar's Balls, man. You paid a fortune for those!" the master exclaimed, looking up through one huge eyeglass attached to a band around his head.

Wyl shrugged. "It was for high stakes."

"You're a fool!"

He could see this man was not impressed by Romen's noble rank or purse. "I'm sorry," he replied. "It won't happen again."

"No, it won't, because you're not getting any of my precious weapons again."

"Oh, come on, Wevyr. Yours are the only blades that kill neatly," he said, grinning.

It did not work for him. The old man seemed genuinely miffed. "I have crafted blades all of my life for the likes of the Thirsks of Argorn. Armyn Thirsk killed three hundred and seventy Briavellians in his time with one of my swords and Fergys Thirsk admitted the sword I made him thirty years ago needed sharpening only twice in its lifetime." He coughed after his angry outburst.

Wyl was stunned by the mention of his family name. He had admired his father's sword on countless occasions and, as was the Thirsk way, the Generals were buried with their blades. When he had lost his father he was too young to know important things like where to get the best swords crafted. Gueryn had held all of that information. Hearing his father's name spoken aloud moved him, as did thinking of Gueryn, and he began to consider how he might be able to find out about his friend's fate in the Razors.

He came out of his sorrowful thoughts. "Pardon?"

"I said, are you all right, Koreldy?"

Wyl took a breath. "Yes, apologies. You mentioning Thirsk made me think of the loss to the kingdom."

The old man sighed and his voice softened. "Indeed, a great loss it is. I hear a rumor that the son is dead to us too. Is this true?"

Wyl nodded. "I was in Pearlis for the funeral."

"A very sad business. The son should never have followed his father to the grave so soon. I did not even have a chance to forge a blade for him. Did you learn how it happened?"

"Treachery, I'm told." Wyl could not help himself.

"Oh? Whose?"

"They say Celimus was jealous of him—wanted him dead."

Wevyr looked horror-struck. "Hush, man! Walls have ears even in this remote town."

"Sorry. It's what I heard."

"I don't want to know any more," Wevyr said, holding up his hand. "I am too old for intrigues. What is it you require?"

Wyl grinned. "A sword and two knives?"

"Come with me."

The old man took off his eyepiece and walked around his work table to a display cabinet. He slowly unlocked it before reverently picking up a sword that had unique markings engraved on the blade itself as well as the hilt. It was magnificent.

"My finest ever," he said, presenting it.

"And you'd let me have it?" Wyl said, incredulous.

The man made a face. "There are very few swordsmen I'd allow to even hold this beautiful weapon, Romen." Then he scowled, voice scathing. "You are fortunate that you wield a blade with such exquisite finesse that you deserve something as fine as this." He poked Romen Koreldy in the chest for good measure and his humor was not improved by the wide grin that greeted his efforts.

"Thank you." Wyl took the handsome blade and weighted it. The balance was perfect. It was as if the sword had its own momentum. "May I?" he asked, gesturing toward the open door, which led to a courtyard.

"Of course. There are matching knives."

"Bring them," Wyl said, marveling at the sword's lightness and grace in his grip.

Outside he went through some of his old practice routines and felt Romen's skills intruding, guiding his hand to new movements, and through it all the blade glided effortlessly through the air. As the sunlight hit the sword, it glinted blue, which in itself Wyl found fascinating.

"Did you make this especially for someone?" he asked Wevyr, who had arrived carrying the pair of knives.

"Yes. For me. It is the sum of my training and experience—my life's work, you could say."

"You know I want it," Wyl admitted.

"It is yours. The price is exorbitant, of course."

"Naturally," Wyl said, amused. He exchanged the sword for the pair of knives.

Wevyr looked towards a hessian dummy hanging fifteen or so paces ahead of them. "Try them," he said.

Before he even threw, Wyl knew they would land true. Romen's skill with throwing blades was already obvious to him but the knives themselves were as perfect as their larger counterpart and they moved sweetly through the air, one landing in the dummy's face, the other in the gut. He had not even taken aim but spun on a heel and threw from instinct.

"If you lose these, Romen Koreldy, don't ever come to Orkyld again."

With his purse significantly lighter, Wyl felt renewed at the feel of the sword by his thigh. He had purchased a special crossover body belt recommended by Wevyr for the knives. The clever part of this soft, malleable belt was that it was designed to be worn inside the shirt so the knives could be concealed. He could lift the blades from their holder in the blink of an eye and, although Wyl knew he probably did not need to, he was looking forward to practicing with them in the woods behind Orkyld.

Wyl had changed into his new shirt and was getting used to the feel of the belt next to his skin. He was beginning to feel comfortable yet something nagged at him through the evening, which he spent leisurely in the common room of the Old Yew Inn. He knew the thought was there. His keen soldier's sense combined with Romen's naturally suspicious nature tried to make him sit up and take notice of it. The trouble was he was feeling especially relaxed on this night as a half-decent musician sang a lament in one corner and the kitchen served up his favorite dish of steamed fish. The vague notion of danger dissipated instantly when a particularly good-looking woman strode up and slapped him hard around the face.

"Romen Koreldy, you dare to sit at this table!"

Wyl rubbed the stinging mark of her hand and, with his mouth wide open, watched her flounce off, magnificent in her anger.

Other patrons laughed, enjoying the spectacle and his embarrassment.

Another girl sidled up to clear his table. "Arlyn is really cross this time, Romen," she warned.

"So I can see," he said, wondering what Romen could have done, although he could probably guess. "Can I make it up to her?"

"I don't know—how do you make it up to a woman who was preparing for her wedding?" asked the girl.

It was worse than Wyl had first guessed. "I can explain," he offered, feeling helpless.

"Not to me, Romen, to her!"

"Where can I find Arlyn later?"

The woman rested his dishes against her hip and said with no little exasperation, "Forgotten already?"

He sighed. "Life's been a bit hard for me lately—I just thought she might have—er—"

"No, nothing's changed. You'll still find her working her hands to the bone out the back."

Wyl nodded and thanked her although it did him little good. He needed to sober up and so decided to take some fresh air. *Perhaps I might find a place to buy Arlyn a gift as a peace offering.*

On the rare occasion his parents had had cross words, his father had always made the first move to reconciliation, usually with some beautiful item that he knew would please his wife and hopefully soften her toward his spoken apology. Wyl felt helpless at being held responsible for Romen's fault—all he could do was try to remedy the slight by making Arlyn a Thirsk-style apology. Also at the back of his mind was the notion that this excuse to meet with Arlyn and make his peace offering might give him an opportunity to learn more about the man whose body he walked in.

Wyl left the inn and strolled into Orkyld's main street. It was a busy enough town. Apart from its fame as a place to buy weaponry, it seemed to be a busy hub for people moving into the north. Walking without clear direction he began to consider how to make amends with Arlyn without finding himself trapped.

"Marriage! Shar's Wrath!" he murmured. It was the last complication he needed.

They had been careful. Jerico was not a man to take chances and following Koreldy had been challenging. The mercenary's trail had disappeared at Farnswyth and, although Jerico hated to do it, he split the men up into four groups. They were handpicked by him; all trusted cutthroats who would slit the jugulars of their own grandmothers if paid enough coin.

At Farnswyth he had briefed them all with care and then sent them off in different directions. He and two other men had traveled north. His only reason for this direction had been the small item of information he had gleaned from a conversation he had overheard between the King, who was then still a Prince, and Koreldy.

When the Prince's spies had first noted Koreldy arriving in Morgravia, he had been requested to meet with Celimus. It just happened that Jerico was attached to a network of spies that Celimus paid handsomely for information and, although Koreldy had not seen him, he had been present during their first meeting. Celimus had asked the mercenary directly about what he was doing in the realm. Koreldy had been guarded, had tried to laugh it off and hold on to the mystery, but the Prince had persisted and finally the mercenary had admitted he was escaping the clutch of a woman determined to marry him. Jerico recalled how Celimus had laughed at this.

It could have been a ruse but Koreldy's sour tone suggested otherwise. And so, with no other ideas to follow, he and his murderous companion had headed to Orkyld, where Koreldy had mentioned the scorned woman lived. Jerico's intense joy at spotting the mercenary walking into Orkyld with a lame horse held no bounds. He had even let out an inadvertent whoop of surprise before cupping his hands over his mouth. Koreldy had looked his way but the glance had understandably slid over him. They had never met, fortunately. A large part of Jerico's success in his trade was the fact that he was so ordinary-looking and thus forgettable. Not a single feature of his person would ever win comment. He was neither thin nor fat, tall nor short. His hair was sandy-colored and his face hardly handsome but then it was not especially ugly. His voice was low and unremarkable. But his mind was quick and he had no qualms about killing.

He had given over the day to observing Koreldy. A room at the Old Yew and a hearty meal of pigeon. Following him to the baths was easy enough and then to purchase garments. Jerico had then expertly shadowed him to the famous blademaker, Wevyr, but although he saw him enter the man's workrooms, he did not see him leave and after waiting what he considered was long enough, he made his furious way back to the inn, hoping he had not lost his prey.

The killer had been rewarded with the information that the man had recently returned. He had waited, toying with a jug of ale. His companion meanwhile kept a watch outside in case Koreldy decided again to take a back door out of the inn this time. Later Jerico surmised that obviously their quarry was not suspicious, for he had descended the stairs into the common room in the evening wearing a wide grin for the serving girls and a fine new sword. Jerico's companion had returned to sit beside him.

Jerico had admired the sword from a distance and promised himself the fine weapon as a special prize after killing Koreldy.

"He'd better not have spent too much of his gold on that sword," his companion had murmured, his back deliberately turned toward Jerico so they were not taken as friends.

Jerico had snickered. "I couldn't agree more, but remember there's only the three of us now to split the spoils."

"Shame we can't split that sword into three," the man grumbled.

Jerico smiled to himself; he had decided against mentioning to his companions that the King had offered to double the figure on Jerico's return to Pearlis, should he be successful in ridding Celimus of Koreldy. "I'll tell you what, you can take a bigger share of the gold he's carrying, as I have need of that sword."

The man had nodded. Jerico had returned to his ale and his observation of the mercenary. He spent the time considering whether to cut off Koreldy's ring finger while he was still alive so they could enjoy the screams or whether to do it after he was dispatched and silent. Jerico favored live torture and thus had begun to hatch his plan for capture when a voluptuous woman had appeared from the back of the inn and belted Koreldy hard enough that everyone heard the slap. He had noticed the angry words she muttered before her departure and then the low conversation between Koreldy and the other serving woman. Jerico had downed his cup of ale as Koreldy stood and righted his sword, and then he followed his prey out of the inn, giving a low whistle to the other of his companions.

They watched Koreldy now as he strolled off but were in no hurry. Jerico, ever cautious, heeded the fact that he had been present at the funeral feast for Wyl Thirsk. Just in case Koreldy had seen him, he suggested to his companion to go ahead of their victim while he brought up the rear.

"Any plan?" one of them asked.

"Play it by ear, although your talents might come in handy as a distraction. We're looking to catch him unawares in one of the side streets or better still an alley. And listen!" he warned. "It won't be done here. The woods will give us the cover—and privacy we need," he added.

His partner smiled grimly and set off, digging into his pockets for the distraction his companion had referred to.

Wyl was lost in his thoughts. He looked up and saw a man juggling wooden balls—at least seven of them—and the juggling was skilled enough to stop Wyl in his tracks to admire the performance.

He watched for a while and laughed when the man performed a small jig while still not disturbing the rhythm of the balls. It occurred to him that this fellow might know where the sideshow alley performers might be in the realm.

"You wouldn't happen to know where the fairground traders are right now?" Wyl asked. As he continued to juggle, the man screwed up his face in thought. Wyl pressed. "It's just that I met someone at the Morgravian royal tournament and have a message for her."

"Can't say I do, sir. I'm just a wandering performer. I follow my own path."

"Well, thanks anyway," Wyl said, tossing him a coin. He made to move on and then turned back. "Oh, by the way, where can I buy a nice trinket for a very angry lady at this time of night?"

The juggler expertly gathered in the wooden balls and a few passersby clapped as they walked on. He grinned at Wyl's dilemma. "I believe I might know just the place, sir. If you're prepared to pay a very small fee, I can take you there."

"Oh? What sort of place?"

"Would a silversmith suit, sir? My cousin crafts very pretty jewelry at his shop just down the back here. He'll give you a good price too—I'll see to it."

Wyl was tired. He felt uneasy about Arlyn but was it really that important to settle Romen's old scores? He decided it was, now that he was to all intents and purposes Romen Koreldy. Tongues wagged and if he was going to wear this body, this face, for the rest of his life, then he certainly did not want women around the kingdom hating him. He sighed.

"Yes, why not? Is it far?"

"Not at all," the juggler said with no little glee. "Just a minute or two. My, that's a fine sword, sir, that you carry . . ."

Jerico smirked as he overheard the juggler making trivial conversation, leading their prey like an innocent animal to slaughter.

The world went dark for Wyl soon after.

Wyl came back to consciousness abruptly but he was badly disoriented. It took him several moments to realize he was hanging upside down from a length of rope tied to a tree and that he had been beaten very effectively. He hurt everywhere. The mournful hoot from an owl told him few sensible people would be abroad in these woods at night. The burning sensation on his face led him to believe his captors had emptied their bladders in an attempt to revive him.

Obviously it had worked. He shook his head, noted that at least his arms were free, and tried to get a bearing on his surrounds. Not far away lay his scabbard and the blue sword. *Damn them! They're not getting that!* He felt at his chest and realized with a tingle of relief that they had not yet discovered the concealed knives. He marveled again at Wevyr's work—the knives were so slim and flat that he was not surprised his captors had not noticed them. He surreptitiously undid a button of his shirt so he could reach them.

The men turned.

"Time for some fun," the juggler said.

Jerico walked closer.

"I presume you already have my purse and I see you've claimed my sword," Wyl said in Romen's calm manner. "Is my life that important to you?"

"Not to us," Jerico replied.

Wyl felt a chill settle about him. So this was not about theft then. "To whom?"

Jerico grinned. "Far higher-ranked individuals. We're just the means to the end."

"Well then, whatever he is paying you I will triple," Wyl offered.

"No, Koreldy," Jerico said firmly. "I have made a point of doing business with care. I never double-cross a client I have made a bargain with. This policy has kept me alive."

"But not necessarily rich," Wyl answered, playing for time as his mind raced. Romen's instincts told him he had to get the three men a bit closer to him and to each other before he could risk a strike. But then even what was left of Romen reminded him that at best he could only cut himself down and take one of them out. At worst he could possibly injure or even kill one but remain hanging like a pig on a rope waiting for its throat to be slit.

The juggler laughed and walked forward. "How would you know, mercenary, what we are worth?"

"I don't," Wyl admitted.

"Well now," Jerico said, taking a dagger from his own belt. "There is this ugly business of having to cut off one of your fingers."

"Why?"

"The man who is paying for your death requires it."

"Well, I suppose it keeps you lowlifes honest."

Jerico stepped forward. "From one assassin to another, I take offense at the word 'lowlife.' "

The men were in range. He would go for the leader. No more time to think—at least he would die taking one of them with him.

The men were standing close enough that even dizzied and upside-down he felt confident of hitting one of them. In a smooth movement Wyl crossed his arms and lifted the two knives from their belt and, using the same momentum, hurled one toward the man he considered leader. At that same moment, out of the darkness leapt a huge shadow that enveloped the juggler, who went down screaming with terror.

Shocked, Wyl held his second knife close to his chest, ready for what might attack next. The gurgling sound of a man dying was blotted out by the deep, guttural sound of a beast ripping at flesh. He spun around again on the rope and could see Jerico lying still on the ground while his companion writhed in agony. And then he too went still very quickly. The beast gave chase after the third man, who senselessly ran deeper into the woods. Wyl heard a muffled scream before the woods became silent again.

"Knave?" Wyl asked into the dark fearfully and he flinched as the dog appeared at his side, his warm breath smelling of blood.

Wyl struggled upward, bending himself double to reach the rope that bound him and slashed with the knife. He fell in a heap and Knave loomed over him. For an instant he felt a thrill of alarm. This dog had just mauled two men to death. He could do the same to him, his still-jumbled mind thought. Instead Knave licked Wyl and sat down, a gentle whine of pleasure escaping from the dog's throat.

Wyl was trembling. He looked over at the dead bodies and back at the dog. Knave had saved his life, there was no question about this. *But where had he come from and how did he know where to find me?* He tried to stand and promptly fell over again. He had broken ribs, he realized. It added up that his attackers had enjoyed some fun with him—not that he could remember much.

Knave was rooting about in the undergrowth and returned now carrying a flask. Wyl had seen the treacherous juggler sipping from it and gratefully took a draught of what turned out to be strong liquor. He felt it burn all the way down his throat before its comforting warmth hit.

Knave regarded him intently.

"I gather Fynch is not with you," he commented and the dog lay down, putting his head on his paws. "Hmm, thought not. I have to presume he at least has obeyed instructions and remained with Valentyna, which is where you are going back to right now."

The dog growled and moved closer to his side.

Wyl searched the bodies in an attempt to discover who these men were. There were no clues, but he recognized one of them: Celimus's man! He was sure of it. He remembered catching sight of him at the funeral feast for his own true body.

And that probably explained the vague feeling of threat he had felt all day. He remembered now; he had sighted the killer this morning as he walked into Orkyld. A noise—a man yelping—had caught his attention but only for a moment.

That was it. Celimus had sent the killer after him. It was the King who wanted his finger. He looked down at his hands in reflex and noted his signet ring. It and the finger it sat on was probably what was required as proof of his death. Wyl growled to himself now, anger overtaking his fatigue. He would give Celimus something to consider.

Hauling himself to his feet, he reclaimed his sword and, ignoring the intense pain, in one powerful hack lopped off the head of Jerico, its tongue lolling out of the mouth. He pulled off the dead man's shirt and wrapped the head in it several times, hoping the blood would not show through too soon. Fortunately it was a black shirt and would hide the seepage for a while.

With disgust now he rolled the bodies into the bushes. Wolves or other scavengers would find them soon enough and that was fitting. He cared not. Wyl staggered from the woods carrying Jerico's head, which he had already decided would have special ironic significance for Celimus. He spent an hour trying to find a suitable container among the rubbish of the town and, when satisfied, he hid the box and its vile contents to be dispatched as soon as he could arrange it.

Only then did he collapse.

21

HIS TIME WHEN WYL REGAINED HIS SENSES HE WAS LYING IN A bed. At first he thought he was dreaming as memories of an ugly night returned. He touched the feather coverlet and it was real enough to convince him he was not imagining these comfortable surrounds, and the spicy fragrance that lingered around him definitely smacked of a woman. Its owner, familiar to him, suddenly leaned over.

"Don't hit me again, Arlyn," he croaked and smiled crookedly.

She gave a full-throated laugh this time. "I'm tempted, Romen. What in Shar's Name happened to you last night?"

"Long story. Would you believe me if I told you it all happened because of you?"

"No, because you are a liar, a cheat, and a low, good-for-nothing scoundrel whom I shall toss from my bed just as soon as your body can stand it."

He winced. "How bad?"

"The physic says you can't move for a couple of days at least."

"Then I am at your mercy," Wyl said, surprising himself. He liked women a lot yet he felt tongue-tied among them. He thought of Valentyna; the thrill of her touch and how his throat had closed up when she had turned her attention fully to him. And yet here he was in this woman's bed, acting the roguish flatterer using Romen's confidence.

"Mynk for those thoughts?" Arlyn said, squeezing out a rag into a small bowl of water. She smoothed the linen gently over his face, her expression suddenly tender.

"I was just contemplating how sorry I am," he said softly.

Arlyn paused in her ministrations and fixed him with her green gaze. "You hurt me so much."

Wyl reached over with Romen's large hand and cupped hers to his chest. "I know. I have a lot to explain."

"But not yet," she said, reaching for a cup and handing it to him. "Rest and heal are the physic's orders. Drink this."

He did so and made an expression of the worst sort of disgust.

"Sleep now," she said, a smile passing across her face.

"Arlyn," he said drowsily. "How did I get here?"

"A huge black dog dragged you to my doorstep," she said indignantly.

He started to laugh as he drifted away. "His name's Knave."

"It could be King Celimus for all I care," he heard her say as he lost his grip on the bright morning. "I've told him he stays out of this bedroom. He's outside."

"Thank you," he said and slept.

Two fierce needs woke Wyl. It was dusk now. He was starving but even more pressing than the desire of his belly was the desperation of his bladder. He would have to move fast or make a fool of himself in front of Arlyn. He scanned the room desperately looking for the chamber pot and, after finding it, dragged himself out of the bed. Arlyn must have heard him moving because she entered the room just as he finished.

"You shouldn't be up," she scolded.

He looked around. "It was urgent," he admitted sheepishly.

"Let me feed you and then we'll talk."

Arlyn's food was delicious and as Wyl ate he wanted to ask her questions but he knew he could not for fear of showing his ignorance. He had decided that Romen must have got himself trapped and no doubt did flee Arlyn's arms rather coldheartedly. The man's manner, his whole ease among people, suggested he was a womanizer. Wyl was the opposite sort of character. He needed to try to right the wrong, at least in her eyes.

After helping him eat, Arlyn brought a bowl of scented water for him to wash his hands and face. Then she took a seat on the bed near to him.

"So, Romen. Will you tell me what went wrong?"

Wyl had already given the situation much thought and decided to tell a lie of such extravagance that she could never blame herself for being abandoned so callously.

He took a deep breath. "I am a marked man, Arlyn. When I left here it was not because I did not want to marry you but because I had to flee for my life."

Whatever excuse Arlyn had expected, this was far away from it. She remained silent despite the obvious questions in her expression and Wyl pressed on.

"King Celimus wants me dead," he said. "I suspect it has to do with a friendship I had with his former General, Wyl Thirsk."

"Former General?"

"He's dead. Murdered by assassins sent on the express wishes of the King."

She was going to say something but thought better of it.

"But here's the worst of it," Wyl continued. "What happened last night was one of a series of attacks. The first occurred after I ran from you. They tracked me down and left me for dead but in fact they had knocked me unconscious. When I came to I had lost my memory."

It was thin but he had been convincing. He watched Arlyn's hand move to her throat. He hated himself for lying but he would be damned if he would risk hurting her again. This at least gave her the dignity she deserved.

"I did not even recall my name." He had to be careful here. "How long have I been gone?" he asked casually as though trying to search for the answer from himself.

She readily gave him the answer, not realizing the subtlety of his ruse.

Wyl had to stop himself from looking at her in alarm. What a bastard Romen had been. "Is it really that long?" he muttered instead. "I spent a good part of that time in a monastery convalescing from the stabbing injuries but mostly trying to find myself again." He thought she might cry but she soldiered on.

"And your memory?"

"I still have not recovered much of it, which is why I must ask your forgiveness if I appear vague." He liked the neat excuse—it might permit him to make errors.

"Oh, Romen, this is shocking news, and there I was thinking—oh, never mind. And last night it happened again?"

He nodded. "I've been safe for a while and perhaps I got too confident coming back here but I was drawn to Orkyld. I was drawn to you, Arlyn, but I can't remember anything of what happened between us. I'm so ashamed. So sorry to have hurt you."

His sincerity melted her and Wyl despised himself.

"What happened to the men who attacked you last night?"

"They ran away when Knave joined in the fray," he lied. His last lie, he promised himself. "If not for him, I would surely be dead. Where is he anyway?"

"Terrifying people."

He smiled, knowing he needed to press home the point now. "I am a fugitive. I will be until Celimus succeeds in killing me. Already I have tarried too long and I must get myself away from here. By staying here I put you in danger."

"They would kill me too?"

He shrugged and it hurt to do so. "They are ruthless. The King uses common cutthroats—unscrupulous bastards. No honor."

"Where can you go?"

Wyl shook his head this time. "I intend to keep moving. Perhaps I'll go across the seas. You understand why I cannot marry you, my love. I don't know when I might next see you, if at all."

"Romen, let me be honest now. I don't believe, after all this time, we could find that special affection we had before. It's been too long." This was music to Wyl's ears. "But can we not hide you here?" she said, taking his hand.

"No. Too dangerous. They are on my trail now. I must lose them again. As soon as I can walk, I'm leaving. Forgive me."

"Never mind how we feel now, I hated seeing you so hurt yesterday."

"Next time they won't fail," Wyl said, hoping it was the last nail to drive into the wretched coffin of their relationship.

She rallied. "How can I help? Money?"

"I have money. I want you to forget about me. Wipe all trace of my stay here after I leave and tell anyone who knows you have me here to keep their wits about them and not answer any questions."

She nodded. "No one saw you come to my house."

"Good. I'll leave tomorrow at nightfall."

"So soon?"

"Would you be kind enough to hand me my pouch?" he asked. It was a small leather bag with a long strap designed to be worn across the body. She gave it to him and he delved inside, bringing out Ylena's brooch. She would not miss it and it was going to a worthy person who had brought him the good luck his sister had wished for him.

"This is for you. I do remember choosing it but not where or when," he said, smiling regretfully as he put it into her palm.

"Oh, Romen, it's beautiful."

"Then it will do justice to its owner," he said, this time with sincerity. "Keep it as a reminder of what we shared once."

She kissed his hand, which was still entwined with hers, and could not help but feel a surge of desire for the handsome rake who lay near-naked in her bed. "Then I must return the gift."

Wyl felt compelled to shrink from any mention of a gift from a woman. "Oh?" he said.

"The only one I have at hand," she said, unbuttoning her shirt.

The next day Romen's arms held Arlyn close but it was Wyl who, with great fondness, kissed her goodbye. Her tender attentions had allowed him to forget himself for a brief time. Lying beside her, loving the incomparable sensation of her flesh against his, he lost his senses in a glut of affection. Although hampered by his injuries, this did not prevent their lovemaking and it helped immeasurably toward disguising his inexperience. If he had been healthy she would have known he was not Romen, or at least not the Romen she had once known. Wyl Thirsk had not bedded a woman in quite some time. The last memorable occasion was with a young soapmaker in Pearlis who supplied her produce to Stoneheart. It was a brief fling between two young people with little experience. He had seen her a few times around the castle and had once been nearby when a horse shied toward her and she had spilled her basket of soaps in fright. Wyl had called for two pages to help her pick them up and then he had graciously apologized for the skittish horse. The girl had a sweet smile and had accepted his apology shyly.

She had not been so bashful the next time he had come across her in one of the better taverns in the city where she was making another delivery. On this occasion she had invited him back to the tiny, airless room where she lived with her father above their shop and undressed herself. It had been quick but nonetheless memorable, Wyl groaning as he reached his height of pleasure and she enjoying his look of ecstasy more than experiencing much of her own.

He had thanked her and pressed some coin into her pocket to buy herself some new fabric for a dress or ribbons for her hair. He thought he might see her again but their paths had not crossed. A half-dozen other joyless, mainly urgent couplings—more from necessity than anything else—he had chosen to put out of his mind. That was the sum of his sexual experiences in recent years.

But Arlyn, he would always remember her—

"I can't come back," he whispered as he hugged her, being careful not to crush his body against hers too hard.

She nodded, long resigned to Romen not being in her life. "I know. Be safe."

And with one last warning for secrecy, Wyl left. Like him, his horse was glad to be out of its confines and on the dusty road again. They did not linger and he did not look back, although he suspected she might still be watching him.

"One more errand," he promised the beast as they rounded a bend and mercifully fell out of her sight.

As he expected—though he did not know why he should be so confident—he found Knave waiting for him in the undergrowth at the spot where they had hidden the box containing the assassin's head. They sat together for a few moments, Wyl stroking the dog and weighing his thoughts about the animal's enchantment. It seemed futile to pretend Knave was not part of Myrren's magical world and yet if he tried to explain it to a stranger, they would laugh at his reckonings.

Finally he spoke, glad that it no longer felt odd giving Knave instructions. The dog always seemed to understand anyway. "Now you know you must return," he said sternly. "Go back to Fynch. Keep Valentyna safe until I come," he added, hoping that his instincts were true. The Widow Ilyk had cautioned him to keep Fynch and Knave close, yet he had sent both away.

Knave fixed him with his intense stare. Then he gave a single bark. Wyl had no idea what it meant but when his dog licked him and then bounded off, turning once only as if in farewell, Wyl had to assume the dog knew his duty. He felt a twinge of sadness at its leaving. Something about Knave made him feel safe, invincible even. But that was every reason why the dog had to return to Valentyna. Perhaps Knave would offer the same comfort to her.

He rode back into town to where the coaches left for the south. The driver he approached agreed, for a price, to deliver the box, which Wyl had now carefully wrapped in several hessian sacks, to Pearlis.

"Where can I leave it?" the man asked.

"At the palace."

"Who for?"

"Just leave it with the guards at the main gate. They're already expecting it."

"No message?"

"There's one inside," he lied. "It's for a very high-ranking noble. Don't touch it please—he will scream hell and high murder if it is tampered with."

"Shar! What's in here, man?" the coachman asked.

Wyl knew it might be tempting for the fellow to take a peep if he did not give him a better reason to leave it well alone. "It's a witch's talisman," he explained and appreciated the look of alarm that spread across the man's face. Good. It seemed the fear of witch curses was still rife in the north, even though the Zerque influence had faded. "If it's looked upon by any but the true recipient, the intruder is blinded." Thank the stars that what was left of Romen in him found it very easy to embellish all truths, he thought, amazed at how such falsehoods came to him.

The man looked ready to toss the box off his coach.

"Look here, I will give an extra gold piece for your trouble. I appreciate your help with this and I too don't care much for the contents. I didn't look either—I'm simply the courier to this point," Wyl added, and the money seemed to soothe the man's concern. "How long?"

"About four days, sir."

"Safe travels," Wyl called as the coach drew out.

The weather became decidedly cooler as Wyl began to ascend into the higher northern counties of the realm.

He was glad of the cloak and ensured the horse moved at a slow, steady pace to prevent the uneven terrain from jarring Romen's injured body any more than necessary. Wyl was grateful to Arlyn for packing some of the strong-tasting potion. It was even harder to take as pure medicine than the brew she had plied him with at his bedside. Nevertheless he sipped it morning and night, grateful for the relief it brought. He traveled for two and a half days through increasingly barren land as the terrain became more rocky. He recalled that the villages were scattered and there were no major towns in this part of the north. Wyl was not interested in any of them for now. His attention was firmly focused on reaching Yentro, where the Widow Ilyk hailed from; it would be a small place, he imagined, of little note.

Half a day's ride later he was stunned to enter what was clearly a bustling frontier town.

Wyl stopped the horse in no little amazement. This was a major trading town, he could tell, and business was brisk. First stop was the stables. Then he went in search of a decent inn. There were far too many people around for him to worry about being noticed and the population was so varied that Wyl felt sure he would appear to be just another journeyman.

He was wrong.

I t's him, I swear it," the man said, deferentially. The person he had addressed was eating. He ate with care, reflecting his careful, neat thoughts as he chewed and considered the information he had just learned. His men were reliable, especially his friend and counsel, Lothryn, who spoke with him now. He scratched at the newly grown beard he used for disguise.

So, Romen Koreldy had returned. *Why?*

Green, unreadable eyes looked back at Lothryn. "Why now?"

Lothryn shrugged. It made no sense for Koreldy to be back in the north. "Spying?" he offered, instinctively.

"My inclination lingers there too. Spying for Celimus

perhaps. The Morgravian brat is hungry for more Mountain blood, then," he mused. "We foiled their recent incursion attempt with that team of useless spies—Haldor help the Morgravian King if they're the kind of dullards we're up against! Only the leader was worth his salt as a soldier. We'll kill them all, Lothryn. And we'll spread the Mountain Kingdom beyond the Razors, mark my words."

Lothryn said nothing, waiting for his superior to make the inevitable decision. It came swiftly. The strapping, golden-haired man pushed his plate away, no longer hungry. He stood to his full, intimidating height and looked toward his loyal deputy, his friend for more than thirty years. "Take Myrt and one other. Follow him for a few hours. Let's find out what he's up to. Then take him. I'll see you back at the Cave."

Lothryn nodded. "It will be done, my lord."

Lothryn watched from the shadows as Romen Koreldy entered the Scarlet Feather and, according to the innkeeper, was fortunate to buy the last room in the house. It was expensive but Wyl was looking forward to some comfort and a chance to recuperate after days in the saddle. He desperately needed to give his ribs a chance to heal further. He was still sporting a bruised eye, which drew a comment from the nosy man behind the counter.

"A lady didn't take too kindly to catching me kissing her best friend," Wyl remarked easily and winked, not aware that he had been trailed since entering Yentro.

The man laughed. "She's got a good punching arm then, sir. I'd avoid that one again."

"I don't believe she'd have me again," Wyl said archly, adding, "though it would be worth another shiner." This time they both enjoyed the jest. "I could use a smooth. Are there some chambers nearby?"

"Yes, sir. When you've settled in your room I'll give directions. It's attached to the bathhouse."

Wyl nodded. He took the stairs slowly, having already been warned there were four flights to his room. These were mercifully short but he still collapsed on his bed, glad of his small sack of luggage. He undid his scabbard, took off his shirt, and undid the hidden belt and knives. Such relief. He leaned back and immediately began to doze. Rousing himself, he realized he had actually fallen asleep, which would not do. He needed to establish quickly whether the Widow Ilyk was in Yentro. Time was working against him. He had to get back to Briavel to meet with the Queen, then keep his promise to his sister and convey Alyd's remains from Rittylworth to Felrawthy. He hoped to escort Ylena back to the safety of Argorn and her own people as well. And still the question of treachery niggled. Would he try and overthrow the Crown? He had to stop thinking about all that was still ahead or he would be overwhelmed. He recalled Gueryn's advice to deal with one issue at a time. His mentor had trained him to clear his mind and concentrate on the most important demand. *Prioritize!* He could hear Gueryn's voice now. The priority was to find the Widow. Everything else came after that.

Yawning and stretching carefully, he hid his weapons in the bed linen and, after dressing, locked the door and headed downstairs, where the innkeeper was giving instructions to a brace of serving girls and boys.

He noticed Wyl watching. "Very busy, today, sir."

"Is there something going on?"

"It's our annual trading fair. I thought you might be here for it. No one actually passes through Yentro without a reason." Wyl heard the curiosity in the man's voice.

"Ah well, perhaps you can help me. I'm actually in Yentro to pass on a message to the Widow Ilyk. Would you know of her—she's rather old and is a local?"

"I can't say I do but then I'm fairly new here myself, sir. Bought the Feather only a few moons ago."

Wyl gave a casual wave of his hand as though it were of no importance. "I can make inquiries, thank you. Now those directions?"

The innkeeper busied himself with a detailed account of how to find the bathhouse and Wyl was glad to escape the man's watchful gaze. The directions were accurate and, looking forward to the intense pleasure that only an expert smoothing could bring, Wyl was once again oblivious to the dark-haired stranger who followed at a safe distance.

He was soon luxuriating in fragranced, steaming water. He paid for a private room, preferring not to share his bruises with the rest of the men enjoying their dip. After soaping his hair, he rang a bell and a young woman came in and poured fresh warm water over his head. The rinse was scented with gardenia, which sharply brought back a distant memory for Wyl, although the nature of it was blurred. He searched his own thoughts and understood the recall was not his.

Someone in Romen's life had obviously used the scent.

He stored that thought away, realizing that the woman who waited on him stood patiently holding drying linens. Wyl forced himself not to be self-conscious of his nakedness. Romen would stand and probably even stretch for her, he thought, and found the courage to be still as she rubbed the fabric around his body.

"I cannot help but notice that you are hurt, sir?" she inquired, large eyes darting toward the worst bruises.

"Yes," he said, elaborating no further. "I shall have to ask you to be extremely gentle with the smoothing around my ribs."

She nodded seriously before gesturing toward the table, where she invited him to stretch out. He did so with difficulty. Lighting several scented candles, she burned oil above them and when heated she poured some into her palms and with great care smoothed the warmed oil over his body. Wyl felt his body relax under her touch. Working silently, she avoided his midsection and concentrated instead on his sore buttocks, legs, and shoulders. Her fingers were strong and skilled.

Wyl finally broke from his relaxed stupor and spoke to her. "I'm trying to find someone called the Widow Ilyk—would you know of her?"

"No, sir."

The response was too quick, he thought. "That's a pity. I have a message from the south for her. I promised a lady by the name of Thirsk that I would deliver it." Wyl figured that if she did know the old woman then the name Thirsk would be memorable and the seer might give her consent to see him.

There was a pause as though she was considering. "I'm sorry I cannot help you, sir."

He left it alone, now sure that the Widow Ilyk was known to people in Yentro. He hoped his instincts were right about the girl, and soon found out they were. He took his time finishing up. After the smoothing he took a plunge in a tepid, salted pool attached to his private room. It roused him from the drowsy state he had fallen into. He dressed and left the building, already noticing that the young woman who had done his smoothing was following him. She waited until they had rounded a corner before stopping him.

"I do know the Widow Ilyk's niece, sir," she called to him.

"Go on."

"I sent a message. Widow Ilyk will see you today."

He hid his elation. "Thank you," he said, giving her a silver duke, grateful for her involvement. She had clearly not held that much money before for her eyes shone. "How will I find her?" he asked.

"My friend—her niece, Elspyth, will meet you at this corner shortly. I have described you to her."

Romen's heartbreaking smile broke like sunlight. "I hope you told her how handsome I am?"

She laughed despite her serious nature. "I did. Farewell, sir."

"Thank you," he said, adding, "you have excellent hands."

The smoother hurried away but he caught the flush at her cheeks.

Lothryn was close enough to catch the blush of the woman. He also saw the flash of silver. No smoother was paid so highly for her services, not unless she belonged to a brothel that offered some very special additional comforts. The Mountain man watched as she fingered the coin. A lot of money for a girl like this. His eyes narrowed in concentration.

"What information have you just paid for, Koreldy?" he whispered, noticing that after the girl hurried off, his quarry was in no rush himself to leave the breezy, cold corner where he now stood. "And so we wait," Lothryn murmured.

He turned to where his companions sat discreetly mulling over their ale. Lothryn gave a sign, which they understood to mean that they would be waiting now. His companion nodded, turned away from Lothryn.

The three men of the Mountains who now stalked Romen Koreldy blended into their surrounds. They would not normally. If dressed in their preferred garb, they would be conspicuous, but Cailech's men had taken the precaution of equipping themselves with appropriate clothes that did not attract that sort of attention. Lothryn did not fool himself into believing the northern Morgravians did not recognize him or his compatriots for who they were but the simple disguise just made it easier for them to be accepted as traders—albeit illegal ones—from the mountains rather than barbarian warriors.

This had been a successful trading week. The King would be pleased and in his usual way he would plow the gold from the sale of the prized horses bred in the Razors back into goods for the Mountain People, seeds especially. Paper and stylos were high on the King's shopping list this time—he was determined the children would write with the correct equipment from now on. His plans for the future were lofty indeed, but why not? Lothryn argued to himself. Cailech had a vision for their harsh Mountain Kingdom, and if anyone could realize it, this man could.

Lothryn had grown up loving Cailech and although he rarely dwelled on it, he knew he could flatter himself in saying that the feeling was mutual. They had played side by side since they were old enough to walk and had been inseparable since. And now Cailech ruled. A self-proclaimed, magnificent King; Lothryn his unfailingly loyal second. Lothryn smiled. Life was good—almost perfect in fact, if not for the increasing upheavals with the new King of Morgravia.

Celimus had already made what was surely a challenge to war by sending a team of spies into the Mountain King's territory. And Lothryn was quietly worried that Cailech's well-known temper might lead them into deeper waters. He was already talking up the notion that his people deserved the plentiful southern lands for themselves, to grow their crops and raise their children. It was an audacious dream and one that Lothryn did not agree with. He had suggested time and again that their people should keep to the safety and obscurity of the Razors. Their arable land was small but rich, their animals fat and healthy, the people themselves happy. But he knew Cailech wanted more. Cailech always wanted more—even as a youngster he had dreamed big. And now he wanted to teach the new sovereign of Morgravia a lesson in kingship. Lothryn shook his head. In truth, if they were going to attempt to take the south then Lothryn believed they should attack weaker Briavel first, thus effectively encircling Morgravia.

He shook his head clear of thoughts of war. All he wanted right now was to be gone from Morgravia, to head back into the Mountains, where his child was preparing to be born.

He watched Koreldy pace in the cold and smiled at his discomfort. The man had obviously softened in his time south. A young woman was approaching him. Lothryn had not seen her before in Yentro but that was not necessarily surprising. *She's lovely*, he thought, *small but a lovely handful*. And he grinned to himself.

"Here we go," he muttered to himself, as the young woman paused to speak with Romen. Lothryn looked behind, caught the gaze of his companions, and nodded. It was time to follow their prey.

22

LSPYTH CAME UP BEHIND THE MAN WHO HAD BEEN DEscribed to her. She had been watching him for a brief while, wondering what his true interest was with her aging aunt. His story was a ruse, she was sure of it, but her gifted aunt had recognized the name Thirsk, had been startled to hear it in fact, and had immediately given her agreement to meet with him. Why she herself felt so wary she could not say.

Her aunt had only just made the long trek home; she was weak and fragile and Elspyth was tired. Tired of the fairgrounds and weary of life on the road. She loved the rugged north and Yentro seemed to have swelled to twice the size even in the time they had been away. She was not sure the south knew how this place was flourishing and Elspyth wanted to be here to enjoy it. She liked their cottage in the foothills and for the most part did not mind the lonely life, although she dreamed of one day having a family.

Why do I think this stranger will bring us trouble? she thought as she approached him. "Koreldy?" she said.

He turned, looking down at her from his height. Her friend told no lie with her description either. Elspyth could sense this was a man who enjoyed the company of women.

"You are the niece?" he asked, affably.

She nodded.

"Thank you for coming," he said and bowed.

Elspyth was not going to let him work his charms on her. "Follow me."

"Is it far?" he called to her back, for she had already turned and left.

"Why? Are you lame?" She did not mean to be rude but his easy smile clashed with her mood.

He did not take offense—laughed in fact. "No. No, I'm not but I am hurt."

She turned, her expression a question.

"I took a beating from some bandits. It's my ribs," he said in explanation.

"Our cottage is in the foothills."

It gave Wyl no more information than before. He protested no further. "I'm sure I'll manage."

They walked heading north out of Yentro and then veered east. Wyl regretted not wearing his knives at least, having had no idea he would be leaving the main town. The woman called Elspyth strode ahead but he had gradually made up the ground with Romen's long stride, admiring her shapely backside and the way it swayed as she walked. He finally drew level with her.

"Another mile," she warned.

"When did you get home?" he asked, mainly to make conversation, but realized it was an error.

She glared at him. "How did you know we've been away?"

Yes, how could Romen know this? Fool! "Er—I saw your aunt at the Morgravian tournament."

"Oh?"

"She met with a friend of mine," he added, hoping that was enough information.

"My aunt took unwell on the night of the tourney. We started the long journey home the next day."

"Well, it is wonderful countryside," Wyl said, trying to turn the conversation away from that particular day. "I can understand why you would want to be home here."

"Can you?"

He nodded. "I don't care much for cities myself." It felt like this was his first truth in days.

Elspyth went quiet after this and Wyl soon began to labor. The pain was back.

"What's that?" she asked, returning to where he had stopped at the roadside to tip something from a bottle into his mouth.

"Something to ease the pain." He grimaced as the vile-tasting stuff slid down his throat.

Her brow creased at his expression. "That bad?" He nodded. "May I?" she said holding her hand out.

Wyl gave her the tiny bottle and she smelled its contents. "Powerful stuff. I have something else, less harsh on your belly, that you may care to try."

He nodded his thanks as his eyes picked out the thatched roof of a cottage, partly hidden behind a mound and some trees. It seemed Shar was smiling on him. They were here. Elspyth led him out of the sharp sunlight and into the darkness of the small cottage.

"I'll not be long," she said, gesturing at a scrubbed table

and chairs. The young woman disappeared into the back of the cottage and reappeared a few moments later.

"My aunt will see you now."

Wyl had not realized he was holding his breath with tension. He followed Elspyth into the back chamber, which was darker still, and the familiar odor of burning sticks took him back to the seer's tent at the fairground.

"Welcome," the old woman's voice croaked.

Wyl bowed to the Widow Ilyk out of courtesy even though she was blind. Somehow he felt she would sense his good manners anyway.

"Elspyth, my dear. Would you fetch us some wine?"

Her niece glanced toward Wyl as she departed. He suspected her glare was to warn him not to tire the old woman. Meanwhile the wine was obviously her aunt's manner of requesting privacy.

"It is good of you to see me, Widow," Wyl said.

The old woman swayed slightly as her whitish eyes stared over his shoulder. "Your name is unknown to me, Romen Koreldy, but I am familiar with Wyl Thirsk. That one had an aura about him."

Wyl felt a chill settle across him. She was definitely no trickster.

"No aura about me?"

"Not that I can detect," she said and a small smile snatched at her mouth. "Where are you from?" she asked.

"Grenadyn, madam," he replied. "Originally," he added for truth.

"Yes, I hear its soft lilt in your voice. A nice voice, belonging to a handsome man, I'm told," she said, her eyes crinkling as she smiled.

"That depends only on the opinion of the beholder, madam," Wyl replied.

"You've obviously come a long way to find me. How can I help?"

"Take my hands," Wyl suggested.

"Why?"

"Isn't that what you do?"

"Sometimes. Other times I just listen."

"To what?"

"Oh, the voices around you, the aura surrounding your person. I might add you are closed to me."

"Please, take my hands," he asked.

"If it pleases you," she agreed, reaching forward. "I imagine—" At his touch she instantly swallowed what she was about to say. Instead what came out was a terrified gasp.

"Widow?"

Now she trembled. He could feel her fright beneath his fingers, could see her garments shaking against her frail body. Her lips began to move but no sound came out.

"Widow!" Wyl repeated, worried.

"It is you." She spoke hardly above a whisper. "It has happened, Wyl Thirsk."

Relief flooded through him. "You remember." There was a hint of sadness in his voice.

"I could never forget you. When?"

Wyl told her what had occurred.

"A curse or a gift, Wyl Thirsk?" she demanded.

"I'm not sure. It saved my life but it took another."

"He would have taken yours."

"This is true. He was, I suspect, a good man."

"You will make him better," she comforted, sensing his sorrow. "You've tracked me down because you have questions."

"Yes."

"I will answer as best I can, though I warn I know little."

He nodded. "Are you a witch?"

She chuckled at this. "No, son. I have no magics. Only the Sight."

"But you deliberately masquerade as a trickster."

The old woman shrugged. "I cannot risk the truth. You have witnessed firsthand the suffering of those they suspect are empowered. Those dark times are behind us now, thank Shar's Mercy, but still I find it easier to hide my talent than flaunt it. If people suspected I could really see into their lives, I think they would fear me for what I might tell them.

They prefer the notion that fortune-telling is just some harmless fun."

Wyl understood. "Tell me what the Quickening is."

The widow sighed and sat back into her chair, releasing her hold on his hands. "That's not as easy to explain. I cannot answer it as you wish. All I can tell you is that it has no remorse, no empathy . . . and you have no control over it."

"Can I rid myself of it?"

"No." She had nothing to add.

"So I will remain Romen Koreldy for the rest of my life," he murmured. It was not a question. He felt grief and yet in his soul he had expected nothing less.

"I have no knowledge to confirm or deny it," she said sadly.

Wyl stood and paced the tiny chamber. He did not trust himself to speak for a few moments.

"Elspyth!" the widow called and her niece appeared around the door, answering softly. "Bring the wine, my love."

The young woman came into the room with a tray. After setting down its contents she withdrew silently.

"Drink!" the seer ordered. "It will help."

Wyl did, gulping down the sweet wine, needing to feel its sugary warmth within him. She was right, it steadied him.

"Why did Myrren do this to me?"

"I imagine she saw something in you, Wyl. A need perhaps? A burning desire? Who knows? It could even be that she wanted something of you . . . something she wanted you to achieve."

"All because of a sip of water," he said, laughing sadly to himself.

"There would be more to it than that but what that is, I cannot guess."

Wyl took another couple of swallows of the wine. Mixed with the potion, it was making him feel lightheaded. He sat again.

"Tell me about the dog."

She made a small circle of her mouth as though they had stepped onto a hallowed topic. "A very powerful one, that."

"He's enchanted?" he asked, trying to make it sound like the most reasonable assumption.

"Not in himself."

"What do you mean?"

"He is a channel for magic."

Wyl did not understand but pushed on. "What else?"

"Keep him close. I told you that before. I meant it then as I do now."

"And the boy?"

"Strange."

"He is strange?" Wyl wondered aloud.

"No. Strange that I cannot read him. A complex child with an adept mind. He is very susceptible to magic, although he does not know it. That's why the black dog chose him. Trust the boy. He begins to understand Knave—and you."

She sounded as though she was falling into a trance but Wyl pressed on. He was frightened but determined to wring every last ounce of information he could.

"My sister, she—"

"Is in grave danger. You think you have her hidden but he will find her."

Wyl was astounded. How could she know these things? He felt suddenly violent, wanted to hurl something at the wall, at her, at the stupid cottage they stood in. Ylena was safe . . . safe with Brother Jakub.

Now the woman's voice sounded dreamy. "Jakub cannot protect her, nor himself," she droned. "And the other woman—the Queen. She is strong but her realm is weak. It makes her vulnerable."

This was not a revelation to Wyl but it still terrified him to hear her say it out loud.

"You must never speak of this to anyone," Wyl warned.

"I am only a sideshow alley trader," the woman said, more focused now. "No one takes me seriously."

"Is there anyone who can help me?" he asked desperately.

"Seek Myrren's father!" Her voice was hard. It sounded deeper all of a sudden.

"The physic?"

"No! He was not her real father," the low voice said angrily. "Seek the manwitch."

Wyl felt his world tip on its axis. This was too much. He was about to demand more about the father when she suddenly screamed out. "Wyl! Beware the barbarian! He knows you. He's coming—coming for you—coming for you—" Her voice trailed to a whisper and then she seemed to pass out.

"Elspyth!" Wyl yelled.

The woman ran into the chamber and bent down by her aunt, lifting the closed lids before rubbing the old woman's chilled hands. "She forbids me to witness these sessions but look what it does to her. Saps her strength. I swear it will kill her. Quick, help me with that blanket . . . she's freezing."

Wyl did as asked and together they wrapped the birdlike frame of the old woman in a thick woolen shawl.

"Will she be all right?"

"I hope so. She went too far that time. Tried to see too much. She'll sleep now for many hours," Elspyth answered matter-of-factly. "She will give nothing more to you," she added and it sounded like a challenge.

Wyl swallowed. The widow had already told him plenty and none of it pleasing.

"She's the real thing, a seer," he said, nodding and just a little awed by the tiny woman wrapped in a cocoon of blankets.

"And if you ever mention it outside of this room, I'll come after you, Koreldy," Elspyth whispered. "Remember, it was you who pursued her."

He felt suddenly dizzy. "I shouldn't have drunk that wine on top of the medicine," he said, reaching to steady himself on something.

Elspyth grabbed him. "Let's get you some air," she suggested, eager for him to be gone.

As they stepped outside beneath a darkening afternoon sky, Wyl's world went painfully blank for the second time in too few days. The club hit him so hard he did not even have time to react . . . did not even hear Elspyth scream. It mattered little, for her cry was cut off as quickly as it arrived in her throat. The man's punch clipped her jaw so effectively, she was unconscious before she hit the ground next to the prone body of Romen Koreldy.

"Take them both," Lothryn said, regretting his companion's blow to the woman. "We ride immediately for the fortress."

23

ELIMUS WAS BORED WITH THE WOMAN AND HER FAWNING manner, as well as her parents' smiles and knowing looks. Did they think he might make their daughter a permanent arrangement in his life? *Fools!* She was nothing more than an amusement. And now the novelty had dissipated for him.

He pushed her aside. "Leave me," he commanded and ignored her pout. "Now!" he yelled when she did not move immediately and it gave him pleasure to see fright flit across her face as she gathered her clothes and fled.

Soon enough, Jessom arrived—a man Celimus had appointed to the newly created position of Chancellor. The middle-aged man had appeared at Stoneheart a few weeks previous, presenting his credentials for employment to the King. Celimus cared nothing for Jessom's background— which was suspect—only for his willingness to serve, and he had already proved himself to have a slippery mind with a propensity for intrigue. He was perfect for Celimus.

"Shall I have her things sent back to her family home, sire?" Jessom asked, setting down a tray of sweet pastries and the King's favorite juice of the parillion fruit. It was chilled, just as he liked it. "I took the liberty of telling the

servant I'd bring your breakfast," he said by way of explanation, now busying himself with tying back the curtains on
the King's bed.

Celimus was flattered that Jessom had so quickly understood his needs so well. "Please. She is tedious and is no
longer permitted visitation rights."

"As you wish, sire. I will see you shortly in your study,
majesty," the Chancellor said, walking toward the door.

"No, wait. Tell me, what news from Briavel?" Celimus
asked, expecting none. He rose and pulled on the robe Jessom held out for him.

"No change, your majesty. Our second messenger has returned with the same courteous words. Her majesty, Queen
Valentyna, graciously thanks his majesty, King Celimus—
la la la."

Celimus almost laughed. Jessom really did have his measure. He knew when he could take liberties and when to
play the groveling courtier.

"What is her plan, do you think, Jessom?"

"My opinion only, sire, is that she wishes to hold you
at bay."

"Are my advances that distasteful?"

"Yes, sire," he said, handing his King a cup of the juice.

Celimus approached the window and sipped thoughtfully. "Why? She has met me only once and she was merely
a child."

"It is my guess that the dearly departed General might
have something to do with her attitude, sire."

"No, I don't believe so. According to my sources, Thirsk
won her father's permission."

"But he did not win hers, your majesty," Jessom cautioned.

"Because he did not discuss it with her," Celimus countered.

"Perhaps he should have, sire," Jessom said, bowing politely and offering the King a plate of the treats.

Celimus waved them away for now. "True. But that is not
relevant, surely?" The man shrugged and Celimus noted
Jessom clearly had more to say but was holding his tongue.
"Speak freely."

"Well, this young woman is now a Queen, sire—and there is no King or husband to advise her. No parent to demand things of her. She is the highest-ranking decision-maker in the realm. I would suggest that Valentyna may well make up her own mind about whom she entertains as a suitor."

"But she does not know me," Celimus bleated.

"Ah, there you have it, my King," Jessom said.

It was a deliberately cryptic statement and the man idly adjusted something on the mantelpiece, waiting for the obvious response.

Celimus knew his servant waited. He considered this sudden appreciation of the older man's views, wishing he felt less dependent on them. "Explain what you mean by this, Jessom."

"Only this, sire. Perhaps you should no longer rely on third parties. Go to Briavel, my lord. Let her see you for herself. A woman needs to be wooed, your majesty. Make her feel special . . . desired . . . loved."

Jessom had warmed to his subject; suddenly he was the teacher guiding the student. "This is no bedmate, your majesty. This is an equal. She is the reigning monarch of the land you want to rule. You need to make a very direct approach yourself. I dare a woman to ignore your looks or your charm, sire. Use them well. If you want Valentyna to marry you, ask her yourself. Tempt her with your honeyed words and your dazzling gifts. Bring all the pomp and ceremony of Morgravia to Briavel. Allow her to see your strength and understand how her own realm can benefit from the sacred union of marriage between these two great nations." He paused only long enough to take a breath. "She wants peace, your majesty. Be sure of it. I suspect Valentyna is already well-advised that there is only one way to secure it. But she is playing the coquettish virgin, sire. You must woo this woman properly."

Celimus was stunned. He regarded the man carefully. Jessom was right. It was no longer time for missives and messengers. He, King of Morgravia, must take direct action.

Jessom pressed his point. "Word from the north, sire, is

that the Mountain Dwellers are getting more bold. I suggest Cailech is flexing his muscles for his first raid out of the Razors."

"You really believe this?"

The man nodded. Celimus knew it was likely. Apart from the reports back from his northern guard, led by the Duke of Felrawthy, his own father had warned him of the dire need to shore up defenses on the northern border. Weeks before his death Magnus had firmly counseled his son that Briavel should no longer be the Morgravian focus. "A new threat emerges," he had warned. "Cailech grows restless in his mountain fortress."

Celimus had already known that, of course, but it had suited him to have his father believe he had no idea of the politics of Morgravia and beyond. In truth, it enraged him that to think that Cailech might have delusions of building an empire. A barbarian! What next?!

Furthermore, the ease with which Cailech and his Mountain Men scuttled into and out of Morgravia infuriated him. Part of Gueryn's mission had been to discover the paths they were using—a dangerous task with a high probability of failure. It had been Celimus's intention all along that Gueryn's party be caught. In fact, his recent order to the Duke of Felrawthy to kill any Mountain Folk found on the wrong side of the border—including those who might have stumbled across accidentally—had been a deliberate ploy to increase the ire of the Mountain King. Felrawthy and the Legion had balked at killing innocent women and children, so Celimus had hired mercenaries to carry out the public executions.

After learning of the cruelty inflicted on his people, Celimus was sure Cailech would retaliate equally brutally should any Morgravian be discovered in the Razors. All had gone according to plan and Celimus had been thrilled to receive a rumor that Gueryn and his spies had indeed been captured and were almost certainly meat for the mountain wolves by now. He was also captivated by the idea that if Cailech's fury could be so manipulated by something as simple as killing off some of his Mountain sluts and brats, how easy it might be to provoke the hot-tempered King into waging war on Morgravia—or, better still, Briavel.

His cunning mind began to wrap itself around this notion. If such a thing could be achieved, he could contrive for Morgravia to come to Briavel's rescue, causing Briavel to be hugely indebted to its neighbor. Celimus had no doubt that not only was his Legion more than capable of successfully punishing any army Cailech cared to bring across the border but also of crushing Briavel in its current weakened state. And he would have demolished two monarchs in one clever plan, removing the need for marriage at all. However, there was no harm in a contingency plan and he would be wise to keep the union with Briavel and its subsequent takeover foremost in his mind.

The sound of Jessom clearing his throat drew the King from his plotting. "I shall make a state visit to Briavel," he said firmly, "but I will not take the Legion. Let's keep it more informal. We don't want to terrify the Queen. Instead we must further bolster the supervision of the northern border."

Jessom nodded and Celimus hated himself for feeling pride at the man's acknowledgment. "You make a wise judgement, sire," Jessom said. "Would you like me to make preparations for Briavel?"

Celimus was glad to be back in charge. "Yes, go ahead. Keep me posted. I wish to be on our way as soon as possible."

"I shall need a few days, sire."

"As you see fit," the King said, waving his hand casually as though it were of no further consequence to him.

As Jessom bowed to take his leave, there was a knock at the door. It was one of the King's many secretaries. He whispered something to Jessom, who closed the door.

"The front gate has a delivery for you, sire."

"So? Send it up."

"I gather it is somewhat grisly, my King. They preferred that I seek your permission on this."

"Grisly?"

"A box carrying a head, sire, I gather," Jessom replied as easily as someone else might have said "a box of pastries."

"Whose?" Celimus was pulling off his robe and grabbing for clothes.

"That I can't tell you, your majesty."

Celimus shook his head absently. His mind was racing. "I wish to see this head."

"As you command, my King. I shall come with you."

The box was brought to the King's private garden, which Magnus had previously cared for so passionately. Celimus rarely bothered with it but, knowing the value of appearances, he commanded a team of gardeners to take care of the old King's handiwork.

The box was placed down in front of him by an embarrassed senior member of the guard.

"Who?" Celimus demanded.

The man licked his lips. "Sire, my apologies. I do not know this man."

"Is there any correspondence with this delivery?" Jessom asked, enunciating his words as though speaking to an imbecile.

"I'm sorry, my lord," the guard said, deliberately addressing his King rather than the newcomer most already despised. "We thought it best not to tamper with the package once we realized what it contained."

"Very good," Celimus said, no longer caring. "Let me see this head, then."

The sacks were opened and the man gingerly reached in. He lifted out the head of Jerico.

Celimus felt his stomach twist with a knife of hate. Romen had escaped, then. He would be a dangerous foe out there, now that he knew of Celimus's betrayal. He realized all eyes were upon him and was glad he had kept Jerico's presence as much his secret as possible. He suspected Jessom was not as ignorant as he pretended, though.

"Check again for any note!" Jessom ordered.

The man looked inside the box. There was nothing else.

Celimus forced himself to shrug very casually. "And no one has any idea who this is?" he demanded.

The two other members of the guard who had accompanied the box shook their heads fearfully.

"Well, this unfortunate fellow is not known to our King. I suggest this is a prank. Get rid of it. Burn it," Jessom ordered. "Your majesty, I shall personally make inquiries about this insult."

Celimus had already turned to walk away, anger rising, his parillion juice curdling in his stomach. Out of earshot he stopped as they crossed a courtyard.

"Jessom. That was the head of an assassin I sent off to deal with a renegade—a dangerous one. The renegade's name is Romen Koreldy."

Jessom had suspected the King knew very well whose head he had just clapped eyes on although he himself had not recognized the man. That was annoying but he was glad Celimus was conspiring with him now. "You have mentioned Koreldy to me before, sire."

"Yes, he departed just before you joined us. I want Koreldy dead, Jessom. I am making you personally responsible for this special task. Hire who you need, pay what you will. Just kill him and do it quickly. Are you up to this duty?"

The servant made a gesture indicating it was little trouble for him. "Of course, sire. I will see to it. Um . . . may I make a suggestion, my lord?"

Celimus's eyes narrowed. "Go ahead."

Jessom looked around furtively. "I know of someone. A spy of such talent that this person can go unnoticed in any circle. I think what Morgravia needs, sire . . . what you need is someone reporting back to you on the comings and goings in Briavel. Then with that flow of information, you can safely turn away and focus on the north as well as matters—such as this Koreldy—closer to home."

"Who is this person you speak of?"

The servant put his finger to his lips. "Best not shared, your majesty. The less involved you are, the less damage can be done to the Crown. Allow me to see to this for you. You know nothing of it and can claim that truly."

Celimus could appreciate the sense of this. "And can this person track down Romen Koreldy should I ask it?"

"If we assume the renegade is likely return to Briavel to

stir up trouble for us during this time of delicate negotiation, then the moment he sets foot in that realm, our spy will know of it."

"Can this spy also kill?"

"Better than any man alive, sire."

"Have it done! Pay whatever he asks," Celimus commanded, before stalking away.

Jessom smiled to himself. It was perfect that the King assumed the spy was a man. Well, she would enjoy hearing of this.

24

ELSPYTH REGAINED HER WITS FIRST.

She awoke to find herself on a horse and tied securely to the man who rode it. It was a clear night and so chill that she knew immediately she was nowhere near home. Only in the Mountains would it be this cool. She had not seen the men who hit her, had no idea what she was doing here, but somehow she did know it had nothing to do with her. This was all about the stranger from the south. Romen Koreldy was the reason she was freezing on the back of a horse, tied to a man and heading higher and deeper into the forbidding Razors. Elspyth had sensed Koreldy would bring trouble. Her thoughts fled to her aunt. It came back to her now. She remembered that the old woman had fallen into one of her trancelike stupors. She would sleep deeply, probably all night and possibly most of the next day. She would rouse and feel so weak she might not be able to support herself. She would be thirsty rather than hungry, exhausted and unable to move easily. Elspyth felt her grief snap to anger.

How dare they! How dare they come onto her land and

strike her out cold and then cart her off like some animal. She tried to piece it all together. Why had they stepped outside? Ah, that's right. The stranger felt lightheaded. She had thought he might collapse and did not feel like moving his dead weight around her cottage. She had suggested going outside more as an excuse to get him out and off the property. If he fell over inside she would have had to care for him and she did not want to be involved with Koreldy.

Elspyth had been so starved for male companionship she often wondered if she would ever have the joy of living and lying with a man. Marriage was not so important to her. But family was. She was alone except for her aunt. When the old woman died, that was it. Just her and the cottage. But to share it with a family—that would be her idea of an idyllic life.

Her smoothing friend had breathlessly described her client to Elspyth. But no, not Koreldy, even though his eyes had looked over her with appreciation; she would not risk her heart being broken by a flirtatious man such as him. She tried to look around surreptitiously for where he might be. Ah, over there on the spare horse. He was trussed to its back. She wondered if he too had regained consciousness—possibly not with the blow he'd taken.

"If you're awake, you can stop leaning on me," the man in front of her growled.

She immediately sat back. "Who are you?"

"The name's Lothryn."

"That means nothing to me."

"Nor should it," he said. Then he spoke briefly to his horse, encouraging it to take the higher of two paths they were approaching.

"Why am I here with you?" she demanded.

"Why not?"

"I mean why have you brought me here against my wishes? We have no argument."

"Unless you keep bleating on."

"Answer me!" she said, furious.

"I didn't think we needed to leave behind a witness."

"You left behind my aunt!"

"I didn't think she'd care for the ride into the Mountains."

"Well, neither do I."

He laughed and said nothing more. She saw that he had two other companions. They were strong-looking men, all of them. The odds were stacked against escape. But they wanted Koreldy, not her.

She tried a more placatory approach. "Why not let me go? It's him you want."

He remained silent.

"I have no goods, no money. I have nothing of any use to you."

At this Lothryn chuckled deeply. "Myrt over there may well argue that," he replied.

It was Elspyth's turn to become silent. She had not considered such a turn of events. How stupid was she? Three lonely men, Mountain Dwellers too. Why not? Who would even care? Suddenly Romen Koreldy was the only friend she had.

Lothryn seemed to read her thoughts. "Don't worry. No one will lay a finger on you. Not yet anyway."

"Until what?" she dared ask.

"Until—and only if Cailech sanctions it."

Elspyth became still. Cailech! King of the Mountain Horde. There were so many stories about him, and she believed he was stuff of legend only. No one in Yentro had ever seen him but then how would they know if they had? Increasingly more members of his race were ignoring the Legionnaires and finding ways into the border towns. She herself had seen them brazenly coming into and out of Yentro. They kept to themselves, caused no bother, and so the people of Yentro began to relax around them. Trust was not the right word but their gold was as good as any in the taverns and other merchant outlets. Their interest, of course, was trade; selling their skins and furs, utensils and jewelry.

For all she knew, Cailech could unobtrusively slip into and out of the border towns without anyone knowing who he was. How right she was in this assumption.

"Forgive me," she said, a little intrigued despite her perilous situation. "I didn't believe he was real."

Lothryn snorted. "Trust me."

Wyl was heartily sick of being knocked unconscious. This time he deliberately kept the fact that he had regained his wits to himself. It was night, very cold, and he was lying on the ground; mercifully he was near a small fire but his hands and legs were bound. He could see Elspyth was sipping something. She was lost in her own thoughts, staring into the flames. Nearby he could hear, but not see, men speaking in low voices. He wondered how many there were.

Realizing he could get no further information from his prone position, he shifted his body around.

Elspyth looked over. "At last."

"My head hurts horribly," he admitted, after which he felt the blade at the back of his neck. "I don't have the strength to do much more than lie here," Wyl said and the pressure of the sword was removed.

He was hauled into a sitting position, and his mind swam with dizziness.

"Drink this," Elspyth said, handing him a cup. "This is Lothryn, by the way. "

Wyl blinked the blurriness away and looked across at a large, barrel-chested man who grinned at him. The man was familiar.

"Sorry about the club. Didn't think you'd come willingly," he said.

"You might have tried asking first," Wyl suggested.

Lothryn nodded. "Aye, I might have."

"Why did you bring the girl?"

"He didn't want witnesses, apparently," Elspyth chimed in.

Wyl thought of the Widow, knew Elspyth would be worried. "Let her go."

"I can't now," Lothryn admitted. "No spare horse, too far to walk, too dangerous—can't have you dying in the Mountain, can we?"

"Only in the fortress, I suppose," Wyl countered and won a smile from the big man.

"Nice to see you haven't lost your sense of humor, Romen," Lothryn said.

"You know him?" Elspyth exclaimed at her captor. "How nice for you both!" she snapped and was infuriated at the way the big man grinned at her waspish response.

Wyl racked his mind for any detail from Romen's memory. None came. There was a sense of familiarity about the man but no information bubbled to the surface. There was also a sense of foreboding at the suggestion of the fortress. Wyl could not put his finger on why he felt so suddenly fearful. Romen had given him the distinct impression that he and Cailech had been on reasonably good terms.

Elspyth's expression was as fiery as the flames that lit it. "Neither of you care about me anyway, so let me go—I'll worry about my own survival, thank you. The Mountains don't frighten me."

"They should," the man replied. "They kill without remorse."

She was not to be deterred. "You want him!" she said, jutting her chin toward Wyl. "Not me. I have to get home to help my aunt."

Lothryn shook his head sadly. "Myrt checked on her. She was dying then. Is probably already dead."

The words hit like a slap. "You lie!" she spat.

He said nothing. Just stared at her with dark eyes. She hated that she sensed compassion in them. Elspyth threw the contents of her cup into the fire and left the warm spot. She would not gratify them with her tears. Myrt followed her like an obedient dog.

"Why am I here?" Wyl said.

Lothryn glanced at him in surprise. "Did you think he'd allow us to sight you again and not bring you in? You were stupid to return to the north, Romen."

Wyl felt the twist of fear again. What was it? It had to be Cailech whom this fellow spoke of. "So Cailech ordered my capture?" he confirmed, hating feeling so lost for information.

Lothryn nodded.

"And how far have we come?"

"You've been out for the best part of two days. Sorry, we kept you drugged. We reach the Cave tomorrow. Now eat, we saved you a share."

Two days. Combined with the couple of days' traveling to Yentro, Wyl assumed the box containing the severed head had been delivered to Celimus by now. He smiled to himself although there was little satisfaction in it. This diversion into the Mountains could cost Valentyna her realm. He needed to escape—and fast. They untied a hand so he could eat and relieve himself and then, still feeling the effects of the blow, which had left a lump the size of an egg near his ear, he drifted again into a fitful sleep.

The next morning Elspyth hardly uttered more than two words from the time they stirred and broke camp. She was deep among her unhappy thoughts and Wyl decided it was best to leave it that way. He too had plenty to consider, not the least of which was learning from his captors as much as he could about Cailech, the man who had ordered his capture.

The scenery about him was achingly familiar and Wyl found himself holding his breath. He sensed the darkness of Romen's past was in the process of being brought into the light. The Razors were forcing it back to the surface, as though with each step closer to Cailech's mountain home, another fragile bond holding that mystery in place was being broken.

J essom waited patiently. The Old Plough at Sheryngham was a popular tavern with the merchants who plied their goods between Morgravia and Briavel. It was always busy, usually filled with strangers and the ideal spot for him to meet her. He ate, not bothering to stay alert for his guest. She would hardly announce herself anyway. She would just arrive, as was her way. The medley of roasted meats and buttery mashed parsnip was excellent tonight and he ordered a second helping to satisfy a ravenous hunger.

She had been watching the thin, wiry man for a while now, knew he would not bother to look out for her, but still she liked to observe. Knowing people's habits down to their eating and sleeping preferences was a practice most in her profession would scoff at. But she was thorough in her work, studying her clients as much as her victims.

Jessom's message had been curt. He preferred to deliver the instructions in person, which suggested to her that he planned to have someone killed rather than simply observed. So be it. As long as he brought gold with him, she had no qualms about her role. She could not help but marvel at the amount of food such a lean man was tucking into. After the second order was delivered and half-eaten she decided it was time to make herself known. Surreptitiously touching the fake hair around her face to check it had adhered securely she sucked on the foul-smelling pipe that hung from her lip and shuffled over to his table to sit down.

He looked up, unperturbed by what faced him. "Can I get you an ale?"

She nodded.

"The disguise is impressive. I noticed the old man," he said, his voice very approving of her talent, "but thought it too obvious to be you. I would enjoy knowing what you really look like."

"Let's talk business," she croaked in a low voice, smiling and revealing blackened teeth.

He blinked, dabbed at his mouth with the square of linen he habitually carried, and pushed his food aside.

The ale was delivered and they raised their mugs to each other.

"To success," he said.

She put her mug down and licked the froth from her lips, careful not to disturb the carefully applied beard that she had had made and shipped from Rostrovo. "What is the job and who orders it?"

Jessom steepled his hands and rested his narrow, clean-shaven chin on them. "Highest possible source."

"I see. And the money?"

"Left in the usual spot. Three bags this time, which I think might more than cover your fee." He grinned and it struck her that he looked like a vulture.

She did not return the smile. "Let me be the judge of that," she said in her affected voice. "Who is it?"

Jessom became businesslike. He briefed her. "A noble from Grenadyn who in recent times has adopted mercenary status. Be warned, he is good. His name is Romen Koreldy, a skilled swordsman and canny soldier."

"And how has he offended?"

"He carries dangerous information in his head, the sort that could damage the Crown. He also killed Morgravia's commander of the Legion, General Wyl Thirsk."

At this she lifted her eyebrows. "I'd heard he died in dubious circumstances."

"Koreldy also stole a ward of the Crown. Thirsk's sister has disappeared with him."

She did not pursue this, considered it irrelevant. "And my instructions?"

"We believe he is likely to come into Briavel to make contact with Queen Valentyna. I want you to watch for his arrival. When the opportunity presents itself, you are to kill him."

"I will need time," she said, sipping her ale again. "If he is as skilled as you say, a more elaborate disguise is essential. You will require patience."

"You have it. I have never questioned your methods before."

"You have never ordered someone's death on behalf of a third party before."

"True. Will you do it?"

"Describe him to me."

Jessom did so. He too was an accomplished observer of people and before he applied to the King for the position he now held he had spent some time watching the comings and goings of Pearlis, most especially what was happening in and around Stoneheart. He had witnessed Romen's arrival and subsequent departure with Wyl, although none, not even the King, knew this.

"You would make a good spy with that talent for description."

He nodded. "Thank you."

She sucked on the pipe and then blew a long thin stream of smoke from the corner of her mouth. He almost smiled at the audacity of this woman. Her affectation as an old codger was perfect.

"The payment," she said.

"Yes?"

"It is not enough. Triple it."

"Shar's Wrath! Are you mad?"

"No. He can afford it and I suspect there is no limit on the price."

Jessom regarded the old man with the young woman's eyes looking out under bushy gray eyebrows. She was the best. Her price was worth it. "I'll arrange it."

"Don't try to make contact with me again," she warned. "I'll be disappearing for a while."

"How will we know of your success?"

"You will know when it is done," she said, lifting herself slowly as an old man might, breaking wind loudly as she did so. Only one person who was eating very nearby took offense but she ignored his curses. She did not look back as she limped from the tavern.

As they rode in single file—Elspyth now in front of Lothryn on the horse—they passed through the narrowest of openings in the rocks. Suddenly a flood of emotion assaulted Wyl. He could not attach it to a memory of any particular event but once again he felt twisted inside. It was fear. But it mingled with despair and guilt. This time the sensation did not dissipate but instead intensified with each step his horse took closer to the Mountain fortress.

The mostly silent Myrt made the sound of an animal and this echoed cleverly up the close walls, where presumably lookouts passed on who had arrived.

The four exited the pass and came face-to-face with the unforgiving sheer rock frontage of Cailech's fortress. It was known as the Cave to its dwellers but was in fact a breathtaking stone building, fashioned from the surrounding rock, that appeared to cling to the cliff edge they found themselves on.

Elspyth, no longer silent in worry, was in awe of where she found herself. The two Mountain Men were used to its effect and were simply pleased to be back with their people. Wyl, however, inexplicably leaned over from his horse and in a state of utter bewilderment retched as the weight of Romen's secret overwhelmed him. Still the truth evaded him.

A swirl of vague notions came to him: unpleasant notions of ugly deaths. Then they breezed away as fast as they had arrived, leaving him grasping helplessly after nothing. He delved hard in his despair but came up wanting— Romen's memories yielded no answers this time. It was terrifying. How would he be able to keep up this pretense with so little knowledge of the man's past and in the company of others who presumably knew it well? He retched again. If he could not carry off this pretense then Ylena and Valentyna were as good as dead and all that he treasured would be destroyed by the madman masquerading as the King of Morgravia.

"Romen!" Elspyth called, shocked by his actions.

"Leave him," Lothryn said quietly. "This place, particularly the vineyards at Racklaryon, holds dark memories."

She twisted to look at her captor. He was a man of few words and yet she sensed the kindness he worked hard to conceal with his gruff manner. It was there in his eyes now and he looked first at Romen, then at her, and finally away.

"Will you tell me?" she asked out of earshot of Romen and was surprised when the Mountain Man responded.

"There were needless deaths here in the Razors. He holds himself responsible."

"And is he?"

"Yes," Lothryn replied and she knew she would get nothing more from him on the subject.

"So this is his first time back—is that why he sickens?"

"I imagine so."

There was no point in pursuing Romen's past but now that she had Lothryn talking, Elspyth was not prepared to give up too easily. "Do you have family?"

"I do."

"A wife?" she wondered.

"I am married. Our child should have come by now. He is late."

"He?"

"She . . . I don't mind."

"You sound worried—are you?"

"No."

And again the tone was final. She was impressed she had coaxed this much from him. Legend had it that the Mountain People ate children. As huge and imposing as Lothryn was, she guessed he would probably be the most tender of fathers.

He waved at the guard who began to raise the massive portcullis to permit entry.

"One way out only?" she said.

"Only one way in, no way out," Lothryn replied.

The huge iron gate squealed as its chains rolled to lift it up. The horses moved through and entered a bailey. The size of the fortress was awesome. Men came toward them; some to take horses, others to escort the prisoners.

"I will leave you now," Lothryn said to them once Wyl, pale and embarrassed, had caught up. Myrt had already disappeared. "These men will take you to chambers where you can freshen yourselves."

Wyl nodded, said nothing.

"I hope your wife and child are both safe," Elspyth called after their captor but he did not look back. Wyl looked at her with a query but she shook her head. "I trust you've got a plan to get us out of this?" she said.

The guards were not so interested in his response and pushed them forward, deeper into Cailech's clutch.

25

THEY WERE SHOWN TO SEPARATE GUARDED CHAMBERS. THE rooms were warmed by hollowed clay pots, standing half as high as a man, in which small fires burned, their smoke exhausted via cunningly concealed flues. Painted frescoes adorned the whitewashed interior walls; even the ceilings were painted with vines and intricate border designs. Animal skins were laid on the floors and carved beds were decorated by woven spreads, simple and beautiful in their bright coloring. In such a forbidding place, beauty abounded and this was a surprise.

Wyl dozed briefly and woke to make full use of the fresh water and fatty soap that had been left for him. With Romen's hair washed and neatly tied back, he scratched his new beard, wishing he could shave as well. There was not much he could do about his clothes, he decided, and so fetched a chair to the window, which afforded him a breathtaking view of the pretty meadows beyond the lake. Intuition—only Romen could give him this—told him that those meadows led to a cove with a sandy beach. Why was this significant to him? He settled back in the chair, cleared his mind as Gueryn had taught him to do in readiness for a sword fight, and allowed any random thoughts or information to flow in. He cast a prayer that Shar might guide the truth to him of Romen's dark past.

He sat for a while without any thought. Still and unfocused he stared out toward something he knew was significant. It was beyond the meadows but before the sea. It evaded him, although he sensed it was tantalizingly close to revealing itself. Wyl heard a noise from below; it disturbed his clutching search into Romen's history. He leaned out of the window to see a team of men rolling wine barrels. He sat back down hard on his seat, his pulse suddenly quickened. *Wine!* What was it that Lothryn had said earlier? It was subtle but it was loaded with meaning and it was connected with wine. A place called Racklaryon—he had suggested that was why Romen's physical reaction to seeing the fortress again had been so strong. Wyl remembered now how some trace of Romen had unwillingly stirred at the naming of that place. Why was that?

Racklaryon. The name was painfully familiar but he could not say why. He leapt from his chair and summoned the guard from outside his chamber.

"Where is Racklaryon?" he inquired.

The guard nodded. "The plains are after the meadows," he replied abruptly.

"Before the sea," Wyl added.

"The vineyards eventually lead down to the sea, yes."

Wyl felt his heart leap. Vineyards. He was close. "Am I permitted to go there?"

"I will check," the man replied and left Wyl standing in his doorway. The guard then muttered quietly to another man who was passing by. "We wait," he called back to Wyl.

Wyl returned to his room to wait and soon enough the guard knocked on his door.

"You are permitted," he said. "Then you will meet with the King."

Wyl nodded. He needed someone to show him the way and presumed he would not be allowed to roam free. "Will you accompany me?"

"Yes. I will arrange horses."

Leading the horses away from the fortress, Wyl gave up trying to be chatty with his companion. The man's stern countenance and monosyllabic answers to polite questions were sufficient to warn him off. So now they cantered in silence, two more men bringing up the rear.

"I have no intention of riding away anywhere," Wyl reassured him.

"Orders," his captor said.

The ride was pleasant enough and lifted Wyl's spirits for

a while, which was perhaps why the shock was even more intense when he caught his first glimpse through some trees of the picturesque vineyards of Racklaryon.

He galloped toward it, skirting the trees, his escort following just as fast. Finally seeing the rows of resplendent vines rolling down the plains to a sandy cove was too much even for Romen's buried memories. The force of the sight's terrible impact smashed through whatever thin veil had kept Romen's recall of this time so remote from Wyl and the full tragic event exploded into his consciousness as though he were watching the horrific scene unfold once again.

Wyl jumped from his horse, all but falling to the rich earth of Racklaryon, and there, on his knees, his arms uplifted to the heavens, he screamed his despair as the truth of his host's mysterious background unleashed itself on its guest.

It felt like an age before he could compose himself and he was grateful that his escort had finally dragged him from the vineyards, forced him back on his horse, and returned him to his chamber where he remained, numb, until they came for him. The men spoke only the words necessary to ask him to come with them and he appreciated that they used his own language to communicate. Their own was a guttural, bastardized version of an ancient language from lands to the northeast of where the Mountain Dwellers' ancestors originally came. He suspected Romen knew this language but he no longer wanted to delve into Romen's past. What he had learned today he wished he could give back.

This new escort, like the first one, wore nothing warmer than shirts and sleeveless leather jerkins over woolen baggy pants tucked into sturdy boots, while he was glad of the several layers he had donned back in Yentro. He tidied himself quickly once again until he was neat and presentable for the King.

There were no stairs in this part of the fortress but gently swooping circular ramps, smoothed from the stone, ran between the floors. Wyl noted sconces burned at frequent intervals on the walls. He presumed they must remain lit constantly as only very little daylight would seep through into this vast place of cavernous halls. He soon lost his bearings. The men escorted Wyl through a wide, dark passage that ended at a great oak door. Guards were posted down this corridor and two burly men stepped aside as Wyl's entourage arrived. One banged on the oak door and it was opened from the inside.

Cailech was obviously a cautious leader.

Inside, the large room lost all the austerity of what had gone before. Massive windows allowed maximum light and overlooked a picturesque scene of the lake, which was home to thousands of water birds. Snowcapped mountains in the background stepped jaggedly down toward the valley and its pastures, over which the fortress hung.

Huge pines lined the slopes. Late winter flowers were bursting into bloom everywhere. Wyl found himself entranced by the spectacular panorama and was tempted to squint against the blaze of light and color as he emerged from the dark of the corridor.

The chamber he stood in was enormous.

A familiar voice greeted him now from one of its many nooks. "Romen Koreldy. *Tsk, tsk.* I told you what I'd do to you if you ever set foot on my path again."

Wyl turned to his right where Cailech, King of the Mountain Dwellers, stood relaxed by a huge open fire, its stone mantelpiece intricately carved with beasts and birds. A bare hint of a grin played around the man's mouth. The King's light-colored hair was long and loose, carelessly held back from his oblong face by a leather thong tied around his head. He wore no beard but Wyl imagined he could grow one with ease. He did not bother with a shirt but wore only his leather jerkin over his skin, which was burnished from sun and wind. His arms were thickly muscled, ending in large, blunt hands.

The King held one out now, palm down, in the Mountain way.

Wyl stepped forward and intuitively placed his own, palm up, against the calloused hand, which dwarfed his. As he did so, he bent over that large hand to show his respect for this self-proclaimed royal.

"To tell the truth, my lord Cailech, I did not deliberately set foot on your path. You had me stolen from Morgravia."

Hard, unreadable pale-green eyes held Wyl as he straightened. For a moment he worried that the man might see him for the impostor he was.

"Why were you so far north, Romen?" The voice was pleasant enough but the question was pointed. Cailech knew no other way.

Romen had warned Wyl not to trifle with this man. He gambled. "That's a rather long story."

"Share it with me. I'm in no hurry and you are certainly going nowhere." Cailech glanced toward his men who then withdrew, although Wyl noted they remained in the chamber itself.

They sat. Wine was immediately served.

"Hungry?" his host asked.

Wyl shook his head, recalling how violently he had emptied himself earlier. "But I will gladly take wine with you, my lord." He slipped into a topic he was familiar with and which came naturally to him. He had seen the wine barrels, noticed the vine designs in his chamber and on various items—Wyl felt he could risk this conversation as a polite opener. "Has the harvest been generous?"

"Bountiful last year and this year shaping up to be just as good. This is some of our finest from the plains of Racklaryon."

Wyl flinched at the naming of this place. He looked over the rim of his goblet at the strong features that regarded him. His father had cautioned so many times about the threat from the north and how Morgravia should never underestimate its wily King. Wyl could appreciate that now, staring into the face set in an expression that seemed carved from the same granite as the Mountains he called home.

Wyl sensed he must not show any further proof that the word disturbed him. "How old are you anyway, Cailech?" he asked, falling back on Romen's nonchalance, which had saved Koreldy so many times.

"Odd question," the man replied, showing a smile that Wyl noted touched his eyes and changed his demeanor into one of pure amusement. "I would hazard that you and I are around the same age."

Wyl nodded, estimating thirty-five or so summers. "You have achieved so much for one still relatively young."

Cailech snorted. "I don't feel young."

"Tell me how it all came about . . . how you united the tribes."

"I thought we were discussing you. Anyway you would have heard it from others during your last stay, I'm sure."

"I'd like to hear it from you," Wyl said carefully.

"Why?"

"You said you were in no hurry and you have never told me much about yourself," Wyl gambled again, all but holding his breath.

Cailech sipped, watchful, obviously carefully considering Wyl's question.

"There really isn't much to tell," the King finally said. "We were a rabble. A horde of scavengers who would just as soon fight over a neighbor's goat than look to the bigger prey of neighboring kingdoms and fight over something worth winning."

"Such as?"

"Land, horses, wealth."

"Go on."

"We were never going to amount to anything more than vandals whose best success might be raiding another tribe's region. I suppose I had a vision."

"How old were you when you had this vision?"

The King tapped his goblet in thought now. "I could see it clearly from childhood. As soon as I was considered old enough to wield weapons and join the raiding parties, I began preaching that vision. At every opportunity I'd beg my father, the leader of our tribe, to call talks. After a raid, whether we were successful or not, he would sit with his counterpart and they would discuss what I suppose could be called terms of war. It became infectious and my father and I would travel into different tribes as the mediators for such talks. As my voice deepened into a man's, I think they began to pay more attention to me. For this, you see, was only the beginning of my vision. My plan was always to unite the tribes into one race, one leader, one aim." He broke off and shrugged suddenly. "All history. This fortress took almost two decades of my life to build."

"I was impressed all those years ago, your majesty. I'm even more astounded by its simple beauty now."

"Thank you," the King said. "And Racklaryon? How was your ride?"

This time he did not hesitate. "Painful."

"I expect it was," Cailech replied carefully, then switched topics as smoothly as his wine slipped down Wyl's throat. "We are wondering why Morgravia would use you to spy on us."

Wyl balked and the surprise showed on his face. "I am not spying for Morgravia, your majesty. I would sooner join you in cutting its King's throat."

It was Cailech's turn to be surprised. "Is that so?"

"He has done me many wrongs. That's why I was in the north."

Cailech raised a cynical eyebrow. "Well, Romen. It's your turn. I shall have your story about this trip so close to our border."

Wyl took a careful breath of relief. This was something he could speak about without fear of error.

After an opportunity to wash and neaten her appearance, Elspyth enjoyed a most acceptable meal of warm bread and a thinly sliced meat she did not recognize. As she finished off the light but nonetheless deliciously buttery wine, there was a knock at the door. She took a deep breath and crossed the room, brushing crumbs from her clothes. She was pleased to see it was Lothryn who had come for her.

"How is your wife?" she asked before he said anything.

Lothryn's expression did not change but she would never know how much her gentle-mannered inquiry meant to him. "As well as can be expected. She began her pains before our arrival. She's still going."

Elspyth could sense the anxiety he did his best to disguise. "Not long then before you can celebrate your son's arrival," she said brightly.

"Haldor willing," he replied softly, calling on the Mountain god.

"Have I been summoned?"

"Not yet. I thought you should see how barbaric we really are."

She frowned, not sure what this meant.

"Shall we take a walk?" he offered.

This took her by surprise but she quickly rearranged her expression to a smile. "I'd like that."

He showed her through sections of the fortress and Elspyth admitted to being delighted by the beautiful decoration on the walls and ceilings, on the timbers and in their fabrics.

"You are a most artistic people," she observed and meant it. "More talented than us Morgravians."

"Skills passed down through generations over centuries," he explained, not showing it but pleased by her compliment. Outside he guided her past the busy kitchens.

"There's a feast in the making," he added, which explained the frenetic activity.

They continued beyond the stables and into the orchards and vegetable gardens. These were vast and a small army of people were busy tending to them. He left her momentarily to reach up and pick some late apples. Lothryn munched on one and offered her the other. They strolled in silence as they ate.

"Tell me about Koreldy," Elspyth suddenly blurted.

"I can't imagine there's anything I can tell you about him that you don't already know," he responded cautiously.

"Please, Lothryn. He's a stranger. I'm having enough trouble working out what I'm doing here. Perhaps if I knew more, I could help with what you want," she offered.

The man paused a while as if measuring whether she was trying to trick him.

"We want to see if Koreldy is a threat to our people."

"But you know him already, surely? And how can a single man be a threat?"

"We knew him a long time ago. Cailech would like to know what he's doing in Morgravia."

"Well, I can tell you that," she said, puzzled. "He's somehow connected to that General who recently died."

"Thirsk?"

"Yes."

Lothryn shook his head. "He was an old man, bound to eventually die on the battlefield. Connection or not, I suspect this is not what my King pursues."

"No. I'm talking about the son. His name was Wyl."

"Wyl Thirsk is dead?"

It clearly came as a shock to him, she realized. "Well, yes. My aunt and I heard about his state funeral on our travels back to Yentro from Pearlis. I remember her saying we hadn't heard the last from that one but I don't know what she meant by that."

Now she had Lothryn's interest piqued. "And what is Koreldy's connection with Thirsk?"

"I have no idea but my aunt may have known. She agreed to meet Romen only because he mentioned the name Thirsk."

"Then what are your aunt's dealings with the former General?"

"Very little. She did a 'speak' for him when we were in Pearlis for the tournament."

"A 'speak'?"

"That's her talent. She's a seer. She speaks about what she sees in people, although I would not admit that on Morgravian soil."

"Do they still burn people?"

"Not for several years now, but the old suspicions die hard in the south. In the north we believe in empowerment, we always have."

He grunted. "Us too." Lothryn tossed his apple core aside. "So what did she see in Thirsk?"

"Truly, I don't know. I wasn't present. It wasn't anything serious—just a bit of fun fortune-telling to earn a few pennies."

Lothryn nodded thoughtfully. "What else do you know?"

"That's it. We arrived home and not long after Koreldy appeared in Yentro asking after the Widow Ilyk, my aunt."

"Perhaps we should have grabbed the old woman," Lothryn muttered ruefully.

She took advantage of his mood. "All you had to do was ask me—I would have given you this information willingly. You didn't have to knock me unconscious and drag me up here to learn it."

He did not respond, although she sensed his amusement. They continued walking.

Elspyth tried again. "So what is Romen's secret?"

Lothryn looked at her with no understanding and she returned it with an expression of exasperation. "It's clear he hides something which you know about. You two greeted each other amicably; how does a Mountain Dweller know a Grenadyn noble?"

"Grenadyn is but a short boat trip away."

Elspyth shook her head. "You're avoiding my question," she admonished.

"Perhaps you should let him tell you his past."

She made a sound of scorn. "Lothryn, you didn't bring me out here for the fresh air. I suspect Cailech asked you to find out what I know. I've told you what information I have. I also suspect the walk helps take your mind off your laboring wife. First child? I'd say you have hours to go. We're in no rush. Talk to me—I'll keep you company but only if you're honest. I've told you the truth."

She was easy to like, this one. Lothryn found her fiery nature attractive. He hoped Cailech would not order her defilement as some sort of example to the Morgravians, although he was more than capable of something that brutal, especially now the young Morgravian King had showed himself to be more aggressive than his father. Magnus had left it to General Fergys Thirsk to ensure the Legion's presence at the border was a sufficient deterrent, but Fergys had never been heavy-handed with that weapon. In contrast Celimus had, and his recent act of slaughtering innocents who had inadvertently stumbled across the border had plunged Cailech into an unpredictable mood. It might have been eased had Celimus sent immediate apology but the silence from the south was both deafening and damning.

Lothryn hoped his influence might count for something when he met with the King later—perhaps he might help avoid some brewing trouble. He came out of his musings, realizing Elspyth was staring at him, waiting for his response.

"All right. I'm sure it can't hurt," he said. "Sit here." Lothryn gestured toward a low wall that led into rockier pastures where the fortress's goats were grazing.

"He is from Grenadyn. He belongs to a wealthy noble's family—I mean real riches. There were three children. An eldest son—the heir—and then twins, Romen and his sister. I gather that Romen was the wild one of the three and always leading his sister into trouble. His antics became more reckless as he grew up and it was the brother who saved Romen's lot countless times."

Elspyth smiled. She had never had any siblings to know that kind of love. "They were close then."

He nodded.

"I sense from your expression that this story doesn't have a happy ending."

"No," Lothryn admitted. "Grenadyn's south island is really not that far from our mainland. Cailech passed a law forbidding any visitors beyond our borders without prior permission being sought. He really meant it against the Morgravians and Briavellians who treated us Mountain Dwellers as nothing more than barbarians."

"If only they knew," she said, trying to ease his obvious wrath for the rich southern realms.

"I don't think he really worried about Grenadyn. They had no argument with us; never sought our lands, never gave cause for us to regard them as anything but friendly neighbors."

"Until?"

"Until some of our people mistakenly got themselves washed up on a Grenadyn beach. Some panic-stricken idiot sent out the word that the barbarians were raiding. It was a ludicrous claim considering our people were in a smallish rowboat but it was night and the thugs the alarmist called were drunk. I presume they decided to take matters into their own hands. Our people fought back as bravely as they could without many weapons but they were slaughtered. The children, too, who were hiding in the boat. One of those children was the King's cousin. He loved her very much."

Lothryn threw a stone into the distance. He stayed quiet for a few moments and Elspyth wondered if he would continue with the story.

"Cailech did not respond as predicted—he took us by surprise, to be honest, and I imagine the Grenadynes held their collective breath waiting for the onslaught that never came. Instead he simply issued a warning. His instructions were clear. If anyone from Grenadyn was ever sighted on our land they were to be killed with the same speed and lack of sympathy that had been shown our people."

Elspyth did not need to hear any more. She could guess the outcome but Lothryn's tongue was loosened now and he seemed compelled to tell it all.

"We sent word to Grenadyn of his decision. Everyone sensibly heeded the warning—except Romen Koreldy. Arrogant and possessing that sense of invincibility all young braves have in abundance, he devised a dare for the young folk of the south island. Bring back a bunch of Cailech's prized grapes from his vineyards of Racklaryon and you won what he called the dare gold."

"You don't need to go on," she said, touching his arm gently.

Whether he noticed the gesture or not, he ignored it. "Several took him up on the dare but were unsuccessful. Thankfully that channel of water that divides us is usually perilous. But I gather from Romen that he goaded his sister unfairly, for this girl was not scared of anything, as I understand it—very much in his mold . . . a worthy twin, you could say. She was every bit the adventurer Romen was and always trying to prove she was a match for him.

"The short of it is that Lily—that was her name—took the dare. And Romen, delighted and filled with bravado, said he'd join her. They rowed across the channel. Fate calmed the waters on that particular day. When the elder brother found out their folly he was understandably furious and rowed after them." Lothryn put his head in his hands. "You know she almost made it, that brave girl. She had the grapes in her hand when she was discovered. The elder brother had the presence of mind to bring his sword and he wielded it gallantly. I was there, I witnessed him fighting for their lives."

"And Romen?" Elspyth enquired.

"Ah, that's the crux of this dark tale. He lost his nerve. Cringing in a copse near the vineyard, he shielded himself and watched us take his brother and sister. Cailech ordered their deaths instantly. Our King made the right decision— the only decision he could under the circumstances—but it made me feel we earned our title of barbarians that day. We crucified those two young people in the Racklaryon vineyard for nothing more than a bunch of grapes.

"It was a bright, clear day and the Grenadynes could probably see the two crosses and their victims through an eyeglass. The brother died first but she lingered throughout the day and night, punishing us all. She called to Romen. Begged him to save her. Poor, tragic Lily. She fought death all the way to her last gasp and he would have heard every groan, would have watched every moment of her suffering."

Elspyth was rigid with tension now, both sickened and despairing of this sad story. "What happened?"

"The next morning their stiff bodies were cut down and burned, their ashes scattered on the waters that brought them to us. Romen watched it all and when it was over, his fighting spirit, it seemed, made a return."

"What do you mean?"

"He tried to kill Cailech."

"What?"

"It's true. He's a dead-eye marksman with knives, did you know that?" She shook her head. "Cailech was at the burning, or so people thought. Knives hit him clean in the chest and killed him outright . . . or would have if the man had been Cailech."

"I'm not following you now," Elspyth admitted.

"Cailech had his Stones read the night before by Rashlyn, the King's practitioner, and they told of an attempt on his life that next day. He is very mindful of any advice given through the Stones and took precaution. From a distance, any big man with long hair of similar color could fool an intruder such as Romen. He threw true, killed his man, and when captured was obviously stunned to learn the truth."

"How has he survived to this day, then?"

"A miracle, I would suggest. Perhaps Cailech had had enough of the killing. He can be ruthless, don't be fooled, but he is a deep thinker. My feeling is he admired the fact that the brother had finally found the courage to do what was right. They were of an age and he spared Romen, allowed him to live and work among us for a while and tried to help him come to terms with his loss. He never did, I might add. When he was ready to leave, he was given back his weapons and escorted to the southern border. He promised never to return to Grenadyn. Cailech told him that if he ever set foot near the Razors again, he would die."

Elspyth ran her hands through her hair. "How long has it been?"

"Has to be ten summers or so."

"And still you recognized him?"

"A man as distinctive as Romen is not easily forgettable."

She nodded; he was right, of course. "And will Cailech kill him?"

"That I can't answer but now come, we must return. He will wish to see you."

You expect me to believe that, although you were working for the Morgravian King, you have no loyalties to him?"

"I do," Wyl answered carefully. "If I told you I could unite Briavel and your people against Morgravia, would you believe me?" he challenged.

"No," the King answered. "I would not trust them anyway. And I don't trust you. Your tale is too farfetched."

"What can you not believe?"

Cailech sat back in his chair, twirling his wine glass,

highly amused. "You were hired by Celimus to assassinate Wyl Thirsk, which you claim you have done. Then you took his body back to Pearlis to ensure the General's name was cleared of wrongdoing because you suspected Celimus would spread lies about Thirsk's involvement with the Briavellians . . . can you hear how unbelievable this all sounds, Romen?" Cailech scratched his head theatrically before continuing. "You witness the funeral . . . ah, no wait, another intrigue. First you rescue Wyl Thirsk's sister from the dungeon where Celimus is keeping her. You spin him some story about wanting to shame the Thirsk name further by lying with her."

Wyl nodded grimly. It did sound farfetched when spoken aloud like this—how sad then that it was the truth.

"But here comes the good bit. Then you escape from Stoneheart because you know Celimus will never keep his word—will most likely make another attempt at your life. And, of course, you're right, but you escape death even though trained assassins follow you."

Wyl had mentioned nothing of Knave's involvement. That really would be pushing Cailech's indulgence.

The King sipped his wine and smiled. "You kill them and then dispatch the head of one to Celimus . . . why? Why would you let him know anything of your escape? But let's move on to the most intriguing part of all." Cailech was enjoying himself, Wyl realized. "Your actual intention is to track down a seer who did this 'speak' on you because you want more information."

"Correct," Wyl said, terrified by all the holes in the story he had related.

Cailech exploded into laughter, getting up from his seat to return to the mantelpiece. "Priceless! But I'm afraid it's too thin, Romen. You're going to have to come up with something more plausible if you want your life spared."

A servant stepped up quietly and at the King's permission whispered something.

"Bring her," he said and the servant departed.

Moments later Lothryn appeared with Elspyth, who went down on one knee to the sovereign.

"My lord Cailech," she whispered in no little awe.

The King glanced toward Lothryn and Wyl was quick enough to catch the surreptitious nod from the man. What it meant he could not guess.

"You are the seer's daughter, is this right?" Cailech asked.

Elspyth remained bowed. "No, my lord. I am her niece, Elspyth."

"Ah, that's right. Now tell me, Elspyth, what did your aunt say to Romen here the first time she met him? Please stand."

She did so, looking up at the mountain of a man before her. He was taller than Lothryn. A fierce intelligence lurked behind those shrouded eyes and they saw the puzzlement on her face.

"My lord?"

"Would you like me to repeat the question?"

Wyl felt the hairs on his arms lift. This was dangerous. Think fast! He opened his mouth to say something but the King was quick. He held up his finger to his mouth to stop Wyl.

Elspyth glanced nervously between both. "No, sire. I . . . I just don't understand it. My aunt has only met Romen once."

Cailech glanced at Wyl slyly but he spoke to Elspyth. "Ah! And I presume this occurred at your cottage . . . in the foothills?"

"Yes, my lord. A few days ago."

"And to your knowledge your aunt has met this man only once."

"I speak the truth. She told me she didn't know him, did not know his name."

Wyl knew Cailech would turn that hard gaze of his toward him now and whatever Romen said next would have to be convincing.

He had no choice and adopted a tone of soft offense. "Well, she has lied to you, Elspyth. I'm sorry."

Elspyth turned on Wyl and glared. "How dare you! Why would she?"

He shrugged, palms turned upward in a show of helplessness. "How can I possibly know her reasonings? She and I met briefly at Pearlis. It was early afternoon on the day of the royal tournament—the main break had just been called for the midday meal and there were plenty of people milling through the side stalls. You were definitely not around, though, or I would have recalled you." Wyl watched her anger stoke as he pressed on. "If my memory serves me correctly, I did see Thirsk with a companion, a man about his own age I knew to be Captain Alyd Donal. I don't think they went into your aunt's tent because I overheard them saying something about coming later, if all went well or something."

Fury turned to slow understanding on Elspyth's face. She suddenly looked down, embarrassed. Lothryn felt sorry for her when he noticed her blush.

"Sire, perhaps this is my mistake. Romen speaks true. My aunt mentioned that Thirsk came with a companion called Captain Donal and she also told me they had been at her tent earlier that day—she mentioned it only because she was surprised they did not visit her then and that she knew they would return."

"Where were you?" Cailech asked.

"I was at the tournament."

Trying to be helpful, Elspyth recounted for Cailech the Prince reintroducing the old rite of Virgin Blood.

"And they call us barbarians," Lothryn muttered under his breath.

Cailech's wry smile was evident too. "Please go on," he encouraged, fascinated.

"I was close enough to hear what followed the Prince's victory," she continued, looking at Romen while Wyl inwardly flinched at having to hear the torrid account again. "The General, I gather, thwarted the Prince's plans by marrying off his sister the previous day. It was obvious the Prince wanted to bed her—not because he loved her, I don't think, sire. She is a beautiful woman, of course. But he loves only himself, my aunt says."

The King nodded. "So Celimus had good reason for hating Thirsk. Humiliation is a wonderful weapon, isn't it, Lothryn?"

The big man returned the nod.

Wyl grasped the shift in thought and pushed the point harder. "Their hate for each other went back to childhood, I hear. It festered for a decade or more and was complicated—the fathers were blood brothers and old King Magnus was fond of Wyl while never enjoying much of a relationship with his son. There's more to it but Celimus did not enlighten me."

"All right, let's say I do accept most of what you've told me today. I still don't understand your trip north."

"Cailech, you're reading more into it than there is," Wyl said, reaching for the familiarity he sensed Romen once had with the King. "The seer told me my life would become entwined with a Queen. And that I must pledge my life to her cause. It meant nothing at the time—there was no Queen in any of the realms I knew. And then I went to Briavel for Celimus and met Valentyna," he lied. "All the events I spoke to you about then unfolded and I knew, at her father's death, this was the Queen the seer spoke of."

"So you came here to learn more about the vision she saw for you?"

"It's as simple as that. I didn't get a chance to learn much because Widow Ilyk kept calling out that the barbarian was coming. If only I'd paid attention."

Both the men before him smirked.

"Plus he was unwell from the potion he was taking for his pain and I served wine and we thought he might pass out and that's why we were outside," Elspyth concluded in a rush of words.

All eyes turned to Cailech. He swallowed what was left in his goblet, not at all perturbed by the audience's held breath or the awkward pause, which he further pressed by turning to Lothryn. "How is your woman?"

"I might check on her if we're finished here, my lord," Lothryn replied, not at all disturbed by the sudden twist in conversation.

Cailech nodded and his man left.

The King switched his topic back, once again surprising Wyl with his quick mind. "Why do you care about Thirsk, Briavel . . . any of it?" Cailech sounded exasperated now.

"Because Wyl Thirsk, as I discovered, was honest. I'm an outsider and I'm telling you Thirsk was true to Morgravia—as true to his King Magnus as Lothryn is to you. Now you admire loyalty, and so if you had known him you would have admired Wyl Thirsk for that quality alone. Furthermore, he abhorred torture of any kind," Wyl said, warming now to his own pet subjects. "If he had had the chance to go to battle, he would have spared death wherever he could. He was not a warmonger. He was not so dissimilar to you, in fact. Your vision was to parley, to settle squabbles with talk, not bloodshed."

"You seem to know a great deal about him—you must have gotten close swiftly?" Cailech watched Romen blink as though taken aback momentarily, then he saw him shake his head wearily.

"We spent a few days tied together, then we fought alongside each other to save a monarch under attack, then we fought each other because even he understood that only one of us could escape from Briavel alive. He died valiantly and he won my oath, as I've explained, to protect Valentyna."

"I ask again, why do you care?"

Wyl had no more answers. He cared because he was in love with her and that love was as ferocious as his hatred for Celimus.

Cailech sighed as though admonishing a child. "This is that nobility thing again with you, isn't it, Koreldy?"

"It runs in my veins," Wyl answered with sincerity, glad for the excuse. "And I made a pact with him. We mixed our bloods. It is binding, Cailech, and I must admit my loyalties are far easier given to Briavel than Morgravia," Wyl said, lying now. He felt suddenly tired and confused. He hated to think that he was no longer loyal to his homeland.

Cailech missed very little and could see the spirit, the fight that had been there previously had suddenly evaporated from the man he rather liked in spite of himself.

"We shall talk later. I need to think upon what you have

told me. You two are free to enjoy our hospitality. Please don't try and leave the fortress grounds or our archers will use you for target practice. My guards are on orders to kill either or both of you on sight if you are anywhere you shouldn't be. Understand?"

They both nodded.

"Tonight I am holding a feast. There may be a special dish on the menu that I'm sure will amuse you, Romen . . . not so you, my dear," he said to Elspyth. "I will ask you both to join us for some interesting festivities."

26

WYL TOOK ADVANTAGE OF THE AFTERNOON TO SLEEP. HIS dreams were filled with nightmares of a young woman hanging from a timber crossbeam begging him to save her. It became even more disturbing when the young woman's face dissolved from one he vaguely recognized from borrowed memories to one that was achingly familiar. Ylena hung now, beseeching Wyl, wondering how he could have failed to protect her.

He woke with a start, his bed linen drenched. *I have to escape these mountains!* The widow had warned him of the danger to his sister and now his dreams echoed that warning. To calm his anguish he lingered over his toilet, pleased to note that some kind soul had left him a fresh shirt. Washed and refreshed he was able to put aside his fears for the time being and concentrate on getting through this celebration of Cailech's. Perhaps if the King was in a good mood tonight, he might negotiate his own release.

Unable to sleep, Elspyth wandered the fortress aimlessly but felt her presence was unwelcome and all eyes watchful. The sense of alienation prompted her pleasure at seeing a familiar, albeit hostile, face as Myrt lumbered past her.

"Good day, Myrt."

He did little more than grunt but at least he paused.

She wiped her palms nervously on her skirt. "Um . . . would you know where I might find Lothryn? He, er . . . he went to check on his wife's progress."

The man mumbled directions that she hoped she could remember. According to Myrt, Lothryn had private lodgings among the fortress buildings. She had already gathered Lothryn was far more than a foot soldier for Cailech—it was obvious now that he was some sort of deputy. On her way she picked a bunch of wildflowers, hoping to please the new mother.

She lost her way several times but worked up the courage to ask directions of other souls even less communicative than Myrt and retraced her steps. Finally she found the alleyway they spoke of that opened into a small central courtyard with several stone houses built around it. At one doorway a group of people had gathered and she presumed this might well be the welcoming party for the new babe. As Elspyth approached she sensed, however, that the atmosphere was far from celebratory. If anything it was grim. The small gathering noticed her standing back and she was embarrassed by their stares and mutterings.

Elspyth called out carefully, introducing herself and asking after the family, having decided it was probably best not to trespass on what might be a private assembly.

An older woman, perhaps she was family—Elspyth could not tell—looked angrily at her and yelled. "Go away, Morgravian scum!" Then she spat toward Elspyth, who was too stunned to avoid the spittle that landed on her skirt. "You've brought the barshi!"

Barshi? She had no idea what it meant but found the mettle to ask where Lothryn was.

The old woman hurled a string of words at her in a language Elspyth could not follow. So she turned away from her and addressed a girl with red eyes, sore from her tears.

"I have a message for Lothryn," she lied.

"The Mourning Stone," the girl answered.

Elspyth began moving away. "Where is it?" She did not wish to antagonize the group any further.

Someone pointed toward a hill. She fled; her own fears and anguish welled as she ran. She found him finally after falling twice and grazing her palms and elbows in her efforts to climb the steep incline.

He was kneeling on a flat boulder of granite facing out to sea. He keened and the sound of his anguish cut through her. His cries intensified with the wind and were carried seaward.

Elspyth felt herself trembling for his pain and it was only after a few minutes that she noticed a tiny bundle in his arms. The shock of realizing the baby was present forced her to her feet and she stumbled forward again, risking his wrath, wanting to share his grief. It mattered not to her suddenly whether he acknowledged her presence or chose otherwise but Elspyth moved onto the Mourning Stone and put her arms about him and cried. She so badly wanted family of her own that she could more than empathize with this family's loss.

He did not recoil at her touch. Instead he rocked all three of them in his keening, clutching the bundle so close that Elspyth could not even see the baby's face. She assumed the worst, that new life had been snatched away by Haldor, the god in whom Lothryn had placed his faith. She lost track of time, realizing the flood of tears she herself had cried were not just for this Mountain Dweller's loss but for her aunt. Also for Romen and the horrible death of his family.

The wind gradually died down and she caught the unmistakable sound of a gentle whimpering of an infant.

She pushed back on her heels. *The baby lived!* Fresh tears. *Don't let him see them.* Elspyth stepped around Lothryn and reached tentatively toward the baby.

"Lothryn, it's Elspyth. I mean no harm. May I?"

He turned eyes of such intense sorrow on her that her courage almost failed and she would have left him if not for the gentle way in which the huge man held out his newborn baby. She took the child, feeling a fresh wave of grief. Holding this precious infant highlighted her own plight, her own lack of family and belonging. Elspyth cradled the softly moaning baby and without thinking put the tip of her small finger in the child's mouth. It immediately began to suck.

"Your baby needs feeding," she said.

His words came back hard. "His mother is dead. She fought hard to stay with us but she bled so much. They couldn't stop it."

Elspyth swallowed. "I'm so sorry." She said no more, fearful of using the wrong words. Instead she simply laid her hand on his arm. Perhaps through touch she could convey her despair at his loss.

He surprised her by covering her small hand with his own. "Thank you."

He reclaimed his newborn son and strode away, leaving Elspyth empty and shattered on the Mourning Stone where he had cast his wife's spirit to the seas.

Later, exhausted and back in her chamber, Elspyth glanced out of her window toward the meadows. She saw two riders. One was Lothryn. The other, unmistakably, was his King. Elspyth hoped Cailech would offer more comfort to his friend than she had.

She gave a son to our people, Loth. We must celebrate her contribution rather than mourn her death," Cailech said, staring out across the pastures he loved.

"You have good reason to celebrate the boy's birth," Lothryn replied more pointedly than he had intended.

Cailech now looked towards his closest friend and companion, the man he trusted above all others and remained silent. The look exchanged carried much weight. Both knew that whatever stood between them on this subject best remained unsaid. The King nodded in deference to his deputy before they walked their horses on.

"She didn't love me at the end, Cailech, it's all right," Lothryn finally said with a sigh. "I grieve for the unhappiness I gave her and the fact that the boy has no mother."

"We will care for him better than any other."

"I know."

The men guided their horses toward the lake. Cailech liked to skirt the water's edge. It was peaceful here . . . and especially private.

In his typical way he changed subjects. "I want to talk to you about the Morgravian prisoners we captured."

"Oh? I've been waiting to hear your decision on them."

"I've waited, Loth. Waited for my wrath to calm."

The big man spoke gently. "Cailech, our people should not have been there."

"That is as may be. But they were lost. I'm sure they explained this to their murderers before they died."

"If we overreact it could mean war between us and Morgravia."

"Overreact? A dozen innocents were mindlessly slaughtered, mostly our young."

Lothryn stayed quiet. He recognized the dangerous sign of his King's anger stoking. He appreciated how Cailech admired and encouraged the young members of their race. It was through his efforts that so many now lived into older age and did not kill each other in pointless tribal war. It was Cailech who had turned the young's energies to animal husbandry and farming on a more intensive scale. His people now fed themselves easily. Their harvests were plentiful and storage for less bountiful times more concerted and well-organized. It was Cailech who had insisted from the moment he had pronounced himself King that the young would now be taught letters and the history of their people rather than how to kill a man. Cailech encouraged music, singing, dance. He always had time for the youngsters. It hurt his very soul when one died from natural causes, let alone a dozen or so in brutal slaughter.

Lothryn knew, better than any, that Cailech would exact a price for their lives. He held little hope, in truth, for the unfortunate Morgravians they had captured but still he would try.

Cailech pointed towards a small stand of trees. "Race me, Loth."

Their horses, especially bred to be fast and hardy in this

terrain and climate, were spurred into a flat-out gallop. Predictably, the King won on his beautiful mare.

"Isn't she spectacular?" he said, laughing, breathing hard from the exhilaration of the ride.

"She's magnificent," Lothryn answered just as breathlessly, stroking his own mount, who had chased well. "What is your decision, my King?" he added, determined not to let the subject be left.

His friend became serious again. "I'm going to make an example of them."

"Please, Cailech, think it through."

"I have. While you were capturing Koreldy, I gave my attention to nothing else but this topic. I do not reach this decision lightly."

"These prisoners in our dungeons are innocents too. They have suffered enough. Must we react in the same fashion as our southern foe?"

"They are soldiers, not innocents!"

"Only one is a hardened soldier, my King. The others strike me as peasants who wouldn't know anything about killing, other than their beasts for meat."

"What would you have me do?" the King suddenly roared.

Lothryn took his time answering, waiting for his friend's anger to die.

"Release them. Be lenient, be better than the Morgravian King."

Cailech shook his head angrily. "It is his doing! His father would never have condoned such killing of our people. The son is a madman. You know all our spies report that even the Morgravians increasingly despise him. No, I cannot turn away from this, Loth. I want vengeance this time. Celimus will know my fury, he will know not to sleep too deeply. One day I will come for his lands."

His deputy sighed. This was the old mantra. For all his brilliance as a philanthropic ruler, Cailech still possessed the spirit of the conqueror. He remained a warrior and his desire to broaden the scope of his rule and his people's lands burned bright and deep within their mercurial King. It would be his undoing one day, Lothryn feared; had said as much on previous occasions. This was not the time to repeat it.

His sorrow at the King's decision was evident in the weary way he spoke. "What do you have in mind, my lord?"

And the King told him. There was no joy in it. Cailech spoke briefly, grimly, and refused to justify his planned actions. Lothryn had never felt more hollow, could not have imagined that Cailech would take his people to such a low place.

He could not help himself. "This is insane!" he said, risking offense.

"I will—"

"Cailech! It's madness, I say. Do you want to give our enemies the right to retaliate?"

"We are ready!" the King growled.

"For more of our people to die? Are you sure? If you do this war will come here, my King. Have you lost your mind?"

"Be careful, Loth."

The King's friend heeded the soft warning. "Cailech, we've known each other since the cradle. I have followed you through all the trials to becoming King and I have never once shirked my duty to you. There is no one more loyal to you."

"I know this," the King snapped.

"But I don't support this idea. In my estimation it lessens you," he risked saying. Then his voice became beseeching. "My King, this is not at all like you. You are so much better than this."

Cailech's expression twisted in discomfort. "I want to teach them a lesson they won't forget. The Morgravians murdered our children, Loth. Now I will respond in the only way they'll understand. It's horrific, I agree, but I am not going to let my people be bullied by this new and arrogant southern King. If I don't retaliate now and in equal measure, he will think me soft—vulnerable even."

"What does it matter if he does? He is nothing to us."

"It matters!"

"Will you be able to live with yourself after this?"

"You know me well enough."

And then it dawned on Lothryn. "This wasn't your idea, was it? Your mind doesn't work this way."

Cailech gave a small shrug. "What does it matter if Rashlyn devised it—he is right!"

Lothryn grimaced. Rashlyn was the King's barshi. People of the Mountains had always embraced the notion of magic. For a sovereign to have his own barshi, or sorcerer, was considered a blessing, for these practitioners were rare. But Lothryn had disliked Rashlyn since he had first come to the Razors and ingratiated himself into Cailech's inner sanctum.

Rashlyn had shown patience too. Years of quiet counsel and waiting, playing on the King's superstitious tendencies until he had won Cailech's trust. Now he considered himself untouchable; he knew Lothryn despised him but was confident of the King's protection. His sway with Cailech was becoming more pronounced with each year; this latest idea was an abomination.

Lothryn pressed the point, running his hand through his thick hair, the color of wet sand. "They will brand us barbarians."

The King gave a bitter bark of a laugh. "Morgravians and Briavellians, you mean? They already do! I no longer care."

"And this will give them good reason to believe it, my lord. You belittle your people in this and still you will do it, knowing they will blindly follow like sheep . . . as you do Rashlyn?" He had well and truly overstepped his mark. Lothryn anticipated an explosion of wrath.

Instead the gaze was as cold as a mountain spring in winter. Cailech's words splintered like ice through the heat of Lothryn's despair. "Leave me, Loth, before you say something else we'll both regret. Fret not for our people's reaction either. Rashlyn will doctor tonight's wine and our people will feverishly celebrate with me."

Lothryn did not utter another word, did not trust himself to speak further to his sovereign. He would die for Cailech without hesitation but he had never been more horrified at a plan or more disappointed in his friend than at that moment. Something would have to be done about Rashlyn. Lothryn had never trusted the man's intentions. Now Lothryn had good reason to wish the man of dark magics dead.

"Make sure Koreldy and the girl are present at the feast tonight," the King's voice carried to his turned back. Lothryn's cheeks burned with his own anger as he heard the words and the threat couched within.

27

THEY GATHERED IN THE MOUNTAIN HALL, A VAST CAVE OVER which the fortress itself had been built and which gave it its name. This was the heart of the stronghold and right now it was in a festive mood. Flaming torches lit the path down to the main arena where many dozens of trestle-style tables had been set up. There was no central fireplace; instead several scores of clay ovens with their cunning flues burned small fires around the edge of the hall, keeping its guests warmed. Countless numbers of the exquisite lantern flower, peculiar to the north, had been cut and strung across the hall, high above the heads of the gathered. In the bell of each flower a tiny candle had been lit and the flames made the lanterns' pink cups glow magnificently, scenting the air as they warmed and released their fragrant vapors. It was a truly beautiful and majestic setting. The more self-important southern realms had much to learn from these "barbarians," Wyl mused yet again.

The center of the hall had been left vacant and right now it was filled with dancers performing a traditional wheel. It was energetic and lighthearted; the music was loud, bouncing strongly off the walls and intensifying the atmosphere of the party. Dressed in brightly dyed garments, the dancers moved through their complex, fast-footed steps in time with the rhythmic beat of the great Mountain drum attended by two burly tribe members.

Cailech, seated on a dais, was resplendent in a charcoal-colored outfit that set off his height and contrasted with his light golden looks. He wore a linen shirt beneath his short jacket and a thin silver circlet replaced the leather thong around his head. In the elegant simplicity of his presentation he looked every inch a King. The gentleness of the lantern light softened his angular features and permitted Wyl to glimpse an echo of the young idealist Romen had known previously. The King looked proud this evening and oozed the strength and charisma that made him such a persuasive leader. He was in high spirits, too, singing along with the music and loudly enjoying the festivity and happiness of his people.

Wyl was seated at his right—as one might expect an honored guest—yet he knew himself to be little more than the Mountain King's prisoner. He noticed Elspyth, pale and quiet, further down on another table. She acknowledged his arrival with a nod but said nothing and hardly smiled. She was seated near Myrt. Lothryn was nowhere to be seen.

The music died to wild applause, led by Cailech. A troupe of children filed in. They were to sing for their lord King and needed help arranging themselves so he could see all of their sweet faces. Wyl took the moment to inquire after Lothryn.

"Ah. Sad it is. His wife died today birthing their child," Cailech whispered back, while still smiling for the children. Then he looked at Wyl. "It is a son, though—strong and proud—another warrior to wage war on the south." He grinned just for Wyl and there was something extra in that smile, something secretive, but Wyl had no intention of pursuing it. "I expect Lothryn will join us soon enough," the King added.

"How can you sound so callous over his loss?"

"No loss," Cailech replied abruptly. "They were a bad match, those two. Never suited and destined to be unhappy. I told him that before he took vows with her but she was with child and he was determined to be father to it. The child died days after birth, as did the next one. She never recovered her smile—going through life as though each day was a trial for her. Loth hoped this third child might bring some joy into her life—as did I for she came from excellent stock. Her father and his father before him were tribal leaders."

"So her death is a blessing, you mean?"

"I didn't say that, Koreldy. He will feel it no doubt, for he loved her in his own way. Lothryn will recover. I must help him find a mother for the boy."

Wyl shook his head. "And you, Cailech. No woman has ever touched your heart?"

Something passed across the King's face at this question. For a moment the man's eyes seemed to darken . . . and then it disappeared.

"I don't want Loth to miss tonight's special event" was the King's only response.

Wyl left it. It made no difference to him whether Cailech's heart ever warmed enough to love someone. "What special event?"

"Hush, the children are ready," Cailech said, turning back to the arena.

The youngsters sang sweetly—it was a moving ballad of the plight of the Mountain People from the early ages when tribe waged war on tribe. Wyl did not pay much attention although he noticed that Cailech was rapt with the words as well as the performance; the King clearly enjoyed the young members of his people. Instead Wyl turned his focus to what lay ahead for him and how he might argue his release. He had to win Cailech's trust again and the only way to do that was to somehow assure him that they shared the same dislike for Morgravians. The children had finished their song and were taking their applause. Cailech was on his feet and clapping loudly.

There was a feverish quality to the crowd's festivity, Wyl sensed. It was Romen's sharpness that picked this up, noted the glazed look in people's eyes, the laughter so quick and too loud. He dismissed the thought as the King sat down again and looked towards him.

Wine was poured and a course of steamed fish was served as a group of musicians struck up.

"I hope you're up to a long night of feasting . . . two in fact," Cailech said. "It continues on tomorrow. These fish were caught in my rivers today. Enjoy."

Wyl figured it was best to go along with the King's happy mood. After the fish, a delicious press of combined meats was served, their simple flavors enlivened with herbs and spices.

Now he decided it was time to make his first attempt. "Are you satisfied that I am no spy for Celimus?"

Cailech sipped his wine, again unperturbed by a sudden question. "Do you have more to tell that might convince me?"

"There is no love lost between Celimus and myself . . . this I promise you on my own life."

"And yet you worked for him, joined his ugly schemes—"

"Yes! For gold, Cailech—nothing more complicated than money." Wyl had to lower his voice for fear of attracting attention.

Cailech said nothing, although his gaze made Wyl feel uncomfortable as the big man weighed him up.

"What do you want?" Wyl tried a new approach. "How can I prove that I have no loyalties to anyone but myself?"

"Oh, I believe you have grievances against Celimus. We all do," he said. "But what about you and the Queen of Briavel?"

"If I can destabilize Celimus by helping her, I will."

"Why bother at all, Romen, if money is what drives you these days?"

"Revenge," he replied.

"Why do you care?"

Wyl sighed. "Celimus goes beyond craving power. I understand that. It is in a man's nature to want more land, more wealth, more power." Cailech nodded but said nothing. Wyl continued. "If someone doesn't help Valentyna, Celimus will invade Briavel. The Legion is strong and she has no experience with battle. I may be a Grenadyne but

after his betrayals I would hate for him to get another yard
of land, another piece of gold to add to his coffers."

The King considered this before speaking. "It would be
folly for Celimus to underestimate this new Queen, however inexperienced she may be. Sometimes all it takes is
passion."

Wyl agreed with the sage comment, particularly recalling
how stubborn and determined Valentyna had appeared to
him. If any young Queen could lead an army, he reckoned,
she was most likely the one to do it. "Still," he countered,
keen to take the conversation away from Valentyna, "if my
service can assist her against Celimus, I give it gladly, although my prices are higher these days." He added the last
deliberately to keep up the pretense that deep down he
cared little for either realm.

"So that's where you're headed, Koreldy? Back to Briavel? To offer your expensive blade at high cost to the
young Queen?"

"Yes," Wyl answered, hoping this was the response the
Mountain King wanted. He noticed that someone had just
signaled a message to Cailech. Romen's ever-alert eyes
missed little.

"I see. Then all that stored hate for Morgravia will ensure
you enjoy my surprise." The King gave Wyl no further opportunity for discussion. Instead he rose and banged his
mug loudly on the table. "Good people," he hushed the
crowd. "My people," he emphasized in a more patrician
manner. "I have a surprise for you tonight. To honor our
dead . . . those who had their innocent lives taken by the
southerners last moon, I have asked our kitchen to prepare
a special dish in commemoration."

He paused dramatically. Wyl felt a twinge of fear knife
through him, unsure why. Perhaps because he knew this
King to be unpredictable.

Cailech continued, his smile not touching his eyes this
time. "Enjoy something very new and different on our
menu tonight." He banged his mug again and encouraged
his people to follow suit.

They did. The Mountain drum was sounded mournfully

and the crowd fell in time with its beat. Wyl had no idea what was happening and nothing from Romen's memory yielded what this ceremony might signify. He imagined it was to present the King with a fabulous dish—someone had mentioned swan was on the menu, which in Morgravia was served only for high-ranking dignitaries and royalty. Could it be that?

The haunting Mountain horn sounded over the drums.

"Watch over there," Cailech whispered, a savage bleakness in his voice. "They come."

Wyl followed the King's avid stare and encountered a sight so powerfully shocking he felt immediately unsteady. He immediately looked toward Elspyth, whose hands covered her mouth, eyes wide with disbelief.

Wheeled in on special presentation tables were people, still alive, but prepared as though they were dead animals ready for the coals. There were five of them, Wyl counted slowly; four men and a woman—all naked. The woman was spread-eagled on the table dressed with seasonings, hands nailed in place and feet bound. All but one of the men were trussed like pigs, hands and feet together and hung from poles carried in by the burliest of barbarians. The final man, his head hung low, was chained around his neck, hands and feet. He shuffled behind, a pathetic figure, a sorrowful finale to this disturbing array.

Wyl's chest felt suddenly heavy; he could not drag in sufficient air. "Cailech?" he croaked but the King ignored him.

"Behold!" Cailech yelled to his people. "Morgravian meat for your bellies!"

The people, whom Wyl had admired as creators of such sophisticated beauty, now began to chant and hurl abuse at the victims. Wyl took full measure of the atmosphere in the hall. If he had not known better he would have assumed that the people had been drugged. His attention was caught by a man in dark robes. Small eyes, black almost, they seemed to Wyl, watched the proceedings with a hunger. His hands were clasped before him and a wild beard hid the shape of his mouth, while equally untamed hair curled wildly about the face. The man's eyes darted between the prisoners and

Cailech. Wyl saw him nod and then heard the King give the order.

"Oil them up!" Cailech roared. "Fan the flames!" He swallowed the contents of his mug, banging it down and wiping his mouth, his eyes now burning with a passion Wyl could not read. "Take them and wait for my signal," the King commanded. "All but the chained one. He remains. Tie him at the back of my hall so I can gloat before him."

Wyl searched for the strange, dark man but he was already gone. However, Wyl was sure he had been orchestrating events here tonight. *Who is he? Why would Cailech do his bidding?*

The tables were wheeled out and the single man, whose long, greasy hair streaked with gray covered his grimy face, was pulled roughly by his chains to the wall, where he was restrained as one might a dog.

"Music!" Cailech called and a happy jig started up. He turned and then conversationally said to Wyl, "Swan is next. It's our specialty, you may recall, Romen." The King smiled grimly, seating himself again.

People began to talk loudly and laugh with one another as though what had just occurred was a perfectly normal interlude to any Mountain feast. But Wyl's original curious thought—that these folk were drugged—took on high possibility for him. Just watching them dance the jig, it struck him that their energies were too frantic, too out of kilter with one another.

Wyl, still unable to talk coherently, looked over to find Lothryn had finally joined Elspyth and Myrt. Obviously he had not missed the proceedings, for his face was a mask of undisguised contempt. Meanwhile, the shock of what she had just witnessed was etched on Elspyth's face.

Wyl cleared his throat, his nerves still betraying him. "Cailech," he said softly, "who are those people?"

"Morgravians. You should be rejoicing with me rather than preparing to hurl up your fish."

Wyl had to clench his fists beneath the table to remain calm. *Morgravians!* The horror of it.

He had to know more, forced his voice to be steady. "Soldiers?"

Cailech nodded, chewing on bread. "The woman is their whore."

"How did you . . ."

"Fergys Thirsk was always shoring up the border patrols and now Celimus takes the offensive, sending in parties of spies, perhaps with the intention of becoming raiding parties." He scoffed. "They think they know the Mountains . . . they know nothing! The fools we captured were peasants, not even soldiers."

"And will you eat them?"

"Perhaps. Who knows the whims of the barbarians who eat the flesh of their own kind," the Mountain King said, loathing in his voice.

"Why are you doing this? To prove a point?"

"Precisely!" Cailech said, low and angry. "Celimus has ordered the killing of any Mountain People on sight. He is not choosy about whether they are children either. They slaughtered a dozen innocents not so long ago. At least I restrict my capture to soldiers!"

Wyl had not heard of this new law from Celimus but it rang true; nothing should really surprise him. "Cailech, most people in the southern, more populated regions of Morgravia would not even know what a Mountain Dweller looked like, or even that you personally exist," he tried to reason.

"Well, Morgravia's King seems to be taking us seriously enough. I have lost almost a score of lives since he took the throne, too many of them children, Romen, who accidentally crossed an invisible line. Children!" He was just short of shouting now and his people began to look up and wonder what might be making their King so anxious.

Wyl moved quickly. He could not risk Cailech's blood boiling up. Romen's memories told him the man became unpredictably dangerous if his temper was stirred. "Hush, my lord. You will make your people anxious. This is a celebration, is it not?"

The King gulped his wine, forced himself to remain silent as he calmed down.

Wyl filled the pause amongst the swirling noise of the festivities. "Truly, you don't mean to eat those folk."

The King remained silent.

"Cailech, you said yourself these people are peasants, not soldiers! You cannot punish them thus—even in war there are protocols observed. It is Celimus who is guilty; these people are innocents!" Wyl noticed there was pleading in his voice . . . and so did the King, who turned his intimidating gaze upon him now.

"And the people I lost were not?"

"I didn't say that."

"It is implied."

"I beg forgiveness. It was not my intent. Soldiers at least deserve an honorable death. The woman doesn't deserve to lose her life at all."

"For a Grenadyne you seem very concerned about Morgravian lives."

"As I grow older, I am concerned for all life." A woman with a lovely voice began to sing a soft, haunting ballad and Wyl was relieved that it seemed to calm the listeners.

"But I thought you killed without remorse, for money?" Cailech asked, looking back at the woman.

"I don't have to like it, though," Wyl replied, and at this the King finally smiled, genuinely amused. Wyl felt relief.

"You never fail to surprise me, Romen. It's probably why I let you go on living."

"I am grateful for your indulgence, my lord," Wyl said gravely, lifting his cup to the King. "May I speak with the prisoner?" He was relieved that Cailech had not answered his question about eating the prisoners. Perhaps it was all plain theater—something to stir the blood of his people.

"Go ahead. He's tough, that one. We've tried breaking him but his spirit is strong."

"Who is he?"

Cailech shrugged. "Who cares? Someone of rank by the way he spoke up on behalf of the others . . . and accepted their pain."

It was a cryptic statement. Wyl left it. "What is your plan for him?" he asked, suddenly afraid of the answer.

"Rashlyn suggests we cook him bit by bit. We'll cut off his hands and feet first and slice off fresh bits of meat from his sorry carcass each day. And perhaps I can take a leaf from your book, Koreldy. I shall send his head—baked, of course—to Celimus, so he can no longer perpetrate a lie that we eat our enemies. He will know it to be truth!"

Wyl ignored the rhetoric. "Who is Rashlyn?"

"My barshi. He advises, you could say."

The word barshi meant nothing to Wyl. He stored it away to check with Lothryn, though, and he had a very good idea who the barshi was. "Was tonight his idea?"

Cailech ignored him. Wyl had no doubt that Cailech was a ruthless ruler but he sensed he was too intelligent to lower himself to this horrific deed without being influenced in some way. Obviously this Rashlyn fellow wielded some power with the King. He turned away from the table, bowing to Cailech as a stuffed, roasted, and artfully refeathered swan was presented at the royal table to much applause. Trying to regain some composure as he left, Wyl paused by Lothryn to offer his condolences on the loss of his wife.

The Mountain Man only nodded before moving onto the matter at hand. "I'm sorry you bore witness to this dark deed tonight."

"You don't agree, obviously."

"I don't believe the King is even speaking to me after I had my say about it."

Wyl nodded. "Was that man with the beard and long hair Rashlyn?"

"Yes. He's very dangerous."

"I gather this is his doing."

"Unfortunately."

"Where's Elspyth?" Wyl asked, noticing she was not present.

"I think Cailech's surprise was too much for her."

"His course of action is unwise," Wyl said, knowing Lothryn to be a reasonable man.

"I don't like it any more than you, but I have said all I can on the subject. He is determined to retaliate in this contemptuous manner. You know what Cailech is like. We have lost many lives recently and, in spite of anything I advise, he is immovable. He is also wrong, of course. This will simply provoke more killing of our own people but he is proud and he is hurting over the children who died. They killed them for sport, you know . . . Mountain Dwellers are less than animals in Morgravian eyes."

Wyl sighed. It seemed impossible that men under his command would perpetrate such horror. *Except they aren't under my command,* he reminded himself. He looked at the pathetic, chained figure squatting naked against the wall. Something was nagging at his mind; something he knew he should pay attention to but his thoughts were too fractured.

"Would you keep an eye on Elspyth? She doesn't deserve to be a part of all this."

Lothryn nodded, suddenly silent again and Wyl thanked him, walking now toward the Morgravian, whose head was hung between his knees. He was a tall man, Wyl could tell. Slim and hard-muscled, clearly one who had trained hard. As he drew close, again Wyl felt the nudge against his mind. *What is it? What are my thoughts trying to provoke?*

Now he could smell the grimy, unwashed soldier. It reminded him of how he had found Ylena and anger surged. He wondered how much punishment this man had taken upon himself to protect the others. Wyl made to bend down to talk with the man but a guard prevented him.

"It's all right, Borc," a voice came from behind. It was Lothryn.

"Cailech's leaving nothing to chance, then," Wyl said, a hard edge to his voice at being trailed by Lothryn.

"He never does, Romen. You should know that."

Wyl nodded, his fury mingling with despair and a small surge of wisdom advising him against responding to that comment. He ignored the guard and squatted. The overpowering smell of the soldier almost made him stand up again but he reached out his hand and lifted the head to look into the ruined face of a man he knew all too well.

"Gueryn!"

"Is that you, my boy? Is it you, Wyl?" the man croaked,

clearly in some sort of stupor. He was blind; his eyelids had been sewn together.

"You know him?" Lothryn asked, surprise evident.

Wyl could not respond to either Lothryn or, more importantly, Gueryn. He could not bear to see the state of his mentor—this brave man of Argorn, so loyal to Morgravia, so dedicated to the Thirsk family.

"Wyl?" the battered man asked again and then hung his head into its same cowed position.

"He's always asking for someone called Wyl. Must be his son," the guard commented. "Wish we'd got him too."

His malicious laugh was poorly timed. Wyl moved fast. In a blink the guard's throat was being crushed by the large hands of Romen Koreldy. The man's flailing limbs managed to send one server's tray of roast swan high into the air before it came crashing down onto the stone floor, causing quite a commotion. Wyl was grabbed from behind and a more powerful strength than he owned fortunately prevented him from doing any further damage.

"Are you out of your mind?" Lothryn exclaimed, pinioning Wyl's arms.

It was too late. Cailech had leapt from the dais and arrived quickly at the scene. "By Haldor's hairy ass! What happens here?" he roared.

The cavernous hall had become silent, save the sound of the serving woman moaning over her tray of swan meat.

"Koreldy!" Cailech yelled, forcing Wyl to look at him. "You would assault one of my men in my own fortress?"

"I took offense at something he said, my lord," Wyl replied, his mind racing, knowing he would need a watertight reason for this latest act.

"He knows the prisoner," Borc croaked.

Cailech's jaw was working furiously. "Out!" he said and Wyl was manhandled by Lothryn, away from earshot of curious bystanders.

They left Borc coughing and massaging his bruised throat.

"Who is he?" the King demanded.

"His name is Gueryn le Gant," Wyl said, glad to be away

from his old friend as he began to wield Romen's inimitable skill at spinning a web of lies. "He is originally from Grenadyn. I grew up with him." Gueryn was only about ten years older than Koreldy, Wyl realized. He would have to be careful.

"Then what in Haldor's name was he doing wearing Morgravian colors?"

Wyl's gaze flicked to Lothryn, who stood expressionless behind his King. There would be no help from that quarter. He played for time instead. "I can't answer that until I've spoken with him. I haven't seen him in years," he lied.

"Fetch him," Cailech said over his shoulder and Lothryn obeyed.

Wyl realized that Romen's normally easy smile failed him now. And Cailech knew it too as he took a threatening step forward.

"If I find out you're lying, Koreldy, it will be for the last time. You will suffer the same fate as your naked friend here."

Gueryn was dragged shivering before the King. Perhaps he anticipated more beatings, Wyl supposed, as the brighter torchlight showed up livid bruising over most of his body. Lothryn's expression showed that he did not agree with his sovereign's brutal taste for revenge. Wyl assumed the sewn eyelids was Rashlyn at work again.

Wyl turned at a disturbance behind them: Elspyth was trying to break through the guards. When Cailech inquired with a single glance, Lothryn whispered something brief.

"Allow it. She can help."

Elspyth was permitted to join them. She averted her gaze from the prisoner and glared at Cailech instead.

"Ah, Elspyth. I did warn you that tonight's festivities might not be to your liking. Now you can assist us, please. Would you address this wretch here and ask him a question on my behalf? It occurs to me he may respond to a woman's voice—we should have thought of that before, Loth, eh?" He grinned but his deputy did not respond.

Elspyth turned and caught a strange expression on Romen's face. There was pain there and she was not sure what he wanted from her in this moment.

"Talk to him softly," Cailech guided. "Ask him who Romen Koreldy is," he added looking slyly toward Wyl. There was both menace and warning in his glance.

She looked toward the trembling man. It was not fear that made him shake. As far as she could tell he was sick, and little wonder, looking at his battered body. Elspyth's heart ached for this brave soldier who had obviously kept his secrets to himself. If he stood to his full height he would be a tall man and no doubt proud. Her tears welled to see his eyelids so cruelly sewn shut. They had bled and the blood had crusted. Sores had erupted around the punctured skin. Death might be a kinder blow. She pushed that thought aside, realizing the three men were watching her.

"What is his name?" she asked, turning to Wyl.

Cailech did not permit Romen to answer, which she considered strange. They had seemed friendly enough an hour before—now suddenly there was a cloying tension between the pair.

"His name is Gueryn," Lothryn answered, directing a ghost of a smile toward her, from which she took courage.

"Gueryn, can you hear me?" she asked.

Immediately Gueryn turned sightless eyes toward Elspyth. He nodded.

Cailech's expression turned into one of grim pleasure. At last, the man would reveal something . . . all it needed was a woman's touch.

"My name is Elspyth, Gueryn. I am Morgravian from the town of Yentro."

A single tear oozed between the stitches of his lids as he recognized the lilt of her accent and Wyl's heart broke. It was just too much for him to bear. "As one, Gueryn!" He shouted.

He should have anticipated it but he was so intent on reaching Gueryn's blurry mind that Cailech's fist connected unimpeded with Romen's fragile ribs, which fractured again under such direct pressure. Wyl doubled and then fell to his knees, pain engulfing him in a haze of sharp, fragmented lights. He slumped in a corner, breathing with difficulty, desperately hoping nothing was punctured. He did notice that Gueryn stood just a little straighter, a fraction taller; his mouth had found that firm line he remembered seeing as a child when Gueryn was displeased with him. Screaming out the family motto had achieved something far more important than a smashed rib.

It had happened so fast, Elspyth had not even the chance to scream.

"Make a sound, young woman, and I will do the same to you," Cailech whispered.

"It's all you're good for then, my lord," Elspyth rounded on him. "Hurting women. Torturing people. You had me fooled for a while but I see you are a barbarian in the truest sense of the word. You have no compassion, no empathy for your fellow man. Kill me if you must. I will not do your dirty work. I am Morgravian and proud of it. I will not bow to the Mountain race. I would sooner die than forsake my fellow countryman. Trust me when I say that I distrust my King but I love my people. I wish you and your tribe no harm but I will not allow you to torment me or my people any further. I will not join you in persecuting this man or humbling the mercenary. You can find out for yourself in your own barbaric way what you want to know."

Elspyth's a long speech took everyone by surprise, which was probably why she was allowed to have her full say. Her eyes blazed with passion and fury; her chest rose high with her heavy breathing. If Wyl had had the strength he would have cheered. He felt sure the King would strike her too after such high insult.

Instead Cailech sneered. "Take all three to the dungeon, Loth. They can share the same fate over the roasting coals. We shall have to do it tomorrow. Frankly, I've lost my appetite for tonight."

28

AN OBSERVER MIGHT BE FORGIVEN FOR ASSUMING THAT THE King of the Mountains was alone, brooding by a fire he neither needed nor appreciated for its comfort or light. Beside him a cup of warmed wine stood untouched.

Cailech was angry. In fact still angry from Lothryn questioning his actions prior to the feast. He loved Lothryn. He would never have a more loyal subject or as close a friend. But it seemed they no longer shared the same vision. Lothryn was content with what had been achieved. Cailech knew his friend's advice would be to live life happily now and reign well. Look after the people. Flourish among the mountains of their homeland. He could almost hear Lothryn saying it.

But Cailech wanted more. He was ambitious still. Although he was now in his fourth decade, none of the fire in his belly had dimmed. Without knowing they shared a similar dream, he and Celimus could both imagine a sprawling empire beyond their own realm's borders. Cailech's would ideally have stretched from the north throughout the south of the continent spreading east and west to encompass the pompous Morgravians and the naive Briavellians, who paid scant attention to their northern border. Neither realm had ever been more vulnerable. Both had young heirs recently taken to their thrones. It was good sense that Celimus would make an offer of marriage to Valentyna and she would accept, binding their nations, combining their armies' strengths.

Rashlyn was right. If Cailech wanted to claim some of the fertile, easy-to-farm lands south of the Razors and if he wanted some of his people to migrate toward an easier lifestyle in a softer climate, then he must make his move swiftly. *Do I want this?* he asked himself. *Do I really want our people to soften?* If he was honest—which he was not on this occasion—then he would admit what he truly wanted was to humiliate and dominate the new King of Morgravia. Celimus was a menace to everyone's peace and prosperity and Cailech knew that if the southern King got his way and married Valentyna then he would not be content until he had tamed the people of the far north. Celimus was ambitious by all reports and not a coward. Inexperienced but certainly avaricious and of a mind to build his own empire; have his own son sit across not just the southern realms but perhaps the Mountain throne as well.

Into his ruminations came Koreldy, who had made such a curiosity of himself, beseeching indulgence on behalf of the Morgravian prisoners—people he did not care about supposedly, owed nothing. And then the business of offering his services to Valentyna.

"All very generous and righteous," the King muttered to himself. "But what are you hiding, Koreldy?"

Cailech was convinced Koreldy was not telling him the truth. The man struck him as different. He granted many years had passed since they had seen each other but there were very real inconsistencies in this new Koreldy. The old Romen was selfish to the point of distraction and tremendously self-assured. The death of his sister had exacted its toll but the character remained the same. The Romen he now met was far less arrogant. The swaggering personality was there but there was a hesitancy now, even a remoteness that Cailech could not fathom. Besides—and this was the greatest curiosity of all—Koreldy had not even challenged him to game of agrolo and no amount of maturity would change the competitive streak between the two for this game of skill played on a board with stones for pieces. When they were younger men Cailech had taught Romen the game and he had embraced it with a fierce passion. It took high concentration and an inclination to take risks—only those prepared to lose everything they wagered stood the true chance of winning.

Romen was a man who liked to win at everything and he would not have forgotten their last encounter, when Cailech had trounced him. Won his whole purse, damn it, even his lands back home in Grenadyn! Not that they were ever claimed.

No, the King mused. Koreldy had either undergone some extraordinary change in character or they were dealing with an impostor. He had not realised he had voiced this thought aloud.

"Not an impostor, my King," a voice spoke from the shadows. "I have searched him. This is Koreldy."

"You're quite sure?"

"How can it be otherwise? Are you suggesting a glamor?"

"Is it possible?"

"No. A glamor requires immense skill, Cailech," the voice said, no longer quite so subservient. "Who do you imagine could wield such talent?"

The King shrugged. "Just a thought."

"An impossible one. There is only one other person I know who might possess such ability and he is dead."

"Elysius."

A dark shape melted out of the shadows now and Rashlyn's face was lit from the glow of the fire. "Who else?" he said with finality. "And you forget that I am as familiar with Koreldy as you."

"You never really knew him, though, did you?"

"No. I observed him from a distance. But I would know if this was not the same man in the flesh."

"Is it the same man, Rashlyn? I agree with you that I too would know him if he were outwardly different. There is something else, though. But I do not possess your sentience—I cannot determine it," Cailech said, frustrated.

"I sense nothing except that he will bring trouble, my King."

"He can do nothing. He is locked in my dungeon."

"And Lothryn, Cailech? Can you trust him?"

Cailech looked at his barshi for the first time since they had spoken. It was a fierce glare and said much.

"Forgive, my lord," the sorcerer said and bowed contritely to take his leave.

They were locked into the same cell. It was large but with nothing in it save a bucket. A vent offered vague but nonetheless welcome air and the walls dripped with a slimy damp. A single candle had been lit by Lothryn as a small mercy; he had said nothing, refused to answer Elspyth's pleas, but Wyl could sense the big man was deeply unhappy at the turn of events.

Guards had bound their hands and, although Lothryn had left the two men tied, he had undone the rope around Elspyth's wrists, even lingering just long enough to rub them. Then he had left, but not before a final glance towards Koreldy that, for all his intuition and experience, Wyl could not fathom.

The heavy oaken door had slammed with a chilling finality.

"Untie me," he said to Elspyth, then looked anxiously over at Gueryn.

She began worrying at the knots. "I suppose your rib has broken again?"

He nodded. "Don't fuss."

She bristled. "That was particularly stupid of you to incense the King. What was in your head?"

"Love, loyalty, friendship," he replied.

Elspyth heard the sadness in his voice. "Love! For whom?"

"Him." His hands came free and he put a finger to his lips to ask Elspyth to keep silent. "Gueryn?" he whispered.

The man did not flinch. Wyl tried again but with no success.

Elspyth, never one to remain silent for long, decided to intervene. "It's Elspyth here, Gueryn. We're alone for now. The man speaking to you is—"

She was not permitted to finish. "It's me, Gueryn. It's Wyl."

Elspyth sat back astonished. Romen ignored her. He was intent on watching Gueryn's reaction, which was immediate. The man turned his swollen face toward the voice.

"Wyl?"

"I'm here."

"When . . . how . . . your voice . . . it is—"

"I know. I have much to explain but you must trust me now."

"How can I?"

Wyl thought hard. "You gave Ylena a white kitten when my father died but you gave me a long hug of comfort in my father's study that I have never forgotten. You hated not being with my father in the field but you loved our family . . . loved me enough to give up your career in order to raise me and train me in my father's absence. I have loved you for it. I think you might have admired my mother just a little more than duty required, and I think she knew this. She—"

"Stop!" Gueryn said. "Enough . . . enough," he added in a voice that hurt Wyl more than the old soldier could know. "Did he injure you?"

"Not nearly as much as you, old friend."

Gueryn, amazingly, croaked a laugh. "Wyl . . . my boy . . . I never thought I would see you again."

"And I was told you were as good as dead."

"Celimus?"

"Yes."

"It figures." He began coughing.

"Cover him with your jacket. He is sick," Elspyth admonished in a stiff whisper, still trying to fathom this conversation.

"No escape, Wyl. I've tried. It's secure," Gueryn warned as he felt the comforting touch of Wyl's jacket.

Wyl ignored that fact for now. "Why did they sew your eyes shut?"

"Because Cailech didn't like the way I looked at him. He said he could see nothing but contempt in them. He was right."

"I suppose you're fortunate he didn't have them poked out," Wyl offered glumly.

"He's saving that for tomorrow night. He will do only one apparently. Says I should not miss out on watching myself being eaten." He rocked back and forth. "What have we come to, Wyl? Fodder for the barbarians."

"Tell me everything," Wyl asked.

Gueryn began his tale from the moment Celimus ordered him north to his capture. "I was set up for it. Celimus intended for this to happen."

Wyl nodded knowingly.

"By Shar's Name, I swear it. He deliberately had me ordered to lead a reconnaissance into Razors territory with men I was not familiar with. Felrawthy would have been furious had he known but it was all done behind his back. We all know you only send the very best trackers and experienced soldiers on such a dangerous mission. These men were clearly expendable, with little soldiering experience. Fresh from the fields, I'd say. They made much noise and were useless at coping with the mountain terrain. It was not a case of whether we would be picked up but simply when. I realized as much as soon as the orders were given. The woman was probably a special sweetener from Celimus. I learned she was paid to follow us."

Wyl squeezed Gueryn's shoulder in sympathy and his friend reached up to cover his hand with his own. It was an emotional moment for both of them as they realized how low Celimus was forcing his proud Legion. Bound to the King, they had no choice but to do his ugly bidding.

"And Elspyth with the lovely voice . . . who are you, my dear?"

"Entangled in your friend Koreldy's web, I'm afraid," she answered. "Not that I know who he is these days."

"Have you taken a guise, Wyl?"

"Yes," he replied, glad to use that excuse.

"What about your story? Are you going to enlighten me?"

"In good time, Gueryn. Right now you must rest. Your breath comes hard. Please, sleep."

"He's right," Elspyth echoed to the older man. "You're shivering with fever, sir."

"Good. I hope I have plague and make fine eating for tomorrow—infecting all of the Mountain scum."

Wyl had pretended to sleep. He did not feel much like talking or, more to the point, explaining himself

Elspyth. She left him alone, although he could feel her disgruntled stare for some time until she too realized that rest was a good idea. It seemed many hours had already passed since the door had closed on them.

Then came the sound.

A soft thud. Wyl listened intently. There it was again, this time louder and accompanied by a grunt. He heard the jangle of keys and then in the thin, dying candlelight noticed the ring handle on the door move. Wyl silently got to his feet, anxiously looking around for something with which to hit whatever head came around that piece of oak. Barring his own fist for a weapon, he could only see the bucket, which was mercifully empty. He grabbed it, blew out the candle, and stood behind the door as the key turned in the lock.

A large shape, outlined in ghostly light from the torch in the corridor, entered the room as the door swung back. It was such a wide door that Wyl had to step out and around it and he thanked the reach of Romen's long arms as he swung the bucket toward the head. The weapon connected and shattered, accompanied by loud swearing. Elspyth screamed.

"Haldor's Balls, Koreldy! Did you have to do that?" Lothryn whispered angrily, rubbing at his head.

"What did you expect me to do?" Wyl replied, unprepared for the familiar voice. "Walk meekly to the ovens without a fight?"

"Well, before you hit me again, consider why I'm whispering."

Elspyth had already worked it out, leaping to her feet and into Lothryn's arms.

"I knew you wouldn't let me perish," she said.

"How could I?" he said, voice suddenly gentle. "I couldn't bear for you to be hurt."

"I know," Elspyth replied, her gaze searching his as if no one else in the room mattered.

"Lothryn, this is all very touching but what in Shar's 'ame is going on?" Wyl hissed.

"I'm getting you out," the man whispered. "Hurry, rouse your friend. I've brought warm clothes."

Wyl wanted to shake his head and think it through. Lothryn, betrayer of Cailech! Surely not?

The Mountain Man seemed to guess what he was thinking. "I don't agree with Cailech. I grieve too for our dead but butchering our enemies to make a point is heading back to our darkest days."

Wyl gently shook Gueryn, who now awoke bewildered and groggy, the fever still claiming his body. "Loth, it's suicide for you to do this."

"I know. Here's a key to unshackle him. Now help him dress; you need to climb into these clothes to look like we're all from the tribes, and hurry. I've drugged the guards but you never know how luck will hold."

"Who is the man who helps us?" Gueryn wondered aloud.

"Lothryn," Elspyth answered, just a little too proudly, Wyl thought.

"You were the one who tried to break me?" Gueryn said.

"And I failed, I'm glad to say. Your loyalty is stronger than mine," Lothryn replied.

"I bow to you all the same for your courage."

"You can thank me later if we still have our lives," he said grimly.

"Can we help the others?" Gueryn asked, teeth rattling.

"It is too late. We would risk everyone's lives to save them."

"We can't let him eat them!"

Lothryn sighed. "In truth, I don't think he will. Tonight he was fired up, angry. You've seen him like that before, Koreldy." Wyl nodded. "But he will end their lives. Escape with me is your only hope. Is everyone ready?"

His companions nodded, although Gueryn was definitely confused now, knowing full well that Wyl had never met Cailech before.

"Weapons?" Wyl asked.

"None, other than mine. There will be no killing. We either get out without harm to any of my people or we die in the process. Here is your pack."

Wyl could only nod. "Then we're ready."

"Did you bring my cloth bag?" Elspyth inquired of their rescuer. Wyl laughed. What a typically womanly thing to ask. Elspyth understood his smirk. "It occurs to me, Romen Koreldy—or whoever in Shar's world you are—that you may need pain relief. Feel free to go without, though. I will lose no sleep."

Wyl meekly muttered an apology, which she chose to ignore as Lothryn, who had indeed brought her bag, tossed it toward her.

"Here," she said, roughly pushing the small bottle into Wyl's hand. "It's all yours."

He took several sips and felt the numbing sensation begin to ease the pain. He made Gueryn take a few sips as well. It would not touch the fever but it would ease the pain of his other hurts.

"Silence," Lothryn cautioned as he and Wyl virtually carried Gueryn between them.

The early hour worked in their favor. The castle was only lightly guarded, such was Cailech's faith in his Mountain fortress's impregnablity. Very few Morgravians even knew of its existence save what the old stories told and even fewer would know how to reach it. Most would die with an arrow through their throats anyway, for Cailech posted keen-eyed lookouts throughout the passes that gave access to the fortress.

For now the small group tiptoed by several fallen guards, presumably sleeping off the same drug Lothryn had used on the dungeon guards.

"I've tipped off the gatekeeper that I will be leaving with three of our men. Remain silent. I will do the talking. Elspyth, keep your hair under that hood and face covered. We are all dead if they suspect anything."

Wyl whispered to Gueryn, "You'd better keep your head covered too."

Lothryn had planned well. They wore the special hooded cloak favored by the Mountain Dwellers for travel in the higher parts. That hood would serve them brilliantly now, they all hoped.

"Are we trying to do this on foot?" Wyl whispered.

"No. Horses have been readied. Can he ride, do you think?"

"Don't talk around me as though I'm senile. I can ride. Ride the breeches off both of you—even without sight!" Gueryn growled as they both shushed him.

Lothryn led them to stables, where a young lad was rubbing sleep from his eyes.

"Very late for you to be heading out, Loth," the boy said.

"Secret mission, lad. I told you. Now you must keep that quiet, remember. Tell no one, all right?"

"Not even the King, Loth?" the boy joked.

"He'll know," Lothryn replied and they all imagined the cold touch of Cailech's wrath reaching out to them already.

Lothryn kept the nosy stableboy distracted with a request to adjust his horse's saddle straps while the others mounted. Somehow Gueryn managed to clamber onto his horse himself, slumping into the saddle. Elspyth's foot slipped in the stirrup but fear made her quick to scramble up, while Wyl managed easily enough with no pain to hamper his movements. He had little doubt, however, that his rib would be aching again before sunrise.

Lothryn whispered some final parting words to the lad and then waved a silent farewell. The boy responded in kind and then yawned, heading back into the stable.

"That was the easy bit," Lothryn muttered to Wyl. "Just follow my lead now."

Walking the horses softly out of the stables complex, Lothryn led them to the gatehouse. They pulled their hoods even deeper over their faces as they approached.

"Ho!" Lothryn called to the man whose sleepy head poked out of the window.

"What do you call this then?" the guard asked.

"Apologies, Dorl, for the late hour. We are on the King's business."

"Oh, yes, and what might that be, Lothryn?"

"Never you mind that nose of yours, Dorl. It will get you

into trouble one of these days," Lothryn replied, amusement in his voice.

Dorl responded in kind. "It's my job to be nosy."

"Yes, but not about Cailech's private business."

"All right, all right. Give me a moment. I'm off for my supper, just waiting for the relief."

"Who takes over?" Wyl asked conversationally, taking Lothryn's lead and firmly believing that three silent riders might be construed as suspicious.

Dorl was not paying attention anyway. He was already occupied with cranking the wheel which would open the gate. "I think Borc is on his way down," he called out in answer. Wyl and Lothryn threw each other a meaningful glance. Borc would be a problem. "Although I heard there was some problem at the feast. That he had been hurt or something?"

"I wouldn't know," Lothryn lied. "Come on, Dorl. Put your back into it!"

They heard him make some deprecating noise at Lothryn's comment and the gate slowly began to ascend, protesting with creaks.

Lothryn was not prepared to risk waiting any longer and clicked his horse to move on. The animal was reluctant until the gate opened fully but the rider insisted and the beast obeyed, ducking its head. Elspyth was next and was relieved her mount simply followed the lead horse.

"Haldor's Wrath, but you're in a hurry," Dorl called out.

"King's business can rarely wait," Lothryn called back, hoping Gueryn would take the hint and follow next.

He did so and Wyl brought up the rear, lifting his hand in thanks to the gatekeeper.

"Haldor guide you," he hailed at their backs.

Lothryn replied in similar fashion and felt relief flood through himself as the gate began a quicker descent.

"Ride!" he said over his shoulder to his companions and they broke into a canter over the rocky ground and through the first pass. "Don't look down, Elspyth," he cautioned.

"I won't," she called grimly, holding the reins and staring at the back of the Mountain Man.

"Do you think they'll follow?" Wyl called to Lothryn.

"Of course they will. Cailech will track us forever now."

It was probably fifteen or so minutes later that Wyl heard hooves behind them. He yelled to Lothryn, grateful he could see some flatter, open ground for a while. "Run for it!"

No one needed to be told again. The four horses were spurred into a gallop, Wyl calling guidance to Gueryn, who seemed fearless despite his blindness. His horse obediently followed the lead horses and, as the companions' hoods blew off and their identities were revealed beneath a full moon, they heard the roar of anger behind them as Borc tried to shorten their lead. He was brandishing a sword and Lothryn had no choice but to pull his own from its scabbard and turn back to meet the howling man head on.

Wyl turned back too but felt helpless without a weapon. The others slowed their horses and Elspyth took Gueryn off to the relative safety of a craggy overhang. Wyl yelled to Lothryn to give him the sword.

"Don't fight your own man. Let me. I've reason to kill him. You don't."

"I have no intention of killing," Lothryn yelled back.

"I understand. Let me," Wyl begged, mindful of how hard this betrayal was for Lothryn.

Lothryn finally tossed the sword to Wyl, who grabbed it effortlessly from the air and then jumped from his horse. He had only a moment's time to gather his wits before Borc was upon his fellow tribesman, determined to slay him. He swung at Lothryn's head with his sword, only just missing, and if not for the distraction of Wyl running at him with a weapon, might have finished the attempt with a second swing. Instead, he jumped to the ground to face Wyl.

"You traitor!" Borc yelled at Lothryn as he circled his new opponent. "How could you betray us?"

"Because Cailech is wrong!"

"Wrong to kill the enemy?"

"Wrong to murder innocents."

"Since when have you cared about a Morgravian soul?"

Wyl allowed them this time. As Borc continued to circle

him, Wyl could already see that his opponent was clumsy by comparison to his own silky skills. Borc, he anticipated, would simply rush at him. Wyl had no fear of this warrior.

"Since now, Borc," Lothryn replied.

"Just fuck her, Loth, and be done. I'll help you do it, man. You know there will be no forgiveness from Cailech."

"Not another word about her, Borc," Lothryn cautioned, "or I will take the sword and finish you."

"And you think I'm afraid of you?" he countered.

"No," Wyl chimed in, tiring of the conversation. "But you should be very afraid of me, Borc, because I still carry insult from you. How is your throat, anyway?"

Borc narrowed his eyes at Wyl. "When this is finished," he called back to Lothryn, "I shall do her in front of you."

Wyl made the sound of a parent scolding a child. "Very ugly talk, Borc. Let's see if you fight as dirty as you speak."

A whir of sword thrusts left Borc groaning on the ground, holding his leg, with blood pouring from severed tendon and muscle and another slash on his arm.

"That should slow him down," Wyl said to Lothryn, who looked on with awe.

"I knew you were skilled, Koreldy, but not that good."

"I've learned some tricks from a new friend," Wyl replied. "I gather you want him left alive?"

Lothryn nodded. "Leave him some water."

They did so and rode off immediately, Borc howling curses after their backs. Once out of sight of the guard, Lothryn stopped the group's progress.

"What's wrong?" Wyl asked.

"We must use what's left of the dark to get as far as possible," Lothryn cautioned. "Once Borc set off after us, Dorl will not have wasted any time in running to the King. In any case, the guards have probably already woken and raised the alarm that you three have escaped. Cailech won't wait—he'll have sent a tracking party by now."

Elspyth felt a new fear. "What are you saying?"

"He's saying we'll have to escape the hard way, am I right?" Gueryn croaked.

Lothryn nodded, looking at Wyl.

"So leave me!" Gueryn ordered. "I will hamper progress."

"Stop!" Wyl ordered. "There'll be no talk of anyone left behind. Lothryn . . . tell me the worst."

"We'll have to go over the mountains. The horses can only take us so far. It will be on foot for the most part. Very dangerous."

"Lookouts?"

"No," he said somberly, "they're the easier of our problems. Our greatest threat is from the zerkons."

"You mean they're real?" Elspyth said.

Wyl had not heard of them. "Zerkons . . . another tribe?"

Lothryn gave a harsh laugh. "Another species. I hope you never have to see them, let alone fight them. Here," he said, lifting a bundle wrapped in sacking from beneath his pack. "You'll be needing these."

Wyl heard the comforting clank of metal. "My weapons?"

The barbarian nodded. "I took them from your room at the inn in Yentro. I had high hopes of keeping them, to be honest, but they're somehow too elegant for the Mountain style of combat."

"Are the knives sharp?" It was a strange question from Gueryn.

"Very!" Wyl assured him.

"Good. Then you can release these stitches from my eyes."

His three companions looked at each other. It was no polite request from the old soldier.

"Do it!" he commanded with a strength Wyl remembered all too well.

"I will," Elspyth offered. "I have a steady hand."

Wyl gingerly gave her one of the daggers.

"I can't see very well by moonlight," she admitted to her patient.

"Well, that makes two of us," he replied gruffly. "Do what you can."

Laying him on his back, she quietly thanked Shar for his full moon this night. It hurt Gueryn badly, for the stitches were dried. She did her best to moisten and soften them with water but the delicate task was still seriously hampered by the conditions. Wevyr's brilliantly fashioned blade was the only blessing. One touch and the black thread was cut through cleanly. Gradually, painfully, his swollen lids were released.

"They're not perfect," she admitted, looking at the stray threads still embedded in his lids.

"It is to me. Thank you, my dear, and you are every bit as pretty as I imagined you might be with that lovely voice."

She smiled at his compliment. Gueryn now looked for the man who claimed to be his beloved Wyl Thirsk and saw only a tall stranger.

"You're not Wyl." Bitter disappointment gutted the older soldier.

"Gueryn—there is much to say and yet no time."

Understanding dawned on Gueryn le Gant. "Save those words for another time. Thank you for helping me—I presume you are the Romen Koreldy Cailech was so interested in me identifying. If you had not called out the Thirsk motto or pretended you were Wyl back in the dungeon, I might have given up my fight against him, against the fever, against the pain." He found a shaky smile. "You know, you look nothing like Wyl Thirsk and yet somehow you do remind me so strongly of him."

Wyl could only shake his head. He badly wanted to confide in Gueryn and tell him everything about the bewildering life he now led but he knew that right now his old friend would not believe him. It would need careful telling and time.

Gueryn's gaze had already moved on to Lothryn. "Our eyes meet again," he said in his dry manner. "If I was strong enough I would offer to fight you."

The big man smiled, offered his hand to help Gueryn to his feet.

Wyl was anxious at how weak Gueryn really was. "Right," he said, "we'll take our chances over the mountains, then."

Lothryn nodded. "He will not expect it. He will follow the most logical trail, anticipating we will go for speed."

Elspyth groaned. "He'll just send out two sets of track-ers, surely?"

Lothryn flicked a glance toward Wyl. Elspyth was right but he did not want to dishearten them any further. Their chance of escape via the more treacherous and mountainous route was slim at best between Cailech's men and the zerkons but it was infinitely better than the more straight-forward route winding down the Razors.

"Cailech will not send two sets of trackers if he's follow-ing four horses on one clear track." Gueryn said firmly, try-ing hard not to cough or reveal how sick he was.

"I don't understand," Wyl said.

"Koreldy, your chances, I am gathering, are lessening by the moment. If we give them a clear set of tracks and no reason to question it, they will follow that trail blindly, no jest intended."

"No!" Wyl said, suddenly understanding where this was headed.

"Yes!" Gueryn replied just as adamantly. "You three go off on foot across the mountains. They will not suspect it if you cover your early tracks well. I will take the horses and lead them down and away from you. You will win a day, perhaps even two if you move quickly and you'll move faster without me."

"Gueryn, I can't permit this," Wyl said.

"Why? I am not answerable to you, Grenadyne. We have no loyalties to each other but I can do this for you because I want to. Get yourselves to safety and warn the Legion of Cailech's threat to spare no prisoners. The Legion must not be sent in recklessly—perhaps you can persuade Celimus to do that much."

There was so much to say, so much to tell him. Wyl felt the bleakness grab him again. "You will die! It will be for nought."

Gueryn smiled in a way that reminded Wyl of all the rea-sons he loved this man. "I'd far rather die outwitting these bastards—forgive me, Lothryn—than be roasted over their coals. I'll make them kill me, son, and I'll die laughing in their faces. Please, go. Let me do this for you as my thanks for getting me out of that dungeon."

Lothryn felt for Koreldy's pain. "It's a good plan, Romen."

Wyl looked back at his old friend and mentor, fighting back the emotion, demanding that the tears he felt welling did not show themselves for he could not explain them anyway. He nodded. "So be it."

Gueryn held out his hand to Wyl. "I will take the horses as far as my ailing body can get them and still further. You obviously knew someone very special to me called Wyl Thirsk. Looking forward to hearing his story and how he fares will encourage me to live. Perhaps we might meet again, Koreldy . . . if not in this life, then the next."

29

GUERYN LEFT HIS COMPANIONS, TRAILING THEIR HORSES BE-hind him. Wyl's last view of him was seeing his friend take a sip from the small bottle he had pressed into the old soldier's hand. Gueryn had taken it gratefully to numb the pain and win him a little strength. No one admitted that the fever would most likely kill him before those giving chase could, but they all thought it.

Wyl, however, preferred not to dwell on this. Instead he emptied his mind and walked in a grim silence, bringing up the rear behind Lothryn and Elspyth. Each of them deliberately stepped in the next one's footsteps and Wyl brushed a fir branch in their wake to disguise any tracks as best he could. He ignored the pain in his rib and the whip of the wind, which was picking up. He focused only on counting his steps, putting as many between him and Cailech's fortress as possible.

As the first light of dawn glowed gently, Lothryn halted.

"We should rest for a couple of hours. There is a cave not far from here where we can lie down for a short while."

"Can we risk it?" Wyl wondered aloud.

"We must if we are going to conserve energy for the thinner air and harder terrain. This is nothing."

"Really easy," Elspyth said in a tone that belied her words.

They undid the packs and found some dried food Lothryn had the foresight to include. None were hungry but the Mountain Man insisted.

"Forget hunger. Your body needs the sustenance even if your head tells you otherwise. Force it down," he advised and they did, chewing on dried meat, dried fruit, and a small knuckle of bread each.

They drank thirstily, knowing there was plenty of fresh water along the way to replenish what they used.

"So rest. Two hours only," Lothryn cautioned.

Wyl turned his back as Elspyth shamelessly curled up in Lothryn's arms. She felt safe in his embrace, but she also knew she somehow belonged there. Sleep claimed all of them almost instantly.

He dreamed. It was a familiar chamber; the smell of sweat and fear, of feces and urine . . . and curiously the smell of desire. Wyl was himself again; red-headed, young, and frightened as they hoisted Myrren up in the hideous contraption known as the Dark Angel. He heard the pop of her shoulder sockets as they yielded their oh-so-fragile hold on her arms but she did not scream. She did not even groan—not even when her elbows dislocated. The spectators made all the noise as they shuddered and cringed, imagining her pain even if she would not share it.

She was naked, of course. Necessary to please the all-male chamber. He could see the gleam in their eyes but she did not seem to care. Myrren looked at no one but Wyl. For the most part of her traumatic time under torture she kept her eyes firmly closed but when, now and then, they flickered open for just a moment, her faraway gaze rested only on his. He had not noticed previously how her lips kept moving in a constant stream of silent words. Words presumably only she knew. Witch words, he suddenly realized.

Wyl heard the terrible command "Drop!" and then, as if she were falling a hundred times slower than in reality, he witnessed Myrren descending. And he grimaced again in his dream, for he knew what was coming, knew they would hurt her terribly. Suddenly she lurched to a sickening halt in midair and her lips pulled back in her excruciating agony as the limbs, muscles, and tendons tore and wrenched.

It was then that a new dimension invaded the dream. The torture chamber seemed to still. Myrren's bloodshot eyes flew open and she spoke to him alone.

"Find my father!" she commanded.

Wyl woke, trembling in Romen Koreldy's body.

They had slept for less than two hours but it was enough. Again Lothryn paused long enough to make them eat a little cheese and more nuts washed down with a skin of water. Carefully covering up any clues to their visit, they pressed on. Elspyth openly held Lothryn's hand now—that was probably the reason for her higher spirits, not that it interested Wyl much beyond acknowledgment. His thoughts were with Gueryn and whether they really would see each other again.

Gueryn pressed doggedly on. It was warmer in these lower reaches but his fever had gained its foothold and would now run rampant through his shivering, aching body. He swigged again from the bottle, knowing it would not alleviate the effects of the fever. He cared not. His single notion was to stay upright and keep the horses moving forward. Every yard gained was another minute of life for his friends, whom he hoped were far away now. And anyway, any moment he expected an arrow through his throat. He was surprised he had made it this far.

To take his mind off death he considered Koreldy.

A strange one he was. Why did the Grenadyne look at him with so much compassion? No, not compassion. That was too mild a word. It was love. Koreldy was connected to him in some very special way and yet Gueryn could not figure it. And the man's pretense at being Wyl was clever, he would give him that much.

Koreldy had saved him the indignity of being eaten by Cailech. Just thinking about it brought bile to his throat. What an end. Now, because of Romen and the courageous Lothryn, he would at least die honorably, outwitting the enemy, and perhaps when all hope was lost he would turn and fight, dying bravely as any soldier of the Legion should. The Grenadyne had told him nothing, not that he had had much chance to say more than he did, Gueryn admitted. There was obviously much on the man's mind and plenty he wanted to say—Gueryn could see it in the sad gray eyes. How could that be?

And then it hit him. Was Wyl dead? Is that what it was? He was misreading Koreldy's compassion; the man was simply reluctant to pass on news that he knew would bring Gueryn such grief it might encourage him to give up his tenuous hold on life.

Wyl dead? No!

Gueryn slumped in the saddle. What else could it be? If Celimus was prepared to plan his death then his real target had to be Wyl. Gueryn was not important enough to warrant such attention. His clouded mind began to clear and anger began to gather. The new King of Morgravia, when still a Prince, had deliberately separated him from Wyl and then set about destroying both their lives.

The more he chewed at it, the more it made sense. How would Celimus have contrived Wyl's end? It could not have been achieved on Morgravian soil—too much loyalty from the Legion. An uprising would erupt if the army caught even a whiff of such heinous betrayal. But Celimus was too clever for that. So he would have planned for Wyl to be beyond the realm's borders and he would have commissioned outsiders—foreigners, no doubt—to do his dirty work. Mercenaries were easy enough to hire for the right amount of gold.

Mercenaries! Gueryn's grip on the reins slackened. Had not Elspyth called Koreldy a mercenary during the confrontation with Cailech? Yes! Gueryn ran back over the scene in his mind. Elspyth had said something along the lines of refusing to humble the mercenary further. Romen Koreldy, who clearly knew Wyl enough to call out the Thirsk battle cry, was a mercenary. Gueryn was aware that he was making huge leaps and possibly landing in the wrong spot but the temptation to believe that Romen held critical information on Wyl was too strong. He must stay alive. He must know what has happened to his precious boy . . . and what about Ylena? Beautiful girl; she too would be in danger, although he hoped Alyd had the wits to get her away from Stoneheart at least. Yes, her husband was sensible and capable, his wits his best asset. He would not risk her life.

As his feverish mind raced, the arrow he had dreaded finally came thumping into his back and knocked him off his horse with ease. Gueryn dropped like a stone, his head hitting the frosty mountain ground hard enough to send all notions of Wyl into darkness.

Wyl was leading—no need to brush their tracks now— as they ascended a challenging climb and so the others all but stumbled into his back when he suddenly stopped walking.

"Romen, what's wrong?" Lothryn asked.

Wyl was listening. Not to an outside sound but to an inside voice. Something called to him. But it was gone as suddenly as it came, replaced by a wave of sadness he could not explain.

"Gueryn's dead," he said in a flat voice, believing it.

Elspyth took his hand. "You can't know this."

Lothryn tried to echo her reassurance. "His chances were grim, I'll grant you. But he had a good lead on them."

Wyl looked at his friends, Romen's eyes darkening. "You are not me, you cannot know what I feel . . . you don't even know who I am!"

He read their sideways glances as a suggestion that they leave him alone. He knew he made no sense.

"I'll lead," Lothryn said, pushing past.

"They're coming now," Wyl warned and fell silent, fol-

lowing once again in the other man's footsteps, deeper into
the forbidding Razors.

If he's dead, I'll have you strung up by your balls, man!"
Cailech boomed, pointing at the archer. He leapt from his
horse. "Check him!" he called to the man nearest to the
felled soldier.

They waited, the archer holding his breath.

"He's alive, my lord. Just."

"Get him back to the fortress. Bring in the herbalists and
find Rashlyn for me. Now!"

Men rushed off in all directions. Gueryn was wrapped in
blankets; they were careful not to disturb the ugly arrow
that protruded from the lower part of his shoulder. He was
laid across a horse and immediately led back the way he
had fought so hard to escape. The man leading him swallowed hard, casting a silent prayer to Haldor to help him get
the prisoner back to the fortress alive and into the hands of
the herbalists, for he did not doubt the King would carry out
his threat if this man lost his life in his care.

Cailech turned to one of his trusted; it pained him more
deeply than he cared to admit right now that it was not
Lothryn.

"So they tricked us. Where would they go?"

Myrt was not used to being asked for his opinion. He was
loyal to Cailech and a faithful member of the tribe but he
would prefer it was calm Lothryn under the King's scrutiny.
Lothryn knew how to handle the King and his moods. He
regarded himself as a doer, not a decision-maker. The
King's pale-green eyes continued to regard him and he
cleared his throat.

"My lord King, if Lothryn is with them—"

"He is with them! Traitor!" the King raged.

The man tried again. "That being the case, my lord, I
would suggest he might take them via the higher pass."

"Why not the Dog Leg?"

He did not mean to shrug at his King and was grateful
Cailech had not noticed. "Lothryn knows the mountains

like no other, my lord. If I were him, I'd take the most treacherous route because it might give me a better chance. He knows Haldor's Pass."

After several moments of consideration, in which everyone else held their breath yet again, Cailech nodded. "I agree with you, Myrt. It is wise counsel."

Myrt sighed silently with relief. His expression betrayed nothing, however, as he waited for orders, which came quickly.

"You take your men and follow Haldor's Pass. May he preserve you. If you find them you may kill Koreldy and the woman however you please. I want Lothryn brought to me. He will face my personal justice."

Cailech pointed at another of his men. "You, Drec. Take another ten and go via the Dog Leg, just in case."

The man gave a short bow and men he pointed to began to remount.

"Report back to the fortress by nightfall," Cailech ordered. "Have you brought birds?" They nodded. "Use them, keep me informed. Send birds to the lookouts. They no longer have to preserve any life other than Loth's, understand?"

Cailech did not wait for a response. He turned his horse and galloped back toward his stronghold. He would have answers from this Gueryn le Gant.

Shielded by a snow-covered overhang of craggy rock, they rested. Lothryn insisted on an hour despite their protests to keep going. He assured them it was necessary. A hard afternoon's climb was ahead. Each of them sensed that Gueryn probably had reached as far as he could go. Cailech's men, if not the King himself, would most likely have him by now . . . dead or alive . . . it mattered not. His life was over but he had won them some precious time and they would use it wisely.

Elspyth thought Romen looked haggard with his pent-up anger and grief. Perhaps she should relieve it. "What did you mean by us not knowing who you are?" she blurted out.

He had been staring at the ground but looked up. "Forget I said it," he replied.

Elspyth was cold, frightened, and above all angry. She

snapped. "No! Romen, my life has been turned upside down because of you and now . . . I might even die, and horribly. I'm not going to forget you said it just because you tell me to. I am not yours to order. You've been strange since I met you. My aunt only agreed to see you because you threw around the Thirsk name. And then you claim to be Wyl Thirsk to poor Gueryn, who believed you—until he could see again, of course, then he knew you for the pretender you are. There are secrets upon secrets within you. Why don't you tell us the truth?"

Lothryn tried to interject in his calm way but she shook off his gentle, restraining hand, her eyes blazing. "He is nothing but lies. He might betray us in a blink! We are risking our lives for him."

"Then don't," Wyl said harshly.

"What choice have we got, Koreldy?" She was shouting now. "Lothryn has given up everything."

"Hush, you'll bring the snow down upon us," Lothryn said in a soft gibe.

She was going to say more, meant to rail at Koreldy a bit longer, but the sob escaped her throat and the floodgates had opened.

Wyl felt immediately ashamed of himself. His own anger ebbed as he heard her break down. Lothryn said nothing—he did not have to—but rebuke was in his eyes when he regarded Wyl.

"Elspyth, you wouldn't believe me anyway," Wyl said, turning his hands palms up and shrugging.

"Why don't you try?" she dared, her voice tearful but now muffled by Lothryn's embrace.

He so badly wanted to share this strange and frightening story that suddenly it sounded like the right thing to do. "Don't say I didn't warn you," he cautioned as he began the tale of Wyl Thirsk and Romen Koreldy becoming one.

When Wyl had finished speaking, the only sound among the still mountains was the eerie call of a great eagle flying high above them. Elspyth was staring at her boots but Wyl noticed Lothryn regarded him with a hard, penetrating gaze.

"Magic! Pah!" Wyl said as though he was tired of his own hard-luck story.

"I knew you weren't the Koreldy I remembered," Lothryn suddenly admitted, his voice low and serious. Wyl waited. "I just put it down to there being so many years since we had last known you but somehow deep down it was more than that. You were different." Lothryn shrugged, letting out his breath as though he had held it for a long time. "Cailech sensed it first, you know. The face was the same, just older and more handsome than you deserve to be; the voice was the same and the mannerisms all Romen Koreldy. But the person inside had changed. He knew it."

"How so?" Elspyth asked, intrigued.

"The Romen I knew was witty, gregarious, and above all, self-centered. The Romen before us is . . . complicated," he said, having struggled for the right word. "What I mean is, this Romen cares. The other one didn't. This Romen isn't looking for attention and, Elspyth, the Romen I once knew would have had you naked between the sheets as quick as one of his knives passes through the air."

She looked horrified. "That good, eh?"

"Women, even the more cynical Mountain women, could not turn him down but, more to the point, he couldn't resist any woman. It was like he needed to conquer them. He did not love them; he did not feel much at all for them. It's probably why Cailech liked Romen so much—they are birds of a feather."

Wyl frowned. "I like women," he said, defensively.

"But you never made any remark to me along those lines," Elspyth admitted, arching her eyebrows. "Am I not pretty enough?"

"That's my point," Lothryn said. "It wouldn't have mattered to Romen. He would make the remark come what may. He was a flirt just for the pure amusement of toying with a woman's feelings, winning her trust. You did not make any approach to anyone in Yentro, or here, and it would have been so easy with Elspyth."

"I'll speak for myself, thank you," she said, glaring at Lothryn. "I'm not easy but I understand what you're saying."

"There's more," Lothryn said, warming to his subject now. "Romen was brilliant with his throwing knives—no one could hold a candle to him. He was a skilled swordsman but nothing close to what I witnessed back there with Borc."

Wyl shrugged. "That man was clumsy at best." He liked that Lothryn returned the grin.

"And back in the Mountains, no mention of agrolo," the big man continued. "Cailech is sharp. He picked it all up."

"What's agrolo?" Wyl queried and saw the answer on his companion's face.

"There you have it," Lothryn said.

"Is that why you came to see my aunt?"

Wyl nodded. "I don't know why I am Romen Koreldy or what I'm doing in this body. I should have died—my soul gone to Shar—back in Briavel's palace. I hoped your aunt would tell me more."

"And did she?" Elspyth asked.

"No. She knew I wasn't Koreldy, though. She knew exactly who I was when she touched me." He rubbed his hands through his long hair, still not used to the sensation of its smooth texture. "She told me to find Myrren's father. I had a dream or perhaps it was a nightmare while we rested in the cave. It was Myrren. She spoke to me and ordered the same thing—to find her father."

"And where is he?" she asked.

"I have no idea, nor do I know his name. I have no lead to follow," Wyl replied, wishing his voice did not betray so clearly how desperate he felt.

A look of concern passed between his two companions. "So what now?" Lothryn asked, trying to keep his tone encouraging.

"Escape here. Get my sister to safety. Go back to Briavel and protect Valentyna. All sounds simple enough, don't you think?" he said.

Elspyth's mind fled back to the old soldier. "And so Gueryn is truly your former friend and mentor?"

He nodded. "He is . . . was a father to me."

"I'm sorry, I should never have agreed with him . . . to let him go on alone," Lothryn admitted.

"Don't, Lothryn. This is not your fault. Without you, we'd all be feeding the tribe tonight." He forced a smile. "So you both believe me? How incredible."

"My aunt believes you . . . and I believe in her skills. How could I not accept what you say?" Elspyth said. "We accept magic in the far north even if we don't admit to it."

Lothryn nodded. "There are forces more powerful at work in our world than Kings and Queens and petty squabbles over lands. Haldor spoke to me by finally giving me my son. He was a gift from the gods. Yes, I believe in the gods and their magics. This witch you speak of, Myrren, she was a channel for the gods and what they want done in the world."

"Thank you," Wyl said, glad he had finally told someone the truth and more grateful than either would know that his friends believed him without hesitation. "I only wish I knew what was expected of me with regard to this gift."

"Trust your instincts," Lothryn replied sagely.

"And what of Rashlyn—is he truly empowered?"

Lothryn nodded. "He is a sorcerer, for sure. But his influence is all bad on Cailech."

"Where did he come from?"

"No one knows—if Cailech does, he has not shared it with me. And Rashlyn is incredibly secretive about everything," Lothryn replied and nodded assurance when Wyl raised his eyebrows in surprise. "But he knew of Koreldy. The fact that he did not detect the witch magic in you is surprising. Cailech would certainly have shared with me any suspicion of Rashlyn's that you were an impostor."

Wyl shrugged. "I don't understand any of it."

"What shall we call you?" Elspyth wondered.

"Until we're safe, I'd suggest you call me Romen," Wyl said, picking up his pack.

"Come!" Lothryn said, helping Elspyth with her pack. "No more talking. Save strength—we're all going to need it for Haldor's Pass."

30

QUERYN MOVED IN AND OUT OF HIS DREAMLIKE STATE, NEVER lingering long enough in consciousness to react to his surrounds. Soft light eased across his senses now and then, together with hushed voices. Pain accompanied his brief waking moments and that in itself would send him fleeing back to the dark . . . to safety.

Gradually the periods of awareness began to lengthen until the voices belonged to murky faces, which were joined by probing hands. The light that filtered through his fluttering lids, he gleaned, came from candles. The pain itself was all-encompassing but increasingly he could bear it for longer without having to run from it.

He became aware that he was on his belly, his face turned sideways, and the muttering people worked at his back. Slowly, very slowly, like blood seeping through thick fabric, memory returned. He had been struck by an arrow—had expected as much and had fully accepted death as a result.

What am I doing alive? Where am I?

"Drink," a distant voice said.

He was rolled onto his side, flashes of pain arcing through him. An artfully cut reed served as a clever method of allowing him to sip easily from the proffered cup.

"What?" He groaned. It was all he could force his voice to say.

His mumblings made sense, for the man answered: "Poppy."

And then oblivion claimed him, the pain drifting in the opposite direction to where he felt he was headed. At regular intervals this blissful state was interrupted, much to his annoyance. And the familiar fingers would unwrap dressings and push deep into his angry wound. He knew they were looking for infection, waiting for the telltale odor. Seemingly it had chosen to be absent on this occasion, which he regretted. Death, he knew, was his friend. The poppy-seed liquor he so gratefully swallowed was all too quickly diluted until he could hardly taste its bitter presence. They were bringing him fully to his wits now so he could face his healers, bear his pain . . . recover.

On one of these occasions he realized he was fully awake and staring into the leathery face of a man—not especially old but then not particularly young, ageless, in fact—whose single most daunting feature was the amount of dark hair about him. On his chin, around his face. Wild it was.

"Good morning," the man said.

Gueryn tried to speak but coughed instead, a fresh spasm of pain gleefully taking over from his cough, leaving him panting and perspiring.

"Don't speak. I am Rashlyn, healer to King Cailech . . . among other things," the man said.

Gueryn groaned. *Cailech!* He was back in the Mountain fortress.

"You must have a strong will to live, my friend. All the early signs told me you were for Haldor's arms."

Haldor be damned! Gueryn thought, wishing he could say it aloud but he was too weak.

Rashlyn corrected himself. "Ah, but my apologies. You would be a man of Shar, no doubt. Well, let's just say you would not have lived but for an extraordinary desire to hold onto life." He smiled sadly but the words that followed did not match the smile—they sounded cruel. "A pity. I fear death might have been easier."

"Then kill me now," Gueryn managed to utter.

The healer was amused. "I like my own life too much to do that," he said before becoming more serious. "Cailech is to be informed that you have woken. Be brave, Morgravian. He respects courage."

Gueryn gratefully looked away from Cailech's man as he was rolled onto his belly.

"This poultice must stay on for the day," Rashlyn warned.

Gueryn said nothing. In fact he had every intention of ripping off the healing herbs as soon as he was able, hoping to encourage an infection to breed quickly in his wound.

As though he fully understood Gueryn's mindset, Rashlyn added: "You will be bound, I'm sorry . . . just in case you have a mind to discourage your recovery. Cailech would not be pleased."

The man clapped and others arrived to tie Gueryn, belly down, to his pallet. They were thorough. He would not be escaping these bonds with any ease. He had no choice but to lie there and wait, fully conscious now, with plenty of time to wonder at what Cailech had in store for him.

He waited many hours in this position, the once hot, uncomfortable poultice cooling sufficiently to feel cold and clammy against his skin. He had even dozed, waking numb and alarmed to realize the sun had moved from high overhead and was now dipping behind the mountains, casting a pink glow across the sky.

As dusk fell Cailech arrived. He came alone, which for Gueryn made his presence seem even more ominous than when surrounded by his henchmen.

Cailech did not stand on any ceremony. "We meet again, soldier."

"Sadly," Gueryn replied, his voice thankfully stronger and clear. He was determined his courage would not fail him now, although his neck, after being twisted for so long, ached badly enough for him to crave more poppy liquor.

"Your companions are dead," the King offered abruptly.

A thrill of fear initially passed through Gueryn but he halted it, controlled it, and pushed it back out at Cailech, who he believed was bluffing.

"I sense a ruse."

"Why is that?" The King sounded genuinely interested . . . and amused, which Gueryn found more irritating. The King's smile all but admitted he had lied.

"Why am I kept alive with such powerful healings if the others—surely more important to you—are dead?"

"You are too hard on yourself, le Gant. You are important to me."

"How so? Not long ago—forgive me for losing track of time—you were preparing to roast me over the coals."

"That's before I was aware of Romen Koreldy's interest in you," the King replied more slyly now.

Gueryn knew he was being toyed with. "What is it you want from me? I have nothing to offer you but the glee of my death."

"Death is too easy now, soldier. You are far more valuable to me alive."

"I can't imagine why."

"I've already told you."

"Why is Koreldy so important to you?"

"He has betrayed my trust." Amusement was gone. A simmering fury replaced it. Even from his prone position, Gueryn could see the anger glittering in the Mountain King's eyes.

"I cannot help you," he replied flatly. If he could have turned his head away, he would have.

"Tell me of Koreldy," Cailech asked.

"That's the best part, my lord. I know this man you speak of with less familiarity than you, sir."

"Nevertheless, tell me what you know."

How he mustered the laugh, Gueryn would never know. He saw how it infuriated the King, wished he had the strength to do it again—louder, longer. "I know nothing. He is a stranger to me."

"You lie! I saw how he recognized you. Even a fool could not be aware of his concern for you . . . and I am no fool, le Gant."

"Then you have me as baffled as he does, my lord King. I had never heard the name Romen Koreldy until he spoke with me on the night of the feast. I was blinded as you recall, sire, so I could not claim him to be a stranger to me until the stitches were removed. I can assure you, I never set eyes on the man until that moment. In truth," he paused before adding, "I thought he was someone else until my eyes saw him."

Gueryn watched the King's confusion at this last comment melt into fascination as obviously some new thought struck him. He noticed the man's lips purse, go white. The King was struggling to remain calm. Gueryn fully expected Cailech to hit him. He would not care if he did, especially now that his wound was aching again.

"Riddles! I will have the truth, Gueryn le Gant," Cailech said.

"I have spoken it. Romen Koreldy is unknown to me. Why he finds me so fascinating I can not tell you. Why he went to such trouble on my behalf is a mystery. And why one of your most loyal men would help me to escape is even more of a conundrum." Gueryn was just short of smirking. He enjoyed using Lothryn's treachery as a weapon against this man.

Cailech grimaced. His fists clenched. *Ah, that one hit the mark,* Gueryn thought, pleased with his efforts. The King made a sign toward the door that Gueryn was not able to see. He could hear footsteps arriving and suddenly he was being untied and hauled to his feet between two huge guards. He was too weak to even struggle, too numb to support himself and the nausea from being stood suddenly upright threatened to render him unconscious. It was only the arrival of a terrified and painfully familiar woman that caught his attention, held it and did not permit him to succumb to welcome oblivion.

It was Elspyth. Bruised and ragged. She was sobbing.

"Behold another proud Morgravian, whom I've allowed some of my men to . . . well, soften up, shall we say," Cailech said, turning back to watch Gueryn closely. "I have Lothryn too . . . he is a guest of my dungeon for the time being. It's true Koreldy eludes me."

Gueryn ignored him. "Elspyth," he muttered, all hopes dashed, but the woman did not respond.

Elspyth appeared vague and disoriented. He could see nasty welts across her face and a cut in her hairline that had bled down the side of her face and now dried. She looked abused and distant, frightened. Her mouth was shockingly swollen and bruised.

"We have cut her tongue out, le Gant. I'm sorry she cannot talk back to you," Cailech said, motioning to a guard who held her. The man pulled open her jaw to reveal a black and bloodied mass. Teeth had been broken in the process.

Gueryn felt waves of fury now. He could feel his despair pounding at the site of his wound, his blood pumping angrily around it. Gueryn wanted to wreak violence on this heinous man who could perpetrate such horror on a woman . . . on any innocent.

"Shar will see you rot for this and your name be spat upon and ultimately forgotten," he raged, ignoring the pain.

"I do not fear your god, le Gant. But you should fear me."

"What do you wish to hear?" Gueryn yclled, feeling his wound burst open again and a trickle of something warm ooze down his naked back.

"I wish to know your connection to Romen Koreldy," Cailech replied in a soft tone, deliberately giving the impression he was bored as he lifted a huge dagger from his belt. He stared at it for a moment and then back at Gueryn, his eyebrow arched in a question.

Gueryn looked from the pathetic, bleeding figure of Elspyth back to the man whom it appeared would be her executioner. Nothing in Cailech's expression told Gueryn that he was bluffing this time. The evil-looking blade rested loosely in the man's large hand and it was clear he would not hesitate to use it.

Gueryn shook his head in silent disbelief. He was helpless. He could no more save this woman's life than his own. All the years of training, all the skills and talent at his fingertips, all the arrogance of being from a noble line and attached to a family of such prestige and power was suddenly worthless. He could not help her. She would die because he was so helpless . . . so worthless . . . so pointless.

He lifted his eyes back to the searing gaze of his keeper, King Cailech. "I beseech you, lord King. Let her be."

"I have run out of patience with you, Gueryn le Gant. She is Morgravian. She is little more than worthless scum to me."

The words cut as sharply as the blade the King held.

Rage returned to Gueryn le Gant. "Romen Koreldy knew a man called Wyl Thirsk whose family I worked for. That is our only connection. I have never seen Koreldy before—I can tell you no more . . . nor would I if I could!"

He regretted his tone and his harsh words the instant they fell out of his mouth. Anger—normally something he had in control—betrayed him and the woman. He watched with horror as Cailech calmly turned away from him and punched the blade into Elspyth's belly. As she doubled up, the King stepped away momentarily to ensure Gueryn could see him wiping at the spattering of blood that had hit his jerkin.

"Let him watch," he said and the guards held her upright as Cailech ripped the blade, still embedded in her, across her abdomen.

Her face became waxy white, and a terrible sound issued from her throat. She gurgled as blood welled up and spewed from her ragged mouth. Cailech calmly removed the gutting blade, wiping it on the woman's garments as her head slumped forward. The guards and their King made a show of avoiding the spume of blood and turned their heads from the smell of ripped bowel. Gueryn could not tear his eyes from the horrific scene. He watched her lifeblood creep slowly yet inexorably toward his boots in a thick line and then curl around one of them, molding itself to his feet . . . forever marking him with her death.

Forever reminding him that he had killed Elspyth.

She shuddered and groaned once more before mercifully letting out her last wretched breath. Fiery Elspyth with the kind voice and tender, steady hands was dead.

"Take her away. Throw her to the wolves. We need to give them a taste for fresh Morgravian meat."

As she was dragged away, Gueryn took his guards by surprise as he hurled himself at the King. It was the young woman's blood that undid him; he slipped and, before he could reach Cailech, he was falling heavily on his face, his legs flipping under him. The ravaging pain newly erupting at his wound was the last thing he was aware of. When he woke he found he lived an even bleaker existence.

Cailech had imprisoned him again in the dungeon. There would be no escape this time.

Cailech sat brooding over a spiced wine. In the shadows of his great chamber overlooking the lake, Rashlyn waited patiently. They had been like this for some time. It was a familiar scene for both. The King finally hurled his clay goblet at the fireplace where it shattered loudly, breaking the silence, klaxoning his fury.

Rashlyn spoke quickly. "The glamor was effective, my lord. The likeness was extraordinary."

"But it didn't work, Rashlyn! He still didn't break."

"Perhaps it was too effective?" the sorceror said.

Cailech turned on his man. "What do you mean?"

Rashlyn shrugged. "Only that I imagine for him there was no point in cooperating beyond her death. Perhaps he never thought you would do it, my lord?"

"Trust me, he knew. And he allowed her to die. You're right, the likeness of your glamor was extraordinary—he could never have guessed it was not her. Who was it, by the way?"

"The Morgravian whore we captured him with."

Cailech nodded. "Why is he protecting Koreldy!" This time the King kicked over a small wooden seat in his frustration.

"Calm, my lord," Rashlyn soothed. "Send out more men. The Stones tell me they have followed Haldor's Pass. In the meantime we must think hard on this. It will come to us . . . we will find a solution."

Hours later—Gueryn had no idea of day or night—the door swung back and Cailech was outlined menacingly in the archway. Gueryn pretended he was asleep but the King ignored this fact. He knew full well the Morgravian would hear him and he was filled with energy at having resolved his dilemma. Rashlyn's advice was sound. Keep him alive. If he was so important to Koreldy, use him as bait.

"I hope you like it here, soldier, for this is your home

now. Make yourself familiar with these granite walls, welcome the damp and embrace the darkness. There is no light for you, no warmth . . . very little sustenance will I offer, save what will keep you alive."

"Why bother? Koreldy's escaped your clutch. He won't be back," Gueryn said, not even turning toward the King. It was the only way he could show that the Morgravian spirit remained strong in him.

"Because as long as you're alive I know Romen Koreldy will find my Mountain fortress irresistible."

"I don't know him!" Gueryn roared with the little strength he possessed.

"Ah, but he knows you, le Gant, and he has saved you once—he will do it again."

The door slammed with finality.

Gueryn wept. Rashlyn was right. Death would have been much kinder.

31

THE THREE OF THEM TRUDGED HIGHER. LOTHRYN HAD BEEN right to warn them of Haldor's Pass. This was its earliest stages and already the going was treacherous. The air was thin enough to discourage any conversation other than odd grunts and noises to check on each other. Wyl's thoughts rested with Gueryn. As much as Lothryn believed Cailech would kill him, Wyl did not share this notion. The subtlety of Romen's thoughts—what tiny residue was left of them—reassured him that Cailech would not kill any man who might have some value down the track.

Cailech is too shrewd, he reminded himself. Why save Gueryn? Because up until Wyl declared his knowledge of him, Gueryn was a stranger to Cailech . . . nothing more than a Morgravian soldier of rank, and worth the satisfaction of killing. Now, Wyl reasoned, Cailech might view him as worth saving, if just to taunt Koreldy.

All of this was hypothetical, of course. Wyl had had a premonition that his mentor was dead. None of them had any idea whether Gueryn survived the descent. The likelihood of him surviving his rampaging fever was slim enough. Still, Wyl clung to his notion that Gueryn's spirit was stronger than his body and Cailech's shrewdness would overcome his desire to slake his thirst for revenge. Wyl reasoned that Cailech might spare Gueryn even just to find out what he knew of where his companions had headed. At the heart of it Wyl accepted that Cailech's real thirst was for Koreldy and, no doubt, Lothryn. Gueryn was of negligible interest against such tempting prey but if his being kept alive could help trap them, Cailech would not hesitate to use him.

He came out of his tangled private thoughts only because Elspyth had signaled a stop. She was breathing hard, ignoring the advice of Lothryn to take shallow breaths. The Mountain Man walked back to where she had slumped on a rock.

"I need a few moments," she begged.

Lothryn nodded. It clearly was not to his liking but he refused to waste precious breath and strength arguing. He pointed to a small circle of boulders that would offer minimal shelter but a break nonetheless from the icy wind. He helped Elspyth back to her feet and the three of them gratefully collapsed among the circle of stones.

"If you tell me to eat anything, I am going to be sick," she haltingly cautioned, eyeing Lothryn.

"No eating. Drinking is important, though. That's what our bodies need."

She took small sips from the skin he offered.

"I've been thinking," Wyl said, glad to be out of the wind momentarily, "does Cailech have an actual healer he trusts?"

Lothryn nodded. "More than a healer. It's Rashlyn."

"Ah, of course. Tell me what you know of him."

The big man sighed. "He is dangerous, as I've said. In ancient times, when we were separate tribes, each had their own barshimon. The barshi, as he is known, was called upon for everything from blessing a birth to cursing an enemy. He does readings, he interprets visions, reads the Stones, he performs enchantments . . . and he heals."

"You say only in ancient times."

He shrugged. "Perhaps the magics were more genuine in ancient times or, more likely, most were pretenders. In the last few centuries we've discovered that true sorcerers are a rarity . . . most people could move through a lifetime and never meet someone with the true gift of magic."

"And Rashlyn?" Wyl asked.

"As I said, he's the real thing. And he's ambitious."

"You think he's using Cailech."

Lothryn nodded. "I know it, and none of it towards good."

Elspyth joined in. "I heard one of the women use the word barshi against me when I came looking for you at the time of your son's birth." She instantly regretted mentioning his baby.

Lothryn smiled sadly. "Yes, barshi can also be used as a way of calling down darkness . . . bad things. They needed something to blame for my wife's death. You were an easy target . . . and a stranger."

"So Rashlyn is barshi to Cailech?" Wyl reasoned.

"He is barshi to the united Mountain Kingdom," Lothryn admitted.

"You don't sound approving," Wyl risked, already knowing it to be true.

"I hate him. He has no soul. I have wished all too often that Cailech had not aligned himself with a man of such darkness."

Wyl nodded. He would store away this knowledge. "But he is a healer?"

"Yes. I can see where you're headed with this conversation, Koreldy. You believe Cailech will spare Gueryn's life . . . save it, in fact, with powerful healings of the barshi?"

"You read my thoughts well!"

"You are as easy to read as a book when you're being this Wyl Thirsk person. If you are to outwit Cailech you need to be Romen through and through," Lothryn counselled.

"He's right," Elspyth admitted. She smiled. "Now that Loth mentions it, you do flit between personalities. I can believe there are two of you. As Wyl you seem naked, too honest."

Wyl considered what they said. "Wise words. I must learn from them."

"If it's any consolation, Rashlyn has the power to save Gueryn if Cailech permits it. But what he is being saved for he may prefer to escape through death," Lothryn added. "Cailech will go this way only if he can benefit."

"He can," Wyl said. "He can lure me back."

"Romen, no!" Elspyth shouted. "Gueryn chose. He gave his life to save you. The two of us aside, he wanted you to get away. You make his sacrifice worthless if you consider returning."

"I don't mean to turn back now," Wyl reassured her. "I just have a feeling that Gueryn will be preserved for the one reason that it might bring Koreldy back to Cailech's fortress. I was so transparent at the feast. It was obvious I knew Gueryn well and cared for him. Cailech's too wily to not notice such things."

Lothryn nodded. "He misses nothing."

"Then if Gueryn is alive—and I choose to believe he is—I think he will remain a prisoner to entice Cailech's enemy back."

"If you believe this, then you must not fall for such a plan," Elspyth reasoned.

"I won't, I promise," Wyl said but his glance at Lothryn said differently.

"We must press on," Lothryn cautioned and wearily they hauled themselves back to their feet and stepped out into the biting wind. "Use your hood tails," Lothryn shouted against the howl. "Wrap them about your mouths. You must keep the icy air from entering as best you can." They followed his lead. "One more thing," he cautioned. "We're entering zerkon territory. We must be wary."

The first indication that one or more of the beasts were near came some time later, when Lothryn, becoming suddenly rigid, stopped and smelled the air swirling about them.

"What?" Wyl mouthed, careful not to make a sound.

"Zerkon," Lothryn replied in the same manner.

Elspyth's expression queried how he could know this.

"The stench," he whispered. "Can you smell it?"

They both lifted their noses and inhaled. A vague waft of something musty and unpleasant crossed their senses and they nodded.

"Not close enough to threaten yet. But if we can smell him, trust me that he can smell us. He will stalk us."

"What can we do?" Elspyth asked.

"Distance is all we have," Lothryn admitted. "But if he signals any others . . ."

He opted to say no more.

"Let's go," Wyl said and took the lead, setting a rattling pace.

Cailech's tracking group had made good ground on horseback but the terrain was fast becoming too precarious for their precious animals. They did not know it yet but they were getting close to their prey, who had been laboring for a much longer distance at a slower pace.

"They've passed this way—and recently," the leader called back to his second-in-command. He scrutinized the footprints and broken stems of nearby bushes where the trio had rested in the circle of boulders just a short while ago. "Send a bird," he said. "Let the King know they're in Haldor's Pass and we're following."

The man he spoke to nodded. "Immediately."

Myrt, close friend of Lothryn, turned back and squinted into the snowcapped Razors. He despised leading this mission, knowing how it must end. But he hated more Lothryn's betrayal and the fact that his own loyalty was now being called into question. It was no coincidence that Cailech specifically picked him out for this task. The King was testing Myrt's faithfulness to the tribe.

Myrt grimaced at the thought. "Hobble the horses, we're on foot from here," he ordered.

Wyl and Lothryn were just hauling Elspyth up a slippery series of rocks when they heard a sound that made Lothryn almost let go of her hand.

"That's our zerkon. He's calling in another. They often hunt in pairs."

"How close?" Wyl asked, dragging Elspyth up onto the flatter ground.

"Too close. No longer any use fleeing, they're much faster and sure-footed than us."

"Can we hide?" Elspyth gasped, still out of breath.

"No point," was the terse reply.

"Right then," Wyl said, shedding his pack and dragging the blue sword from the sheath he now wore across his back. Instinctively he touched the knives at his chest. "So we stand and fight."

Lothryn dropped his pack onto the ground and brought out a crossbow.

"I've been wondering what you carried in there," Wyl admitted.

"This might be more effective than your beautiful weapon," Lothryn said.

The men shared a knowing smile, one shared universally by soldiers needing bravado to go into battle.

"What was that thing you called out to Gueryn?" Lothryn asked.

"As one . . . Thirsk family motto and war cry," Wyl said proudly.

"As one, then, Wyl Thirsk," Lothryn said and they stood back-to-back, watchful. "He won't strike immediately. If there's two, they'll watch us for a while."

"Elspyth, you hide," Wyl ordered.

"No point apparently. Give me a blade!" she replied.

"No!" Lothryn was determined. "We're enough to satisfy them. You hide for now and then you run the moment you get your chance. Don't you dare cross me on this."

Lothryn's glare was enough to dissuade her from arguing further. She grabbed their sacks and backed into a depression in the rockface.

And so the two men found themselves alone on a freezing plateau, awaiting sure death.

"I've been meaning to say something about your son, Lothryn. I'm sorry you've had to leave him."

"He's in good hands."

Wyl should have left it at that but, embarrassed by his inept first attempt at raising the subject, he pressed on. "I fear we've forced you into making the most damning of all choices. Blood should come before duty."

There was a difficult silence before Lothryn spoke again. "He's not blood," the man said in a soft voice.

The words hit Wyl like a blow and he was glad they stood with their backs to each other, eyes roaming the rocks for any sign of the beasts. His pause gave Lothryn the opportunity to fill it.

"He's not my son. My wife birthed him as ours but he was sired by another. Duty came ahead of blood," the man of the Mountains admitted.

Wyl was confused. "What do you mean?"

"I regret it but I permitted my wife to be used in this fashion. Perhaps I am making amends now for bad judgment."

"I don't understand." Wyl said.

"He is from Cailech's seed."

"What!"

"I've never told anyone. I hate myself for being so weak and allowing Cailech his way. You shared your secret with me. I will do the same with you. Cailech made me promise I would swear it was the death of our first two babes that soured our marriage but it was nothing of the kind. If anything after such tragedy we felt closer than ever, more committed to each other. Ertyl saw my capitulation to Cailech as betrayal. She accused me of many things, the most hurtful, I suppose, was the most truthful—that I was his puppet. She said I had no mind of my own. And that made me less of a man in her eyes."

"Why would you permit such a thing?" Wyl knew he should not ask it of Lothryn but the words tumbled out.

"My King demanded it for the line. Ertyl's father was the strongest of the tribal leaders before Cailech united them. He believes in lineage. His family blood and Ertyl's family blood would make a powerful mix."

"Cailech strikes me as too intelligent, respectful—loyal even—to ask such a thing."

This time Lothryn grunted, although Wyl could not see the twisted set of his face. "It wasn't his idea, of course."

"Oh, Shar's Wrath!" Wyl cursed, understanding dawning. "Rashlyn?"

"He advised—he had a vision—and Cailech followed it."

"So the boy is where?"

"He was taken from me. Cailech wants him raised away from my influence. He will keep the child close—be his father. I would have loved him as my own, because he came from Ertyl. When he was taken from me on the day of his birth something snapped . . . and then the feast and the events surrounding it gave me the excuse I needed, I suppose."

"To strike back, you mean?"

"Well . . . to let him know I am my own man. He took too much from me—my wife died because of him. And my son is now motherless."

"What is the child's name?"

"He is called Aydrech . . . golden warrior."

"We shall stay alive, Lothryn, and we shall see the boy grown, I promise."

The Mountain Man grunted but before he could say what he intended they were spotted by Myrt and others, who were climbing up the escarpment to where they stood.

"Lothryn!" Myrt cried. "Traitor!"

"Run, Elspyth!" Lothryn screamed. "You too, Wyl, it's our only chance."

They heard Elspyth take flight like a startled deer and leap from her hiding spot, crashing down the ridge into the undergrowth below.

Wyl refused. "We face this together."

At that moment, the zerkons leapt down from their vantage point above the plateau and pandemonium broke out.

It was a bloodbath. The zerkons' long and agile bodies landed with the greatest of ease. Their white coats were striped with a dark brown, a brilliant camouflage in this environment. Yellow eyes sat above vast snarling mouths; their paws were huge and their spines strong enough to support them on two legs if need be. The daunting razorlike teeth were intimidating enough, but a barb on the tip of their strong, swishing tails that could inject a fast-acting paralyzing poison completed what was arguably the most effective killing beast Wyl could imagine.

Momentarily stunned by their arrival, he could only watch as the duo instantly killed two of the men with teeth and barb. Another two who rushed toward them with swords met a similar fate.

"They should know better," Lothryn said almost conversationally as he slowly went about the business of loading his crossbow with a mean-looking bolt. "Myrt!" he called calmly. "Use bows!"

Myrt nodded and began barking orders, rallying the remaining men as another went to his gods.

"Wyl." Lothryn spoke softly. Wyl could hardly tear his eyes from the carnage. "You must go. Fight on for another day. Take Elspyth. You'll come out at a place we call Straplyn—a narrow deer track leading into your realm. Get into Morgravia to safety."

"Lothryn, I can kill these men now! I can give us a fighting chance."

"No! This is the right way. No killing of my people. Go—before they even realize you've gone. Save her for me. They won't kill me, Wyl. Cailech will want that pleasure for himself. I'm not afraid."

Myrt looked back. "Hurry, Loth, loose that bow!"

A man screamed as an zerkon ripped into his flesh. Wyl saw carrion birds begin to hover as words sunk in.

"He will torture you!"

"He has nothing to get from me. No. He won't torture.

But he will make me pay somehow. Please, Wyl . . . escape, for all of us. Make this count."

It was the big man calling him Wyl that broke the spell. Lothryn saw his words get through and took the opportunity. He pushed Wyl away and ran toward his friend Myrt. Side by side once again they fired death bolts toward the animals as men died about them. Wyl finally turned and ran, hating himself. No one noticed him leave the wind-riddled escarpment . . . no one cared right now. Except Wyl. He made a promise that he would return. Return one day to claim back Gueryn and Lothryn if they were alive and if not, he would seek terrible revenge on the King of the Mountains.

Eighteen men died that day on the escarpment. The zerkons were riddled with bolts before they too fell. Only four of the Mountain Dwellers could claim to have outlived an zerkon attack.

Myrt finally turned to Lothryn. "We are to bring you back alive."

"I thought as much."

"You let him go, of course."

"Yes. I'm glad I got him this far."

"Why, Loth?" Lothryn knew Myrt was not referring to Koreldy's escape.

"Oh, it's complicated, my friend. Don't immerse yourself in the web. Stay pure. Stay true to the tribe." Lothryn offered his wrists and Myrt reluctantly nodded toward one of the others to bind them. "Did the Morgravian soldier live?"

"Cailech spared him for reasons he keeps to himself."

Lothryn felt a twinge of satisfaction that Wyl had been right. "And me? Is there a plan?"

"I'm not sure any of us would want to know it, Loth," his friend admitted sadly.

32

WYL WORRIED AT NOT FINDING ELSPYTH. BY NIGHTFALL HIS anxiety had tripled yet he dare not risk a fire, which might attract Cailech's scouts or worse, a curious zerkon. He hoped Elspyth would have the same sense. He decided to find shelter before darkness closed in completely. One blessing was that he was already in the lower levels of the Razors so the air was far milder and breathing was normal again.

His fighter's hearing and instincts combined to sense danger before he saw it. The noise came from behind and his sword was out of its scabbard and pointing at Elspyth's throat in a blink.

"Shar's Wrath. You've cut me," she complained, although the wild look in her eyes suggested she had intended far worse for him with the thick branch she was carrying. "I thought you were one of the scouts. Thank the stars you're safe."

He slid the sword back. "Let me see how bad it is."

"It's fine, really," she said and he could see it would stop bleeding very quickly. She looked as weary as he felt. "Where's Lothryn—is he coming?"

This would not be easy. "No."

Elspyth dropped the branch and balled her fists instinctively. "Dead?" she asked, her face without any expression.

He shook his head.

Now she just looked beaten. "He made you leave, didn't he, like he made me run?"

"Lothryn is too brave for his own good. We had a chance at escape but he wouldn't agree to my killing any of his people. He chose to face Cailech."

Her shoulders slumped and she sat on the leafy ground amid the small grove of trees they found themselves in. She wept quietly, her wound already forgotten.

Wyl knelt and put his arms around her. "I know you were fond of each other."

"Cailech will execute him," she muttered through her tears.

"I don't believe so, Elspyth. I can't promise you that but as I sense with Gueryn, I think Lothryn might be more useful to the King alive . . . if he can get past his rage, that is."

"He will hurt him, though," she muttered.

"Perhaps, but he is strong. He will survive. I know it."

She wiped her face, trying to gather herself. "So we just leave?" she said flatly.

"For now," he offered as gently as he could. "But I give you my oath. I am coming back for them."

She turned to him now, her wet eyes searching his for any sign of guile. "Swear it!"

"I do swear, on everything I consider precious to me. I will return, I promise."

"With other men, you mean?"

"With a plan and when I am equipped to deal with Cailech."

"And so what happens between now and then?"

Wyl had not thought beyond escape. Now that freedom seemed very real for them he considered his options. Elspyth waited while he thought, digging in her pack absently to fill the silence. It was Lothryn's pack. She had mistakenly grabbed it in her flight. In it Elspyth found a little food. She was no longer hungry. She offered it to Wyl.

He had no appetite either but obliged, chewing as he spoke, tasting nothing but knowing his body needed it. "All right. This is my plan for us now. As soon as we enter Morgravia we split up. You must not go home, Elspyth. It's too dangerous right now. They know where your cottage is—"

"But my aunt," she protested.

"They have no quarrel with her. If she is dead . . ." He saw how the words cut her. "Forgive me but it must be said. She may be dead. And if not, she is safe. You are not."

"So where do I go?"

"Travel to a place called Rittylworth."

She nodded. "I've heard of it. There's a monastery there, is that right?"

"Yes. Good. That's where you need to go. Brother Jakub will help you. But you mustn't linger. Promise me."

"I promise," she said, confused. "So then what?"

"My sister, Ylena Thirsk, is at the monastery. You must take her with you. Tell her and Jakub that Romen Koreldy insists. Mention nothing of Wyl Thirsk. Do you understand what I say?"

She bristled. "You're speaking our language so of course I do."

"Apologies. I am worried for Ylena as much as I am for you. Travel northeast. Under no circumstances allow her to return to the Thirsk family home in Argorn. You need to get to Felrawthy. I will tell you what to say to the Duke when you get there. It is important you give him some information—I'll write it all down in a letter for him. He will offer the protection you both require for different reasons."

"I'm confused."

"Just trust me."

"And where are you headed, may I ask?"

"Into Briavel. I made a promise to its Queen that I must fulfill."

She crossed her arms and eyed him suspiciously. But he was offering no further information.

"I need you to keep my secret, Elspyth. No one is to know that Romen Koreldy is really Wyl Thirsk, especially Ylena. No one will accept or even try to understand—the fact that you do is some sort of miracle. You will be safe and anonymous at Felrawthy so long as you keep our secret. I will send word as soon as I can and I will not break my oath to you. I need you to be patient."

It was toward dusk of the next day that they found themselves at Straplyn. The path, as Lothryn had said, was little more than a deer track, which by Wyl's estimation cunningly entered Morgravia in the northwest. Energized by their success at getting this far, neither felt tired enough to sleep and agreed to press on through the night until they could establish exactly where in Morgravia they were. It was a clear moonlit evening and very mild in comparison to the chill of the Mountains.

"It even smells like home," Elspyth commented absently.

"Will you be all right?" Wyl finally asked the question.

"Yes, you're not to worry about me. I have been alone, save for my aunt, most of my life. Lothryn and I never did get the chance to speak of how we felt but we felt it all the same. If Shar decrees we be together, we will be."

"You're wonderful, Elspyth, do you know that?"

She stole a glance and grinned, obviously flattered by his words.

"No, truly," he said. "You're courageous and honest, you're resilient and loyal. You and Lothryn share many qualities and you deserve each other." He reached out to take her hand as they walked. "I won't let you down. If he lives, I'll get him back for you."

Elspyth squeezed his hand, finding his touch comforting and filled with friendship.

"And you're very handsome, Romen Koreldy, but I prefer the man inside . . . Wyl Thirsk."

It was Wyl's turn to be evasive. "Romen helps me be all that I can't, though," he admitted.

"I'd like to have met Wyl, the man. I saw you fight at the tourney. You are a magnificent swordsman."

"I was a bit short, though, eh?" he said, as ever unable to handle a compliment from a woman as Romen might.

She laughed. "Don't be too hard on yourself. They say there's someone out there for each of us," she said. "After all, look at Lothryn and myself. What an odd match we are—him so huge and me so tiny."

"I believe in love at first sight."

"Is there anyone you love, Wyl?"

"Yes." He could not help being honest. Now that he was free, getting back to Valentyna meant everything to him. "But she is untouchable. Way above my station. An impossible relationship . . . and probably one that exists only in my mind. Doomed to be an unrequited love." Wyl finished with a dramatic flourish of his hand, hoping to turn his comments into something more lighthearted.

"Ah, the Queen," Elspyth said intuitively.

He looked at her, shocked to admit she had learned his other secret.

"I'm right, aren't I?" she said, tapping her nose. "A woman can guess these things. Does she know?"

It was a loaded question. He shook his head gloomily. "No and no. She knew me as Wyl and thinks he is dead but she has never met Romen Koreldy."

"Wyl . . . may I call you that?"

"Of course." It was refreshing to hear his own name spoken.

"Can I suggest you take a look in a mirror sometime? At the risk of understatement, the body you live in is very pleasing on the eye. You have no idea right now how she may view you."

"I don't know about that but what I do sense is that she is in terrible danger. I must get back to Briavel."

"I understand your motives better now. Thank you for telling me." She pointed to a milestone ahead. "There, Wyl! Now we can see where we are."

"Sharp eyes," he commented and they hurried to the small stone pillar. "D four miles," he read out. "Where's D, would you know?"

"Has to be Deakyn, which means we're about twenty miles from Yentro."

"And several days from Rittylworth for you. Can we get horses at Deakyn?"

"Yes, I should think so. It's only a village but it's on a main road which feeds south. It has an inn called the Penny Whistle and I imagine horses should not be a problem."

"Our problem, of course, is paying for them. They took my purse when Cailech had us imprisoned. Damn!"

"But they didn't take mine," she said, reaching beneath her skirts.

Wyl could not help but hug her. It was good for them both to hear each other laugh.

"Right, I'm happy to keep going," he said and saw her nod. "You can spend the time telling me all about Wyl and how he turned into Romen. I must know the whole story . . . in detail this time."

They had hidden their cloaks to rid themselves of all links with the Mountain People. The travelers standing before the innkeeper were dusty and disheveled but thankfully the man did not so much as bat his sleepy lids when they arrived at the Penny Whistle in the early hours of the next day. It was still dark outside and he was too burdened with yawns to be even mildly curious. They had coin to pay and that was enough. Wyl and Elspyth shared a room to avoid drawing attention to themselves, and there they slept.

After cleaning and tidying themselves later in the day, they enjoyed a hearty midday meal, having missed breakfast. Elspyth then spent all her money on a horse for Wyl's long journey.

"Thank you for this," he said, after she turned from paying the stableman. "Ylena has money. Use it. Remember what I said about how fragile she is—she may not be ready to care properly for herself anyway and your companionship will be a blessing."

Elspyth had slept only lightly. Wyl's story had left her mind reeling with possibilities and no little terror. Ylena's story touched her heart. She wanted to believe that Lothryn would survive his ordeal but to hear of Ylena's husband so brutally murdered made her shudder.

"Now, have you got that letter for the Duke?"

She tapped her skirt pocket. "I could hardly forget it, having watched you labor over it this morning."

Wyl grinned. "I'm better with the sword."

"Are you leaving now, then?" she asked. She did not mean for it to sound so sad.

He nodded. "I must."

"Oh, I forgot to tell you!" Elspyth suddenly said, reddening at her oversight. "I overheard some travelers in the inn this morning. They were from Pearlis. Apparently the King is preparing to make a state visit to Briavel."

Wyl looked aghast. "When?" he asked, grabbing her tiny shoulders.

"I don't know. I got the impression it was imminent, if not already happening. They seemed excited, talking up a possible union between the realms and peace at last."

"I have to go," he said, his mind racing. "Do your best to travel with people. If you get the opportunity just link up with others headed south. A woman traveling alone is vulnerable."

"Wyl, I'll be all right. Just send word as you promised. I have no money to give you for your journey."

"I'll be fine," he said, his thoughts already in Briavel. He leaned down and kissed her and was delighted when she suddenly hugged him fiercely.

"Be safe, Wyl."

"You keep yourself and Ylena out of trouble. Just get to Felrawthy. I'll meet you there."

She nodded and let him go, mustering a brave smile as she waved.

33

YL PUSHED HIS HORSE HARD. ONCE AGAIN HE RELIED ON INtuition to guide him over the terrain and was grateful that the spirit of Koreldy lived on, albeit vaguely. He rode diagonally across the country for two days in a southeasterly route until he hit the border between Morgravia and Briavel. Sleeping rough did not bother Wyl, although he imagined he looked quite a sight when the Briavellian Guard finally picked him up less than half a day's ride into Valentyna's realm. He was reassured by their promptness; the security in place was at least working.

His worn and dusty appearance seemed to belie his story

that the Queen was expecting him. However, Koreldy's
high-mannered tone and clipped accent reinforced his claim
of noble status and discouraged the Guard from ignoring
him. He knew his luck was holding when a man called
Liryk recognized his name; even better, the man had been
briefed by Valentyna that should Koreldy make application
he was to be brought to Werryl immediately.

With Liryk's sanction he was permitted to join the party
of Guards heading back to the city with taxes and missives
from various townships. It was an uneventful couple of
days during which Wyl could eat well and sleep without
worry of ambush by bandits or the like. In truth he rather
enjoyed being among the company of soldiers again. He deliberately did not foist Romen's large personality onto them
and was quick to share the general workload of making and
breaking camp, keeping company with the foot soldiers.
Mostly he kept himself to himself.

Wyl only discovered toward the end of the journey that
Liryk was not just a senior member of the military but in
fact Commander of the Briavellian Guard. He gleaned this
information over a meal at an inn obviously quite used to
the comings and goings of soldiers, for the serving girls
smiled and joked with the men.

"You're rather lofty in status to be doing this sort of
task," Wyl commented, tucking into his roast chicken.

Liryk had chosen the pie and was neatly shoveling in
forkfuls of beef and gravy. He saved the pastry for last and
Wyl smiled. Ylena did the same. He wondered how she
fared and prayed to Shar that she was well enough in her
mind to welcome Elspyth into her life. He realized Liryk
was talking.

". . . I thrive on it, though. Hate being cooped at the
palace. I take these duties whenever it is feasible, although
increasingly I think they will become fewer. I need to be
around her majesty."

Wyl nodded. He already liked his man very much and
was glad that Valentyna had his years and wisdom to
draw on.

"Besides," Liryk continued, "it's a nightmare organizing

so many men to return to Werryl. I have been personally rounding them up because I want as many as we can spare back in the city for this state visit by the Morgravian King."

"You don't trust him?"

"Apart from the fact that we are sworn enemies, you mean?" Both men laughed. Liryk waved his fork at Wyl. "You peaceful Grenadynes could never understand the animosity between our realms. Suddenly we have to act courteously and be diplomatic when only a few years ago they slaughtered us on the battlefield. I was there—I witnessed hundreds of our young bloods die—and for what? So Morgravia could say they won that time! Pah! I may not care much for the young King but I support the notion of this marriage because it means peace."

Wyl put down his chicken leg. "How advanced are negotiations?"

Liryk made a face. "I'm sorry, Koreldy, I can't discuss that matter with you but suffice to say that most of our people would welcome the union for all the right reasons."

Wyl nodded. "I understand. When do we get there?"

"Tomorrow afternoon."

"And the King?"

"Expecting his arrival in a week or thereabouts. Apparently he's slowing his journey deliberately to call in on towns along the way."

"So they can all fawn over the man they hate," Wyl said, wishing he had not.

Liryk eyed him. "We'll be making our last stop at Crowyll. It's a major town about ten miles north of the city. Has the best brothel in Briavel, by the way. You should visit, Koreldy . . . get rid of that bile on your liver."

Liryk was as good as his word. Wyl had not visited many brothels in his day but he soon realized that the elegant stone building at Crowyll with a sign that read "Forbidden Fruit" enclosed one of the most salubrious establishments of its kind in any realm. It seemed to him that the Briavellians were not as straitlaced about sex as their more powerful neighbour. These were people who made a point of enjoying all of life's pleasures and he was taken aback at how Liryk encouraged his men, many of them married, to spend a few hours with a desirable woman.

Wyl commented on this and Liryk shrugged. "These men have been on the road for many weeks. They need to relax before they head back to the strict duties imposed because of the royal visit. Normally they would get some time off but not on this occasion. They deserve a night of, er . . . relaxation and will work harder for me because of it."

Wyl felt his own strict upbringing coming to the fore. "I wonder if their wives feel the same way."

Liryk laughed. "I'm surprised at you, Koreldy. You look like a man of the world. What the women don't know cannot hurt them."

"And you? Do you intend to partake of the, er . . . relaxation on offer?" Wyl asked, casting a general gaze around the Welcome Chamber. Here the men were invited to enjoy a few ales or wines, and some songs from the women before then moving onto more intimate activities. In Briavel, as in Morgravia, these activities normally began with a soak to be followed by an oil and smoothing.

"Of course, but then I'm not married and so do not suffer even the slightest guilt," Liryk replied. "I've got my heart set on that rather interesting creature in the corner . . . she looks like she'd be good value, although I fear she has eyes only for you, Koreldy."

Wyl grunted a dismissal but looked toward her anyway. She was intriguing. Not traditionally beautiful in the way that Ylena could turn heads, this woman was striking by her sheer force of presence as much as handsome looks. She was watching him as she entertained a small group of men, tilting her head as she laughed at their jests and flicking her shoulder-length hair coquettishly. Most Briavellian women preferred to wear their hair long. Still, hers somehow suited her tall, strong build.

He continued to stare, fascinated by her feline manner. There was no other way to describe her liquid movement. He sensed she could move fast even though she gave the impression of being unhurried. As she fetched drinks for her guests, he noticed she moved as lightly and lithely as a dancer . . . or even as one trained in what was known as the Simple Art. Gueryn had never had much time for that style of fighting without weaponry in which the hands and feet were used to inflict injury and the fighter's only protection was his own speed and strength. Consequently Wyl had never learned the techniques although he had intended to some day. Many of the younger soldiers coming up through the ranks had studied the Simple Art and Wyl had seen for himself the damage such skills could cause to an enemy during a fighting exhibition in Pearlis. He had promised himself that he would acquire the techniques—once the royal tourney was over. He no longer possessed that young, agile body and would probably never learn those skills.

The woman's limbs were long and angular. Wyl could see a sculpting of muscle on her bare arms and her belly was flat and tight. Here was someone who perhaps took care to keep herself trim, supple, and strong. He looked away, embarrassed, when she caught him staring. Romen would not look away, he admonished himself. Romen would meet her gaze and return it with lust.

Wyl was disappointed with himself as once again a nagging thought nudged at his mind. The longer he lived inside Romen, the less of Romen there was. When he had first moved across, everything that was Wyl had felt tightly contained and he had depended on the Grenadyne's personality and character. Increasingly, it was Wyl who was shining through and it was becoming harder, sometimes impossible, to find Koreldy within. Did this mean that Romen was finally lost? Had what had been left just evaporated over time?

Answers would come only from Myrren's father, the manwitch, as Widow Ilyk had cautioned.

Someone accidentally elbowed him and it brought him out of his thoughts. He found his gaze once again drawn helplessly toward the woman. He noticed her eyes were a soft murky brown, and with the darkly golden hair, it was an enticing mix. None of her features were particularly beautiful either, he had to admit. It was more her vivaciousness and mannerisms that were so appealing. Confidence was not lacking and she held her audience rapt with what Wyl assumed was witty conversation. Her companions seemed to be laughing a great deal.

Men around the chamber finally began to drift away with chosen partners. The woman deliberately excused herself from the attentions of several men and found a reason to approach Wyl.

"You don't look like you belong in this group," she said. She had a low voice, oozing appeal. "But you are most welcome. It's a treat to have someone so attractive visit us."

Wyl had no retort for such directness and desperately wished Romen would surface to save him. His command was ignored and he watched a slow grin move across her face.

"Where are you from, stranger?"

He was glad to be on safe ground with a question he could answer by rote. "Er, Grenadyn."

"Then you are a long way from home. Do you have a name?"

"Koreldy!" someone answered for him. It was Liryk, who appeared to be in a suddenly expansive mood. Wyl felt sure the older man was nothing like this back at the palace. "Don't worry about him, my dear. Us older men are much more fun." He winked.

But she did not see it. Her gaze had not moved from Wyl and he felt compelled to answer a question he was not sure had been asked. "Look, you two go right ahead. I'm happy savoring this rather superb Alsava. I haven't tasted such a good wine in many months," he lied, instantly regretting such a weak remark.

"There, you see," Liryk said and beamed at the woman. "Now what's your name, my lovely?"

"I'm called Hildyth," she replied, still watching Wyl with narrowed, searching eyes.

Liryk wasted no further time in conversation. "Come, Hildyth, we have only a few hours." And he led the way.

She turned back. "Pity," she said to Wyl. "I think we might have enjoyed each other."

"Next time, perhaps," he said, regaining some composure.

"I hope that's a promise." Her voice made him feel hot in places he preferred not to.

He nodded and again the wry smile hinted at her mouth as she turned and left him with his wine.

Wyl felt out of sorts after his meeting with Hildyth. He did not feel like going back to the inn in which Liryk had arranged for them to stay. Instead he made the lonely walk back a few miles to the field where some of the foot soldiers had made camp, far preferring the company of these men right now to a whore or his own troubled thoughts.

The next morning, when the small company had reunited, Wyl was astonished to see Liryk—normally so neat and tidy—looking much the worse for wear after his night in Crowyll.

The elder soldier spotted him. "Shar's Mercy, man, you're safe!"

"Of course. What's happened?"

"There was an incident at the inn where we were staying. Where were you anyway?"

"I came back here. I didn't feel like sharing my own company last night."

"Good job you did too. There was a fire. I thought we'd lost you."

Wyl frowned. "We saw some smoke—is everyone safe?"

Liryk sighed. "Yes, our boys were vigilant. Even on these occasions I post lookouts and so the fire was noticed early. Lucky for you that you stayed at camp."

"Oh?" Wyl asked.

"The fire broke out right near your room. There's nothing left of that wing of the inn. Your room was gutted and collapsed first."

"How did it start?"

The soldier shrugged. "No one seems to know. An oil lamp left unattended, someone said, but it's just a thought. There's no proof. Anyway, we leave now."

Wyl thought no more about the incident, his spirits lifting at the thought of seeing Valentyna again.

The assassin stood alongside the rest of the onlookers, making similar noises of despair and disgust. They were all waiting with morbid interest to see the charred remains of whichever poor sods had been trapped by the fire. The innkeeper stood with them, assuring the townsfolk that the inn had been relatively empty the previous night—just a few soldiers staying. He rubbed at his eyes, exhausted from a night of fighting the blaze. Fortunately for him, the section of the building damaged was separated by a walkway to the main inn.

"We did a check this morning. Every guest bar one is accounted for," he said.

"Who?" someone asked.

"Commander Liryk said it was a stranger, not a soldier. He was travelling with them. A person from Grenadyn—goes by the name of Koreldy," he answered, eager to allay fears that one of their own may have perished.

It would be tragic for business if word got out that he was careless with his lamps. The innkeeper could not understand it. He had checked everything before turning in for the night. It was ritual for him to walk the length of each floor, trimming wicks, blowing out candles mistakenly left in corridors by guests. Even more baffling for him was the fact that he only kept a few oil lamps burning at any one time and he did not remember lighting one that previous evening. Perhaps one of the girls had but why would it have been burning near that particular room? He had to accept he had been tired and not thinking altogether clearly but he could not even remember seeing the distinctive stranger return to his room that night.

One of his own people trotted up. "Innkeeper Jon."

He came out of his grim thoughts and looked up. "Any news?"

"None. We've picked through the wreckage. We can't salvage anything, sir."

"I reckoned as much. What about the"—he hesitated, "body?"

"No sign of that. If the Grenadyne was in the room, he's gone up in smoke with it."

The carefully eavesdropping assassin frowned and turned away. It had been risky but worth it to ignite oil at the door of Koreldy's room and again just beneath his room in the empty chamber below. The added precaution of beginning a fire on the bottom floor beneath his window was inspired. He had had no easy means of escape. Hopefully all signs of Romen Koreldy had gone up in flames, as the lad had said. However, this assassin was too thorough for presumptions.

She wanted her other half of the gold from Jessom when he came into Briavel any day now with King Celimus. She wanted to believe her victim was nothing more than ash but deep down her instincts told her otherwise. She left the gawking audience to return to her rooms feeling unsettled.

On the way, alert to her inner voice of caution—for she never took chances with her prey—she concluded that it would be prudent to remain in this town until she had gleaned word that Koreldy was definitely dead.

34

FYNCH BURIED HIS SMALL HAND INTO THE RUFF OF FUR ENcircling Knave's neck. The dog turned and looked at him—deep brown eyes all-knowing. It was as though the animal sensed his moods, his thoughts. Even more astonishing was the fact that increasingly Knave seemed to be able to assist with Fynch's decision-making. As the boy pondered his problems, he felt that Knave could tap into his feelings . . . press thoughts and notions into his mind.

He did not know when this began to occur and he could not explain himself, so he did not try, although he had ad-

mitted as much to Valentyna. To tell any others would be to
bring down much ridicule upon himself. It would be a ludicrous claim anyway among people who no longer believed
in magic. Magic was the stuff of myth. Tales to scare little
ones and give the bards something with which to spice their
lyrics.

But magic must have existed in the world at some time,
Fynch reasoned, for superstitious people still walked
around puddles in case their soul was reflected there. Or
said a special warding if they found their butter had soured,
their milk had curdled, or salt had been spilled. His favorite
superstition was the wearing of something violet the day
before the night of a full moon.

Fynch's mother had been especially "connected'—as she
had claimed—to the spiritual world and she had recognized
something in her eldest son—she never told him what—
that made him vulnerable to unearthly matters.

"They can talk to you," she would caution.

Many people had called his mother lary, which Fynch
came to realize was a kind alternative to being called mad.
He knew she was not. It was simply her "connection" that
made her appear odd. She had heard voices, experienced visions, but had never spoken of them to anyone, including
his father, and only by chance once confided in Fynch, her
favorite. Oh, yes, he was one of the few Morgravians who
firmly believed in the presence of magic.

Valentyna, perhaps not as cynical as most, had agreed
to go along with his notion that Wyl was present among
them and that his connection to Romen Koreldy was far
less obvious than the Grenadyne was leading them to believe. Fynch could not be sure whether she was simply hu-
moring a child but he chose to believe she honored his
reasoning, even if she did not believe. Their discussion of
Wyl's link with Romen had been left behind on the Bridge
that first morning of his return to Briavel and not referred
to again.

Knave, however, was considered in a different light.

"He's definitely touched," she had admitted recently,
though she would never use the term sorcery or enchantment.

"He belonged to a witch," Fynch had replied, leaving it at that.

"There are occasions," she confided on one of their many long walks together, "when I feel transparent to him. Does that sound stupid?"

He had shaken his head. Fynch had known precisely what she meant.

To Fynch it was enough. Valentyna, in her own rigid way, was acknowledging the possibility of magic—for witchcraft was the only way he could describe Knave's ongoing strangeness. The animal's behavior had become less predictable over the past weeks. The dog had disappeared soon after their arrival back in Werryl. He had gone missing the next morning, in fact, having spent the night with Valentyna, or so she claimed when she woke Fynch, anxious at the loss of the dog. Fynch had been inconsolable for the next few days. And then on the fourth day, Knave had reappeared at the palace.

After the initial flurry of excitement and tears of relief, Fynch had scolded the huge dog. He had waited until they were alone.

"Where have you been?" he had exclaimed, holding the dog's huge face in his small hands.

Knave had looked at him strangely. There was something in the dog's stare that had frightened him and then he had felt suddenly dizzy. He shuddered even now remembering it . . . seeing the blood as Romen had hacked off someone's head. The mercenary too was hurt. Then he saw Knave dragging Romen, unconscious, lifeless—he knew not where. The vision had faded and he was staring once more into the eyes of the dog.

"You've been with Romen! He's injured. Where is he?"

A voice, distant and soft, had then echoed across his thoughts. "Safe for now," it said and then it was gone. He had shaken his head. Surely he had imagined the voice? Fynch believed he had even made it up just to reassure himself after the unsettling vision.

Knave had given one of his loud barks. He did that to get Fynch's attention. It was as though he were dragging Fynch back to the present. After that the dog had fallen back into his familiar pattern of traipsing around with him. There were moments during this time when Fynch could believe he was just being fanciful in believing Knave was anything but a lively, buffoonish dog.

Valentyna liked to keep Fynch close. She often used him as a runner for her personal errands and this day was no different, beginning with running some important messages for the Queen. She, however, had felt restless and unable to concentrate on her regal duties and she had suggested a canter through the beautiful woodlands of Werryl.

"I'm determined that you learn to handle a full-sized horse," she had said early in their relationship and she had taken it upon herself to teach him. And so rides together occurred relatively often—the Queen needed little encouragement to leap onto the back of a horse. These days they were always trailed, of course, by half a dozen other riders but their escort was discreet and there were moments when Valentyna felt the thrill of freedom from duty.

Her relationship with Fynch had strengthened to the extent that she felt he was the brother she had never had, had always wanted. Young as he was, Fynch's serious nature and quick mind melded neatly with her intelligence and she loved having him around her, using him to bounce ideas off and work through problems. They were rarely matters of state—she had many councillors to advise her on such things. No, Fynch was a soulmate for her. He was her closest friend, her most loyal subject.

Together they shared discussions on life, love, hopes for Briavel, horse-breeding, gardens, and especially how next they could tease her rather stiff and starchy head of house. On this particular day, they hardly noticed the escort insisted upon by Commander Liryk. The woodland around Werryl was breathtaking at this time of year; it was Valentyna's favorite place to ride, although she could not break into the empowering gallop she preferred. Instead they rode more sedately, Valentyna correcting Fynch's seat and his grip on the reins from time to time, both enjoying the freedom and peace.

Later, leaning against their horses while the animals drank thirstily from the woodland's fast-moving stream, Fynch began telling her a funny story about his former days as a gong boy at Stoneheart. She was laughing hard and leaned across to touch his arm in an affectionate way when she felt his body suddenly go rigid.

Her smile froze. "Fynch?"

He was silent. She noticed his hand was clutching Knave—that was not unusual, for the pair of them were rarely separated—but her attention was caught by how Knave was looking back at her. There it was again, that disturbing gaze of the dog's that seemed to see right through her. They were connected—she touching Fynch and he gripping Knave with the dog's eyes locked on her. She tore her own eyes away from the compelling hold of Knave's stare and saw that Fynch's mouth was slack and his gaze faraway but she could still feel the tension in the muscles in his arm. He was trembling slightly.

She took him by the shoulders this time. "Fynch!" she yelled. "It's Valentyna. Please, Fynch, talk to me."

His small body slumped against hers and, had she not caught him, he would have fallen. She picked him up—he was so light it was no effort—and walked toward the soft grasses in the shade of one of her favorite oaks.

"Rawl," she called to one of the men. "Water, please."

The man immediately broke from the pack of soldiers nearby. He appeared by her side with a flask and she wet her handkerchief and dabbed it over Fynch's face. Rawl was dismissed the moment Fynch opened his eyes. Knave, as usual, was sitting close—next to the boy's head, in fact—and she stole a glance toward the dog as Fynch struggled to sit up. Fynch immediately put his head in his hands as though it hurt.

"What was that all about?" she finally asked. "You scared me."

"It happened again," he muttered, barely above a whisper.

"Again?" This has happened before? "Look at me," she said and he did. "What occurred just now?"

Fynch shook his head. "I can't explain it."

"Don't try to explain, just tell me."

"I had a vision."

She had not expected this. "And what did you see?"

He looked at the Queen and detected no amusement or disbelief. There was concern but also interest in hearing what he had to say. He decided to tell her everything. "I saw you."

"Me?"

He nodded. "You were with Celimus."

Her lips pursed. "What were we doing?"

"Watching an execution." Fynch noticed how she struggled to respond. He pressed on. "He kissed you after it was done."

It was too much for her. Valentyna was glad she had dismissed the guard.

"Fynch, what is this about?"

"I told you, I can't explain it."

"And this has happened before, you say?"

"Yes. The last time I saw Romen and yet somehow he was Wyl Thirsk."

The Queen sat back and crossed her arms around her knees, hugging them close—this was disturbing. "Why didn't you tell me about this?"

"I thought I had imagined it . . . dreamed it."

"Fynch, you are the most sane person I know. You would not be duped by a dream."

"It was frightening."

"Tell me about that other dream," she said, suddenly feeling very much the adult comforting a child.

"I saw Romen. He was injured but he was cutting off someone's head. I think there might have even been another dead person in it but I can't be sure."

It sounded to her as though he had simply experienced a nightmare. She remained patient. "Your dreams are brutal. Public executions and private beheadings." She shook her head gently. "And what else?"

Fynch looked distraught now, almost angry with himself. "I was looking at Romen but my impression was that he was Wyl."

She was careful not to sound condescending. "You know that makes no sense."

"Of course. But it doesn't change what I saw or how I felt about it, your majesty."

"Well, you've mentioned before that you believe Wyl is somehow strongly connected to Romen. Do you think you could have just wanted to see that?" She hated the placatory tone creeping into her voice.

"Yes, your majesty, I have told myself it was pure fancy." There was no sarcasm in his voice, only honesty.

She looked at Knave, who was gazing at her intently, and she hastily looked back at Fynch. "But you don't believe it is pure fancy, do you?"

He shook his head miserably. "It was as if they're both together."

"Is there more? You seem to be hesitant," she encouraged.

"I heard a voice. It was so soft, again I thought I had made it up. It answered my question to Knave."

The Queen took a deep breath. "Go back to the beginning, Fynch."

It was his turn to sigh. "I was cross with Knave for leaving as he did, and you know how you talk to your horses?" She nodded. "Well, I talk to him like that. I asked him where he had been."

"And?"

"The vision happened. I was shocked and must have said something along the lines of 'So you were with Romen and he's hurt.' I think I must have asked Knave where Romen was."

"And a voice answered you—is that it?"

He nodded. "It said, 'Safe for now.' " Then he grimaced. "I know what you're going to say next."

"Oh?"

"You're going to ask me if it was Knave who answered and then dismiss me as lary, like my mother."

She looked at her hands. "I didn't know your mother, Fynch. I know you rather well and would never consider you as anything but intelligent and sane."

He said nothing but she sensed he was pleased.

Valentyna could not help herself. "Well?"

The vaguest of smiles played around his mouth. "No. Knave did not speak to me."

"So someone else—who?"

He shrugged. "It was a man, that's all I can tell."

Valentyna had no idea what next to say—this talk of magic always unnerved her—so she retreated to safer ground by returning to his more recent vision. "And now in this second vision you say you saw me with Celimus?"

Fynch nodded. He chose not to speak, pulling at the grasses around his feet.

"Anything other than the kiss, Fynch?" she asked, holding out the flask so he could drink.

He took it but did not put it to his mouth. "I don't know the man he's having executed, of course, but it's being done with a sword."

"A noble then?"

"I suppose. The prisoner's looking at you, though."

"I know him!"

"I don't know."

Intrigued despite herself, the Queen held her hand out for the flask of water and took a sip. "Describe him for me."

"I'm not sure I can—"

"Oh, come on, Fynch. You have the most acute powers of observation. Think hard!"

He closed his eyes and screwed up his face.

"Large man. Sun-weathered face. Rugged features."

"Hair?" she prompted.

He shook his head, eyes still closed as he strained to concentrate. "I can't tell the color. It's tied back and dark with his sweat."

"And they're about to execute him?"

"Yes, that's all I saw. I did not see him being executed." Fynch opened his eyes. There was nothing more he could share.

"Well now, that certainly has me baffled."

"Best not to dwell on it, your majesty," Fynch suggested. "You've enough on your plate."

She grimaced. "It's bad enough that Celimus is coming here—will be here any day—and I have no doubt what's on his mind for our royal discussion."

"You can't marry him, your majesty."

"I know this, Fynch, believe me," she lied to herself as much as him. Marriage would be her only solution for guaranteed peace. She felt the rise of expectancy among her people. They all wanted the marriage to take place . . . they wanted the young men of Briavel to survive, grow old. "I don't want to marry him!"

"And yet I think you may," he said, even more miserable now.

She looked at Fynch, her frustration weighing heavily on her at the strength of his conviction. She saw what a small and frightened little boy he was and yet he found courage, he was always so strong for her. His eyes finally met hers.

"I'm sorry, your majesty."

Knave shifted closer to Fynch and the animal's move was not lost on Valentyna. The dog at times made her feel so safe and yet on occasions, like now, she could easily feel so threatened by him. In just that slight movement the dog was communicating something to her or to Fynch—she could not be sure but she believed it was directed at her. *Trust the boy,* the dog seemed to say. *Trust the vision.* She knew she needed to behave rationally and not dismiss Fynch's words as lunatic ravings. Fynch had not let her down previously and above everything else she loved him, trusted him.

"I must somehow achieve peace for our realm without giving offense to Morgravia. I cannot even begin to deal with the prospect of war—we are ill-equipped. Marriage is the most diplomatic path to take." She sounded sad. "Perhaps I could learn to love him."

"No, majesty, you would never be able to do that. You could not love the Celimus I know."

"Maybe I could change him?" The words sounded hollow.

"And the oxen may well skip over the lavender bushes, your majesty," he said and was rewarded with a smile. He had not meant it to sound funny but was pleased he had eased the tension.

"How do you feel now?" she asked.

"My head hurts but I'm fine," he said. "Let's forget my visions," he added. "You have enough to think about in trying to make the King of Morgravia feel welcome, even though his advances may not be."

As she nodded her agreement a messenger from the palace made himself known.

"What is it?"

"Your majesty." The lad bowed. "Riders. Commander Liryk and party are two miles from the palace. He has sent word ahead that a man called Romen Koreldy is with the party and that you are expecting him."

Fynch's spirits lifted instantly at the news.

"Thank you, Ivor." She smiled at the lad. He had become one of the best messengers in the palace. His parents had succumbed to the Fainting Fever, which had been sweeping the land, and Valor had ensured the baby was taken into the care of the palace. Thinking of her father now made her feel bereft all over again. She knew she would be a good ruler for her realm—she had learned well—but oh, how she craved his guidance right now, especially after what Fynch had just told her of his vision.

There was no doubt Fynch was honest—he could not be otherwise—which made his telling of what he had seen all the more unfathomable as well as frightening. *Celimus kissing me!* The man who had contrived the death of her beloved father. And deep down, tucked away tightly in her heart, Valentyna knew that she would most likely have to marry this man she did not know, would not love. Hated! How could she marry Celimus after all that she knew of him through Wyl and Fynch? She would give anything for her father's strength beside her now and, much as she hated to admit it, she was gladdened by the news that Romen Koreldy had returned.

The words of his letter burned brightly in her mind.

I will come soon—I am yours to command, my Queen. My loyalty to you will never waver. In the meantime I give you a special gift. I give you the dog Knave, who will be true to you. Trust him alone and his faithful companion, Fynch. They will protect you.

Be brave, beautiful Valentyna.

She did trust Fynch and, as much as Knave scared her at times, she knew the dog would never harm her. Koreldy believed they would protect her and now he was coming to Briavel to offer his service. It made her heart feel lighter.

"Rawl, we ride now—make haste everyone."

As she climbed into her saddle she looked at Fynch. "Romen's here, you must stop worrying."

He smiled but she could tell he was still distracted, worried. "You ride on ahead, your majesty."

Valentyna nodded and kicked her horse into a gallop and the riders charged in her wake.

He could tell Knave was eager to go too. "You want to see him, don't you, boy?"

Knave did not flinch; he waited for Fynch's signal. "You go then. I'll be back soon."

The dog cut across open fields toward the palace, making it back before the riders.

35

VALENTYNA LEFT INSTRUCTIONS FOR ROMEN KORELDY WITH her Chancellor before ascending the palace's central staircase to the first floor. She deliberately slowed her walk through the corridor toward what was formerly her father's study and main reception chamber for important guests.

It was from here she tackled the daily business of running the realm, as her father and his father before him had.

She stroked the back of her father's battered chair as she stood by the window in his old room. From this chamber she could look down into the main bailey and watch the arrival of Liryk and his men. His presence had been sorely missed but she understood his need to reevaluate security in the realm and bring many of their soldiers back to Werryl in readiness for the Morgravian visit . . . just in case. The King was apparently bringing only a light escort by his standards— but that still meant five score Morgravian soldiers on their soil. She would not be taking any chances. Should trouble occur or Briavel be duped, they would be ready for any eventuality.

.She looked for Koreldy and, even though she had no idea of his appearance other than the description from Fynch, she picked him out with ease. It helped that he was dressed in civilian attire but even from this height she could tell that Fynch had drawn a supremely accurate picture of this man. Once again she marveled that such a young boy could offer such precise information.

I shouldn't be surprised, she scolded herself silently. *Fynch has a mind like a vise for detail.*

Valentyna watched as her message of summons was delivered to Koreldy. He was to be brought immediately to her. A guard from the palace politely asked for his weapons, which he readily handed over, including two curious knives he pulled from within his shirt. She smiled to herself, not sure why, as she watched from her vantage. She presumed the guard must have apologized and asked if he could do a quick search—orders and all that—but Liryk stepped in and seemed to wave away the necessity for that.

A short discussion and the guard left, carrying the weapons. She noticed a friendliness between Liryk and Koreldy—that too was positive. She trusted Liryk implicitly and he would have made it his business to get close enough to this relative stranger to make an assessment. She remembered how dubious Liryk and old Krell had been about Koreldy. But it was Fynch who had persuaded them that he was very much on Briavel's side. He could be trusted.

She watched the two men in the yard share a few words, a quick laugh, and then Koreldy took his leave, following the page.

Soon enough she heard footsteps and the only outward sign she showed of the sudden nervousness she felt was to touch at her wayward hair, wishing now she had taken a moment to comb it back at least. She was not one to pay much heed to vanity, however, and the thought was dismissed almost as soon as it had come.

A knock at the door and her Chancellor entered. "Your majesty, Romen Koreldy is here to meet with you."

"Thank you, Krell, please show him in."

He nodded. "I will have the refreshments sent up immediately, your majesty."

She smiled her thanks. His intuition as well as his experience was precious to her.

Valentyna remained by the window, just a little unsure of herself. She hated that her normally effortless confidence had momentarily evaporated and she had only just begun to grasp the reason for its absence when Romen Koreldy finally stepped into her chamber. They stared at each other just a bit longer than protocol dictated. She noted that Romen's eyes were sparkling—it was as if he already knew her and was gladdened to see her again.

A small smile of bemusement played at her lips as the silence lengthened. He had not made a step since the door had closed quietly behind him. Koreldy became aware of her gentle confusion and was now quick to stride across the room before kneeling and taking her hand.

"Queen Valentyna." He kissed her hand, again lingering, she thought, for a moment or two longer than strictly necessary. "Your majesty, I offer my service, as promised." His head remained bowed, her hand still resting in his, she noted. He was clearly not keen to let it go and if she was truthful with herself, she was in no hurry either.

"Be welcome, Romen Koreldy. It is a pleasure to have you among us."

Now he stood up to his full height, taller than her, she realized, which was unusual. Most men she could look straight in the eye or down at; to reach his gray gaze, she found herself tilting her head just slightly. A rare and pleasurable experience.

Emotions she could not immediately pinpoint passed through her and threatened to unbalance her poise. In the same instant Valentyna recognized what had sapped her normally unflappable nature. It was him. For the first time in her young life Valentyna understood what it was like to be strongly attracted to a man.

Oh, she had experienced infatuation with older men when she was a girl. In fact she recalled having a crush on a tawny-haired stable boy when she was barely ten summers, and one of the squires in training had chanced kissing her once. She had kicked him. There was a tutor when she was twelve who made her breath catch when he smiled or leaned in close but since then no one. Not a single man to send her heart skipping out of control. The feeling unnerved her in truth, for it made her feel weak inside, like her knees felt right now. Weakness would not help her rule.

He was watching her closely with that sardonic expression, those knowing eyes. She had expected someone more arrogant. Krell had met Koreldy briefly on his first visit and had described a swaggering, confident sort of fellow with an easy laugh—someone used to getting his way. She did not sense much of this right now but it was too early to be making judgement. Koreldy cleared his throat and she realized the silence between them had stretched too far. She should say something.

"Thank you for coming back."

Now he smiled broadly and it changed him, lighting a fresh spark in his eyes and handsomely wrinkling the skin of his tanned face around his eyes and mouth.

"I could not stay away," he replied.

I could get lost in that smile, she thought. Valentyna was rescued by a knock at the door; Krell announced refreshments, which a servant brought in on a large tray.

Relief flooded through her. "You must be thirsty after your ride," she said to her guest.

"Please forgive my appearance, your majesty; we have been on the road for several days."

"Don't mention it," she said, thanking the servant with a small nod as he left the room. "I too have been out riding this morning." She wanted to tell Koreldy that she liked his dusty look, the smell of horse about him, his unshaven chin and the unruly dark hair falling near his shoulders.

Here's a man to lose one's heart to.

As Valentyna cleared her throat with embarrassment at her private thoughts, Wyl was feeling very glad for Romen's unflappable manner, for he was sure without that he would be stammering like a youth. He wondered at how intriguingly unpredictable Romen's essence was, sometimes fading to nothing and at times, like now, potent. Looking at Valentyna again lifted his spirits and filled his heart. He could not imagine ever being happier than this precious moment. Just the two of them. Both a little awkward, his heart hammering in his chest and that familiar sensation of shortening breath. He recalled it from the first time they met. *She is so lovely,* he thought, *and just as I remember: her unaffected manner, her hair easing from its clasp, her man's riding clothes.*

I have missed you, Valentyna. I love you more than I can begin to explain, he so desperately wanted to say. Instead he nodded at her gesture to be seated and joined her at a small table and chairs by the window. He hoped Romen's cheeks did not flush as easily as his own used to.

She grinned. "I'm still trying to get used to this room. It was my father's, you know. I can often feel his presence."

He could tell she was uncharacteristically nervous. "He was a brave man. We were outnumbered, I'm so sorry, your majesty, for letting you down. . . ."

"Don't," she said, instinctively reaching to touch his hand reassuringly, only to be thrilled once again when he did not hesitate to cover hers with his own. She did not shrink away. She allowed the dry warmth of his palm to seep through the back of her hand. It was the most sensuous moment of her life. She caught her breath; those flinty eyes held her too directly.

Valentyna resisted the temptation to clear her throat again and begged her voice not to tremble. "I know that you and Wyl Thirsk fought valiantly to save him. I owe you heartfelt thanks . . . a Morgravian and a Grenadyne fighting for a Briavellian. It's ironic."

Wyl remained quiet. Her pain was evident. The silence stretched.

"There's a small boy and a huge dog eager to see you," she said brightly, forcing herself to move away from the subject of her father's death and from Koreldy's touch.

"Fynch—is he well?"

Taken off guard momentarily by his earnest manner—which certainly did not fit with the description Krell had given her of this man—Valentyna liked him all the more for it. "He seems well."

It struck Wyl that the Queen did not sound so sure. "But?" he asked, releasing her hand and she instantly felt the loss.

She covered her disappointment by handing him a goblet of wine, wishing she had not cast doubt in his mind. He spoke to her as if they were old friends, such was his easy manner, but she did not know this man well enough yet to share secrets. "No 'but.' He is well," she confirmed, favoring him with a heartbreaking smile. "Please," she said, encouraging him to taste the wine. "This was one of my father's favorites."

Wyl sipped, Fynch forgotten momentarily as he allowed the warmth from that smile to wash over him. "It's superb. Thank you."

Valentyna enjoyed the compliment. "Father always counseled that this wine is best when young," she admitted, sipping from her goblet. She took a deep breath. It was time to move on from the pleasantries. "Romen, may I be candid?"

He nodded. "I'd prefer you to be."

"Well, it's just that I find myself in a precarious situation. You tried to save my father's life—with no reason for doing so—and you fought alongside a man we trusted. A man you had been sent to kill, I'm assured. Wyl Thirsk died that day and we have no one's word but yours as to how that happened. The saving grace, of course, is that you could have simply left him and fled. However, you returned his body to Morgravia and then took his sister to safety, which we can only assume is a sign of your honesty in this matter. And now I have to trust that your pledge to Briavel . . . and to me"—she felt herself blush—"is true."

He moved to say something but she held her hand up.

"No, please. Let me say this. It needs to be said. I must have honesty from you in this because I cannot fathom what you have to gain, whereas I have everything to lose by putting my faith in you."

"Your majesty." Wyl took her hand again—how he wished to caress it. "I wrote in my letter that I am yours to command. I meant it then and I mean it now. I am true to you, Valentyna, Queen of Briavel."

"But why?"

"Because Celimus is as faithless as a snake. His loyalty is to himself alone. I have no people, your majesty," Wyl said, hating to hear himself say it. "I no longer have a home. I have no roots I care to claim. I liked Wyl Thirsk. He wrung a blood oath from me that I would protect you with my own life."

"So I've been told," she admitted. "Why would he ask that of you?"

It was his chance. Perhaps as Romen he could say what he never could have uttered as Wyl. "Because he was in love with you, your majesty."

Her mouth opened to speak but no sound issued. She closed it again, eyes wide with surprise. "We were strangers," she finally said softly, in disbelief. "Knew each other for only a couple of hours."

"Have you never felt the stomach-churning, heart-stopping sensation of meeting someone for the first time and knowing they were the only person in the world for you?" He said it lightly for fear of sounding condescending, and followed it up with the dazzling smile he knew Romen did so well.

Valentyna blushed instantly. She hoped he could not read her thoughts. "I have heard of it happening," she said, not daring to admit the truth.

He continued, ignoring her discomfort. "I liked Wyl from the moment I met him." Now he fashioned the lie. "I witnessed Celimus's brutality toward the Thirsk family firsthand and decided then that I would not be Wyl's murderer but I was in too deep to pull away from the mission. I could not allow Celimus to know that I had turned traitor. Wyl knew of my instructions—he heard of them through Fynch." She nodded. "The more I got to know of him on the journey to Briavel, the more I knew I could not execute him. We hatched a plan. Of course he did not know you then, your majesty, or the plan would have been very different."

"Go on," she said, embarrassed but intrigued.

"Well, of course, once he had met you, it all changed. He no longer wanted to encourage you to marry Celimus, even though to fail would threaten his sister's life."

She nodded. "Yes, he said as much to us. He told us everything. His hatred for Celimus was the reason he was prepared to fight for Briavel's King, I presume. He was the bravest of men, for to turn traitor takes the hardest courage of all, especially with the name Thirsk."

"Very true," Wyl said, touched by her perceptiveness. "Thirsk had witnessed his closest friend killed ruthlessly. His sister, wife of that friend, was made to kneel in her husband's remains. The length of their marriage could be counted in hours." Wyl's tone was so raw he had to clear his throat. "Ylena was imprisoned, held as ransom against her brother's success in persuading your father to agree to the marriage. His guardian and mentor, Gueryn, had been almost certainly killed in the north, he was told. He suspected foul play on the part of Celimus and I have since discovered he was right to believe this. But he was cornered. Wyl had more than enough reason to hate the new King and after meeting your father and you, your majesty, it was easy for him to choose Briavel's cause despite his loyalty to Morgravia." He rushed toward the end of his emotional speech. "After you and Fynch had fled the palace, Wyl let me into the chamber and told me what he could about the ambush. That was when I realized I had been double-crossed. He asked me to fight alongside him. I had no choice." His tone became tentative, not wishing to reopen old wounds. "After your father was slain and we thought we had killed his attackers, Wyl admitted his heart was already lost to you. One last man murdered Wyl, I'm sorry to admit."

A small choked sound escaped from the Queen. "We had shared a brief meal together—that was all. How could he claim to be in love with me?"

"Your majesty, when love's arrow bites hard into the flesh, there is no escape, no preferred length of time for its delicious poison to take effect. For some, its magical potion can be instant. There is no doubt in my mind that Wyl spoke from the heart. He was prepared to die for you—and he did. But he made me promise over a blood oath that I, of no loyalty to any crown, would protect you with my blade and his sister with my connections."

Wyl deliberately stopped himself from biting his lip or betraying any other sign of anxiety over the cleverly crafted lie. Would she take it? Would she accept him?

"I sensed he was a good man," she said, turning to stare out of the window as she considered all that she had heard. "I believe my father trusted him, even though they were sworn enemies."

"There can be true honor between enemies, your majesty, although I can assure you Celimus has none—he is so much less than his father was."

"Oh? Did you know Magnus?"

"Er, no." *Fool!* "I heard much about him and Wyl Thirsk convinced me the old King was everything his son is not."

She smiled sadly. "My father highly respected Magnus, though he hated him—does that makes sense?" Wyl nodded. "And he held Fergys Thirsk in enormous regard. They fought many battles," she said, a wistful note in her voice. "I should tell you that my father also approved of the marriage. The union will bring peace."

"It no doubt will—but a peace weighted heavily in favor of Morgravia," Wyl cautioned.

She turned away from the window and regarded him steadily now. "Go on."

"Celimus wants to rule Briavel. Once you have agreed to this marriage, you will relinquish any hold over your own realm."

She balked. "I would only agree to rule together."

Valentyna watched Romen shrug. He sighed. "Yes, and

he would promise you the world until you had taken your vow. Be warned, your majesty, Celimus will not keep his word to you on anything. Look through the handsome exterior. A serpent lives beneath."

She stood, pacing distractedly. "He will be here soon. I have no doubt he comes in person to make a proposal of marriage. I have kept his advances at bay, as you suggested, but now I cannot avoid him. There are no more excuses . . . unless I wish for war, which I cannot put my people through again so soon. They crave peace."

"I'm sure the Morgravian people feel the same," Wyl admitted, knowing it to be true.

"What am I going to do?" she said, swinging around. For the first time Wyl saw beyond the regal facade and sensed how alone she was.

Wyl stood and approached her. He wanted to kiss her but he fought the impulse. "Valentyna, will you trust me?"

She cast her blue gaze at him. It was direct, unwavering, strong. He loved her for it. "You have pledged your sword to us . . . your life to us. Yes, I must trust you because I love Fynch and he does trust you . . . and Wyl's strange, unfathomable dog trusts you. You are surrounded by mystery, Romen Koreldy, which troubles me, but yes, I must believe you are true."

He bent and kissed her hand, relief flooding through him. "I am true to you, Valentyna. Let me ponder the situation with Celimus. We will talk later, if that suits your majesty?"

She nodded. "Perhaps you will join me for a walk at dusk? We can talk then."

He bowed, hardly wanting to leave her but knowing he must. He had been lucky this time but she would be more focused during their next meeting. He needed private time to gather his thoughts and find a solution. He was a master strategist—it was what he was born to do—and Wyl knew he would never rely more on that talent than now.

He had only a few days to foil Celimus's plan.

Wyl was escorted to his chambers and the young maid who blushed, curtsied, and stammered a few words as she opened his door was horrified when a huge dog barged past from behind her and leapt toward the handsome guest, knocking him backward. Although he had not anticipated Knave's welcome, Wyl did not lose his footing completely.

"Shar's Wrath, my lord. I'm sorry," the maid shrieked.

Predictably, Knave now had his forelegs up on Wyl's shoulders and had pinioned him against the wall.

"Don't upset yourself," Wyl said to the pale and panicked servant. "I know this dog. This is his most friendly hello."

"Shar preserve us," she begged, calling mightily on the god's indulgence. "That dog of Fynch's will be the death of us."

"He's fine. Please don't worry on my account. We go back a long way. Incidentally, have you sighted Fynch today?"

"Er, yes, sir," she said, hardly daring to move her eyes from the dog. She knew she would be blamed if their guest was in any way harmed or his clothes ruined—not that they could get much dirtier, she decided. "He was riding with her majesty earlier but I have not seen him since."

"Thank you. I'll be fine from here."

"There's warmed water in the basin, sir, and fresh linens. Her majesty requested some garments be laid out too. I hope all is to your liking. I believe young Stewyt has been assigned to you, sir, so he will run any messages for your needs."

She curtsied.

"Thank you again," he said, disengaging himself from Knave and stepping into the room. The dog followed, much to her disapproval. "I'll let him out later."

The maid nodded and, mercifully for Wyl, left. He closed the door and turned to his dog, who was sitting on his haunches and staring up at him. "What are you, Knave? You're no normal hound, that's for sure." The dog lapped up the affection, panting happily. His master shook his head and stood. "I'll clean up and go in search of our young friend," he said to his companion, who slumped noisily to the floor to wait.

Wyl left his boots outside the door, hoping when Stewyt showed up he would take the hint. In the meantime, the basin, as it turned out, was actually a large metal bath. The water was hot, scented, and inviting. Instead of a simple wash he was soon luxuriating in soapsuds and the decadence of soaking. Tension and pain floated away with the grime gathered over many days and when he finally stepped out from his haven he felt like a new man. The notion amused him. He *was* a new man. Koreldy had certainly appealed to Valentyna—he was sure he was not reading her wrongly. But there was little of Romen left now, except his attractive shell and those fleeting sensations of his essence; the rest was all Wyl Thirsk. That made him smile. Perhaps there was hope that he might become more than just loyal blade to Valentyna?

He pushed the thought aside and shaved, wincing at the pain it provoked in his sore rib. After trimming his moustache back to its precise line, he tackled his hair, combing out its dark tangles, glad to feel it clean again, and then bound it back tightly into a single club.

"Ah, that's better, Knave," he said and the dog pricked his ears at his name. Wyl snorted. He had begun to believe that Knave could hear thoughts—he needn't have bothered speaking.

He inspected the fresh clothes that had been laid out for him and was pleased they were of a simple cut and neutral hue. Romen would have preferred them more colorful perhaps. Wyl grinned wryly to himself: when you grow up with orange hair and the plainest of faces, the last thing you want to wear is bright clothes and attract more attention. He would never shake the tendency, even though he now boasted such fine, dark looks. His boots had been polished and returned to his chamber while he bathed in the small side room and, just as he wondered where the elusive Stewyt might be, a soft knock was heard.

"Enter," Wyl answered.

A lad stepped in. "Good afternoon, sir. I'm Stewyt."

"Thank you for the boots."

Stewyt grinned. "Is there anything else I can help with right now?"

"I wonder if you've seen Fynch around the palace recently?"

"Ah, yes, sir. I have a message for you. Fynch asks if you could meet him down by the stream."

Wyl nodded as he pulled on his second boot, hair still dripping.

"Apparently Knave will be your guide," Stewyt offered, shrugging.

"He can always find Fynch," Wyl replied casually, deflecting any suggestion that there might be something mysterious about Knave. The fewer people who picked it up, the better.

"And her majesty has asked you to join her by the herb gardens later."

"Dusk?"

"After the evening bell from the chapel."

Wyl stood, stamping his feet into his boots. "Excellent. Well, Stewyt, I'm all done here. If you care to have the, er . . . basin removed, that would be fine."

The lad bowed and departed. It occurred to Wyl that the boy had sharp eyes, taking in everything in surreptitious glances while they spoke. He dismissed the thought that Stewyt was deliberately spying on him but he had little doubt that Valentyna's trusted Chancellor had ensured his best page was on the job. Wyl presumed the lad had been taught well to absorb as much visual information as possible should he ever be required to report back. It did not bother him. He had nothing to hide other than his identity and that was already in perfect disguise. Knave was whining softly at the top of the small landing, waiting for Wyl to follow him down the narrow staircase.

"Lead the way," Wyl said.

Wyl enjoyed the walk through beautiful woodland. This was where Valentyna liked to ride, he remembered. He could understand her desire to be here among the elms and their shady peace, especially now that duties to the realm were making such demands on her. He thought about Fynch and wondered why he'd chosen such a secluded place for their meeting. Perhaps he was frightened or he wanted to pass on some information in private. Whatever it was, he was not ready to be greeted by his friend—one of the few true ones he had, he realized—with hostility.

The small boy was standing by the stream, hurling pebbles into the rushing waters. It was the first time Wyl had noticed him do anything so childlike and carefree, and yet when Fynch turned he looked anything but.

"Fynch! It's good to see you again."

Hollow-eyed and obviously under some strain, Fynch did not respond. He simply stared back.

"A warmer welcome would have been nice but I'll settle for a handshake," Wyl said carefully, approaching slowly, unnerved now by the boy's attitude towards him. *What is scaring him?*

He continued with slow but steady steps until he was close enough to see that the little boy was shaking. Knave sat on his haunches by Fynch's side. *What a strange pair,* Wyl thought, *my only allies.*

He bent down, kneeling on one leg so that he was on eye level with Fynch. Perhaps Koreldy's height was too imposing but he doubted it. Fynch was not scared of him. The real reason for this cool welcome was in his eyes. Fynch did not trust him.

"Speak to me . . . please," Wyl said.

"I have a question for you," Fynch said, voice somber.

"Ask it."

"Will you be truthful?"

Wyl nodded carefully. "I promise."

"Promise on something you care about."

"On my life, then. . . . What is this about, Fynch?"

"No. Your life is worthless, I think. Swear it on her life."

Wyl was taken aback. This was more than simply strange behavior. Something had rattled Fynch, made him doubt their friendship. "Who do you mean by 'she'?"

"You know who. Swear to tell the truth on Valentyna's life."

Wyl cleared his throat; he had a good idea now of what would be asked. Intuition told him that Fynch had somehow guessed his dark secret. The boy was sharp and extremely perceptive—although how he could have pieced it all together, Wyl had no idea. Nevertheless, the terrified expression on Fynch's face left him in no doubt that he would have to be honest now. It was no longer time for guises or half-truths. Fynch deserved more. He spoke clearly, gently ensuring the youngster understood that he was being taken seriously. "I swear on Queen Valentyna's life to answer your question truthfully."

Fynch stopped trembling and took a deep breath as he reached out to lay his hand on Knave's head. "I suspect you are not Romen Koreldy, even though you look like him. I believe you are Wyl Thirsk . . . and I must know the truth, are you the General?"

"Why do you ask me this?" Wyl said, trying to avoid answering immediately.

"I've been having visions."

Wyl digested this carefully. *Myrren's gift is perhaps reaching out further.* "Oh?"

"One occurred only this morning."

"What have you seen?"

"In one I saw you injured but hacking a man's head off before being dragged by Knave to somewhere—he does not know where."

Bells of alarm. *Surely not. How could Fynch know this?*
"Is it true, Romen?"

Should he tell the truth? What would that do for Fynch, especially if—Shar forbid!—Celimus were to follow in his mother's footsteps and encourage the Zerques to find a foothold in Morgravia once more.

"Fanciful," he declared.

"Answer me!" There was a hint of desperation in this little boy's tone and it hurt Wyl to hear it.

"How would you ever believe me if I told you the truth?" Wyl could hear the resignation in his own voice.

Fynch frowned. "Knave will help me to understand. Tell me."

Wyl's shoulders slumped and he let out a sigh. He sat down and pulled his knees to his chest. "You were there, weren't you, when Myrren was burned?"

The boy nodded gravely.

"And you were also by my side when I passed out at her death?"

Fynch forced himself not to overreact to Koreldy suddenly speaking as Wyl Thirsk. His question was already answered then and Fynch felt his throat constrict with tension at the truth about to be revealed. "I had some water with me and gave it to your friend Gueryn. He was frantic."

Wyl nodded now, recalling what he could of that confusing time. "I remember very little of those moments. But I need to take you back before that event, back to where it began in the torture chamber. Are you up to hearing this?"

Fynch sat down, his face a mask. Knave lay down by his side and the little boy's arm instinctively reached toward the dog. Wyl saw it, was reminded once again of the prophetic words of the old widow. He told the boy everything he could remember about Myrren's trial and how he had interfered with proceedings.

"We shared a few words before the fire was lit. She said she wanted to give me a gift and that I was to use it wisely; she asked me to fetch her puppy from her home and raise it."

"And you thought that Knave was the gift," Fynch added, now freely joining in, both of them silently acknowledging that the man sitting here was Wyl and not Romen.

"Yes. I didn't understand it; I was a child trying to find my way, trying to grow up and be the General I was born to be. I just accepted her words, terrified that I had to witness her death after so much torture."

"And?" Fynch quietly said.

"Then she began to scream, as I recall, and"—he shook his head—"after that it's all a blur. The next thing I knew Gueryn was hovering over me looking frightened and I do remember you briefly nearby."

"I saw your eyes change color," Fynch said in a determined voice now. "We never spoke about it but your friend saw it and exclaimed as much at the time."

Wyl nodded sadly. "It frightened me when he told me about it—I wasn't sure what to believe. He didn't dwell on it—I suspect he was uncertain if that's what he'd really seen—but I imagine it never stopped worrying him."

"That was her true gift, wasn't it?"

It was painful to have this all brought back to him so vividly. "Yes. She was accused of being a witch for no reason other than her oddly colored eyes, and according to Gueryn and now yourself, my eyes echoed her strange coloring at the moment of her death."

Fynch said nothing but his gaze was direct. He wanted the full story—he knew there was more and he knew this was difficult for the man sitting before him. He would be patient until his question had been fully answered.

Wyl continued. "After that event everything was normal—well, as normal as it can be when you're being constantly baited and ridiculed by Celimus. You know what you heard that day while hiding in the drophole? He wasted no time setting up the situation whereby I could be murdered along with Valor. He had me brought before him—Koreldy was present—and he told me of the mission he needed me to take on. I agreed readily when I heard about it for it was the move of a far-sighted King aiming to achieve peace. Except I was to travel with mercenaries and, of course, I sensed a trap was being laid. When I refused to accompany anyone but men from the Legion he had me dragged to the window to witness the beheading of Captain Donal."

Fynch showed his shock at hearing this. He had no idea that Alyd was dead, although he had wondered where the Captain had been when he had met Koreldy with Ylena at Stoneheart. Now he knew.

"It was worse, though, Fynch. When Alyd was killed it just made me more resolute, more determined to overthrow this man who now called himself King. But he knew me as well as I knew myself and he had taken brilliant precaution to also hold my sister. She too was dragged into the same courtyard where her husband had just been murdered. He would have killed her too in a blink if I had not capitulated. Cunning indeed; his plan was beautiful in its simplicity and

perfection. Use those I loved to coerce me into doing precisely what he wanted—and that was to win Briavel for
him. Then kill me, as well as the King who might stand in
his way; then kill my assassin, Romen, as well, no doubt, as
all the other mercenaries connected with the mission. Ironic
that Romen and I managed to kill off the mercenaries for
him. So perfect!" He said the last two words with savage
bitterness.

Fynch nodded, stunned by the information he had
learned. "I know everything to the moment Valentyna and I
escaped the palace. From then I believe I have been fed
your lies."

Wyl held his head. "Not intentional, Fynch. I had to protect you."

"You are Wyl," the boy stated firmly.

"Yes," Wyl admitted looking up, suddenly drained.

A chilling silence lengthened between them.

Finally Fynch spoke. "That's her gift? I mean, that you
did not die when Koreldy killed you?" Fynch's voice was
choked—as much as he believed this was what had happened, it was still distressing to have such a terrifying notion confirmed.

Wyl nodded. "We made a pact. If we both lived after the
assault from the mercenaries, then we would duel honorably. Whoever remained standing would protect Ylena and
Valentyna with his life. We made a blood oath."

"And Koreldy killed *you*?" the boy asked, astonished.

Wyl grimaced. "A lucky pass with his sword. I had him
but misjudged. Koreldy's a brilliant swordsman but not as
brilliant as I." He smiled at this. It seemed Romen's confidence was infectious. Wyl shrugged at the question on
Fynch's face. "I suppose I had more to lose and so I took
more risk . . . and paid dearly for it," he said.

"And then . . . how did it happen?"

Wyl looked up, confused. "Oh, how did I become
Romen? Hard to explain. He entered my dead or perhaps
dying body—I could not tell because I had already moved
into his. I am fully myself. My soul is here. His has
gone."

Fynch's eyes were sparkling with wonder now. He spoke one word. "Magic."

"Indeed."

With that, Fynch launched himself at Wyl and clung to him. It took Wyl so by surprise that he only had time to catch the tiny lad and hold him close before he could feel Fynch's tears against his neck. And then he too was weeping. It was as though Fynch's interrogation had opened the floodgates of emotion as well as memory and they both poured out as boy and man held each other.

The boy finally pulled back but his arms were still around Romen's neck. "And Knave?"

Wyl grinned. "The strangest dog to ever roam Morgravia or Briavel."

"He's part of the magic, though, isn't he?"

"I don't know, Fynch," Wyl said with honesty. "But I believe he is enchanted somehow and, yes, our lives are definitely linked through Myrren. You know that vision you had of me?"

"It was horrible."

"It is also true. Knave saved my life. I was in the north, in Orkyld then. How he reached me or even knew where to find me is beyond my comprehension."

"He was gone for three days."

"And he sat with me for one full day of that, waiting to see that I would recover. How could he cover such ground?" Wyl said, astonished.

"Magic, that's how," Fynch replied gravely. "Were those men sent by Celimus?"

"Yes. His intention was to kill Romen Koreldy. It still is. I know too much. They won't be the last who make the attempt."

"There's more." Fynch told him about the second vision.

"Valentyna married to Celimus?" Wyl said, aghast.

"No, I'm not saying that, I couldn't tell from what I saw—I was more interested in the odd circumstances of the execution."

"And you don't know who the victim was?"

Fynch shook his head. "I described him to Valentyna but

she didn't know either." He gave Wyl the same description: "Large man, sun-weathered face, rugged features."

"It could be so many men," Wyl said, thinking of the Mountain Dwellers. "It reminds me of at least two I know personally. There's only one certainty here—I can't let her marry Celimus. He will destroy her."

Fynch shrugged his tiny shoulders. "It was only a vision, Wyl. It doesn't make it real," he offered, hoping to find some comfort himself in the words.

"Mmm. But yours have a way of being true, my friend. By the way, you have to call me Romen."

The boy smiled and Wyl was amazed at how it changed his demeanor. "I'd prefer to call you Wyl."

"Then they'll definitely have you and the dog carted away!"

"What do we do?" Fynch said, sitting in Wyl's lap. Suddenly he was just a little boy looking to the grownup to make decisions.

Wyl wrapped Romen's long arms about his tiny friend and held him close. "We must protect her. Valentyna is the only obstacle to Celimus getting what he wants. And only you and I know how ruthless he will be."

"He arrives soon," Fynch warned. "You cannot be seen."

"That is true. And we are going to sit here until we have a plan. We alone share the truth of Myrren's gift."

"You won't tell Valentyna?"

"No! She is the last person who must know. Briavellians are more suspicious of talk of magic than any Morgravian could ever be. We are scared of it because we quietly believe it. The people of Briavel dismiss it. She would not trust us."

"She trusts Knave."

"She trusts you and now, hopefully, me. But Knave frightens her."

"Well, she believes he is somehow touched."

"That's a fairly tame word, Fynch. She's hardly admitting to having an open mind on the subject. To start explaining that a witch gave me the gift of a second life and that I am really Wyl Thirsk will push her too far. As it is she is frightened and confused. No, we tell her nothing of this. Can I rely on you to keep our secret?"

Fynch nodded. "Can it happen again?"

"No," Wyl snorted. "She's gifted me a second chance at life; I have to protect this one." He suddenly remembered Lothryn and Elspyth. "Fynch, I did tell two other people, to be honest. One might already be dead. The other, a woman who helped me greatly these past few weeks, is, I hope, protecting Ylena. She is true to us." He gave Fynch her name.

"She believed you?"

"Yes. She and the man of the Mountains have strong spiritual beliefs. Magic is part of their lives—at least, I should say, they accept it. Elspyth will tell no one."

"You must tell me of your northern adventure, Wyl."

Wyl nodded. "It is a long story—when we have the time I will share it with you. For now, though, you must call me Romen," he corrected. "You cannot let it slip, my young friend. I am Koreldy, although that name too is not to be murmured around Celimus."

Fynch nodded solemnly.

Wyl could not help taking the tiny hand in his. "I thank you for your trust and friendship, Fynch."

They spent the afternoon in deep discussion, building and tearing down each other's ideas, and Wyl was once again grateful for the brilliant mind for detail Fynch brought to their final strategy. He would take their fragile plan to the Queen and hope she might go along with it.

36

A LIGHT BREEZE CARRIED THE SCENT OF MINT AND BASIL AND the seductive fragrance filled the mild early evening air. He loved this light most of all, dusk descending upon the soft, dying sunlight. Wyl knew he would forever associate Valentyna's radiance with sunset and the perfume of herbs and lavender.

"Forgive me, am I late?" she asked, approaching quietly. She was dressed in a simple and unadorned gown of soft, dark blue velvet that matched her eyes in this evening light. The bodice was cut low. She was ravishing.

Wyl felt his throat go dry. "No. I was early, long before the last bell," he admitted, silently amused by her long boyish stride, which even her formal skirts could not disguise.

She arrived at his side and he bowed. "I love it here at this time of day," she said, allowing him to gently kiss her hand.

"You keep a wonderful herb garden."

"Not me," she admitted sheepishly. "I'm hopeless at any sort of gardening. It's fortunate my mother is not alive to despair of me, for I'm told her fingers were ever green." She bent to pick a flower from the lavender bushes that edged the garden. Crushing the head to release its oil, she held her hand up so he could smell the perfume.

He held her slightly self-conscious gaze as he leaned toward her palm and inhaled. "Do you miss her?"

"Not really," she replied, beginning to stroll the path that would lead them to a magnificent sundial. "She died when I was still very young. And you? Do you have family?"

Wyl did not know why he lied—or was he being truthful? It was hard to distinguish. He so badly wanted to be Wyl with her and not Romen. "My father died not so long ago but my mother died when I too was very young. I still miss her, though."

"You must have a rich memory." And she knew that this was true by his nod, which seemed weighted with sorrow. "Do you have brothers?"

"No, just a sister. Mother died at her birth." This was dangerous, telling his story and not Romen's.

"Then we are kindred spirits, Romen. We both know the same loss of family."

He offered his arm and she took it, much to his delight. "Did you feel pressured being the only royal child?"

"Yes, of course. After my mother and brother died, I worked out early that I must be more of a son than a daughter to my father, even though everyone was determined to treat me like the finest of glass."

"Is that what he wanted? . . . I mean, for you to have been a son?"

"No. If his son had survived, I don't believe he would have loved me any less—just differently perhaps. I only strove to please. I always wanted to make my father proud of me," she said and then added in a sad voice, "I still do." She walked on, picked some rosemary to twirl in her fingers and continued more brightly. "In the early days I felt I had failed him for not being born a boy, especially as he had been too enraptured by my mother to consider remarrying, starting afresh with the possibility of a male heir."

"He was enormously proud of you . . . you do know that, don't you?"

She shrugged, a little embarrassed. "Yes, I am very lucky that my father never found it hard to share his love and his emotions. He told me every day how much joy I brought to his life, although I'm surprised he would share this with a stranger."

Wyl realized he must be more careful. "We knew it was a hopeless fight. All three of us shared thoughts we normally would not," he lied.

She nodded gently and then pointed toward a small copse. "There's a beautiful summer house in there that my father built for me. I still like to go there often. Shall we walk in that direction?"

"Please. I would be privileged to see it. I was admiring your woodland today."

"My woodland?" she laughed. "I suppose I have made it mine in a way. Did you meet Fynch there?"

"Yes."

"And?"

"Let me just say that I have put his mind at ease and given a promise that I am here to stay." He hoped he had said the right thing.

"Good. He has seemed withdrawn lately," she said carefully, not wishing to reveal anything further about the boy's visions—they had such personal meaning for them both. "No doubt your arrival will cheer him," she added, "so I can stop fretting over Fynch and worry about the King. How serpent-like is he?"

"More slippery than an eel, let me assure you."

Valentyna could not help but laugh. "A snake and now an eel. Tell me about him . . . describe his looks to me."

Wyl did so candidly.

"What a waste," she admitted. "And if he's really as handsome as you describe then surely he can have the pick of brides . . . although perhaps not so readily a Queen," she added wistfully, knowing all too well the politics driving the proposal.

"For sure, but he wants Briavel more than a bride, your majesty. The only marriage Celimus craves is that of Briavel to Morgravia. He would control all land south of the Razors . . . and no doubt, once the south is unified, it is his plan to control what lies north too."

"So marriage really is the means to the end," she said, confirming what she knew, but wishing it did not have to be so.

"I would put my life on it. Celimus cares for no one and nothing but his own greedy desires. I will never forget how he killed Donal so heartlessly and he would have killed Thirsk's sister without remorse or a moment's hesitation if Wyl had not capitulated in that second. Let's not forget that he paid men to assassinate your father."

"Oh, Romen. Don't let's talk of Celimus any more. I know my duty. Let me enjoy a few moments' peace instead."

They had arrived in the copse.

"Here it is," she said, a wistful note in her voice. "Isn't it perfect?" She sat down on a nearby log.

Wyl looked at the fairytale-like structure, which had been built around the hollowed trunk of one of the trees. It was artful the way it blended into the forest—a canopy of leaves disguising and yet decorating it. A haven for a little girl, especially one who played alone and dreamed of being a Princess the equal of any Prince.

"It's stunning," he replied.

She was pleased he was impressed. Valentyna brought no one here. This was hers. Her private place, which she shared with no one . . . not even her father. She had surprised herself in offering Koreldy a chance to see it. She also inwardly smiled over the fact that she had taken extra care with her ablutions, deliberating uncharacteristically long over whether to roll her hair up or let it flow free. This fussing was a new experience for Valentyna. And her clothes, though simple, were more feminine than she had donned in a while. Valentyna had always ignored the curves of her own body. She rarely looked at herself in the glass and yet this evening she had lingered and even fussed a little. Still tall and lean as ever, she was nevertheless delighted earlier this evening to rediscover that her hips rounded nicely over her long legs. Her maid had commented on how beautiful she looked in her dress. She appreciated how much more shapely her breasts became when she was more elegantly attired. It pleased her fiercely all of a sudden.

More than anything, she hoped it pleased Koreldy.

"Pardon me?" she said, realizing he had asked her something.

"I just wondered if I might sit?"

"Oh, please do. I'm sorry, I was far away just then."

She loved his smile when it suddenly broke like that across his face.

"What were you thinking of?" he asked, making himself comfortable on the log next to her.

Now she dithered. *How can I possibly tell him?* "Oh, just remembering good times here when I was little."

"I had an idyllic childhood too. So we have more in common."

An awkward silence followed. She felt that if they were lovers they would most likely kiss now but they were strangers. She pulled her gaze from his mouth and covered her agitation swiftly by turning the conversation to business.

"Have you found us a plan yet, Romen?" She felt her heart lurch when he looked at her with such intensity through those clear gray eyes and took both her hands into his.

"I believe I have, your majesty. It is risky but Fynch agrees, Celimus cannot pass up a challenge to his manhood—for want of a better word."

"What have you in mind?"

"I must admit first that it was our young friend who suggested this. Have you realized how clever he is?"

She laughed. It relieved her fluster and she was able to sit beside him without trembling. "He is so serious sometimes and yet he bedazzles me with his sharp mind."

"He is bright, that's for sure," Wyl said, pulling her hands into his own lap; he felt her tense and wondered if he had been too presumptuous. "Fynch believes we should hold a tourney."

"Whatever for?" she asked, hardly able to focus on her words, looking down at her hands in his for she dared not risk looking into his searching eyes.

"Because Celimus will love it. We hold it in his honor. We invite him to participate and we let him win at everything . . . cleverly, though. He must never know."

"This would certainly put him in a good mood, but how does this help my cause, mercenary?" she inquired, intrigued, nervous about her hands resting in his lap.

"Ah, here's the clever bit. We let him win at everything until he meets the Queen's mysterious Champion."

"Who is you, I presume?" she said, catching on quickly. He nodded.

"And?"

"And I punish him mercilessly. This will put him in very bad spirits. Celimus is prone to bleak moods, your majesty."

"How do you know all this? You are not Morgravian."

"Fynch notices everything," he replied. "He assures me that Celimus does not handle humiliation with any aplomb."

"All right, so we have him embarrassed and furious—I can't see that is any more of a help to my cause."

"Well, when Celimus falls into his black humor he is good for nothing. He locks himself away and rants. Fynch says he usually likes to hurt someone or something. When he was young, apparently it was the castle dogs or cats, even younger children. As he became older, he began to take his fury out on women."

She made a face of disgust and Wyl continued.

"He will certainly not be of a mood to propose marriage if I humiliate him, so we must ensure the tourney takes place immediately before formal talks are held."

"This is it—our only plan?"

"It's the best we can come up with. I know it sounds risky—"

"Risky? It is suicidal. Why won't he, in his black mood, take umbrage and simply declare war?"

"Because he is not stupid, your majesty. He is petulant, erratic, often dangerous, but never stupid and he will not risk his wealth at war when he can secure the land he craves simply through diplomacy or a strategic union. Anyway, I'm assured by my small friend that Celimus has learned to recognize this particular frame of mind of his, and when it occurs he removes himself from public eye. He will not wish you to see that side of him, your majesty. It might make you think less of him."

"If that's possible," she sneered.

"Fynch believes, as do I, that he will take his soldiers and depart Briavel swiftly on the pretext of being summoned home on urgent matters or similar."

"And then he'll simply propose marriage through his minions again?" she said sarcastically but her defiance had disappeared. Wyl could tell she was warming to the idea, in spite of its thin premise.

"That may well be but we will have bought ourselves more time to plan ahead. Right now we have a few days at best. Our aim is to deflect his proposal without you causing direct offense."

"You're sure of this, Romen?" she implored, chewing at her lip in consternation.

"No," he said and laughed when she looked at him in shock. He lifted her hand to his lips and kissed her palm. It was a brief kiss but bold beyond belief. He was thrilled to realize that the courage came not from Romen Koreldy but was all Wyl Thirsk. And Valentyna did not flinch. "But I will kill him for you if you ask me to. He will not get near enough to you to intimidate. This is a state visit of pure diplomacy. Celimus will not risk it getting ugly. And neither will his advisors."

"Will he sense a ruse?" she asked, doing her best to disguise the waver in her voice at the sensation of his kiss.

"No, your majesty, for you will be bright and friendly, ever amicable and welcoming to this suitor. You will compliment him constantly and you will give him the very strong impression that you are overwhelmed by his looks, stature, wealth, and pomp. His vanity is incalculable. Furthermore, he will not expect to lose, for he considers himself the finest swordsman in the land, now that Wyl Thirsk has been laid to rest."

"But you know better, is that right?" she said, shaking her head in worry as well as amusement.

His eyes sparked with mischief. "I know much better, majesty."

She could no longer act responsibly. His closeness, his charm, and his confidence seduced her. When he spoke like this she felt safe . . . no longer alone. Romen would kill Celimus if she asked him to—not that she would but the notion was comforting. She dare not use the word "love" but this was the closest affection she had felt for any man bar her father.

Without thinking on it for a second longer she leaned close and kissed him.

Wyl could hardly believe it until he tasted her lips on his mouth. When she began to pull away from the fleeting, gentle kiss, his arm quickly encircled her, guiding her back so he could return her gesture and confirm that his own heart was incredibly vulnerable where she was concerned.

She had meant the kiss as a thank-you, knowing it was more than was required. But at Romen's insistence it took on a more ardent nature, continuing until the crickets quietened their song and dusk had turned to dark.

Love had spoken to her this night. *The poisoned arrow has bitten,* she thought to herself, recalling his earlier words—and Valentyna knew there would never be another man for her but this one she held close to her now.

It was not just Fynch who noticed the change in Valentyna's demeanor. Everyone from the maid who laid out her clothes to Commander Liryk saw that their Queen had a lightness to her step and a vague smile constantly threatening to break out. She appeared distracted, flighty—dare they think it—even happy. Perhaps her mourning for her father had finally passed and she had decided it was time to lock away the grief and open herself up to life again, rediscovering the breezy optimism she had been known for.

No one complained at this fresh manner in their Queen. It had a positive effect on everyone's spirits and some even began to believe that it might be the imminent arrival of a suitor—a King, no less—that had brought about this change in their monarch. Marriage, peace, unified nations . . . the possibilities drove the Briavellians harder in their preparations for King Celimus.

It was Fynch alone who worked it out. Without realizing it, he absorbed every glance, every smile, every blink of Valentyna's eyelashes . . . every minute movement when Romen was near. It took him only until noon the next day to understand what all of this information meant. Confirmation came from Wyl, who he realized was showing all the same symptoms in the presence of Valentyna. *So it is true. They are in love. Am I shocked? No. Was it so unexpected? Perhaps not,* he decided. *Valentyna is not aware of how striking she is*—it was one of the reasons he liked her so much—*and Wyl, now in the guise of Romen, is a dashing, irresistible man,* he concluded. *If I cannot help but like him, why not Valentyna?* He felt more secure than he had in many moons now that his two closest friends were involved with each other. The neatness of it appealed to his tidy mind and to the child he still was.

Fynch watched too as Romen won hearts very quickly all over the palace. He was always ready with a jest or a smile; he was not averse to helping with any chore that needed to be done to set up the tourney; he struck up friendships with everyone from his page to the cook. Most of all Fynch took comfort in the fact that Knave seemed to overwhelmingly approve of Wyl and Valentyna being together. Fynch could not articulate how he knew this, he simply sensed it. The dog appeared to be less watchful, more playful. He did not stare at Valentyna the way he so often had.

Fynch was not fooled, of course. Knave knew things, saw things, communicated things . . . he was sure of that now. Did Knave cause the visions? This he did not know nor could he guess but he was pleased the headaches were gone for now. Wyl's arrival had put a stop to them, he presumed.

Wyl had been in Werryl now for three days, absorbed both by Valentyna and the bustle of preparations for the King's visit. All of the palace staff including the Briavellian Guard, strong in numbers, had worked tirelessly. The palace sparkled and plans for the tourney were well advanced; many hands had certainly made light work of the preparations. It was not on the grand scale of Morgravia's annual royal tournament but it was festive and would attract a large and excited crowd, which was already pouring into the city's many inns and taverns.

Wyl, at the Queen's direct behest, had taken charge of all the behind-the-scenes arrangements while Krell handled all formal communications. The only people who heard the Koreldy name were Valentyna's close staff and the hardworking team below stairs. For the majority of those working or visiting the palace, the tall, dark-haired man was merely a professional organizer hired especially by the Queen, rarely seen in public and never referred to by name.

The Morgravian escort had been on Briavellian soil for two days now, and it was anticipated the King would arrive in the late afternoon of the next day. "Just enough time for you to see him made comfortable in his suite and then wear him out with the banquet," Wyl thought aloud as he lay back on the grass.

It was just the four of them. Fynch sat cross-legged, leaning against Knave, while Valentyna, back in her trousers again, sat near Koreldy. Near enough that the pulse between them was palpable, Fynch decided, knowing if he was not present they would be sitting much closer, touching even.

"You won't be there, of course," Valentyna said, looking worried.

"You can do this, your majesty. You know you can. It will be all protocol. We have ensured you are surrounded by many dignitaries. The singing, dancing, and special events planned for the evening will make it pass quickly. I promise you he will not have the opportunity to press his case."

"And if he does?" she said, determined to be gloomy.

"I have taken precaution," he answered.

"You're being evasive."

"I'm being optimistic. You just concentrate on being irresistible and charming so he can have no complaint against the hospitality of the Queen of Briavel. Let me worry about everything else."

She sighed, looked toward Fynch.

"And even you can't be seen, I now realize."

Fynch stirred from his comfy position against Knave. "No, your majesty. We cannot run the risk that he or one of the Morgravians may recognize me."

"Romen, how are you going to disguise yourself when you duel with him?"

"All taken care of. Fret not."

She dragged a tuft of grass from its roots and threw it at him. "Ooh, you can be maddening. How are you so confident?"

"Soldiers get like this before battle, your majesty," he said, grinning and dusting the grass from his chest. He desperately wanted to roll over, push her back, and kiss her, but Fynch was present.

As if on some silent signal, Knave suddenly nudged Fynch, barking and nipping at his heels.

"Game time," Fynch said, shrugging. "He's been feeling a bit ignored with all the activity of the last two days. I'll just give him a run through the orchard. He likes to chase a lemon in the absence of a ball."

Fynch stood, glanced at Wyl, who winked at him, and then ran off after an hysterically happy Knave.

"What was that about?" Valentyna queried, frowning.

"He knows."

"About us? How can he?"

Wyl nodded, sitting up. "He's clever, remember. He's giving us time alone."

"Him or Knave? The dog started it," she said playfully.

He looked at her and saw behind her merriment; she was fighting her intuition that Knave was much more than an ordinary hound. "Both, I suspect."

"Well, then, we should not waste the time they've given us. As it is I shall have to do without your lips on mine for the next two days."

As she laid her head against his chest Wyl remembered Fynch's vision of her and Celimus. He buried his face in her thick, dark hair and pushed the vile thought from his mind.

37

ELIMUS HAD NEVER FELT MORE SURE OF HIMSELF. HERE HE was, riding through Briavel, enemy territory, and he was being welcomed as a savior.

His dream of himself as the all-conquering emperor of the southern lands was beginning to seem as if it could be-

come a reality. The journey through Morgravia had proved
an unprecedented success. On Jessom's suggestion, prior to
setting out he had announced a significant reduction in
taxes for the next four moons as part of his coronation festival. It had worked beautifully. The people had greeted him
with smiles on their faces and food in their bellies. He had
even tossed silver coins into the crowds of well-wishers
who lined the road into Briavel and bade him bring back a
Queen.

At each stop, ale and free food had been made available
to all who came to welcome their new King. The generosity was seductive. As Jessom rightly pointed out, people
must view him as benevolent so that when the hard decisions needed to be made—when taxes needed to be
raised—they would be less likely to revolt, understanding
that their good King would not do this to them without
reason.

"You have captured their hearts, my King," Jessom
flattered as they rode side by side on fine horses. "They
adore you."

When Jessom was elevated to the new role of King's
Chancellor, no one in any position of prestige could understand why Celimus had chosen an unknown outsider—
someone so new to the palace—for the role.

Celimus smiled. He too was impressed. This trip through
the townships was inspired; he felt elated at the spectacle he
imagined he must present to the commoners. Jessom had
cautioned him against using that word, "commoners," suggesting that "subjects," "civilians," even "my people" were
far more endearing alternatives. Privately, Celimus considered them all peasants who should be grateful to have so
magnificent a monarch to cringe before. He could tell they
were excited at the prospect of their King marrying young
and to the neighboring realm's Queen. Everyone believed it
was the perfect match, bringing unification and peace to the
region at last.

Pah! he thought, *peace and unification be damned.
Power alone is what this is about. Power and wealth. When
I have Briavel cowed and under my control, I shall look*

north and deal with the hoodlum who dares to cross my borders and offer death threats to my soldiers.

Celimus conveniently overlooked the fact that Cailech's aggression had been entirely in retaliation for the execution of his own people, or the fact that Celimus himself had hoped that one Morgravian party in particular might be captured and killed.

Cailech will eat his words. No, Cailech will eat humble pie before me, Celimus told himself. *I shall see him trapped and cornered. I, Celimus, will be hailed Emperor.*

Celimus continued to amuse himself with notions of his grandeur and majesty all the way from the fertile plains of Morgravia to the lush meadows of Briavel. It only waned as he felt the first tension of being on enemy soil.

"Do you think we brought enough reinforcements?" he queried.

"Yes, sire. Five score from the Legion is more than enough to make a firm statement about who is the greater power here. I gather in the last war Briavel lost thousands of her young men. Your father punished Valor the previous time they battled."

"My father was a soft touch—him and that other aging idiot, Fergys Thirsk!" The King hawked and spat. "Any other soldier worth his salt would have completely demoralized the enemy by inflicting a far greater death toll. As I understand it, Briavel was reeling, her throat exposed, just waiting for Morgravia to rip it out . . . and still, still my father showed compassion." He made a sound of disgust. "The only good thing to come of that battle was the death of Thirsk, may Shar see his soul rot in hell."

Jessom, realizing this was a sore subject, smoothed the King's ruffled emotions with honeyed words. "Nevertheless, your majesty, they were humbled and have not recovered. They are in no position to threaten us. If anything, you are their future, their salvation . . . you will bring peace and prosperity to two lands that have known countless eruptions of war."

Celimus felt soothed by the encouraging words and noted with pleasure that the Briavellians were already gath-

ering to greet him—it had occurred to him they might act
hostile but such a notion was apparently unfounded. He saw
nothing but smiling faces and cheering people. Valor's
death had never been fully laid at his own feet then. People
would have their suspicions, he knew. But Valentyna's advisors were obviously playing a clever game.

Better yet, reports back from various messengers confirmed that the Queen of Briavel was not the plump, frumpy
sort he remembered from childhood but a slender, gracious
woman . . . some went so far as to describe her as a rare
beauty. Romen was right, then. That at least would make
the task of siring an heir on her less distasteful.

Producing an heir whose birthright would straddle both
realms was his paramount wish just now. It consumed him.
If he was going to risk all-out war with Cailech and the
Mountain Dwellers, then he must secure the throne of Morgravia and better still, ensure it was irrevocably linked with
Briavel. His son would rule both realms—there would be
strength, wealth, and men to call upon. There were moments when he almost wished his father were alive to hear
of his grand plan so he could show the stupid old fool what
a truly great King could achieve.

"How much longer?" he asked.

"Riders have been sent ahead, majesty. The palace will
already know your arrival is imminent. I would hazard a
guess of two hours at most."

The King relaxed. Not long then. He would drink in the
fine scenery, accept the well-wishes from the crowd, and arrive ready to greet his new bride with the appropriate
amount of discretion and flattery.

As if reading his thoughts, Jessom interrupted them.
"There is a huge banquet planned for tonight, I'm told,
sire."

"Do we have to?"

"I'm afraid so, your majesty. Briavel is turning out its
finest for you. It is a high compliment; you must attend."

"I could use a long sleep after all this riding."

"I understand, sire. And you will certainly enjoy some
rest, for sure. However, they wish to honor you with this."

"And the formal talks?"

Jessom took a breath. He hoped the King would hold his temper. "After the tourney, sire," he replied evenly.

Celimus turned in the saddle and glared at his advisor. "You jest?"

"No, sire. I was only informed of it this morning. Queen Valentyna has heard of your prowess and wishes to highlight your skills with a tournament in your honor. In her letter she outlined how much the people of Briavel would feel privileged to witness your skills, and how fitting it would be for her lesser subjects to be able to see their Queen and her suitor together on such a social occasion." He hoped he had chosen the right words of appeasement, even though Valentyna had expressed nothing of the sort, other than to say that the tourney was being presented in his honor.

Celimus no longer bristled. Predictably, he lifted his chin. "Yes, well, I suppose I should let them see what a lucky woman she is to have snared the attentions of the Morgravian King."

Jessom offered a conspiratorial chuckle. "Yes, my lord, and a chance to reinforce our prowess too, my King. War will seem an even more undesirable choice when they see how brilliantly our monarch fights. The Legion too will put on an exhibition."

"Yes, good. I should be told these things in advance, though, Jessom."

It was a gentle rebuke but a rebuke nonetheless. Jessom bowed his head. "As you wish, sire. I simply like to keep much of the frippery from you."

"And the marriage proposal?"

"You are free of duties, as is her majesty, for that afternoon following the tourney. It would be an appropriate time to make her aware of your, er . . . shall we say, affections? Formal talks will occur late that afternoon. It is my intention we sign all papers and exchange seals before supper, your majesty."

"Excellent," Celimus said. "Well, carry on. I think I shall ride ahead alone now, Jessom."

"Of course, sire. Let them see your full majesty," the

Chancellor said, smiling benignly as the King cantered toward the front of the column, though the contrived brightness of that smile did not touch his eyes.

Valentyna looked magnificent. Even Liryk, used to her natural beauty, took a deep breath upon seeing how their Queen presented herself this afternoon. Her cheeks were flushed from her morning's ride and matched the close-fitting dusky rose-pink gown she had chosen to wear. The richness of the color set off her smooth, polished skin and loosely clasped raven hair to perfection, while its softness of hue complemented the lightly rouged full lips and gentle smile she wore as she waited on the steps of the grand palace.

Liryk was impressed. She was paying Celimus full homage. No monarch was ever required to meet their guests, royal or not, in person outside the palace, so this was a departure for Valentyna, a cunning and courageous move to ensure her visitor felt more important than any other. He was proud of her and knew her father would be too.

She stood alone, tall and erect. Her bearing was regal, there was no doubt, and Liryk wished old Valor could see his superb daughter now as she held court, preparing to pull off one of the greatest coups in Briavel's history. If she could find the courage to put what had gone before behind her and somehow make a good match with Celimus, their marriage meant instant peace and prosperity for Briavel.

Liryk glanced toward the battlements, where the realm's top archers trained their sights on the approaching column. Soldiers were positioned to show a very strong presence. The Briavellian Guard stationed around the palace outnumbered the Legion by ten to one and still his eyes darted around, taking in and juggling all possibilities should trouble arise. He had no doubt that this was a visit made in true peace—one of diplomacy, aimed at securing a brilliant and strategic marriage agreement—but he ensured every one of his men was ready and focused. There would be no surprises this time.

Valentyna smoothed her skirts, wiping her clammy

hands, as the King's party approached. She lifted her head and smiled radiantly as Celimus, King of Morgravia, brought his magnificent horse to a halt not far from where she stood.

He was utterly beautiful. She smiled inwardly. *Stop admiring the horse and make him welcome!* she admonished herself. Romen would laugh if he knew she was watching the stallion more than the King.

Celimus alighted gracefully and handed the reins to his man. He held her gaze and although she was unnerved by the dark, intense stare, she forced herself to curtsy as he finally bowed very low, very elegantly before her. And still having said nothing, he took her hand and kissed the back of it softly.

"Your majesty," he said, straightening, unashamedly impressed by the woman who stood before him. "The King of Morgravia, at your service."

She looked at his broad white smile and unwavering gaze. She imagined she saw a hunter, sizing up his prey. "The honor, your majesty, is ours. Be most welcome to Briavel," she lied.

A refreshing drink of crushed, chilled parillion fruit was served in the rose garden to Celimus and his immediate party, which included Jessom and the present General of the Legion, a bluff, middle-aged man who exchanged no pleasantries other than the bare words of greeting. Valentyna thought of Wyl Thirsk and how he might turn in his tomb to see his successor. The Legionnaires had already been shown to their barracks, their horses stabled, and three lesser dignitaries were presently being shown to their guest rooms.

"Do you have spies, Valentyna, to know my favorite fruit?"

She noticed they had moved swiftly to first names. Two monarchs, two equals. *He would do well to bear that in mind,* she thought.

"Why, how curious, but it is always my first choice too," she lied smoothly, remembering Romen's advice that she be charming. In truth she did not care for the parillion's overly sweet flesh. Still she sipped its juice politely. "We harvest them daily in season from the palace orchards."

"I should enjoy strolling those orchards with you, my dear," he said and the condescension was not lost on her.

"Of course, it would be a pleasure. And how was your journey, Celimus?"

"Very successful, thank you. It was ever rare for me, even as Prince, to get out into the provincial areas to meet with Morgravians," he said. "They made me feel most proud to be their monarch."

You probably would not even bother with them normally, she thought and then checked herself. This would not do. She knew this man only through other people's eyes and reports. *Do him the courtesy of at least conversing honestly with him. Impress him,* she told herself, *and it will all be over by tomorrow evening.*

"I have no doubt that you are in need of a rest, my lord," she said, deliberately showing deference. "Perhaps you would care to visit your suite and see that all is as you like it?"

He nodded, pleased with her sudden servility. Tomorrow he would participate barechested in some events. He had already planned this so the Queen and her people could view his magnificent physique as well as his prowess as a swordsman, archer, rider, whatever they wished . . . he was pleased to showcase his talents.

"I understand we have arranged for basins to be sent up—sorry," she corrected herself, "baths, as you call them. Please be in no hurry on my account. You must relax and take your time."

"It is very kind of you," he replied. "I gather there is to be a banquet tonight?"

"Yes. It is in your honor, Celimus. We are privileged that you have come in person to Briavel and we would do homage to our special guest with this feast." *Romen would be proud of me,* she thought, batting her eyelids and turning on her smile.

"Until this evening then, my lady," he said, standing so

she could admire him close up as he towered over her. He took her hand and once again laid a soft kiss on it. "Thank you for your gentle welcome."

The other two men had milled around quietly in the background but now they joined their King, bowing to Valentyna, and she gave a small, polite nod to each as they took their leave.

She sighed with relief. The first hurdle was crossed but much worse was to come. She gave her royal guest sufficient time to have ascended the grand staircase before she fled toward her own chambers, using the concealed back passages. Romen and Fynch were waiting for her.

"You shouldn't be seen here," she said, her heart beating faster at seeing Romen. She loved this feeling of being in love. It made her feel powerful.

He kissed her full on the lips and she withdrew, shocked, looking toward Fynch.

"It's all right, your majesty," the boy said and left it at that.

"I'm sorry, Fynch, you deserve to know about us," Valentyna said, embarrassed.

Wyl squeezed her hand. "He already knows, my love. Anyway, he's our cover. If I'm discovered by your staff, I will be seen with Fynch, which gives our tryst respectability." He tugged once again at her pounding heart with his heartbreaking smile. "Stop worrying, and tell us how it went."

"Exactly to plan," she replied, turning to enter her chamber and inviting them in. "He is as you describe. Arrogant, conceited, condescending, heartbreakingly handsome."

"Not too handsome I hope?"

"Anyone who calls me 'my dear,' and is not old enough to be my own father, is not so attractive on the inside," she said in answer. "Outwardly, though, very handsome but with a wolfish attitude and a smarmy manner I find repulsive. Does that cover it?"

"More than adequately," Wyl replied, feigning brightness while really feeling dangerously reckless at the knowledge that Celimus was close enough that he could run him through. Better, he could hurl Romen's daggers with deadly accuracy. He heard a familiar growl from the doorway and shook his head. *Can the dog read thoughts?* Well, if he could he did not approve of the idea of doing away with Celimus so obviously. He ignored Knave. "Are you all right?" he asked, holding her hand.

"Yes, yes, I'm fine. I've got to get through tonight's festivities, that's what's bringing me grief."

"You'll be magnificent, your majesty," Fynch reassured.

She ruffled his hair. "I wish you could both be there," she admitted.

"We will be, in our own way, I promise," Wyl said. "Now we'll disappear and let you start preparing."

"And I'll do my best to look alluring, I promise."

Wyl turned back toward her. She loved the way his moustache twitched like that. "Valentyna, you don't have to try. You are always very beautiful, especially in your riding clothes with your hair about your face and your cheeks so flushed from activity. You are the most desirable woman I will ever know or be lucky enough to love."

She could not help the tears that welled. "Do you love me?"

"From the second I saw you," he said truthfully.

"Romen"—She had no time to say anything else as they came together in an urgent embrace. Fynch had already discreetly closed the door and no doubt stood patiently on the other side with Knave, keeping a close watch.

"You must go," she said, suddenly pulling away and catching her breath.

He nodded, said nothing, trusted himself to say no more. He backed to the door and departed.

Despite her sense of power, Valentyna had never felt more vulnerable. She had never had anything so precious to lose as the love of Romen Koreldy—she would marry him tomorrow, no, tonight, if she could. But there was a banquet to get through and a dangerous, unpredictable suitor to discourage in the most gracious of manners.

38

HERALDS IN FULL REGALIA BLEW BRIGHTLY ON THEIR INSTRUments to announce the arrival of their Queen. Valentyna held her breath behind the doors at the sound.

"Your father would be so proud of you," Krell murmured, unable to keep a shaking admiration from his voice.

It was what she needed to hear at this moment and she cast a shy smile of thanks to him before she swept through the opening double doors and into her palace's Great Hall. It was the first time she had hosted any formal occasion, and she knew it was important to not only impress the King of Morgravia but more so her own subjects, who were looking now to the leadership of their new monarch. There was a collective intake of breath as her guests saw their Queen for the first time looking every inch the rightful sovereign. She was breathtaking in dark green and violet, echoing Briavel's colors. Everyone immediately dropped into bows or curtsies and she surveyed the lowered heads looking for one alone—the only one that was not formally required but certainly expected to offer her homage.

There he was, equally glorious in his own Morgravian livery of crimson, black, and gold. He sketched a bow in her honor and she could not help but be quietly relieved that he had and there would be no hiccup at this point.

As she descended the short flight of stairs, Valentyna's exquisite gown rustled its silks and the gems sewn artfully down its length sparkled. She had designed it herself and her seamstresses had worked day and night since they had learned of the King's visit to have this particular gown ready for her. It was far more spectacular than she had imagined it might be and it was a unique feeling for Valentyna to wear a dress with pride. Wearing the colors of Briavel made her feel fiercely patriotic and she would be damned if some other monarch might think he would crush Briavel and make the realm his.

The soft light cast from the oil cressets made Valentyna's skin glow. Hanging from her neck she wore the Stone of Briavel, which had been passed down through the ages. It was a square-cut, dazzling emerald surrounded by deep amethysts and it now sat against the throat of Briavel's most precious jewel of all.

People parted and the Queen expertly glided as she had been taught, suddenly grateful for all those simpering, irritating tutors. She approached the King of Morgravia to pay him correct courtesies.

Valentyna curtsied before him. "Your majesty."

"Your majesty," he replied in a husky voice. "How in Shar's Name has Briavel kept you secret for so long?"

And she could not help but smile at his comment. "Please, my lord. Join me," she said, offering her arm.

Celimus was, for the rarest of occasions, lost for words. He took her proffered arm and guided her toward the dais where the monarchs of Briavel and Morgravia would sit alongside each other for the first time in history. It was a breathtaking moment, its import lost on none of the guests. Music struck up as everyone was now invited to seat themselves, and the royals were permitted some privacy as staring, admiring eyes were averted momentarily with the arrival of trays of drinks and hot savory pastries.

"Valentyna, you are magnificent," Celimus admitted, finally finding some appropriate words.

"Thank you, my lord. I must say you look most elegant tonight."

"Our royal colors clash," he said and grinned.

She enjoyed his subtle jest. She had not expected him to have a sense of humor. "Strong colors for strong nations."

"Which I hope you and I will find a way to mold around each other, stand proudly alongside each other?"

It was a question she was not ready to answer. She shook her head slightly. "Emerald, violet, crimson, and gold . . . a heady mix."

"A potent one, Valentyna. One we can both be proud of."

She was rescued by the arrival of the server of wines. "Ah, you will enjoy this, I hope, sire. It is a dry Bostrach from our southern vales."

Celimus sensibly allowed his previous statement to rest. No point in hurrying her. He sipped his wine and his eyes widened in appreciation at the crisp citrus explosion in his mouth. "Excellent! I hope you will visit Morgravia soon and allow me to introduce you to some of our fine wines?"

She nodded politely and looked towards the servant to fill her goblet as well. "To a happy visit in Briavel, sire," she said, raising her cup.

"To you, Valentyna . . . for you alone can make me happy," he replied.

She was taken aback by his declaration. He saw this and immediately diverted their conversation toward less confrontational territory courtesy of Liryk, who passed by to pay his respects.

"Good evening, Commander Liryk."

The soldier bowed. "Good evening, your majesty. I hear you like to hunt, my lord?" Liryk added.

"I love to hunt. I see you have some fine woodland nearby," Celimus answered.

"Well, sire, that woodland has been my playground all my life," Valentyna ventured. "My father hunted stag and wild pig very successfully in those woods."

"There may not be time for a hunt, sire," Liryk replied, "but perhaps the Queen will show you around her playground before you leave us?"

Valentyna wanted to glare at the old soldier for the suggestion but she knew it was pointless. Everyone around her, including dear old Krell, was determined for this marriage to go ahead. All of them had set aside the fact that this man sitting beside her and smiling so artlessly in her direction was responsible for the murder of King Valor. She checked her rising emotion. Valentyna knew only too well why her counselors were pushing so hard for the union to take place. Peace was what Briavel craved and freedom from the burden of war and loss of her fine young men. A chance for the realm to flourish. She was the sacrifice. Valentyna could achieve peace and prosperity for her people if only she would say yes to the man beside her.

"Do you like to ride, Valentyna?" the King asked, a little surprised.

A small laugh escaped her. But it was Liryk who answered the King's question.

"Sire, if you did not know better, you'd think our Queen was born astride a horse." He stopped himself saying anything further along those lines, having caught the sharp look of pain from his monarch. He cleared his throat, embarrassed. "Well, anyway . . . do let me know if we can arrange anything for you, King Celimus. It would be a pleasure."

Celimus grinned. "I shall." They watched the red-faced soldier take his leave. "I'm sure he meant it kindly, your majesty," he whispered, leaning toward her.

Valentyna was not upset. She hated polite talk anyway and far preferred the camaraderie of being up on the battlements with Liryk's men, even though they were in awe of her. "I know. He's known me since I was born. And it's true, as soon as I was old enough to hold myself erect, I climbed upon a horse."

"Truly?"

She nodded, a little smugly. "I can certainly ride the pants off you, your majesty." She had not meant to be quite so direct; it had slipped out and she dearly wished it had not. Her father had ever criticized her for her familiar, confronting manner of addressing people. *"At its least it's flirtatious, Valentyna, and will get you into trouble,"* he had warned on more occasions than she cared to remember.

Valentyna felt a thrill of alarm now as she waited for the King's response. It came, loud and full of mirth. Celimus put down his goblet and threw back his head in full-throated laughter.

The man she loved was hovering in the minstrels' gallery observing everything—or at least as much as he could from behind his mask.

"I think we're almost ready for a rousing jig, gentlemen,

then we'll go into the masked bombero," he warned his musicians and the lead player nodded.

"At your signal, sir."

Wyl looked surreptitiously down toward the dais and flinched at the fun that Celimus was clearly having with Valentyna. He had laughed uproariously at some jest she had made and now they had their heads together, whispering. Well, he alone was to blame, having counseled Valentyna to be flirtatious and charming. She was only sticking to their plan. He decided on a whim to change his plan.

"Fynch?"

"Yes?"

"Get them to serve the first course now."

"But—"

"Please," he said firmly and the boy disappeared down the stairs toward the kitchen, where the overworked head cook shook her head.

"We can't work magic here," she tsk-tsked but she liked Fynch sufficiently well that she did not berate him. "All right, all right," she said wearily. Flapping away his thanks, she gestured toward the goose and capons team in one of the corners of the kitchen. "Are we ready?"

A chorus of "Yes!" responded.

"Then serve away, my lovelies. Make sure our royals get the special ones."

Valentyna had to admit that Celimus was more charming than she had expected and close up just as heart-fluttering in looks as he had seemed when they had met earlier. He really was physically the perfect man, as many of the dignitaries' not so subtle, sometimes open-jawed stares attested. Everything about him was perfect . . . everything. A painter would give a limb to have him as a subject—best naked, she thought, imagining one of the friezes in the bathing chambers featuring the King. She stifled a smile at the notion as he turned toward her now. She gazed into the depths of his dark olive eyes and came up wanting. Why she hoped she might find some warmth and softness there she was not sure. Valentyna wanted to dislike Celimus—

and did so—but his persona tonight was hardly that of an avaricious, single-minded man capable of anything. So far he was how a palace courtier, Lady Jane Breck, described him: *jaw-break charming*.

Except right now, she realized, the chill of the thought cooling even her smile. His eyes were hard, calculating. In them she found nothing of comfort. His wide grin did not touch them. And she suspected this man would not hesitate to trample on anyone who stood in the way of getting what he wanted . . . including her. Briavel was in his sights and she was the obstacle.

Valentyna feared her grave misgivings over her guest were written all over her expression when his own clouded as he watched her. She composed herself quickly. "Ah, here we are, my lord," she said brightly, relieved to see Cook's famous roasted goose being trundled into the hall together with roasted capons. "First course, fit for a King."

Celimus's gaze lingered a moment longer on her own, weighing her up. Then he smiled. "My favorite," he said and the moment of transparency passed. He was all charm and frivolity again.

Valentyna had deliberately paraded a dozen courses worthy of a royal banquet. No Morgravian present would leave her tables unimpressed. The goose, duck, and other poultry were melt-in-the-mouth delicious. A broth of oxen was served before the beef, then venison. Red deer were presented on huge salvers carried in by a team of people who wore antlers, winning huge applause.

Celimus leaned across. "Magnificent spectacle," he said. She nodded and smiled. "In your honor, my lord."

Mutton was next, served with fresh bread and a minted sauce, together with boars' heads. Swan followed and the centerpiece, baked stork—its beak stuffed with vegetables and wings outstretched—brought the first series of dishes to an end. A second remove of dishes was composed of jelly, spiced wine, and an exquisite almond cream for which Celimus sent his compliments back to the kitchen. These dishes were followed by practically every bird in the sky including pheasants, partridges, plovers, gulls, pigeons, larks, and even tiny sparrows. Then came fish dishes: ling, coney, pike, salmon, haddock, bass, and lamprey. Once again a centerpiece was the highlight—this time it was stuffed and roasted porpoise and seal. The applause was rapturous. Tenderized lamb and goat completed the banquet before tarts, cakes, and cheeses were served to anyone who had the stamina to keep eating.

Celimus was further prevented from conversing with Valentyna by the seemingly endless line-up of entertainers and singers that filled every gap of the proceedings. It was hopeless to attempt intimate conversation with this woman, who he had to admit intrigued him. He had not expected to be in any way fascinated by her. Winning her agreement without resorting to war had been his sole intention. It had not occurred to him that he might actually like the woman who would hand him Briavel.

Briavel's specialty, its honey from the famous Magurian bees, permeated many dishes, the most obvious being the syrupy, fabulously sweet poppycakes. Drenched in the aromatic honey, mixed with liquor and other herbs, the cakes were a rare treat for high occasions. The seed of the poppy that they contained helped along the happiness in the room and Valentyna noticed Celimus ate several.

"Sweet tooth, sire?" she couldn't help but ask.

"Wonderful. You must bring this recipe to Morgravia and introduce it to our people. Your fare is fit for the gods, Valentyna, not just royalty."

She bowed her head gently at the high compliment he had already expressed in a stirring speech he had made to her guests in her honor. His words were polished and perfectly chosen to enamor the Briavellian nobility to his cause . . . not that they needed much prodding, she thought unhappily. Celimus had an undeniable presence—one could hear a pin drop, such was the eagerness to hang on his every word. If only they knew he had her father's blood on his hands.

The tables were being cleared for dancing and the royal couple was invited to lead the people onto the floor. Valen-

tyna loved to dance and was happy to be in the thick of it,
and Romen was right—the first half of the evening passed
swiftly as a result. She stifled her amusement at the dances
selected for the evening's entertainment. Romen had
planned everything, down to the music. The rousing jigs not
only got everyone into high spirits—as well as thirsty,
which meant they consumed plenty of intoxicating ales and
wines—but left little opportunity for the men to hold the
ladies' hands for longer than a few seconds. It kept the King
sufficiently distant.

She noticed Celimus was enjoying himself too and was
very much the center of attention, with every female present—married or otherwise—vying for a few moments of
his regard. He lapped it up, of course, and hardly noticed
that no sedate dances had been arranged. In fact, as they
clapped, cheered, and jigged loudly to the music, it seemed
that Celimus was very much in his element, for he was an
accomplished dancer with such suave grace to his movement that even Valentyna found him irresistible to watch.

So far so good, she thought on one of the rare moments
she had to catch her breath.

Liryk was now calling for quiet. The chattering voices
and laughter gradually dimmed.

"Your majesties, my lords and ladies. Please choose your
headpieces for the masked bombero." His words were
greeted by cheers and squeals of delight as huge trays bearing an assortment of fabulous masks were brought in. As
guests began to make their choices, a special pair of trays
was walked to the dais by two servers.

"Your majesties," they murmured, holding out their
wares.

"It's a local custom, my lord," Valentyna said laughing.
"The bombero is our most feisty yet sensual dance."

"Of course, but you'll have to teach me," he said, grinning and reaching for his wolf's head mask.

Very apt, Valentyna decided, not daring to look up at the
gallery, where she knew she would find Romen watching.
She picked up her mask and wondered at the lack of caution in fashioning a dove's head for her.

Their meaning was not lost on Celimus, who, sharp as ever, was quick to make a remark. "Someone in your retinue has a sense of humor, Valentyna."

"Whatever do you mean?" she asked innocently, taking his hand and not giving him a chance to answer. "We start in rows, sire, but it gets manic and complex. Just trust each of your partners . . . they're all dying to touch you anyway," she said, smiling beneath her mask.

The music began and Celimus had no further opportunity to say anything to her for he was quickly shunted down the fast-moving line of partners. The women at the front of the line affected a more complex dance step in a round, while women at the back twirled more sedately with their partners, awaiting their turn to move forward. Valentyna heard a familiar voice from the man opposite, wearing an enormous grinning horse mask.

"I love you," he whispered before he vanished, leaving her breathless with the emotion he had provoked deep within her, yet laughing at his comical headpiece; again its meaning was not at all lost on her, for no one loved horses more than the Queen of Briavel.

Jessom, nearby, gave Celimus reassuring smiles that said *all in good time*. He could sense the King's quiet frustration at not being able to get close to the Queen but this was diplomacy and the royal way. Soon enough—tomorrow in fact—there would be time for them to converse more intimately. It was not as though those present did not understand why they were here. It was simply a case of moving through the required protocols. This was one of them and the tourney was another. Then they could get down to the business of making this young Queen realize that marriage was all that could save her realm from devastation. Morgravia would unify the south, one way or another. Marriage was certainly the less painful way.

Jessom could tell Valentyna was not entirely enamored with Celimus—who he had to admit was being utterly charming. He wondered why. In contrast he noticed that his King was more than a little interested in the Queen. Jessom could see why: intelligent, candid, unintimidated, modest in spite of having so much in her favor, young, regal, and gracious. She had style and presence. She was wealthy, sitting on the rich throne of an uncrowded, fertile realm. She could make Celimus a grand partner, perhaps even work with him to build the empire Celimus dreamed of. If she would relinquish her hold on Briavel, far bigger prizes awaited her.

He watched her closely. Her attentions were certainly not given over to any other male in the room, which he assumed indicated she had no former affiliations. After all, what lover would allow her to look as good as she did tonight and be wooed by a King? And yet she was decidedly distant. At no point had she been impolite or inattentive, as such; she was simply remote from Celimus, clearly sticking to safe ground, discussing the food, the music, tomorrow's tourney, without venturing into the real reason this whole pantomime was being played out.

A lull occurred after the bombero and people were removing their masks to laugh with the partner they had ended up with. As the musicians retuned their instruments and some couples got themselves into position for the next dance, the Queen excused herself and she saw the King also break from the dance formation to join her.

Valentyna knew she must be very gracious now. "I noticed your beautiful destrier, my lord. You obviously love to ride." It was a weak statement, for she had heard much of his prowess, but it would have to do. She was surprised by his modest response.

"I do . . . although since taking the throne I don't get any opportunity to ride alone any more. Now I have to take a cast of thousands behind me," he exaggerated.

She nodded with sympathy. "Oh, yes, privacy is what I miss most."

"I suspect you ride only the best horses too," he said.

"Well, I've had plenty of practice. My father always bred excellent beasts and ever encouraged me to ride them."

"Perhaps we can take that ride together as your Commander suggested?"

"Surely," she said, regretting her polite answer the instant she said it.

"How about tomorrow, then? The tourney does not commence until midmorning and I am an early riser. I can imagine your woodland is magnificent at sunrise."

She was trapped. She was also stupid, she thought. How could she have left herself so open? It was everything they had contrived against.

He took her hand and the gazes of many around the room immediately picked up the affectionate gesture. He cared not for gossip or what people thought right now. He wanted time alone with this woman—away from Jessom or any other counselor. He would decide when and where. She would see him at his best. "It would mean a great deal to me if you would see fit to join me, Valentyna."

She hesitated. *Give no offense. It is only a ride, after all.* "Of course, Celimus. It would be lovely to share a sunrise on our horses. I'll make the arrangements."

He smiled, clearly pleased.

She felt ill. "I shall look forward to it," she said, bringing their conversation to an end. "Now, my lord, please excuse me, I must go and thank our dedicated people in the kitchen for their hard work tonight. I'm sure you are tired after a very long day. Please don't wait for me."

He bowed, a little surprised at her sudden change in manner. Still, he must be patient. "Until tomorrow, Valentyna."

She curtsied and moved swiftly away wondering how she would explain this new turn of events to Romen.

She lay awake, despairing. Liryk had appointed two guards outside her suite of chambers and tripled the guard in the corridors and landings leading to her wing of the palace. The shuffling and soft voices of men outside her door helped to keep her awake. She felt inclined to pull on her robe and join them outside for a chat . . . better than lying here alone and so worried. She had not seen or heard from Romen since their clandestine moment during the dance. He was reckless taking such a chance . . . but she loved him for it. *And he loves me!*

So now she counted the minutes in the dark, wanting tomorrow to be over but dreading the hint of dawn when she must face the King of Morgravia alone. Would he try to kiss her? She recoiled at the thought.

It was then she heard the soft sound of the secret door opening slowly. Why she thought it was Celimus arriving unexpectedly to make a proposal of marriage in the middle of the night she would never understand, but it was fortunate she took those few moments to consider the possibility before screaming, for they saved Romen Koreldy.

"It's me, Valentyna!" he hissed, sensing her fright.

She felt her body relax at the familiar voice. "I thought you were *him*," she whispered. "What are you doing here?"

"I couldn't bear to be apart from you," he admitted.

He began to pull off his boots and she pulled the sheets up higher. "What are you doing now?" Her voice sounded squeaky and terrified.

Wyl, infused with love and that new sense of recklessness, suddenly had the confidence of Romen.

"I just want to hold you, feel you against me. I promise I shall not—"

"Stop, don't say any more," she said, pointing to the door to warn him of the guards. "Just get in," she whispered and threw back the sheets, glad for her own modesty that it was a coolish night and she had put on a gown.

He was now pulling his shirt over his head. It fascinated her how men did that—women would always undo the buttons— but that thought was lost at the sight of Romen's near-naked body. Wyl slipped in beside her, gently pulling her toward him, and she relinquished all control of herself. *If it happens now I will let it,* she thought to herself, turning so she could feel the full length of his long, hard body against hers.

"Thank you," he whispered.

"Hush," she replied.

Later she clung close, knowing she had to tell Romen about the ride that was to occur in just a couple of hours. She could already hear the first lone chirping of a bird sounding the start of the dawn's cacophony. She had no more time to hesitate.

"How did you know how to find this chamber, anyway?"

"Fynch," he said, stroking her face. "Valentyna, if I die today—"

"Stop it!"

"No, listen to me," he pressed. "If I die today I will die the happiest man in the southern lands because I have known you and I have loved you . . . and I have held you and touched you like no other man."

She trembled at his words. They frightened her a little. "Let's not talk about death."

"I'm not, I'm talking about life—and how suddenly important mine is to me because of you."

"Was it not before?"

"Not until I met you."

She took a deep breath and turned to face him. "Romen . . . I need to tell you something."

"What, my love?"

"It's about Celimus."

"You must not worry about today, I promise—"

"It's not about the tourney. It's about this morning," she said and he could see she was anxious.

"Tell me." He had not stopped stroking her arm but she could feel the sudden tension in his body now, could see it reflected on his face.

"I was cornered into agreeing to take a dawn ride with him today."

He did stop the stroking now and he sat up, wincing at the pain the sudden movement brought to his healing ribs. "This was not the plan."

She hurried on. "There was no way out. I had to agree or risk offense and you had cautioned me to be friendly . . . flirtatious, you even said."

Wyl ran his hands through his hair repeatedly as he considered this new twist. It was not her fault and he told her as much, although she could sense his despair.

"I'll keep it short and we'll have an escort—I shall see to that. Perhaps I can steer the conversation to neutral territory."

She hated that he smirked at her last remark. "It's no good, Valentyna. He will ask the question this morning. He wants time alone with you, without his courtiers and advisors about him, and now he has achieved it. Never, ever underestimate him—it will be your undoing."

She nodded, not knowing what else to say or do. Sitting up, she leaned against his broad warm body.

"I wish you had taken my virginity last night, Romen. Then we could just tell the truth and be done."

He smiled as one would to a child. "Things are so black-and-white for you aren't they? It would not be over for him. It would be just the beginning of the horror, not the end. Admitting such a betrayal would mean choosing war for your realm. He would put the full might of the Morgravian Legion toward destroying you and right now he would achieve it. No, you are the reigning monarch of the realm he covets and as pure as this King would want you. You are perfect in his eyes, especially now that he has seen you. No one in the Great Hall last night could mistake what he was thinking. He wants to own you. That's why I stopped, Valentyna. I want you so much and yet I cannot have you like that. I must love you from afar."

"Not forever, though. Say it isn't so."

"I can't. We are walking along a cliff edge right now and the only thing that matters is your safety and your realm remaining intact. Our love is secondary to that. You know this. You know your father would expect you to think of Briavel."

"Then he would encourage me to marry Celimus."

"Perhaps," Wyl admitted. "But knowing what you do of him now, perhaps not. Anyway, we must worry about this morning. You'd better get yourself readied while I think."

"Perhaps I could say I am unwell?"

"No. You must attend. And I must come up with an idea that prevents you having to say yes to his inevitable proposal of marriage."

39

HE WAS FLATTERED BY HER GENUINE ADMIRATION OF THE stallion he rode this morning. It was a thoroughbred from the most famous of studs in Grenadyn, a country renowned for horse-breeding.

"He's even more beautiful close up," she said, unable to stop touching the magnificent beast, whose flesh twitched and shivered, eager to be moving again. "How old is he?"

"Two years," Celimus said, in turn marveling at how much more desirable this woman looked in her plain riding garb. She had taken his breath away last night but this morning she was even more alluring. "You don't suffer from vanity, do you, Valentyna?" he commented.

She glanced toward the four men who escorted them; they stood too far away to hear this conversation. The King had wasted no time becoming intimate.

"I have no time for it."

"It is most unusual. I don't believe I know another woman who cares less about her appearance."

"Is that a compliment, my lord?" She laughed, hoping to make light of the topic.

"Of the highest sort, truly," he assured and there was no condescension in his tone this time. "The women at the court of Morgravia fuss and fiddle with their hair, they talk earnestly about silks and colors, their only conversation centers around newest acquisitions or how they look and whom they might marry or marry their kin to. They bore me. But you . . . you would rather talk about horses than gossip with other women, I sense."

She wanted to accuse him of being hypocritical. He possessed enough vanity for her entire court. Instead she explained why she lacked conceit in her appearance. "It's true. I have no interest in clothes or coloring my face, my lord. I wear fine garments only when occasion demands it, such as last eve. Otherwise I am happiest in what you see and even happier sitting on my horse . . . shall we?" she said, eager to move on; she did not want to pursue this particular conversation.

"Perhaps when one is as young, intelligent, and handsome as you, Valentyna, it is easy to ignore the tendency toward narcissism." She smiled at his words but it put a chill through her when he added, "You will be refreshing when you are my Queen at court in Morgravia."

Valentyna did not reply, pretending she had not heard his final comment as she busied herself remounting her horse and settling herself in the saddle. "Come," she said, "we can take a canter along the line of the orchards—I believe I promised you would see them."

Celimus smiled to himself at her evasiveness. The more distance Valentyna tried to put between them, the more fascinated he became with her. She was such a surprise. He had anticipated so much less. Until yesterday, his only thought had been to possess her realm. Now he wanted to possess her as well. He let her go ahead, enjoying watching her ride. She held her seat well and rode her beast strongly, like a man. From this vantage he could also admire her neat behind, which he was very sure now he was going to enjoy soon enough.

The sudden thought of feeling himself against, between, within her, aroused him instantly and he had to shake his head free of the notion of taking her here and now—throwing her down and ripping off those riding breeches, pushing in from behind. He took a deep breath and kicked his horse into a gallop. She laughed indulgently at his challenge.

"Apparently, you can ride the pants off me, your majesty?" he called and she saw the arch of his eyebrows, heard the challenge in his voice.

The soft-natured horse she was riding was no match for the proud stallion but she gave friendly chase all the same, ensuring her escort kept in close range.

Their time was almost up. It was nearing third bell—midmorning—and when Valentyna felt she need not linger any further she politely suggested they return to the palace so she could prepare for the tourney. She felt she had adeptly avoided all potential for intimacy, often deliberately straying toward the escort and querying her men as though she did not know how to respond to some of the King's questions. This brought the others into the conversation and kept her safe.

She knew Celimus understood what she was doing but she did not care. Right now Valentyna clung to her memories of the previous night, embracing Romen, feeling his bare skin against herself and his mouth on hers, his hands roaming her body . . . it was what helped her get through these past hours. The thought of holding him again tonight drove her on to get through what she knew would be a trying day.

A serious error in judgement snapped her mind back to reality. Valentyna had strolled from the party to pick some apples for the horses and when she turned back at the sound of the King's voice she realized they were alone.

"I've told the escort to walk the horses over to there," he said, pointing, "that we would join them in a couple of minutes for the ride back."

She prayed the fright did not show on her face. She turned to pick another apple. "Thank you. I'll just get this last one. I'm sure your horse will appreciate the ripest."

"I'm sure he would," Celimus agreed, stepping closer—too close, she felt. "As I do too," he said.

Valentyna tensed. She knew exactly what he meant in that clever retort but she made an attempt to deflect his innuendo. "Oh, well you're welcome to have it. I'm sorry, I didn't think to offer," she said, holding out the apple.

"I meant you," he said, direct now. "You are ripe for the picking, Valentyna, and I want no one else to taste you first. You know why I am here and I am glad I came. I have seen for myself what a perfect Queen you will make beside me, presiding over Morgravia and Briavel."

"My lord, perhaps we should discuss this—"

"Right now, I prefer. Just us. I want you to be my Queen. Will you marry me, Valentyna?"

He was shocked when she laughed. "Yes," she said. "I will marry you, Celimus, but you must win me first," she added in a gently mocking voice. She had no idea whether she could pull this off but Romen had counseled her on how and when to spring this last trap if it was needed.

"Win you?" Celimus said, his surprise evident in his tone.

"Yes, my lord." Her voice was crisp and confident and she was grateful for it in this dangerous charade she had put into play. "I don't know how it's done in Morgravia but in Briavel our men must earn the right to their chosen woman."

"Is that so?" he said, more playfully now, entering into the spirit of her suddenly flirtatious manner.

"It is." She gathered the apples into a linen and tied them. "At this afternoon's tourney, you will fight for me," she said loftily and then giggled, deliberately stumbling and falling against him so her breast, seemingly accidentally, touched his arm. She hated the sensation.

Another thrill of desire passed through him. "I shall fight for your hand, my lady," he said, playing along. "Who must I duel with?"

"The people will love it!" She laughed again. "You will cross swords with the Queen's Champion."

"Who is?"

She arched her eyebrows, faking high mystery. "Ah, a stranger in black who never shows his face," she said, full of intrigue.

Celimus smirked, only just realizing she had walked them back to where the group was now standing. "And if I vanquish your Champion, your hand is mine . . . is this right?"

Valentyna swallowed. Dangerous now. "Yes, sire."

"Bring him on," Celimus replied, sweeping his hand through the air.

Watching his confident flourish, Valentyna wished Romen had never suggested this ploy. It was not a game to be playing with this man. She could see as much in the dark and greedy gaze of Celimus.

Wyl felt it was the royal tournament all over again. Despite the lack of the grandeur that had been so evident in Morgravia, this homespun version in the King's honor prompted a similar sense of destiny within him. He felt distracted and nervous about facing Celimus again—not because he was afraid of him. No, he was more afraid at what he himself might do in the heat of the moment, especially as Valentyna had now laid down very firm rules about this contest between the King and the Queen's Champion.

"Romen, whatever our personal grudges are against this man, such feelings must not come in the way of what we are trying to achieve here." He said nothing and she did not appreciate the grim set of that mouth she loved so much. "Let us be very clear," she continued, "we are aiming to send him on his way to buy us time. That's what you said."

Again, no response as he inspected his sword. They were in a little-used outbuilding and she was circling him, half-frightened, half-angry with him. Fynch, trapped between them, held on to Knave and watched carefully. He too was worried. He did not like the turn of events. Together with Romen they had been hiding in the stone outbuilding, close to the tourney field, since daybreak and the tension had gradually mounted until the Queen had returned from her ride and told them what had unfolded. If Romen had been relatively uncommunicative all morning, he had now plummeted into a frigid silence.

His expression had grown dark and distant, his normally glittering gray eyes looked depthless. All humor had vanished from a countenance that usually oozed it.

Valentyna accepted that Romen was disturbed, distressed, demented even at how things had turned out. She too hated that Celimus had contrived to speak with her unattended but they had foreseen this, had plotted for it, and although the plan bordered on childish in its simplicity, there was certainly nothing childish about the grave set of

Romen's features. Something sinister was lurking. What did he have in mind?

"Romen!"

"Yes," he said, finally responding but not looking at her.

"I want your promise here and now."

"What am I to promise, my Queen?"

She kept walking around him, not sure if she was deliberately trying to annoy him. Trying to get him to look at her, shout at her, do something other than calmly tend to his sword. *Although calm is really not the word, is it?* she thought. *He is going somewhere I cannot reach. He is deliberately making himself remote from me.*

"First, you will not do anything stupid like die out there today. Give me your promise."

"I cannot promise that, your majesty."

"Yes, you can!" she snapped, her voice cracking with the effort. "For I will order no killing."

Fynch was trembling but Knave leaned his considerable and steadying weight against the boy.

"Then I promise not to die today," Wyl said softly.

"Why don't I believe you?"

He looked up at her with such grief in his eyes that she had to turn away.

"What else must I promise, your majesty?"

She composed herself and adopted her regal voice now, commanding: "I order that you will not so much as draw blood from the King during this contest. Humiliate all you wish, Romen, but no Morgravian blood will be spilled on Briavel's soil." He stared at her and her resolve hardened. "Do you understand?" she enunciated.

"I understand and I give you my promise."

Again she felt a flicker of disbelief. He was lying; she could see it in the darkening of his gaze. She was sure he had other intentions but had no choice but to trust his words. "Then I shall see you on the field."

He stood, bowed, and turned away but she stepped toward him and, not caring that Fynch was present, she put her arms around Romen's neck and kissed him softly on his pursed mouth.

"Just a few hours, my love, and he'll be gone."

The narrowing of his eyes did not suggest he believed her. Romen untwined himself from the Queen of Briavel and bowed once again before she departed.

40

Firyk was impressed by how many Briavellians had made the journey into Werryl to witness the tourney and to lay eyes on the handsome King who pursued their Queen. The excited presence provided an instantly festive atmosphere long lacking since the passing of King Valor. This would do the realm much good, he decided, happy that his security around the Queen and her royal guest was impenetrable. Every attendee had been searched, including all Legionnaires. None minded, good-naturedly submitting to the security measures.

The afternoon had so far provided plenty of entertainment. Valentyna had suggested some highly amusing contests not usually found in tourneys, including the "greased log warriors," which pitched Briavellian Guards against Morgravian Legionnaires and yielded much hysteria as soldier after soldier was dumped unceremoniously into the palace moat as they slid off the rolling oiled logs.

Mayor Belten had agreed to sit on a precarious bench—part of a cunning contraption put together by a team of carpenters hired by the palace—overhanging the same water. For a copper a try, contestants could throw wooden balls from a distance and try to hit the exact spot—a secret—that would release a catch and drop the hapless mayor into the water. All proceeds would be distributed as alms to the poor and a sizable amount was collected before Mayor Belten found himself drenched.

Laughter, cheers, and fun were on the menu alongside sizzling meat on trenchers and some of the best southern ale Briavel produced. King Celimus was very much the center of the attention and the Briavellians, despite long memories, seemed determined to give this monarch a chance to impress them, to woo their Queen and win them all the peace and harmony they so desperately desired.

Valentyna had found her easy smile again and insisted on taking some turns at the special horse races. Neither Liryk nor Krell could persuade her otherwise and Briavellians went wild with cheers when they saw their Queen appear in riding garb, lining up amongst blushing soldiers to compete.

"She has it all, you know," Liryk whispered to a somber Krell.

"Indeed, my friend. Our Queen is all and much more. She has the touch of silk, beneath which is a bedrock of steel. She's better than a man, for she can wield her womanly wiles . . . far more potent."

The old soldier nodded thoughtfully.

They watched, holding their breath, as their monarch leaned down precariously from her mount to grab the colors of Briavel in every contest she raced in. This, of course, won uproarious applause from her people, particularly as she gladly raced against soldiers from the Morgravian Legion. The King declined to enter this particular competition, acknowledging that the Queen was a far more accomplished competitor than he. He won more appreciation from the people of Briavel for his gallantry.

"She's magnificent," Celimus breathed to Jessom, standing close. "I will make her mine," he added as he smiled and waved for the cheering crowd.

Celimus did, however, display his skills in archery, wrestling, and jousting, among a myriad of other contests in which he outwitted and outskilled every one of his opponents. He took his applause and Jessom smiled benevolently on. Things seemed to be progressing perfectly, the King's Chancellor believed. Celimus would be in excellent spirits at having won so many ribbons, each presented by the Queen. And on each occasion he had pressed his lips to her hand.

The master of the ceremony finally took to the stage and called for hush. It took quite a while to silence the happy, ebullient crowd. Not everyone could hear him but those closest gladly passed on the gist of what he was saying in hurried whispers.

"Good folk of Briavel," he began, "let us give thanks that our own realm and Morgravia have, at last, come together to do mock battle in festivity and not the real stuff of war." He paused whilst a loud and heartfelt cheer erupted from the audience. "We welcome our friends—and I don't use that word lightly—from Morgravia, who come in peace among us and we especially venerate today Morgravia's sovereign, who pays us a great honor by making this journey into our realm." He waited again until the appreciation had died down. "I think it goes without saying that the illustrious King Celimus has more than winning mere ribbons in mind for this visit." People chuckled knowingly. "And I think we all wish him only success in his bid to win the hand of our own precious Queen Valentyna. Let peace and prosperity reign through both realms."

At this point the crowd went wild and the master of the ceremony realized there would be no calming them for a while. A glance at his Queen revealed she looked suitably self-conscious about her part in all of this. He waited patiently until finally lifting his hand again for quiet. "However, as with all young suitors in Briavel, our handsome King must earn the right to his chosen one." Clapping and whistles followed this reminder of the local ways. "It is of no matter that he is a sovereign," he said archly, making everyone laugh, "not to mention the reigning monarch of our powerful neighbor." Still more catcalls. "In this mission he is like any eager young fellow, keen to wed the most beautiful girl in the land." Valentyna was now blushing at the direct language. She had not sanctioned such freedom of speech but then again the people loved it and she was glad to see them so happy again after such intense mourning—though she would ask Liryk to keep an eye on the master's liquid consumption for the rest of the day.

"And so Celimus, brave King of Morgravia, has agreed to fight for the right to call our Queen his Queen." A long ooh murmured through the gathered. This was more intriguing than they had first thought. "The King will duel with the Queen's Champion for her hand in marriage. Please make welcome our two opponents."

Wyl listened to the master's theatrical introduction and with each word felt his fury intensify. After Valentyna had left him this morning, Wyl had felt suddenly bereft. Celimus had already taken too much from him. And now he was preparing to take Valentyna—the only woman he could ever love. His thoughts had become morose and convoluted with anger and grief; the faces of Ylena, Alyd, Gueryn, Lothryn, Elspyth, Valor, and his own father began to rear up, demanding vengeance.

"I don't like this much, Wyl," Fynch now cautioned, listening to the frenzied cheering of the crowd.

"You mustn't call me that."

"I know, I know. Whatever is going through your mind, I don't think Knave likes it much either."

"And Knave would know," Wyl replied sarcastically. He looked at the boy then and felt badly about how he had spoken. None of this was Fynch's fault. Fynch was innocent, courageous, and being drawn into this web of deceit and intrigue like water down a drain. And he was suffering for it.

"Sorry, Fynch. I don't mean to mock. I too accept that Knave knows more than we realize. No more visions?"

Fynch shook his head.

"Good."

Fynch was not to be deterred. "But my instincts tell me this is a mistake, Wyl."

Wyl dropped down to his haunches and Fynch was able to look him in the eye, marveling at the dull black helmet that surrounded his friend's face. "There is no other way. You have to trust me."

"I trust you, Wyl. I don't trust Celimus." The boy locked his hand in Knave's fur to stop himself from crying. He would hate it if he broke down now.

"Have faith, lad," Wyl replied, hearing his cue to enter the arena.

Dressed entirely in black, Wyl now pulled down his visor, completing the mysterious outfit that would hide his identity.

"You two stay out of sight," he cautioned and then stroked Fynch's hair. "I'll be back soon, I promise."

As Wyl left the stone outhouse and began striding into the arena, Fynch felt the familiar and terrifying sensation of spinning. Suddenly his head hurt horribly and the overwhelming nausea arrived. The world he knew blanked out as he saw Romen bloodied and dying. There was a woman's voice—it had to be Valentyna, not that he could see—but the voice was not frightened or weeping; she was whispering. *Let go now,* she said. *Die quietly and bravely.*

A new voice floated in his head. A man's voice: *It has to be.*

Fynch passed out. When he fully regained his senses, it was already too late.

As Wyl strode into the loud atmosphere of the arena, he could see Celimus already testing his sword, slashing the air. When the King caught sight of the Queen's Champion he affected one of his most elegant bows in mock homage to the warrior. Wyl ignored him. He could barely bring himself to look at that face he loathed and instead turned toward Valentyna. She looked nervous but only to him. Her cheering subjects saw radiance and laughter. He felt proud of her in spite of his gloomy, simmering mood.

He bowed before her. "A good-luck talisman, my lady?" he requested and she pulled an exquisite silk embroidered handkerchief from her pocket and passed it to him.

"This was given to me by my mother. You must cherish it as I have," she said, loud enough for all to hear. The roar from the crowd was deafening.

As he took it, he kissed her outstretched hand. She looked deep into the visor, looking for his eyes, looking for a sign that he would keep true to her. "Keep your promises," she whispered for his ears only, and he could see she was fighting back tears.

Wyl turned away immediately to pull the crowd's gaze back to himself and Celimus. No one must notice her anxiety at what was seemingly a piece of fun.

But someone did notice. Jessom felt the Queen's discomfort, saw the mist in her eyes, and stored it away. He could not help but wonder whether here in front of them stood the reason why Valentyna had kept Celimus at such a distance.

"Queen's Champion, eh?" Celimus gibed as Wyl approached. He was enjoying today and presumed this fellow in black would put up a brave fight while contriving to lose theatrically and give Morgravia its confirmation of marriage. *Not that I need any help to dispatch you,* the King thought, looking forward to the fun of the fight.

Wyl said nothing as he drew his sword with the bluish tinge from its sheath. It made a sound like a chime as it pulled free. Lightweight and elegant, it felt as one with his hand. He wished he could run it through Celimus right now and wipe that unfaithful smile from his handsome, hateful face. He did not test the sword's weight or movement through the air. Wyl already knew it was perfect.

"Impressive weapon, sir," Celimus commented.

Still Wyl held his tongue. He refused to look again at Valentyna. His gaze was for the King of Morgravia alone.

"Is he mute, your majesty?" Celimus asked loudly for everyone's benefit and they all obliged with howls of laughter.

"No, sire," she answered. "He speaks a strange tongue," she jested, begging inwardly for this mummery to be done.

"Well, perhaps he understands the language of the blade better?" And Celimus, still standing casually, turned like a cat and struck.

Wyl was ready for him, however. He had seen Celimus use this trick so many times on unsuspecting opponents that he was not only waiting for it but was able to deflect the blow with ease and a staged nonchalance. Whistles and cheers from the crowd for their Champion followed.

Celimus preferred it all to go his way. He thrust again, quickly following it up with a low swipe. Again Wyl was ready for him. He had fought him too many times in the Stoneheart training grounds to be caught out by such transparency.

Celimus nodded toward the Queen. So, he was up against a skilled opponent. Perhaps she had not staged this for fun. Perhaps she was still reticent about accepting his proposal and would hide behind this contest. Well, they had no idea whom they had pitched this black warrior against. No one, save Wyl Thirsk, had ever bested him and that fool was ashes to the wind. He would show Briavel his prowess and he would claim his prize. The contest began in earnest.

Valentyna held her breath but she was not sure whether it was from fear for Romen or simply for the beauty of watching these two dashing swordsmen display their skills. It was like nothing she had seen. Everyone else witnessing the fight felt the same way. Their adeptness was mesmerizing. And what had started out as a piece of theater, accompanied by the audience's cheers and whoops, settled rapidly into a duel of such intensity that the voices of those watching died to a whisper.

"They are like artists," Valentyna muttered to Liryk, who was standing nearby.

The way the two men moved reminded her of the grace of the wild, beautiful forest cats her father had once shipped to Briavel from more exotic climes.

"They are of a match, majesty," Liryk admitted, equally awestruck. "Neither has the upper hand on the other," he added before whispering, "Koreldy is amazing." Only Liryk and Krell had been permitted to know the secret of the Champion and Valentyna intended it remain that way.

"Shh!" she cautioned but, though quietly glad to see him flinch under her firm voice, she then made an effort to soften her warning. "It's too dangerous for Romen to be exposed," she added in a whisper. The soldier nodded, abashed.

The King had begun to perspire lightly with his efforts and the warmth of the afternoon sun. This was taking longer than he had planned. He had thought it a fun piece of drama to entertain the masses and an opportunity to show off. There was no one to match his prowess with a blade and yet this masked swordsman was parrying everything Celimus was throwing at him.

A thought began to nag at Celimus. He could not focus on it for his opponent had begun to increase the pace at which he fought. That too reminded him of something familiar. *What is it?* The dance had taken on a darker feel too. The man fighting silently in such dedicated fashion opposite him had a stillness and a calm he felt he recognized. *That is it!* He felt he knew this swordsman. Flashes of familiar movement and balance in the man appeared beneath his flamboyant style.

I'll be damned, Celimus thought suddenly. *He fights at times like the red-headed troll, Wyl Thirsk.* And if the man opposite had not been so tall or lean, he might almost have believed it.

Doggedly Wyl fought on, looking for the opening. He was not permitted to draw blood but perhaps he could flick the King's sword away. Whatever happened he would humiliate the man and send him on his way, his tail between his legs.

Celimus was openly sweating now. The Queen's Champion was relentless. He was no longer allowing the King to showcase his moves before responding with his own. He had just slipped up to full battle tempo. Celimus began to feel the first pinpricks of fear coursing through him. The man meant business. He was dueling seriously. No more posturing or swoops with the sword; no more looking for cheers and grins from the audience. The black Champion meant to beat him. Celimus would not let that happen.

The silence about them had grown palpable and Celimus was grunting with each sword thrust. The more he thought about the orange-haired bastard who had brought him such grief at the royal tournament, the more anxious and ragged his own fighting became.

Wyl, meanwhile, could see nothing but the blur of the blue sword. It felt to him as though he needed no sight. The sword knew where to move and he was one with it. He could kill Celimus now. The King was tired from the previous evening and early start. Wyl sensed his frustration. He knew that the Morgravian monarch had drunk ale and wine last night and danced plenty. The carousing at the banquet would rise up and become another enemy for him this afternoon in the heat. Wyl could see it occurring before his eyes as the sheen of perspiration on the King increased. He could kill him now and surely save Valentyna and Briavel, perhaps even claim the Legion? There was no heir for Morgravia. The realm would lose its momentum for a while until it found itself a new monarch through the various noble families with blood connection to the Crown. And while Morgravia panicked, Briavel would find strength and calm. Valentyna would have the time to settle into her rule and be stronger for it.

Yes! Kill him. End it now, no matter what happens. Finish Celimus, he commanded himself, his wrath hard and complete.

Wyl found a stillness within and his sword began to shine blue with the fast and furious strokes with which he now punished Celimus. He felt he was fighting with the strength of two men. Himself and Koreldy. Perhaps even three or four, adding Valor and Gueryn to the list.

It was all the King could do to fend off the killing blow.

Wyl did not see Valentyna step hastily from the podium on which two thrones had been placed. He could not know she was running toward them now, terrified, absolutely sure that Romen was about to break his promise to her and spill Morgravian blood on Briavellian soil.

All he could see through the grille of his visor was Celimus battling for breath, eyes darting, horrified that the next swipe would be the one to end his life. And then he had him. The King tried to feint but again Wyl knew the move; with Romen's and his skills locked firmly into one, there was seemingly no thrust or feint he could not anticipate. With one sharp snap of his wrist, he sent the King's sword tumbling from his grip and the sovereign of Morgravia falling backward, terror in his beautiful dark eyes.

Now! Wyl and Romen seemingly said together, Wyl holding the blue sword in a double-handed grip, ready to plunge into the chest of the betrayer, the murderer, the faithless cretin who ruled a great nation. Wyl lifted his sword high above his cringing opponent, who yelled cravenly, and then he heard the near-hysterical shriek of a woman . . . the woman he loved, who was now standing before him, eyes wild, breathing hard and screaming directly at him.

"Liar!" she hurled at him. "You traitor! Throw down your sword!"

It was as if Wyl had snapped out of a trance at the accusation. He staggered backward, letting go of the blade, stumbling away now. Celimus was on his feet in a flash. Valentyna was barely in control of herself, tears coursing down her face. The King was touching her, checking to see she would be well.

Wyl hated him more than in any other moment of his life for that touch, that false concern. It was such a clever move to make. Why had he not thought to offer comfort? She would have pushed his treacherous hands away, that's why, he told himself with immense regret. Wyl could hear himself breathing behind the visor—he could swear he could hear his own heart thumping in his chest. Suddenly guards surrounded him, swords drawn. Two grabbed his arms but he did not struggle; he felt useless, limp. He was no longer a threat to anyone. *If only she had let me finish it.*

Celimus was white-lipped with fury despite his breathlessness. His face still pale with terror. "He was going to kill me!" he bellowed at the Briavellian Commander and Chancellor, who were running to their Queen's aid. Jessom slithered to stand by his King.

Valentyna pushed away her tears and dug as deep as she could ever recall to find composure, to steady herself and be the Queen she was.

"I noticed the aggression, sire," she replied. "He will be punished, of course."

"Aggression? Punished? I will execute him right now before you," Celimus raged.

Valentyna turned an icy gaze on her royal guest. "You will do no such thing in my realm, majesty. No blood will be spilled in Briavel this day."

"Except mine!" he roared, spit flying.

"I see no trace of it, sire. Only your sweat of fear." Her words cut deep.

"He must be executed," Celimus insisted, the gentle pressure from Jessom's steadying hand, unnoticed by most, urging him to regain his composure. "I insist."

"King Celimus," Valentyna said, her voice as cold as anyone had ever heard it, "I alone have the authority to mete out his punishment. Please withdraw."

"I demand to see his face," Celimus cried.

A stillness overtook Valentyna. Anger—the depths of which she had felt only at the news of the way in which her father died—was her master right now. Romen had betrayed her. In spite of his declared love for her and hers for him, he still chose his own path. That path now moved away from the one she herself stood upon. Love so newly kindled became tainted. A sense of treachery ran through her veins to her heart like poison.

"Lift his visor," Celimus demanded, impatient with Valentyna.

The guards who flanked Wyl looked only to their Queen for permission. She had no choice. The safety of Briavel now rested on placating this dangerous King. Romen must bear the consequences of his own stupidity and betrayal.

She nodded and Wyl's heart sank. He had lost her.

41

ELIMUS STEPPED FORWARD, KEENLY FEELING THE TRIUMPH, and ripped back the visor on his silent foe. Wyl would later try to convince himself that the shock on his enemy's face was worth the loss of the woman he loved. He forced himself to believe he had won and lifted his chin so Celimus could get a good look at the familiar face, the sardonic, easy smile.

"Hello, Celimus."

"You!" the King roared, disbelief claiming him. But then he surprised everyone, even Jessom, who knew his turns of mood better than any, by bursting into laughter. It was loud and vicious . . . most of all it was confusing for Valentyna. She had no understanding of this.

"Your majesty?" she asked, an edge in her tone. "Perhaps you would share the jest with us?"

"Oh, Valentyna, my poor, witless child," he said, wiping the tears from his eyes and not caring at the way she instantly bristled or that he had shocked her Commander and Chancellor with the pointed insult. "It is priceless, absolutely priceless that your Champion—the one who would protect your life, your virginity, your crown—turns out to be none other than the scum mercenary who ran your father through with a sword not so long ago."

"You dare to bring my father into this!" she cautioned, her voice a knifing whisper.

"Only to save you, my innocent," he said. "This man is Romen Koreldy, a mercenary, who came to me with his hands outstretched for a fortune in gold. He admitted to killing your father; he admitted to killing our very own General Wyl Thirsk. And then he dragged back our General's body for good measure so we could see it with our own eyes."

"You lying snake!" Wyl railed at the King's terrible fabrication, and yet felt helpless at the look of shock on Valentyna's face.

Valentyna felt the dull, tingling sensation at the back of her head that preceded rage. She recognized it even though she had felt it so few times in her life.

"It's true, your majesty. He tried to extort a sack of gold from me, laughing at the way he had murdered your father, claiming he had paved the way for Morgravia to overrun a weakened Briavel."

"I shall kill you—" Whatever Wyl wanted to say next was cut off by a firm arm around his throat.

Celimus had regained full control of himself now. The smile was back as he wiped the dampness from his face with a piece of linen. "I speak true, Valentyna. He is an extortionist. I sent him packing with nothing, of course. Warned him if he set foot on Morgravian soil again I'd hang, draw, and quarter him. Sad as it is to admit, Koreldy was General Thirsk's choice as Captain for the mission to Briavel. He insisted on gathering his own handpicked men about him. Yes, I thought it strange at the time that he did not take Legionnaires but Thirsk insisted on using mercenaries. He persuaded me that taking a troop of Legion men into Briavel could be misconstrued and cause ire. It is all much to my regret now, but who was I to question my General on matters of strategy?" he said innocently. "This man, your Champion, is false, Valentyna. He has betrayed me and Morgravia and now he has done the same to you. Execute him!"

She had listened carefully to the King while her rage bristled beneath the seemingly calm countenance she had forced herself to adopt. She heard the lie in his voice, despite his best attempts to conceal it, and she would never believe that Wyl Thirsk had been untrue—she had met him, heard the sorrow in his voice as he told his tale. Now Valentyna drew herself to full height and squeezed her hands together to keep herself from revealing her fury. "It is my understanding, Celimus—now that we are discussing this—that you planned General Thirsk's death."

Her words fell like splinters of ice before them and Wyl was only sad that none of the Legion's soldiers were close enough to hear this exchange. *Pity,* he thought. *It could have changed everything.*

"Your majesty," Celimus replied just as coolly, but masterfully paying her appropriate respect as this shift in the situation demanded. "I am surprised you know of such a thing and I cannot deny it. But what you do not know is that General Wyl Thirsk was suffering from delusions. He was readying to make war on Briavel."

"What?" both Valentyna and Wyl cried together.

She looked toward her guards and they gripped Wyl tighter. He was meant to stay silent as the sovereigns spoke.

"Yes, your majesty," Celimus continued, ignoring Romen. "Wyl Thirsk was unstable. My father knew it and warned me of it but our two families go back such a long way that I had to know for myself. I liked Wyl, despite our differences in opinion." He shrugged. "I grew up with him."

Wyl began to rant and Valentyna had him removed. Liryk had no choice but to give orders to take him to the gatehouse and secure him for the time being.

Valentyna was in great pain from Romen's betrayal and this new information threw a whole new spin on the story she had been told. She had to hear it in full. She gave a signal and her team of people started a new contest of boulder throwing, which every strong man in the audience was invited to participate in. It achieved the diversion she needed and people began to drift away, stunned at how the contest had turned out—it seemed clear now that the Queen's Champion had attempted to hurt the King. However, the wealth of entertainment on offer soon distracted them and the disquiet and confused murmurings died down.

Relieved, Valentyna returned her attention to the royal party. "Thank you, Commander Liryk. I will call for Koreldy when I'm ready," she said, then addressed the King. "We shall continue this in my solar."

She turned and strode away. Celimus, still fuming, followed along with Jessom. Krell brought up the rear but soon stepped ahead of the royal party to make arrangements for refreshments. Inside the solar the silence was keen as cool drinks were served.

When all servants had withdrawn, Valentyna addressed her sovereign guest again. No warmth had found its way into her voice in the interim.

Celimus bowed and then set about fashioning his elaborate tale. "I was determined to give Wyl every chance to prove his worthiness as a General fit to command the Legion, your majesty. As you may know, we've had our differences but I respected his abilities and his position. I wanted us to work together as my father and his father had before us. I chose to send him on this special diplomatic mission to petition yourself and your father on my behalf . . . such was my personal esteem for Wyl, despite the gossip." He smiled softly. "I realize you and I didn't exactly get off to a good start in our first meeting during childhood and I wanted to approach this matter gently . . . mindful of your sensibilities."

"For which I am grateful, sire," Valentyna said sharply. "You were saying about General Thirsk?"

"Well, it is as you understand it, your majesty. According to Romen Koreldy—and I have only his word to go on—things went from bad to worse during the journey. Wyl's delusions set in and he began talking about needing to kill Valor before it was too late."

Valentyna allowed a small groan to escape; she could not help herself. Could Fynch have been a traitor in all of this, bursting from the privy at the predetermined time?

Celimus was sure he had her now. "He kept talking to the other men he took with him."

"Why did you not use your own soldiers?" she demanded.

"Because I felt it might promote trouble. As I said, I was mindful that Morgravia and Briavel are ancient enemies and I wanted nothing to stand in the way of this potential union, least of all the spark the sight of Legionnaires in Briavel might ignite. At the end of all the discussion, I decided Thirsk made a wise decision in hiring mercenaries."

She nodded. There was some truth in this.

"It so happened that Romen Koreldy had come to our notice before. He was an impressive soldier and assured Thirsk the other men in the party were trustworthy. And yes, I sent Romen along to watch out for Wyl and if he did anything dangerous or anything that compromised Morgravia in the eyes of Briavel he had my permission to dispatch him. It was my own father who had counseled me that Wyl Thirsk was not fit to command our army. He was dangerously unbalanced after an incident at an execution that took place a few years back, majesty. This is perhaps not the time to—"

"No, perhaps not," she interjected, knowing full well that he was referring to Myrren's burning.

He nodded, realizing the Queen was not interested in pursuing the digression.

"And?" Valentyna was determined to get to the crux of this report.

Celimus shrugged. "I have no idea of what was said between your father, yourself, and Wyl. It is my understanding that Wyl began to spread rumors that I executed his friend, Captain Donal and threatened to execute his sister." He feigned a hurt laugh. "It is ludicrous, your majesty. Ylena, bless her, is like my own sister and presumably at her family home right now."

"And the Captain?"

"Donal, I believe, is on the northern borders. I'm not sure I approve of this interrogation, your majesty." There was a subtle threat in his voice.

Valentyna pursed her lips. She needed to remain in control of this conversation, but it would not be easy for her to pursue whether Donal lived. "You know that Koreldy substantiates these claims of Thirsk's. Says he was present in your chambers and witnessed the execution of Donal."

"He lies, your majesty. Koreldy is a cheat, a fabricator, and brigand of the worst kind. Do you know his background?"

She shook her head, suddenly realizing she knew very little of Romen.

"Well, perhaps you should look into it. You would learn that his thieving ways put a price on his head with the barbarian, Cailech, and Koreldy's cowardice resulted in his elder brother and twin sister being executed on his behalf in the most traumatic fashion."

Valentyna swallowed hard. Who to trust!

Watching the Queen blanch, Celimus pressed his point. "I was able to discover this using family connections in Grenadyn. Morgravia had a firsthand report that Koreldy watched his brother and sister suffer for his sins. Cailech would have spared their lives, I'm told, if Koreldy had given himself up but he watched them die on the cross and then stole away, hardly batting an eyelid. I understand he remained in the Razors for some time, but ended up in Morgravia, and more lately Briavel, putting you under his spell."

"So you gave Koreldy permission to kill Thirsk?"

"I did. Koreldy, whatever else he is, is a skilled sword and he controlled the other mercenaries. Without him, they were simply rabble. I gave permission only if Wyl acted in a manner detrimental to Morgravia. And he did. He was threatening to kill your father at the first opportunity. The talk of those mercenaries killing the King is his story, majesty."

"How can you know if you were not there?"

"Because one of them escaped and returned to me with the truth," he lied smoothly, without so much as blinking.

"This is news to me. So what did this man see, what does he know?"

"That Koreldy did kill Thirsk and that he also killed Valor to stir up trouble between the two realms. His aim was to collect gold from both of us. From me by blackmail that he would go to you with a lie that you would easily believe for truth, and from you on the fake promise of protection. He has won from both of us, your majesty. Koreldy is ruthless. He has no loyalties at all, not even to Grenadyn. I believed him when he threatened blackmail. The situation was so delicate between us that I could not risk him coming to Briavel with his lies. So I paid him. I wish only peace for our region. And I could not risk killing him on Morgravian soil because I had no proof of what lies he might already have told you on his mission to Briavel with Thirsk. He is not a trustworthy man, your majesty. This is why I planned soon after to travel to Briavel in person. I needed to prove my commitment to our peace and union."

Smoothly done, Jessom thought, if a little wordy.

"But Koreldy did make it back to Briavel," she said curtly.

Celimus nodded. "He escaped and we lost track of him in the north. I sent a man called Jerico to track him but Koreldy murdered him and sent me Jerico's head as a taunt that I could not catch him. His note said he would create problems for Briavel and Morgravia as he had threatened but I did not realize it would all happen so soon. I am deeply regretful that you have been duped by this fellow. It occurs to me that he was aiming to kill me today, your majesty, to carry out his threat of war between our realms."

"Why?"

"I suppose because I had stopped payments of gold. At first I had no option but to pay, for he was dangerous, demanding larger and larger sums. That's when I sent Jerico out to track him down."

She took a deep breath. It was too much. She needed to think. "King Celimus, I appreciate your position in all of this and would ask your understanding and patience."

He did not quite grasp her meaning. "What do you plan to do with Koreldy?"

"I will need to think on all you have told me before I reach that decision. Please, sire, I am no longer in a position to continue with our diplomatic discussions. I need some time to sort through certain domestic affairs this dramatic event has brought about. Please accept my most sincere regrets that we have brought you here on a fruitless journey."

Celimus could not believe he had lost her. Yet he could tell she had made up her mind. Something in her tone and the set of her mouth made him realize there would be no talk of marriage until this matter was fully cleared up. *Damn Romen Koreldy!* There was nothing he could do except graciously accept her apology.

Jessom whispered in his ear, echoing his own thoughts. "Better to earn her gratitude now and win her hand later, than lose all the favor we've earned so far."

Celimus cleared his throat and nodded. "Of course, your majesty. My man has just given news that we would be appreciated back in Morgravia—trouble in the north. Cailech grows bold, majesty and we must work together against the barbarian. We will talk of this another time." He took her hand and gravely added, "You are aware that harmony for our realms is best achieved by you and I unifying in all senses of the word. We alone can set the tone for our future success and secure peace for our children."

He was right of course but she was relieved he would depart without protest. "Thank you, sire."

"We shall make our preparations to leave," he said, bowing neatly. "Perhaps you would be kind enough to keep me informed of events connected with Romen Koreldy. He will be captured and executed as a traitor if he sets foot in Morgravia. I would suggest you consider the same for Briavel."

"I shall think on all I have learned, my lord, and yes, I will certainly appraise you of the outcome." She allowed him to kiss her hand. "You have been most understanding, sire."

"Be well, Valentyna. I am patient about your dilemma but urgent for your decision."

Valentyna nodded. "We will speak soon," she said, keen for him and his retinue to be gone so she could face the trauma that was looming. "I shall say farewell to you shortly, my lord."

Celimus took his leave, trailed by Jessom. Out of earshot of the Queen, the King spat his anger. "If Koreldy is not executed by her royal decree I want our assassin to move in and finish it, now! The finger bearing his family ring is to be delivered to me within the week, do you hear?"

"It will be done, sire."

When Fynch surfaced to consciousness, parched and muddled, the festive noise of the tourncy had disappeared. There was silence and it sounded grim. He shook his head but the dull headache was still there and he remembered what he had seen in his vision before he had passed out. It disturbed him afresh and he hurried outside the building and retched into the bushes at the memory of seeing Romen dead.

Knave was nowhere to be seen. Fynch ran to the palace well and, after dragging up a pail of water, splashed his face and rinsed his mouth to revive himself. Dripping and feeling only marginally less distracted, he went in search of his friends.

It was one of the pages who finally filled him in. "Ho, Fynch. They've been looking for you."

"Who has?"

"Her majesty's people. I don't know what they want you for but all hell's broken loose this afternoon." His voice fell to a whisper. "Koreldy's been branded a traitor."

"What?" Fynch felt his insides flip.

"True as I stand here," the boy admitted, eyes gleaming with the intrigue. "She's pronouncing sentence now. He'll be lucky to escape with his life, they're saying."

Fynch did not linger to hear any more. He broke into a run, frantically wishing Knave were close, for the dog always knew where to find Wyl and he had not thought to ask the page.

K nave was already with Wyl; he had not left his side, in fact, since Wyl had been carted off to the gatehouse where he had awaited his fate. Wyl had expected to wait longer but it seemed Valentyna had reached her decision swiftly. A hush had blanketed the Great Hall as he was led, hands bound, to a chair before the throne. He sat now dejected, not caring to look at the nobles, dignitaries, and counselors, all in waiting. The atmosphere felt ominous and a frigid bleakness overwhelmed him. For those gathered it was a different tension—a sense of anticipation and foreboding amid excited whisperings.

Liryk came to him and laid a hand on his shoulder. "Sorry, Koreldy," he murmured and moved on. Wyl was not sure yet what the man was giving apology for but he could guess.

Krell also moved by and Wyl acknowledged him. The Chancellor had the generosity to stop.

"Chancellor Krell, I—"

"Hush, Koreldy. We are not permitted discourse with you. Everyone in this room is here to bear witness. They have already been briefed on what occurred, though most would have seen anyway." The man's lips twisted upon the already grim countenance. He nodded and departed. There was nothing else to say.

No one else had spoken much to him since other than a few necessary words from guards. He was grateful that

Knave had been permitted to remain with him in the gate-house, but where the dog was now he knew not, hopefully with Fynch. He wondered where Fynch was, hoping the boy had found the opportunity to petition the Queen on his behalf. He realized his hopes were futile when the horns sounded, the voice called, "All rise for her majesty," and he saw her stern composure.

All bowed low as she entered the hall. When he straightened and looked long into the face he loved, he saw a remoteness that chilled his heart. Her dark blue eyes glanced toward him once. What he glimpsed in that moment was not just sadness or disappointment but wrath. He could only begin to imagine the terrible lies Celimus had wielded to corrupt her mind against him. Wyl felt sick and he looked away, no longer interested in the proceedings. He had lost Valentyna—that was obvious. Nothing much else mattered now.

As Krell had mentioned, the assembled nobles had already been briefed prior to the prisoner's arrival, which was no doubt why the Queen, in a clear, steady voice, had summoned him to stand before her without preamble.

Wyl stood and moved with a sinking heart before Briavel's sovereign, who looked down upon him from the shallow dais with an air of icy detachment.

He bowed. "My Queen," he said but she did not acknowledge him.

"Romen Koreldy, you stand here before us accused of betraying the trust of the Crown of Briavel. I have heard disturbing reports of your clandestine activities, none of which I can substantiate but nonetheless fill me with a dread as I have never known. However, we shall not execute you, Koreldy, as the monarch of Morgravia demands. Briavel extends you mercy, for without proof of your guilt, I cannot condone your death. But I also cannot permit your presence within our borders. For your treachery today, you are banished, to be escorted by my Guard to the Briavellian border."

She paused just briefly to glance his way but he was staring at the floor so she continued.

"You may choose where you reenter Morgravia or you may take your chances by sea to the south, north into the Razors, or indeed far east into the unknown. We care not for your choice, though I would warn that should you return to Morgravia King Celimus will have you captured and executed on sight." This time she looked at him fully, her gaze resting long and sadly upon his bowed head. "Shar speed you, Koreldy, from our sight. Briavel washes her hands of you and your taint."

Wyl felt his body lurch with despair but there was nothing to say, nothing to be gained by helpless, cringing complaints to the contrary. He was cornered by Celimus's lies once again and, although there was the small consolation that Valentyna was not entirely going along with the King's version of events, there was no doubting her desire for him to be gone from this place . . . from her life.

As he searched for something to say a sudden commotion smashed through the silence. It was Fynch bursting through some concealed doors into the Great Hall, yelling.

"No, your majesty. No!"

A loud combined exclamation issued from the gathered, offended that a child should interrupt proceedings but the Queen held her hand up for quiet.

"Fynch," she replied gently, breaking protocol by even acknowledging him at this juncture. "It is too late."

"No, Valentyna," he cried and ignored the further angry murmurings at his familiarity. "You don't understand him." He ran towards her.

"No, I don't," she said but bent slightly to look into the tear-streaked face of the child who had been such a good friend to her. *Will I lose him too now?* "But he must go. I cannot have him in our presence for a moment longer than necessary."

"Your majesty," Fynch implored. "This is not Romen Koreldy . . . this is—"

"Fynch!" Wyl called. "Let it be, son."

They all watched the disheveled boy as his face twisted through a series of emotions, settling on something that seemed to lie somewhere between hate and despair.

"Let's go, lad," Liryk murmured, moving to escort him out of the Great Hall.

"Come, Knave," the boy said. "We have no place here."

Fynch did not look back and would always regret that he did not say a single word of farewell to the man called Romen Koreldy.

Epilogue

Wyl sensed the regret in Liryk, who joined the four-man escort that would see him to the border of Briavel—one man always riding behind, a crossbow trained on Koreldy's back. All knew the weapon was not necessary; still, they were taking no chances.

He had been given no further opportunity for discussion with Fynch or indeed anyone at the palace, save Stewyt, who had packed a sack of gear Wyl could claim as his. The horse he rode was his to keep, especially chosen by her majesty, he was told—her final act of kindness to him. It was a tan mare. He had admired her in the stables once— that occasion felt like a lifetime ago. But Valentyna had not forgotten. He wished he could read more into the gesture but remembering her wintry gaze, he knew they were no longer even friends. Her generosity was simply payment for his service. Now she wanted him gone from her realm. The saddlebags, he noticed, were well stocked with food and supplies. His weapons were in the care of Liryk, strapped to the older man's horse, until such time the Commander decreed it appropriate to return them to the disgraced prisoner.

As for the Queen, after pronouncing sentence she had departed the hall without so much as looking toward him again. She had made it clear that Briavel had washed its hands of him.

He rode in a bleak silence, ignoring his fellow riders, dark thoughts his only company. It was early evening when they set out with little intention of reaching any great distance before night closed in—at best Crowyll perhaps, ten miles from Werryl. It was important to Valentyna that he be removed from the palace immediately. In truth Wyl felt as though he no longer cared about anything. It even occurred to him that should the soldier behind accidentally fire that crossbow it might be a welcome end to his intense grief. The only thought that encouraged him to stay alive right now was Ylena's safety and the need to make amends to Fynch.

He came out of swirling thoughts. The other riders had dropped back, he noticed absently, leaving only Liryk to ride alongside him.

"I did not kill him," Wyl said into the silence. "The deed was done by a thug called Arkol—and he was sent by Celimus."

The soldier knew immediately to what he referred. "But you cannot prove it," Liryk replied, "that's our dilemma."

"Yet you would believe the Morgravian King?"

"I have no choice publicly. But for what it's worth, Koreldy, I don't want to believe you murdered King Valor and just for your peace of mind—if there is such a thing—neither does our Queen."

"Then why—"

The older man interjected. "But what you did on that tourney field today completely overstepped your familiarity with Briavel. It was tantamount to war between our realms. And if we did not punish you for such an affront to the visiting monarch we would risk his personal wrath towards her majesty. Don't you understand, man! We are not equipped to fight another war so soon with Morgravia. We are treading the narrowest of paths here along a precipice and should we trip we could fall into the darkest of times."

Wyl knew Liryk to be right. He had known the consequences before he had even stepped onto the tourney field with the intention to do malice. And he suspected Valentyna's demand for his promises indicated that she never quite trusted that he would not take a chance to hurt the Morgravian King.

"Why could she not say she knows me to be innocent?" There was a plaintiveness in his voice.

"Because she still isn't sure you didn't kill Thirsk in cold blood . . . and frankly neither am I! Whatever Thirsk was, he was honorable by all accounts—as was his father, whom I personally knew. Enemy or not, murder is not the Briavellian way and Thirsk came here in peace."

The sense of being trapped was complete. Briavel was banishing him on behalf of Wyl Thirsk. If only they knew.

"But these days murder is the Morgravian way and you and your Queen are going to have to learn very quickly to fight fire with fire . . . or you are lost," Wyl warned, angrily.

"Let us worry about that. You are fortunate to have escaped with your life, Koreldy. The King calls for your blood."

"I care nothing for his threats. All I know is he has corrupted Queen Valentyna's mind. Tell her that from me. Beg her not to trust him. Not to agree to marry him."

"You know I won't. You understand that I support this marriage to achieve peace."

"You are being duped! Celimus wants Briavel, not peace. He will plunge you straight into war with Cailech."

"How can you know this?"

"Because I know him so much better than you think," Wyl said, exasperated. "He will marry her and he will treat her with contempt. He will destroy her . . . and Briavel."

"Stop, Koreldy! I'll hear no more of this. We're approaching Crowyll and this is where we'll spend the night. You'd do well to appreciate your final evening in a comfortable bed. After this it will be grass for your mattress until we reach the border."

Wyl said nothing, his frustration overwhelming.

"Any preference for an inn?" Liryk asked, friendly again.

His gripe was not with Liryk, who was a good man. "How about the Forbidden Fruit?" Wyl suggested facetiously, remembering the woman Hildyth.

"Aha, so you were paying attention," the old soldier

replied, surprising him. "Yes, why not? I'm sure we can afford the banished man one last glimpse of the good life." He laughed. "Incidentally, in which direction are we headed tomorrow?"

"Morgravia, where else?" Wyl said, his voice hard.

Liryk reminded Wyl that he would be guarded.

"Don't worry, I won't try anything."

Liryk nodded. "Good. Don't, for your own sake. My men are on orders to kill should you attempt to escape and it would not please me to see you as a corpse when we're going to so much trouble to keep you alive."

"Are we all staying here?"

"There are normal rooms for rent so yes, but not all will be partaking of the specialties on offer. However, you may feel free, my friend. It is a farewell gift from me, shall we say. I hope you enjoy it."

Wyl mustered the suggestion of a grin for the older man. Liryk was hard not to like. "And you?"

"Not tonight, son," he replied, his glance flicking behind Wyl. "Ah, there she is. I trust you won't pass her up a second time, Koreldy?"

Wyl turned, knowing it would be Hildyth approaching. He was right. She looked frankly surprised to see him—he could not read what her confused expression meant. Still, he gave no further thought to it, focusing somewhat helplessly despite his mood on how very desirable she looked in a ruched gown of white voile. It was transparent, yet cunning folds of the fabric clung perfectly to the areas of her body which she chose to conceal and tantalize the customers with. Her hair, cut bluntly shorter than any other woman he knew, struck him as unusual again and yet it suited her, framing her square face above very broad and angular shoulders, which were bared.

She smiled and once again he was reminded of a cat—but this time one that had swallowed the pet bird. There was something knowing in those green eyes and he noticed any confusion he might have sensed in her moments before had vanished. She was entirely in control of herself again.

"Romen Koreldy," she said, effecting a graceful and altogether feminine bow.

"You remember," Wyl replied, impressed.

"I would never forget a face like yours," she crooned.
"And Commander Liryk, it's good to see you again, sir."
She returned her gaze to Wyl. "I knew I could trust you,"
she said.

"Trust me to do what?" Neither his body's response to
her flirtations nor Romen's easy grin failed him.

"To return. You said you would."

He nodded. "That I did, madam."

"And I hope you will choose me to give you some relaxation this evening?" she enquired.

"Well, I gather from what you say that I made a promise?"

"Not in so many words," she admitted, "but I took it as
such."

"Then let us proceed," Wyl said, desire sparking through
him, swimming strongly against his mood.

"Gentlemen," she said, bowing to Liryk and the one other
senior officer who had accompanied them into the building.
She offered her arm to Wyl.

"I'll see you in a few hours, Koreldy," Liryk said and
winked. "Remember what we discussed," he added.

Wyl already knew he was a man who needed to love a
woman to enjoy sexual intimacy. He remembered his
night with Arlyn in Orkyld as a blessed physical release,
made richer by her affection. But it was Valentyna who had
made him realize that when love came together with desire,
it was the most potent of confections. Only with Valentyna
had he experienced this viciously addictive cocktail. Wyl
knew he would not recover from the potion. It coursed
through his veins and would continue to poison his
thoughts and his dreams.

Valentyna! he silently cried as Hildyth led him away.

It had taken every ounce of his will to control his ardor
for Queen Valentyna when they had lain together in her bed
the night before. On the surface he regretted it now, wishing they had enjoyed each other fully. It was he alone who

had stopped them from consummating their love. It was right but it was also unjust, considering the next man she would probably lie with might well be his enemy. Yet now as he walked down the softly scented, low-lit corridors of the Forbidden Fruit, he knew she would only have hated him more if they had shared such an intimacy. As it was he could never expect her to look upon him—if she ever did again—with anything resembling affection.

Hildyth had none of Valentyna's raw beauty but there was definitely something about her Wyl wanted to possess, if just for a few hours. He would use and enjoy her hard, taut body and release all of his tightly held aggression. And then he would leave.

No love shared. Just lust and payment.

Hildyth led him into a chamber where a narrow, low shelf ran the length of the walls. Upon this shelf fragrant candles burned, scenting the room with honey and jasmine. A splash pool of heated water awaited where heady vapors of refreshing mint and citrus mingled with the other scents to create a sensuous atmosphere of well-being. Nearby a table held wine and sweetmeats for their indulgence. The smoothing bench was against the far wall.

"What would you prefer me to call you?" she asked, cat eyes shining.

"Romen will be fine."

"Come, Romen, let me undress you."

But first she reached behind herself and flicked the clasp that undid her gown. It fell to the floor, lightweight and wispy, leaving her naked. She stepped unhurriedly from her garment, ensuring that his gaze could roam her body. He had been right; she was contoured by muscle, which did nothing to detract from what he realized was a neat yet wholly voluptuous figure. Her breasts were not large but they were full, curving toward dark, erect nipples.

She turned to pick up her gown. It was a deliberate move so he could admire her round, rather lovely bottom. It occurred to him that she possessed the shape of a beautiful musical instrument. The thought was gone as she turned back to him, the dark downy triangle between her strong thighs arresting his gaze. It was there that he hoped to find solace and relief.

"I hope I was the right choice?" she said, half-smiling at where his look rested.

"Indeed. I chose well," he replied in Romen's sardonic way and began to pull off his clothes.

"Allow me," she said.

It was a slow and sensuous experience being undressed by this intriguing woman. She lingered on certain areas of his body as she unburdened them from their coverings. Wyl felt himself trembling in anticipation and surprised himself by not feeling self-conscious when she removed his breeches and his hard desire for her was revealed.

She looked up from her knees, the half-smile there again. He knew she thought about giving him the much-needed release right then but she decided against it, straightening back to her full height but making sure his naked skin now touched hers, sending a fresh shiver through his body.

Hildyth gestured that he should step into the pool and as he did so, she poured wine for him. She joined him in the water, handing him a goblet and seating herself on the ledge in the pool so he could lean back between her legs as she soaped his upper body. Wyl began to relax as the rhythmic movement of her sudsy fingers played over him. It was a treat to be washed in this manner. She lathered his hair and he drained his goblet of the excellent Kurshor from Briavel's sun-drenched coastal valley, felt its fiery warmth hit the spot as her strong hands massaged his scalp.

As she rinsed his hair, she encouraged him to caress her, and then she suggested he allow her to dry him. Wyl was reluctant to leave the pool, loath to interrupt this pleasure and the state of mind that had permitted him to put aside his angry thoughts, numb his cares for the last hour.

"Let me give you a smoothing as you have never had before, Romen," she muttered in a low voice.

He nodded, allowed her to dry his body with warmed linens. Their gentle roughness against his skin revived his desire again as she dried his legs and buttocks. He realized their time together so far had been mostly silent. She was not curious to know anything more about him, which he found agreeable, and he appreciated that she did not babble, like so many of the brothel girls. Hildyth was comfortable in his silence but not once did he feel she was going about her business with him in a detached manner. If anything he felt a bond with her—as though they were kindred spirits in this comfortable place void of idle words.

She smiled and pointed toward the smoothing bench and he obliged, lying belly down, his face turned away from her.

"On your back, please," she said in a soft voice and he obliged. This was an unusual position to begin the smoothing but he was past caring about details. "I have a warmed pouch of barley I am going to lay across your eyes. It will feel good and help you to relax," she explained.

Wyl nodded. He was familiar with this practice and sighed gently as she laid the perfectly weighted, warmed pouch on his face. He heard her opening the cupboard, and then gentle clink of small glass bottles.

Again the voice soft. "Would oil of lavender be to your liking, Romen?"

"Yes," he murmured, knowing it was dangerous, for it would remind him of Valentyna and the evening they had kissed, the evening their love had first taken flight.

As he listened to her rubbing the oil between her hands he imagined feeling her thighs around him. After the smoothing she would lead him into the adjoining chamber—a bedroom—where they would complete this ritual and she would pleasure him in any way he chose. He desired nothing more complicated than the feel of a woman holding him as he moved inside her. Lost in his lust-filled thoughts, he reached his cupped hands behind, laid his head on them and sighed.

It stretched his body into the perfect position.

He felt her single warm palm touch his chest, not registering that it did not seem quite as oily as it should, and in truth he would later recall that he did not feel the cold tip of the blade when it first entered between his ribs in that sharp upward punching manner. He did, however, jerk and flail almost immediately as it ascended on its killing journey.

The barley pouch was flung off his eyes as the blade expertly and swiftly hit its mark, his heart—puncturing it fatally.

Wyl was strong but Hildyth was surprisingly strong too and she leaned her full weight against his prone, already weakening, dying body and looked deep into Romen's wide, fear-filled silvery gray eyes.

"Hush, Romen. It is finally done," she cooed, demonically stroking his rapidly failing erection as he listened to her gentle words. "Let go now. Die quietly and bravely. The King of Morgravia bids you Shar's speed."

The struggling had stopped, voice had left him, death was claiming him and he felt her kiss his lips as she pushed the knife harder and higher, severing tissue to be sure that Jessom's contract was fulfilled.

They were locked in a lovers' silent embrace now—albeit a bloody one—as Wyl, dying, suddenly felt a terrifyingly familiar feeling. The surging sensation took over as his closed lids, accepting of death, suddenly flew open to reveal two ill-matched and alarmingly different eyes.

Hildyth, as Romen had, stared at him in shock. The convulsive pain was in her too and she had no idea what was happening. She straightened, taking a deep, agonizing breath. Wyl did know what was occurring, although he could barely believe it himself . . . and he hated it.

They both shared death but only one took life. Wyl felt his soul lifting, wrenching free. All that was him and Romen was torn from their body as he glimpsed the dark, angry soul of Hildyth crossing over in terror into the body of Romen Koreldy, where it died.

Wyl staggered back in Hildyth's body now, dry-retching and groaning. Tears streamed down his cheeks in disbelief.

Again! It has happened again!

He lay his burning face against the cold marble of the floor and sobbed . . . deep, dry heartwrenching sobs of intense grief as he curled himself into a small shape and released his pain.

Later, when he could finally bring himself to, he looked over at the body of Romen Koreldy . . . him. His latest corpse. And then he looked down at himself, frightened and disoriented in the naked body of Hildyth the whore.

No . . . not Hildyth, he realized.

My name is Faryl and I am an assassin.

He retched again.

Finally, Wyl composed himself. He had to think and quickly. *How long have I been in here with her?* He looked at the candles. Possibly two hours so far. Liryk would most likely give him up to four hours for this treat but perhaps only three. He looked at his hands—his female hands covered with Romen's blood—and without thinking further jumped into the pool to cleanse himself of death.

He toweled himself and then struggled back into Hildyth's gown, damp and frantic. His fingers could not work the clasp that she had so easily worked minutes earlier. He fumbled and swore quietly, his shock still so acute he had to stop at one point and take a slow steadying breath.

It took him several clumsy minutes to finally be hooked into her gown and only then did he find the courage to face Romen's body. It looked sad and wretched, a vague look of surprise its final expression.

He made his plan. It was thin, as usual, but it was all he had.

Using Faryl's knowledge he removed the wedged blade from Romen's body and then, sickening though it was, sliced through the corpse's ring finger and, wincing, pushed the blade back into the wound in the chest.

He wrapped Romen's finger in a small piece of linen and hid it behind one of the largest candles, taking care to remember its precise location among the others. Then he threw the wine carafe onto the floor, ensuring the golden liquid spilled at the doorway and then wrenched open the door into the main corridor and began to scream. He was amazed at the high female sound that came out, but he used it to full effect, for people came running from all ends of the brothel and with them ran Commander Liryk, whom Wyl deliberately threw his woman's body against.

"He's dead . . . murdered!" Wyl cried.

"What?" Liryk exclaimed, unraveling himself from Hildyth's arms and pushing past her into the room. He sagged against the wall, distraught at what he saw. "How?" he croaked.

Wyl began to weep hysterically. His own fragile state of mind helped him to be convincing as he broke down, speaking through sobs. Briavel's soldiers quickly dispersed the few eager onlookers and closed the door so they could hear privately how such a tragedy had occurred. Through her cries, they pieced together that she had gone to fetch some more wine at her client's behest and in the few minutes she was out of the chamber, someone had come in and killed Koreldy.

"He had this on his eyes," she said, reaching to pick up the pouch. "He would not have known it was not me coming back into the room."

"Did you see the killer?"

"No, not really. I was gone only for a few moments but I did see a man running down the corridor. I thought it odd, of course, but I wasn't really concentrating I suppose."

Liryk put his arm around her. "Hildyth, you need to tell us everything you can remember."

"That's it, Commander Liryk. I . . . I'm so sorry. I know he was your friend. I only saw the killer's back. I dropped the wine. He was big and dark-haired but no more could I tell you. Poor Koreldy." Wyl knew the babbling was effective and real. He felt entirely rattled.

"How was this fellow dressed? Anything distinctive?"

"No, sir. Like any other civilian of Briavel . . . like any other patron of this place."

It was only then Liryk noticed the missing finger.

"Shar's Balls!" he said to his men. "This was an assassination."

"How can you know?" Wyl stammered.

"Koreldy wore a distinctive ring on that finger—he told me once it belonged to his family. It will be proof of his death to whoever ordered it."

Hildyth began softly weeping again. "Do you need me any more, sir? I'm feeling very unwell."

"No, you go home, young lady. I'll send one of my men to escort you back. Please don't go anywhere else, though, we may need you still."

"I'll be fine, Commander Liryk; don't spare one of your men. Perhaps someone from here can take me home," Wyl whispered, mind racing—he had no idea where home was. "You catch the killer," he said, moving to take the old soldier's hand. "I know you liked him, sir. I did too."

"That I did. I'm very sorry it has turned out this way for him."

Liryk turned to one of his soldiers and asked him to fetch someone to help the young woman home. He returned quickly with a kind woman called Remy who took charge of the weeping Hildyth.

"Come on, love. I'll get you back to your rooms," she said as she led Wyl away.

With Remy's consoling chatter and guiding arm, Wyl stumbled in Hildyth's unfamiliar body back to the two rooms in Crowyll amongst the densely populated area near the market. He thanked his companion, shutting the door as soon as it was polite, then he leaned back against it, sucking air in hard to steady his mind.

Myrren's gift was more generous than he had first imagined. So now he was no longer Romen but Faryl. *A woman!* He had to get away from this town. *What to do first?*

Wyl steadied his mind as Gueryn had taught him to do from childhood. He calmed the raging swirl of his thoughts. Then he centered himself and looked at the problem, his strategist's mind attacking it objectively.

Steal my weapons back, was his first decision, then, *fetch my horse. Retrieve the finger. Leave Crowyll under cloak of darkness. Where to?*

Find the manwitch, came his own reply.

Seek answers to the Quickening.

Now available in trade paperback from Eos,
the second riveting volume in
Fiona McIntosh's Quickening trilogy

BLOOD AND MEMORY

"Because I read a lot of fantasy books and books in
general, I am seldom taken by surprise by a plot turn.
When I read *Myrren's Gift*, I thought I could predict
where this tale was going. *Blood and Memory* proved me
wrong. Fiona McIntosh's books move quickly and
unpredictably; if you are tired of plodding trilogies in which
little seems to happen, these books are definitely for you."
—ROBIN HOBB

1

The Queen had suffered a sleepless night, churning over her decision to expel Romen Koreldy. Valentyna had measured the dark hours by listening to the muted noises of the guard changing. The only other distraction was the distant, infrequent howl of a dog—or was it a wolf? She wondered if it was caught in one of the traps laid by poachers . . . or more whimsically she imagined it had lost its mate and was venting its despair.

She understood such things, for the sorrowful cry only served as an echo of her own loneliness.

Valentyna asked herself yet again if she could have hung on to the man she loved and still appeased an angry king? A king, she added, with more than enough fighting power to overwhelm Briavel. The answer, whichever way she approached the problem, was no.

"Damn duty!" she murmured into her coverlets. She punched the feather pillow that brought no comfort this night.

To add to the misery, a vision of Fynch haunted her. How he had looked at her she would never forget. He too had grown to love Romen, despite his misgivings about the man. She and her young friend had shared so much in the short time they had known each other. But all of that closeness was shattered now. Fynch was avoiding her because she had so deliberately distanced herself from Romen and ordered him expelled from Briavel.

She had cast aside a man she loved over Celimus—a man they all hated. A child, not familiar with the way of politics and diplomacy, would believe her actions made no sense.

But this was no ordinary child. Fynch was special in his serious, deep-thinking manner. He understood all too well, but that did not mean he felt any comfort in his understanding.

She did not want to lose his companionship, but it seemed the day just gone had risen solely to bring loss to her life.

King Celimus, she realized, kicking off her blankets with irritation, would probably be close to the border by now, possibly even crossing into Morgravia. She had no doubt spies would keep him updated on Briavel's events, and her standoff with Koreldy would be high on the list of missives. It suddenly occurred to her that the King might have Romen tracked down upon hearing this news. Surely Romen would be cautious? He had been warned that to set foot into Morgravia was to risk certain execution. Failing his own good sense, she trusted that her own Commander Liryk would counsel Romen. Hopefully they had ridden through the night and would be headed north, back to where he had come from.

"Where Cailech, King of the Mountains, awaits him," she whispered sorrowfully.

The last time Valentyna had cried passionately was over her father and the time before that when she had fallen from a horse a decade ago. She considered herself resilient, but silent, heavy tears won now as she accepted the enormity of her orders. Romen had nowhere to go. Briavel represented safety. Beyond its borders to the north and west, people wanted to kill him. The south offered only ocean, no comfort. To the east, only fear in the little-known Wild. Fynch knew it too. That was the reason for the accusation in that chilling final glance he had given her.

It spoke of betrayed friendships.

And he was right. What had Romen been thinking during that swordfight! It was clear that he had meant to kill Celimus, and then where but in intense danger would that have left Briavel?

Romen knew how precarious her predicament had been. What had been his intention? She had not had a chance to consider it, in truth. She had not had the luxury of opportunity to think it through; she had been forced to react, and swiftly, in the only way that a monarch in her situation could have done. She knew her decision was politically correct, but this reassurance was cold comfort.

Her heart ached. She loved Romen and she had sent him away . . . not just away in fact, for expulsion had more serious implications. Briavel no longer recognized him as friend. Romen Koreldy would not be permitted to set so much as a toe inside Briavel. If recognized, he would be captured and imprisoned. Her actions had trapped him. Whichever way he turned; whichever borders he finally crossed, he was as doomed as their new and fragile love.

Valentyna twisted beneath her remaining sheet, banishing thoughts of his touch, which brought a new kind of ache to her body. She would have given herself gladly to him that night before the tourncy, but his was the voice of calm among the waves of passion. It was Romen who pulled back, Romen who made her see the reason for holding on to the most precious commodity for a new queen.

Virginity was wealth, he had counseled. More importantly, it was power. A virgin queen was an irresistible magnet for appropriate suitors. Except she wanted no husband . . . not unless it was Koreldy.

She rubbed her tired but stubborn eyes and sat up. This would not do. Pulling on a soft robe to ward off the chill, Valentyna moved to the window and looked out toward the dark woodland she loved so much.

"It might work," she murmured as an idea gathered resonance in her thoughts. She could meet him somewhere outside of Briavel's borders. Somewhere safe, where they could rendezvous in secret. If only she could feel his kiss just once more, it would be enough, she told herself naïvely, hardly believing it herself.

Her plans to meet with Romen outside of Briavel took rapid shape. She would take Fynch too. Between them they would mend friendships, renew loyalties, rekindle the flame that burned brightly between them all. She could apologize for making the hardest of decisions and she knew

Romen already understood; his eyes had told her as much when they had regarded her so gently despite her harsh words. She could ask him why he had risked so much. They could set things straight between them. Her daydream had even rambled beyond to when perhaps she could find a way around the expulsion order; when time had healed and life was less precarious. Perhaps there was a chance for them in time.

"Where are you now, Romen?" the Queen of Briavel whispered toward the trees, now determined to see her lover one last time, not knowing he was at this very moment just a few miles from entering her own castle's walls.

Far sooner than she could have imagined, Valentyna would cast her eyes on Koreldy; kiss him just once more as she so desired.

⧗

Liryk's expression was grim. Beneath it anger seethed. This should not have happened. The Queen had deliberately granted life, given Koreldy the chance to make a new one elsewhere. She could have easily commanded death. There was friendship between the two, possibly more, if his intuition served him well.

He could not blame her. Who could help but fall under Koreldy's spell?

They had emerged from the cover of the woodland that surrounded the northern rim of the palace grounds. Commander Liryk glanced to his left, where the body of the man he hardly knew but comfortably called friend lay dead in a cart, wrapped in sacking. Combined sorrow and guilt threatened to take over Liryk's checked emotion, forcing him to look away and back toward the castle.

Now they had arrived at the famous Bridge of Werryl, where past sovereigns, remembered faithfully in marble, stood proudly on either side and guided visitors into the palace. Liryk raised his hand toward the ramparts, where he knew his guards saw their fellow soldiers approaching through the light mist of dawn. The gate was up, he noticed, and he grimaced. He would have to take a hard look at security again and ensure the castle remained closed to all visitors until permission was formally granted. After Valor's sudden death, everyone had been so careful, but more recently he had noticed a general slackening of the rules. With an assassin on the loose, who knew what could happen. Their queen must be better protected.

In the courtyard he wearily handed his horse's reins to the stable boy and gave orders for Koreldy to be taken to the chapel and laid out. He, like his men, was tired. They had ridden through the night, determined to bring the body back as quickly as possible to ensure that the gossip fled with the evidence. It would flare and rage for a day and then hopefully be forgotten. There was no body, no sign that the grisly death had even occurred. The Forbidden Fruit's women would be entertaining in that same chamber this very night—no sign of the recent bloodshed in evidence. His mouth twisted at the thought. Poor Koreldy. He deserved better.

Well, no matter how tired he was now, the next hour would be his most difficult. He suspected that no matter how he counseled her, their headstrong queen would want to see the corpse for herself. He shook his head, resigned. Valentyna was an early riser. Best to go see her immediately and get this ugly business done.

Liryk made his presence known to another man he liked. Krell, the Queen's chancellor and former servant to King Valor, was a calm and solid force among Valentyna's advisers.

"May I ask if it is urgent, Commander Liryk?" Krell said, shifting papers around his desk. "This is quite an irregular hour to be requesting an audience."

Liryk nodded. "Something unexpected. She must be told."

"Bad news?" the Chancellor asked. Liryk's expression was enough to foreshadow the fact that this would not be a happy meeting.

Liryk would have told him everything anyway; Krell had

that way of not showing unnecessary curiosity while still finding out what he felt he should know. It was a masterful skill. He was also a man to trust.

"It is, I'm afraid. Koreldy is dead."

The Queen's servant looked up sharply from the neat piles of orderly paperwork he trawled through for his monarch. He had single-handedly eased Valentyna into her challenging role as ruler, allaying her fears, guiding her with informed skill, instinctively knowing what her father would expect. In terms of administering the realm, he was a blessing for them all and could rarely be ruffled. However, the expression on his normally well-guarded face was all shock at this moment. Liryk was convinced that Krell wanted to ask the Commander if he was quite sure but had checked himself.

Liryk confirmed it anyway. "I've had him laid out in the chapel. I imagine the Queen will want to view the body."

"Indeed. She will not be persuaded otherwise," Krell replied, distracted. He walked around from his desk. "This is dark news, Commander. I'm sorry to hear it. He was, in spite of the reason for his expulsion, a good man for Bri-avel . . ."

Liryk guessed that the Chancellor wanted to add that Koreldy was a good man for Valentyna as well. Instead the Chancellor held his tongue, asked him to wait. He would seek an appointment with her majesty immediately. He left Liryk alone with his bleak thoughts and fatigue.